LAW OF ATTRACTION

UNIVERSAL LAWS SERIES BOOK 1

RAEESAH AMBARKER

ISBN: 978-0-620-98539-0

Book cover and formatting design: Books and Moods

Reader discretion is advised

To my readers. I love you endlessly.

And to Ammaarah, my fellow villain and best friend.

Playlist:

Maneater – Nelly Furtado
Barbie Tingz – Nicki Minaj
Bad Blood – Taylor Swift
Maniac – Conan Gray
God is a Woman – Ariana Grande
Cruel Summer – Taylor Swift
Daddy Issues – The Neighbourhood
Running Up That Hill – Kate Bush
Do I Wanna Know – Arctic Monkeys
Teeth – 5 Seconds of Summer
Can't Pretend – Tom Odell
I Wanna Be Yours – Arctic Monkeys
Sweater Weather – The Neighbourhood
Swim – Chase Atlantic
Die For You – The Weeknd
Say You Won't Let Go – James Arthur

Chapter 1

Nyx

Women just had to do everything, didn't they?

Looked down upon until their help was needed, ignored until they were of service to men; situations like these were typical in almost every workplace or school environment. Men who believed themselves smarter would scorn the advice of women, and take the reins until they eventually tumbled off and needed help with getting back up. They considered us the gentler sex, but men's egos were the most fragile things I'd ever come across. All I did was offer help. And did he accept? Big no. Did he need my help now?

Big yes.

My heeled boots clicked against the floor of the foyer as I shoved through the doors leading to the indoor ice rink. A gust of frigid air hit me and I bound my jacket tighter around myself, passing the ice and heading towards the long hallway. The door at the end was my destination and I mentally readied myself. One interaction with him had already taken a hit to my confidence. But I was back now and ready to throw his words back in his stupid face. After a few deep breaths, I knocked, entering once I heard the serious voice.

Coach Stanley Benson was new to USC, having been hired hastily when the previous coach was forced to quit after his wife had fallen ill. It was a major kick in the gut, especially to the team that was left deserted. I'd felt bad at first because it was what the students deemed championship season, although it was an all-year-round thing. It was something we all looked forward to. An all-sports college competition where the University of Southern California competed against the University of California, Los Angeles for the Southern California Crosstown Cup.

But I no longer felt bad. All I felt was rage at the man in front of me, a man who had walked into his new office with the confidence of a god—and told me no because I was a girl.

"You asked to see me," I mused, refusing to take a seat when he gestured towards one. Coach Benson was a tall man, and I wasn't an idiot. My height was five feet and four inches on a good day; when I wasn't slumping in exhaustion. If I were to sit down, Benson would have the upper hand with his long abdomen in his seated position.

My tone was clipped, accentuating that I didn't have time to waste. There were better things to do on a Friday afternoon than stand and listen to someone speak down to you, a man especially. I'd just finished attending my sociology of sports class when a freshman informed me that Coach Benson wanted a meeting. Well, Benson could choke on his toes for all I cared. But the curious part of me wouldn't let it go.

How lovely it was to watch them crawl back.

The last time we'd spoken, he embarrassed me in front of his new team, the USC Trojans. I had offered to aid him, seeing as he was in an unfamiliar environment, dealing with skaters he'd never met before, skaters whom I observed for the past year because I attended every game. I had the marketing and sports event management skills that were needed throughout the duration of the Crosstown Cup. I could've helped him slip into his new role as the coach. But he'd taken my offer as an insult. *Men*.

Now, don't get me wrong. I loved men. I had a vagina, and when I needed some pleasure, I wanted things inside my vagina. What I wanted inside my vagina was a penis. And damn, the penises were great. Hideous, but great. However, once those pants were pulled up, belts buckled up and their mouths opened in preparation for a conversation—I realised why men annoyed me so much. Because they thought I needed to be handled.

It seemed that every man wanted a confident woman, but I'd come to realise it was all just for show. They wanted a strong woman for the image, for bragging rights, but behind closed doors; they wanted submission in every aspect of the relationship. It was a *no* from me, honey.

Benson stared at me, gaze narrowing at my refusal to sit. I smiled innocently and his eye twitched. There were bags under his eyes and his skin was slightly wrinkly.

"Miss Taylor," he began in a throaty voice, linking his fingers in front of him and cracking them. "I wanted to discuss what happened last week."

I raised a brow. "Oh, you mean when you humiliated me

in front of the entire team?" His jaw clenched. "Don't worry, I didn't cry and file a complaint, Coach. Your *job* is safe." My smirk told him all that he needed to know; that I didn't think he was qualified. Uncrossing my arms, I sent him a sarcastic smile. "If that's all, I'll be on my way—"

"Miss Taylor!" Benson called and I halted, hand placed on the door handle, but I didn't turn around. The silence ticked by. "The team and I had a discussion," he cleared his throat as if he was embarrassed, "about your offer to help."

Tossing him a grin over my shoulder I inquired, "a discussion? About me? How absolutely flattering." An angry grunt left him, but I merely smiled, turning around fully. My eyes scanned him from head to toe. "If you don't mind me asking, *Coach*, what exactly happened to me being an insufferable walking encyclopaedia and placing myself in situations where I wasn't needed?"

I found it hilarious, the way his eye was jerking. The man looked seconds away from convulsing in irritation. He muttered something to himself and I noticed that the vein in his forehead looked mighty fine. Just a few more taunting words from me and it'd pop in the same way he'd claimed to pop my bubble of blissful ignorance, declaring that I assumed everyone needed my help and ignored the fact that they didn't want me there.

Oh please. If I had any talent, it would've been the ability to smell the pungent scent of desperation. It was an odour I was well acquainted with, having been drenched in it for as long as I could remember.

Desperate to do good things. Desperate to do better for those that needed me. Desperate to make people proud. *Desperate.* But why have it as a weakness when I could turn it into an advantage? I could sniff out those that stank of desperation as much as I did.

Benson placed his hands on his desk, still glaring at me. Unfortunately, he overlooked my jabs. *Pooh.* I was hoping he'd flip the table in fury and give me something to laugh at.

"It appears that I was wrong about you, Miss Taylor."

"People usually are," I informed him smoothly. "It's a pity I don't exactly care for others' opinions of me, though." I blinked innocently, speaking nothing but the truth. With my previous reputation around campus, it was imperative to have a thick skin. Benson mumbled something again and I nearly choked on my snort when I realised it was a prayer.

I squelched the desire to ask him why he prayed to a god when he already considered himself one, and instead surveyed the office. "Love what you've done with the place." Noting his barren desk, I added, "Of course, back when Coach Ford was still here, the office was more alive. But then again, he was *qualified*, after all."

Coach Ford had known his team like the back of his hand. His desk was always filled with plans. The man was like a hawk at games, studying past matches to prepare for the next. Every week, he'd assess each team member based on his new knowledge and make a list of their strengths and weaknesses, looking for points of change. Individual skill development had been a favourite of his. After that, he would work on line combinations, trying to figure out who worked best together. There'd also always been an event that he was hosting to boost morale and raise funds.

Judging by Benson's empty desk, he clearly hadn't gotten anywhere in the week that he'd been at the university. Poor guy. He didn't have a degree in sports management—which was preferred—just experience with coaching a *children's* ice hockey team. Dean Waverly had chosen him because he was the best out of the lacklustre bunch that had applied for the position on such short notice. Everybody else had no degree and zero experience.

Benson pushed to his feet, face scrunching in irritation. It appeared that his fuse was running short. *How lovely.* "Question my qualifications once again, Miss Taylor, and I'll report you to the dean." He was fuming now, face red and eyebrows furrowed. "I'm fully capable of leading this team to victory—"

"Then why am I here?" I intercepted, lips curving into an elegant smile and fluttering my mascara-coated eyelashes innocently. Benson closed his eyes, taking in a deep breath, holding it for a few seconds before releasing it. "Thank you for that two-second breathing class, truly, I appreciate it." I heaved in a breath and sighed, mocking him. "But I have to get going. Places to be, people to taunt."

Without giving him a chance to reply, I swung open the door and left the office, grinning to myself when I heard him hurrying after me. The man was desperate indeed.

"You'll be paid!" he exclaimed.

I paused my walking. "I'm listening."

He sighed. "Dean Waverly suggested it." That he'd spoken to the dean about me proved how desperately he needed help. His next words sounded pained and I stifled a smile. "You're studying the required courses, have experience with the team and your GPA is one of the highest. Think of it as a paid internship."

I was their only other option and that was *why* I'd offered help in the first place—without needing to be paid. But I wasn't going to say no to money. *He* brought it up, not me. All the other students studying for my degree, especially the older ones, couldn't help because they were unfamiliar with the team or just weren't interested in hockey or giving up what little free time they had. The team needed somebody with a specific skill set. Benson had the coaching experience down, but nothing else.

Turning on my heel, I grinned. "Well, you should've said that in the first place and I would've even given you a spit handshake. The word *internship* sealed the deal for me, one quirk of being a successful woman. We live to thrive." He glowered at me and I laughed. "Only joking," grinning wider, I continued, "Not about being a successful woman. About the spit handshake. That's disgusting."

"You start on Monday," he grumbled, eye twitching again. "I'll email you the papers."

Saluting him, I turned again and was on my way, rounding the corner just as he yelled a string of curses. Once I made it outside, I burst into laughter, pressing a hand to my abdomen as I wheezed. Men were just so easy to aggravate. After my laughing fit, I pulled my phone out of my jeans pocket and dialled the familiar number, smiling the entire time.

She picked up on the first ring, as she always did. It was an unspoken thing of hers. "911, what's your emergency?"

I snorted, leaning against the wall as I watched the passing cars. "I'm afraid I set fire to another man's ego."

"Hold while I transfer the call." Silence for a few seconds, and my grin grew. "Fire Department. You light 'em, we fight 'em! How can I be of assistance?"

Laughing again, I told her, "just come pick me up." She cackled evilly. "I'm at the campus ice rink. I'm already late for my shift at the grocery store because I had to deal with Coach Pissy." The man tended to bring out my murderous side.

"I'm literally down the street, gimme a few seconds." And then she hung up. She was probably at the football field, taking pictures with that camera she always carried around.

Not even a few seconds later, a sleek white Audi pulled up, a blaring siren on the roof as Nailea leaned out the window yelling, "It's the fire department!" Students stared as they passed and I slapped a hand over my mouth as I laughed. I didn't even want to know where she'd gotten the siren from. "Get in, loser, we're going to save a cat from a tree."

Nailea Rubio was the most carefree person I'd ever met. She was also probably the most gorgeous woman I'd ever laid eyes on. And I wasn't even exaggerating. She looked like something you'd cook up in a lab. Her hazel eyes were big—the kind you'd see on an animated princess—and she had a head full of wild black curls that looked flawless every day of the fucking week. There were many times when people would stop to stare at her, a literal angel on earth. And she made me feel way better about my height, seeing as she was barely over five feet tall. If I could tower over anybody, it was her.

We weren't best friends, at least I didn't *think* so? It was weird to talk about because I'd never really had friends before Nailea. But she sat next to me during our shared journalism class and last year; she'd taken a leap and started a conversation with me. She had her group of everchanging friends and no matter how many times she would offer, I'd politely refuse to join them. But she was around when I needed her, and vice versa. Our situation was comfortable, and I wasn't complaining.

I sauntered towards her, laughing at the annoyance on people's faces when Nailea refused to turn the siren off. As I opened the passenger door, a black jeep pulled up next to us. My laughter faded and my lips pulled into a confident smirk as I met the gaze of the driver; Beckham Hunt, captain of the USC ice hockey team.

His eyes were tempestuous as he glared at me, parking the car. He never hid the fact that he hated me and I found it utterly amusing. Whilst he was brooding over my presence, I was laughing to myself. It had taken me a good while to find amusement in the situation between us, to bury the hurt instead of allowing it to dictate my every action. Unlike him.

In the passenger seat sat one of his teammates and housemates, Sebastian Hayes. The latter merely stared at me. They often referred to him as the angel on the team because of his physical appearance, nearly white blonde hair and glass-coloured eyes. But that was the furthest from the truth. As a left-winger, he played offence and I'd lost count of the number of times he slammed opponents into the plexiglass, just for the fun of it.

Beckham turned off the car and slid out, muscular and tattooed arms on display in his white shirt. If he didn't hate my guts, I would've enjoyed admiring him. Broad shoulders, strong nose, sharp jaw, thick eyebrows and long lashes framing turbulent grey eyes. The guy was perfection. And I hated it. No matter how good he looked, he was ugly because of his treatment of me.

Okay, maybe not *completely* ugly. I mean, I had eyes.

Sebastian followed, eying the two of us in suspense. The blonde was a tower of toned muscle, and based on what I remembered from the team's online profiles, he stood at a whopping height of six feet and five inches—four inches taller than the man who stood next to him. Said man was still glaring at me.

I tended to avoid Beckham and vice versa. But the times we *did* run into each other were filled with uncomfortable tension. Nobody knew what to expect. Sometimes insults were thrown around, and other times it was heated glares fired from across rooms.

Nailea finally turned off the siren and smiled at them. "Look, Nyxie, it's the ice princesses."

Sebastian scowled at her but didn't respond. His eyes took a second to focus after being hit by her dazzling smile; a regular occurrence whenever the two of us were out in public. I wasn't joking when I'd said the girl was gorgeous. Her beauty was a fortress that came in handy sometimes. Needed to go unnoticed? Stand beside Nailea Rubio and people wouldn't spare you a glance. I loved it. Who would try and throw disgusting rumours in my face when I had an angel standing next to me?

Answer: nobody.

Sebastian nudged Beckham's arm; the latter boring a hole into my head with his rough gaze. I raised a questioning brow before grinning at him, and his lips tipped into a menacing scowl. I nearly laughed.

"What are you doing here?" Sebastian challenged rudely as I slipped into the car, shutting the door and rolling down the window. "I thought Coach clarified he didn't want your help."

They both smirked at that, probably reliving the humiliating moment for me. I placed a finger on my chin. "Did he now?" Nailea snickered at the annoyed look that crossed both men's features. "How absolutely *lovely*."

With a wink, I grinned as Nailea stepped on the gas pedal, leaving them behind us. Both of us stuck a hand out of the window, our middle fingers waving at the men we'd just left behind.

Once we were off-campus, Nailea rolled the windows back up. She glanced at me, the smile still present in her eyes. "How'd the meeting go?" Her words were coated with a soft layer of an accent she could never shake, no matter how long she'd lived in California.

I held back a laugh. "He practically begged me to help."

She honked the horn as somebody ran across the street. "Damn, I love it when men beg."

Nodding, I said, "It's basically a paid internship. Dean Waverly suggested it, and I'm assuming it's because Benson's so desperate."

Nailea looked bewildered. "Of course he's desperate. The team lost in their division last year and that's when they still had Ford. Benson will be under more pressure to succeed."

Realisation suddenly hit her. "Did you just say *paid* internship?"

The sides of my mouth pulled into a satisfied grin. "Imagine being paid for putting skills you learn at school to use."

My course involved classes such as public relations and marketing, sports marketing and sports event management. Benson would need those skills for the duration of the Crosstown Cup, and seeing as he didn't have them, he needed me. The money was an added benefit, like compensation for the initial humiliation Benson had inflicted upon me. I knew he didn't want my help, which only made it all the more satisfying. I couldn't wait to see the look on the team's faces when I showed up at practice. By the smirk that Nailea was wearing, I knew she was thinking the same thing.

Chapter 2

Beckham

"She's a fucking sociopath," I grumbled, taking a seat in the booth at Daisy's Delicacies. I'd been visiting the place since I was a kid. Despite my parents living in Glendale, they still made the daily trip to their favourite café, their love for it being passed down to me. The familiar place provided me with the comfort I needed. Practice had sucked ass. Benson was failing to adjust to his new role and it was affecting the entire team. Even as the captain, there was nothing I could do until Benson got his fucking shit together.

Coach Ford had always kept all of his plans in his head. He'd memorised them and left no physical copies for Benson to follow from. Marietta Ford falling sick was something we hadn't expected. Ford had planned to work for USC for as long as possible, but the abrupt illness of his wife forced him to take a step back.

And now Benson was stuck, left behind with nothing to work from. The man refused to contact Ford, hellbent on doing this *his* way. We couldn't even argue against him because he was the coach and he called the shots. Now, he had to get to know the team and our skills from scratch. I didn't even want to think about how long that would take. Dean Waverly would probably have to contact the UCLA hockey team to ask for the matches to be pushed even *further* into the year. Our first match was supposed to have taken place in November. It was January already—an entire new fucking quarter. The rivalry was so strong that the Bruins would never let us Trojans live down the humiliation of not being prepared.

How fucking embarrassing.

Sebastian let out a groan of pain as he sank into his seat and I smiled. He'd gotten bulldozed at practice by Tristan, the left-winger in our fourth line. Flattening Sebastian like a pancake against the plexiglass had recently become an unspoken and playful goal during each practice. It was like an accomplishment of sorts. Sebastian wasn't a bulky type of muscular, but he was still a giant and my teammates enjoyed trying to take him down.

"A hot sociopath," Grayson mused, shoving Sebastian over so that he could take a seat as well. The blonde swore when Grayson hit his bruised shoulder.

Leaning back in my seat, I crossed my arms and scanned the café. I spotted a tiny girl in the centre, a broomstick in hand as she hit a book around. The sight made my lips tilt slightly. It reminded me of simpler times when my dad would take me with him to work and I'd spend the entire time hitting a puck around his workplace.

Granted, I'd gotten in trouble a lot because my dad had

been a regular police officer back then, working in a small cubicle where I had to squash next to him on a little stool or even sit under the desk with my building blocks. He hadn't had any control over the station so the Lieutenant went off on me on quite a few occasions, specifically when a teenager getting arrested for petty theft had received a puck to the eye when he was brought in for questioning. My dad had found it funny.

Lieutenant Windsor hadn't.

"A sociopath, nonetheless," I retorted, falling back into the conversation.

"So you agree she's hot," Sebastian expressed through another groan. He knew exactly what I thought of her. My entire team did. She was a minx who cared about nobody but herself.

When I refused to speak, Grayson smirked and spoke again. "Honestly, I think Benson has a point. She *could* help us."

Fucking hell. We'd been over it before. The entire team had been over it and Grayson still didn't see the problem with having Nyx help our team. I refrained from asking him if he remembered what had happened last year, how we all had suffered at the manipulative hands of Nate.

I rolled my eyes, passing Grayson a menu before trying to turn the conversation towards Benson and not Nyx. "Are we talking about the same coach that suggested I remove Oliver and Jasper from our first line of defence because they don't *complement* each other's skills?" I scoffed. "As if he knows what he's talking about."

Grayson flagged over a server, placing our orders, and

Sebastian ogled the girl as she sauntered away. I kicked his knee from under the table and he let out a yelp.

"Fuck," he swore, scowling at me. "Fine, fine. Serious talk, I get it."

"Let's just see what happens," Grayson proposed, snickering when Sebastian rubbed his tender knee. "Give her a chance. Be honest, we're desperate for help right now."

I couldn't disagree with that. With Coach Ford gone, Benson was the only one who met *some* of the requirements for the position. Dean Waverly couldn't find anybody better on such brief notice, not when the annual competition between USC and UCLA had already started. We had a few months ahead and it looked as if Benson would only make it worse.

A loud yell grabbed our attention and we looked to see the manager of the place, Donovan, admonishing the little girl. Donovan's mom, Daisy, had owned the cafe, but after her passing, she'd left it to him. I missed the old woman, even more so because her son was an asshole. Case in point, him screaming at the little girl. He snatched the broom from her and picked up the book before storming off.

Grayson watched him leave before speaking, "She must be the daughter of one of the staff members."

The girl was small, with brown hair in two pigtails, looking no older than six. She watched the ground where the book once was, lips pulling into an annoyed frown. If I was being honest, she looked seconds away from following Donovan and ripping him a new one. I thought back to Lieutenant Windsor screaming at me for getting in the way.

"Serves her right," Sebastian scoffed, breaking me from my

thoughts. "You can't play hockey in the *middle* of a cafe. I've been watching her this whole time. Do you know how many people she nearly tripped with her hitting that damn book around?"

Grayson turned to him, green eyes narrowed. "She's a fucking kid."

"And I hate kids." Sebastian shrugged as if it was the simplest thing in the world. "God alone knows how I managed to put up with River."

Grayson's smile wavered at the mention of the youngest Hayes. "There's a literal three-year age gap between you two," he told the blonde in a dead tone.

Sebastian tutted seriously. "Three years old. Too young to become the parent of a kid you didn't ask for." Two seconds later, Grayson was muttering furiously to Sebastian about how that made no sense at all considering the Hayes duo had both parents to raise them for many years.

Overlooking Sebastian as he began to argue back, I called out to the little girl, "Hey, kid!" Her head bobbed up and she peeked around, trying to pinpoint the origin of my voice. When her eyes settled on me and the two bickering men, she raised a brow in challenge but didn't move. I remembered kids were taught to never talk to strangers. "You like ice hockey?"

Sebastian frowned, looking between me and the girl. "I'm getting major *do you want some candy* vibes." Grayson chortled but was cut off as the girl moved closer. "I can't believe she's falling for this," the blonde muttered when the girl stopped at our table. "Didn't your parents teach you never to talk to strangers?"

She crossed her short arms over her chest, glaring right back at him and I suppressed a chuckle. "If you tell me your name, you won't be a stranger." Grayson smirked. "I'm Indigo."

"Sebastian," he returned, something akin to respect in his eyes.

"Beckham," I told her and she nodded as Grayson introduced himself. Her big brown eyes were still moist with her earlier anger and I remembered why I'd called her over in the first place. "So, you like hockey?"

Indigo nodded, taking the seat next to me and folding her arms on the table. Grayson grinned at her. "You know, we play hockey."

"I know," she responded smoothly, lips tipping into a smile and amusement dancing in her eyes. "I've been to your games before." My surprise must've been clear because she giggled, the sound nearly drowned out by the chitchat in the cafe. She pointed at Sebastian. "Hayes. You have little angel wings painted on the sides of your helmet."

Sebastian stared at her, mouth parting at her words. Many people called him the angel because of his angelic appearance and, as a joke, a few of us had stolen his helmet and painted wings on it. Sebastian wasn't too happy about it, but every time he'd replaced his helmet, we painted new wings. He'd given up trying.

"Carter," she said with a smile, pointing at Grayson next. "You're the goalie. I've seen your uniform, it's hilarious."

I chuckled and so did the man in question. A goaltender's uniform was basically the same as a fort. Wearing it, Grayson was unrecognisable. He was hidden behind a neck shield, chest and arm protectors, and gigantic knee pads. And his helmet was more protective than everyone else's, considering he stopped shots with his body.

Finally, Indigo twisted to face me, tucking her short legs underneath her. "Hunt. You're the new captain this year." I nodded, my respect for her growing. She hmphed. "You're also an asshole." My brows nearly disappeared into my hairline and I felt more than heard Grayson choke.

"What?" I asked, probably looking like an idiot, having a little girl cuss me out.

Indigo crossed her arms, nose scrunching in derision before questioning in a breezy tone, "Spread any other rumours lately?"

My mouth opened and closed, no words escaping. It was probably because I couldn't form any. I'd never seen this girl in my life and she was speaking as if she knew me. Grayson was laughing into his hand and Sebastian was staring at Indigo with narrowed eyes. The gears turning in his head were almost visible.

Rushed footsteps met my ears and I raised my gaze to see a woman hastening over. She was dressed in the red server dress with a white apron around her waist. Her brown eyes were trained on Indigo and I wondered if it was her mother, although she appeared a little too young to have a kid. But hey, who was I to judge? They looked alike. The woman was unfamiliar, which told me she was new.

"I'm *so* sorry," the woman surprised us by apologising as she reached for the little girl, pulling her to her side. "She's not supposed to bother the customers—"

"Annie, look who it is!" Indigo exclaimed, moving out of the woman's hold to point at us. Judging by her expression, Annie had no idea who we were. I couldn't blame her. We were a college ice hockey team, not a team in the NHL.

My brows furrowed when I realised Indigo addressed the woman by her first name. "I'm sorry she bothered you, I'll just take her—"

Indigo pouted. "I wasn't bothering them! He called me over." Her eyes found mine. "If anything, *he was bothering me*."

Sebastian interjected, "How old are you?"

She scoffed, "Old enough to know that boys aren't supposed to hurt girls who try to help them. They shouldn't hurt girls. *Period*."

Her angry words were directed at me. Annie watched the exchange, taking a moment to glance at me and my two best friends. She seemed to be coming to some sort of realisation and her nose scrunched in bewilderment.

Donovan appeared from behind the counter, yelling, "Annie! Back to work while you still *have* work!" The threat in his voice was clear and it caused Annie to visibly panic. The woman was obviously new to her job and he was already being a miserable asshole.

Annie's eyes darted between Indigo and her manager. I sent her an encouraging smile. "Go, we'll watch her for you." Her expression was pained, probably unwilling to trust strangers. Or maybe it was just *us* she was unwilling to trust. There was a familiarity in the way she stared at us. "We'll stay until your shift is over."

Sebastian scowled at my words and I knew it was because

we'd planned to see a movie later. But that could wait.

"I'm *so* sorry, truly. It's my first day and Indigo was supposed to be picked up an hour ago and my shift doesn't end in another *two*," Annie choked out, face turning red. Grayson sent her a friendly smile, promising her we didn't mind. Ever the gentleman.

Indigo took that as her opportunity to speak. "I'll be fine. What are they gonna do to me?" Her eyes found mine again. "Are you gonna hurt my *feelings*?" A mocking pout was on her little lips. "I heard you're good at that."

Annie gasped. *"Indie!"*

"What?" Indigo shot back, shrugging innocently. "I'm just telling it how it is. Boys *suck*." Her final word was emphasised with an exaggerated eye-roll in my direction.

Annie flushed in embarrassment with every word that fell from Indigo's mouth, and she then told me, "I'm sorry—"

"She's alright," I told her, not minding Indigo's presence at all. In fact, I wanted to know how she knew me. If I had to take a few insults to find out, I'd be fine.

As Annie hesitantly walked away, Sebastian groaned. "Of course we mind! What happened to our movie?"

Indigo smiled. "My favourite movie is Shrek. You remind me of that stupid prince." Whether she was talking about Prince Charming or Lord Farquaad, I didn't know. And I didn't *want* to know. The riddle of her words made it all the more insulting and I had a feeling she knew that.

Grayson let out a bark of laughter. "I like her. She's funny."

"I'm funnier with a knife in my hand," Indigo told him seriously and he laughed even harder. With a dramatic sigh, she glanced at me. "It's part of a joke I call *hurting boys who deserve it.*"

I merely offered her a smile and she scowled at my lack of frustration. A server brought over our order. She placed a burger and fries in front of me, alongside a vanilla milkshake. Grayson had ordered two burgers because he was starving, but he placed the other one on a napkin and pushed it towards Indigo.

"Thank you," she said softly and I grinned, splitting my fries and handing her some, even though she tossed a suspicious look my way. I watched her take a bite of the burger. "This is actually really good," she spoke around a mouthful, forgetting that she was my rival or something.

Sebastian popped some fries into his mouth. "You've never had a burger here before?" Indigo shook her head, and my brows furrowed. "But your," he hesitated, trying to think of her link to Annie, "sister?" Indigo nodded, biting more of the burger. "She works here."

After she gulped the portion in her mouth, she answered, "It's her first day. Besides, only employees get free food. And only once a day." Sebastian opened his mouth to ask why Annie didn't just buy food, but I shut him up with a glare.

We ate quickly, the air filled with chatter as Grayson spoke to Indigo about anything and everything. They poked fun at Sebastian's bruised body when Grayson shoved him and he wailed in pain.

"Hurt him again!" Indigo yelled, cackling when Grayson pressed onto Sebastian's aching shoulder once more. I snorted, about to take a sip of my milkshake but found two fries floating in the creamy liquid. Without even having to look, I knew Indigo was smirking at me. "Revenge is best served cold," she muttered, pursing her lips.

I quirked a brow. "Revenge?" I waited for an explanation as to why she didn't like me, but I received none.

Once we were finished eating, someone came to collect our things and I paid the bill. It was only when Indigo spoke that I noticed the server hadn't left. "Ya need a tip, Beth?" The tiny girl asked the server.

The name rang a bell and I glanced up, noticing the familiar dark eyes. But her eyes weren't trained on me. Beth was looking at Indigo.

"*You*," she said in a growl, hinting that the two had a history. Seeing as it was Annie's first day on the job, I figured that Indigo had made another enemy in the period of a few hours.

"Bethany, hey," I greeted her, successfully dragging her attention away from the smirking girl who was no doubt attempting to trigger her anger. "It's been a while."

Sebastian grimaced at my words, knowing that I'd been avoiding the brunette on purpose after the two dates we'd been on. Dating wasn't on my list of priorities, but I'd known Beth since we were kids and when she asked me out a few weeks ago, I couldn't find it in myself to say no, especially since her mom was berating her for not being in a serious relationship yet.

Despite it being the 21st century, Vivian Braswell still believed that a woman's only goal in life was to get married young and start a family. At twenty-one, Beth was practically a spinster in her mom's eyes. I appeared to be the lucky candidate for a son-in-law and husband. Having just turned twenty-one myself, I wasn't looking to get married anytime soon.

Beth sent an uneasy stare Sebastian's way, fidgeting with the bill in her hands as she said, "I've been calling you. My family's planning a brunch this weekend and I was wondering if—"

"I meant to call," I cut her off, feeling guilty when she offered me a genuine smile. She was a sweet girl, one of the nicest people I knew. Her personality just didn't click with mine, in a romantic sense. "With the Crosstown Cup drama, I've been swamped."

The look in her eyes was sympathetic and the guilt churned in my stomach. "Aw, I'm sure you guys will do great. There'll always be a few tables available here for the team if you have a rough day."

I couldn't speak around the block in my throat and I was thankful Grayson did. "You work here now?"

He'd taken the words right out of my mouth. If I'd known Beth was working at the café, I wouldn't have returned until I figured out how to let her down gently. Two dates and it seemed like her mom was trying to plan our immediate wedding. Beth wasn't even attached to me in that sense. Everything she did was to please her mom.

Beth nodded, tucking a thick braid behind her elfish ear. "Too much free time. But hey, at least I get to see you, you know?"

I wondered if my team would be pissed if I changed our hangout spot for the next few weeks.

Indigo rolled her eyes. "Pack it up, Macbeth." Grayson

choked on a laugh and Sebastian was fighting a smile.

"You're a menace," Beth retorted, placing a hand on her hip as she glared at Indigo.

"And you reek of desperation," Indigo replied a second later, scrunching her little nose and perfecting a look of pure distaste that I'd only ever seen on one person before. "The guy's clearly not interested, sweetheart."

There was no way she was six years old, no fucking way.

Beth didn't miss a beat, looking ready to stomp her foot. "Somebody should tell your mom to get you a babysitter, *brat*."

Indigo faltered for a second and then said, "And somebody should tell *your* mom to take you to therapy. " I watched the two carefully. It was weird seeing a grown woman arguing with a child. Eventually, Beth turned on her heel, silently fuming.

Grayson nudged Indigo. "Seems like you've got another enemy."

She scoffed. "Macbeth's been complaining to Donovan since I first arrived. *Apparently*, I get in her way." She then looked at me. "She's probably gonna try and talk to you after her shift. Five bucks and I'll get rid of her for you."

My eyebrow quirked. "And by getting rid of her, you don't mean murder, right?" The twinkle in her eyes was scary.

Indigo burst into childlike laughter, looking nothing like the menacing girl she was a second ago. Her giggles got louder and louder as she burst out, "Of course not!" She wiped at the corners of her eyes, going suddenly serious. "I would've charged more than five bucks, dumbass."

Sebastian couldn't hold his laugh in this time and I allowed a small smile, one she didn't return. She must've remembered she was my enemy because she ignored me after that. Grayson merely laughed at my annoyance.

Indigo moved to the other side of the booth when Grayson made space for her and he handed her his phone, telling her she could download any game she wanted to. She ended up downloading a dress-up game and the two of them took turns to see whose outfit got scored the highest by the judges. I didn't get a chance to question Indigo and I knew Grayson was keeping her occupied on purpose.

Sebastian was people-watching, as he usually did. He didn't like company that much, but he enjoyed watching others and noticed small things; things that people usually overlooked. It was what made him a great asset to the team. He could pick up an opponent's weakness in a matter of seconds and discover their next move just by watching how they interacted with their team members.

I honestly thought we'd have a shot this year against the UCLA Bruins. Annually, our schools hosted the Crosstown Cup. Points were awarded within the 19 NCAA— National Collegiate Athletic Association—sanctioned sports that our schools competed in. Each sport was worth ten points which meant there were 190 total points available to win. At least 100 was needed to claim the overall win.

Last year, our school won the Crosstown Cup because we'd had more points than UCLA altogether. But that was all because of the other sports divisions and their wins. Our hockey team had lost against the Bruins. Although our school had still won, it irked me that our team failed in our division.

At that point, it wasn't *my* team. Nate had been the captain.

And he'd been a shit one. How somebody could make me hate a sport I loved, I had no fucking idea. And I wasn't the only one either. When it was certain Nate was going to be captain again this year, I'd known I had to do something. He'd left the team altogether and the school, and I wasn't complaining.

With him gone, this was supposed to be our year. But then Ford had left and Benson arrived. His words rang through my head when he announced that he'd asked Nyx *fucking* Taylor for help. If only he knew she was Nate's accomplice, adding to the team's torture. Having her back was like being in Nate's presence again, which was something nobody wanted. There were too many bad memories tied to him, and Nyx was a reminder.

I got that she was a sports management major and could help with our events, but that was it. Okay, *perhaps* she had other skills as well. But it was pathetic that Benson had to bring in outsiders because he couldn't do his fucking job. And it had to be Nyx, of all people.

My team hated her.

"Look," Sebastian hummed with a smirk. "It's your girl."

I turned my head to stare out of the window just as Nailea stopped her car long enough for Nyx to jump out. She waved at her friend as she drove off before rushing inside the cafe. I noted she wore a different outfit compared to earlier. Jeans and a white shirt adorned her body and I could make out a nametag but wasn't certain.

Nyx didn't glance around the cafe but rushed straight behind the staff doors. I looked back to Sebastian and he was still watching me with that fucking smirk of his. I wanted to punch it off. Not even a minute later, Nyx emerged from behind the doors. She stood with her arms crossed, blue eyes scanning the cafe. And then they landed on me. My blood boiled. There was just something about her that made me angry.

Not something—*everything*.

Everything about her pissed me off. She glared at me, making the hair on my arms stand up. Slowly, her eyes drifted to the little girl still engrossed in Grayson's phone. Her brow rose in question. Almost begrudgingly, she sauntered towards us, hands slipping into her jean pockets. Sebastian was smirking like an idiot and Grayson looked up, freezing when he noticed her making her way over. Out of all of us, he was the most civil with her and tried his best to stay on her good side.

It never worked.

Without taking her eyes off Indigo, she said, "Bag." The girl tore her eyes from the phone, a frown gracing her lips when she saw Nyx and was ready to argue but got cut off. "Now, Indie."

Annoyed, Indigo gave Grayson his phone back before stomping off to the staff doors. Grayson cleared his throat when seeing that Nyx was glaring at him. "Taylor, long time no see."

Ignoring him, she turned to look at me. "Have you lost your fucking mind?"

My lips tilted at her angry tone. It wasn't every day Nyx got angry. She had a way of pissing you off without even becoming frustrated herself. But this was the first time in a long while that she had any sort of emotion in her eyes when arguing with me.

"Come find out."

Her fists clenched as Sebastian chuckled. "Is this because I agreed to help Benson?" she questioned, her words practically dripping with venom. I didn't convey my confusion and let her speak. "Sending me your manly glares was one thing but involving my sister—"

Old enough to know that boys aren't supposed to hurt girls who try to help them. They shouldn't hurt girls. Period.

Indigo's words played on a loop in my head. Was Indigo implying that I had hurt Nyx? That was the furthest from the fucking truth. Nyx was the villain in this story and she'd stay that way.

Grayson raised a hand, eyes pleading with her to understand. "Whoa, we didn't know she was your sister," he said, speaking for all of us as he turned to see Indigo walking over, pink backpack and blanket in her small hands. "To be honest, she looks nothing like you."

He wasn't lying. Indigo had brown hair and brown eyes, like that woman Annie. But everything about Nyx was the opposite of her name; bright, with blue eyes and blonde hair. She looked nothing like her sisters; sisters that I didn't even know she had. The new knowledge made me slightly nauseous, solely because I'd had no idea.

Realising what she implied, I felt my anger grow. "You think I'd use a little girl against you?" Did she honestly think so low of me? If any of us had to have a low opinion of the other, it would be me. And she had nobody to blame but herself.

Smirking haughtily, she responded, "Wouldn't surprise me. I've come to expect disappointment from men." And there she was. That little crack in her facade was sealed in the blink of an eye. "Have you realised we express disappointment with, *oh man*? I wonder why."

I didn't respond because I knew what she was doing. It was what she always did. She started an argument by provoking us and whilst *we* got frustrated, *she'd* laugh as if it was all entertaining. I could suddenly see the resemblance between her and Indigo.

Sebastian shook his head, his smirk dissolving into a scowl. "You know what I've always hated about you," he began, "your attitude."

Indigo stopped next to her sister, slipping her hand into hers. The brown-eyed girl grinned at Sebastian before saying, "Too bad she didn't ask."

Grayson's jaw dropped and so did Sebastian's. I was too busy staring at the proud smirk on Nyx's face. I knew Indigo's taunting of Beth had seemed familiar. I'd seen it before, even been on the end of it numerous times. Indigo waved goodbye, took keys from Nyx and left through the doors, heading to a red pickup truck and climbing in.

Nyx stared at us. "You say that as if I care what you think," her gaze found Sebastian's and she smirked, "you're a bug under my shoe, *angel*."

Sebastian's eyebrow jerked in restrained anger. He had the worst temper out of all of us and Nyx knew that. She wanted to provoke him.

Luckily, Beth chose that moment to return with complimentary ice cream. "Dessert on the house for my *favourite* hockey boys!"

She didn't even notice Nyx, placing a bowl in front of each of us. Like I knew he would, Sebastian slipped away, claiming to need the toilet. Beth's sugary sweetness always annoyed him, even when we'd been younger.

"Thanks," Grayson murmured, eying Nyx warily as she stood to the side. When he looked at me, I could see what he was thinking; we had to separate the two women unless we wanted a full-blown war in the middle of the cafe.

"My mom said you could come to brunch," Beth continued our previous conversation, one that I was hoping she'd forget about. "She misses having you around. I think she always hoped we'd get together—"

"Drop your panties, why don't you?" Nyx interjected, looking bored and annoyed that our argument was interrupted. If there was one thing Nyx loved, it was arguing, and the fact that Beth acted as a hindrance most probably pissed her off.

Beth scanned Nyx from head to toe, looking satisfied that she towered over her. Nyx wasn't even that short, but Beth had the legs of a runway model, making her nearly the same height as Grayson; who stood at exactly six feet. The look in Beth's usually kind eyes was animalistic. It was as if she concluded she was the predator and Nyx was the prey. But size didn't mean anything. Humans were the number one predators, however, one touch from a poison dart frog, roughly around the size of a paperclip, could take down a grown man.

It felt like I was watching the whole thing play out, an ignorant human coming into contact with a being that could end their life. Grayson straightened, comprehending that two of the only women in my life (other than my mom and River) were about to interact. I'd realised that the second Beth had walked over and it was like waiting for a bomb to go off.

"Beth," my childhood friend introduced herself after a tense silence, one she allowed for the sole purpose of intimidating Nyx. Beth never struck me as an intimidating figure and it was weird seeing her attempt at it.

Nyx raised an unbothered brow. "That short for Macbeth?" With that one inquiry, she managed to snuff all of Beth's attempts at being the predator.

Beth frowned and I fought the urge to laugh at the fact that Indigo and Nyx thought along the same lines. They were definitely sisters.

"It's short for *Bethany*," she replied in the calmest voice she could muster, but both Grayson and I could tell she was flustered.

The blonde girl hmphed. "Macbeth would've been cooler, not gonna lie." It was her turn to scan Beth and I winced inwardly at the bored look in her icy eyes as if Beth wasn't worth her time. "Nyx Taylor."

Recognition flashed through Beth's expression and she glanced at me. "I've heard *so* much about you, Nyx." Her voice was sweet, as always, but carried an underlying meaning. I fought a groan.

"My reputation precedes me, I see. That's cute," Nyx stated with a glimpse in my direction. Beth needed to shut up. She made it seem as if I spoke about Nyx all the time, and that was just pathetic. "Too bad I've never heard a thing about you though."

Beth's lips tilted down and she looked at me for a split

second before she asked Nyx, "Really?"

An evil gleam appeared in her eyes. "Careful, honey, don't sound so disappointed. You might just give me the impression that you seek validation from me. Then again, doesn't make you much different from Beck, does it?"

I wanted to fling myself through the window and Grayson noticed. He tried to intervene. "This ice cream is *delicious*—"

"It's not anything good," Beth continued, her stance becoming protective. I was grateful for her, truly, but she wouldn't last a second against Nyx. "What was it he told me on our last date?" she asked herself, emphasising that I'd taken her on a date and I glanced at Nyx, spotting her glare. "Oh, that you're a *backstabbing bitch*."

Nyx barely reacted. "You shouldn't look so proud of the fact that he speaks about me during your dates." Beth didn't know what to say, seeming to think over her words. "I see you're avoiding blondes, now. Remind you too much of me?" Her words were aimed at me and I felt my blood boil all over again.

"Fuck you, Taylor," I grumbled, watching the look of confusion on Beth's face dissolve into understanding and then hurt.

Nyx laughed, the sound too sweet for somebody as evil as her. "You already did, Hunt. See you at practice, boys. *Ciao*." Her boots clicked as she drifted away. I watched her climb into the pickup truck.

Beth looked at me weirdly before she stormed off. I hadn't told her of what happened between me and Nyx personally, only the hockey team drama with her and Nate. It was a shit way for her to find out, I had to admit.

And Nyx must've picked up on it. She was literally a wild animal, able to sniff out weaknesses. Her mission was to humiliate Beth, who only knew a snippet of our story.

"I'm gonna have to blame Beth on this one," Grayson spoke before I could, seemingly reading my thoughts. "She's always forcing herself into things that don't concern her, as sweet as she is," he explained, scooping more ice cream into his mouth. "It was kinda asking to be humiliated, you know?"

I nodded, feeling more pissed at myself. Beth wasn't a confrontational person. If she knew something had happened between me and Nyx, she wouldn't have inserted herself into what was essentially a fucked up relationship. All she'd seen was somebody that I hated and she'd tried to stand up for me. It was dumb, but completely Beth.

"Never thought I'd see the day Nyx would mention our past," I told Grayson and he laughed in agreement. "And the first time she brings it up is to insult a girl whose mom is forcing me to be with. Sebastian's right, she's a fucking sociopath."

Chapter 3

Nyx

"But they looked so nice!" Indigo blurted as I helped her slip into her pyjamas. Freshly washed, she smelt like a little baby. There was powder on her chin and her hair was brushed flat against her head, pulled into a neat bun. At first, she'd complained she looked like an egg but calmed down when I said she was a pretty egg. "And even though I was a little meanie, they were *still* nice. I don't understand."

I wiped the powder from her chin, pressing a kiss to her cheek. "Just because they're nice to you doesn't mean they're nice to everyone else," I murmured, straightening her pink nightie.

She wrapped her arms around my neck. "Are you angry at me for sitting with them?" Her lips were a tiny pout and I chuckled, brushing my knuckles over her smooth cheek. "You looked angry. I tried to make them hurt for hurting you, but I don't think they took me seriously."

A lot of her pronunciation was incorrect because of her two

missing front teeth. Picking her up, she squealed as I placed her in the rickety bed. "I'll admit, Indie, I was angry. And I'm sorry if I took that out on you." I felt bad about the way I'd snapped at her to get her bag. "And I'm grateful that you tried to stand up for me."

"Always," she countered, curling up into her blankets. "I didn't like the blondie, anyway. I made his eye twitch."

I snorted at that, thinking back to Sebastian. I didn't have a problem with him, but he hated me solely because his asshole of a captain still hated me. I wanted to move on. That hatred was unjustified, but I didn't mind dishing back whatever he served. Thankfully, Nailea took joy in pissing him off, essentially doing my job for me. Something else I had to be grateful for when it came to her.

I kissed Indigo's head, whispering that she needed to get some sleep. She was still filled with energy, wanting to talk the entire time. Her constant bursts of energy reminded me of an aunt that was long gone. It almost seemed like Indigo was born with her personality—like it was the universe's way of apologising for taking my aunt. Indigo stayed talking for many minutes before finally falling asleep.

Annie wasn't home yet even though her shift at the cafe ended hours ago and she wasn't picking up her phone. I tried to calm myself. It was her first day and we hadn't figured out transport yet. Nailea had dropped me so I could get Indigo and then I'd driven home in Annie's truck. I would've asked Nailea to drive us home but she had things to do and I didn't want to be more of a burden than I already was. Annie had assured me that the bus was still an option for her, but for how long? Bus fare was expensive once it piled up.

Turning off the light and closing the door to the room, I stepped out into the tiny living room, seeing Poppy settled at the coffee table, books spread out in front of her.

"Still busy with homework?" She'd been busy since I'd gotten home, having stayed by herself until I arrived with Indigo.

Indigo may have looked like Annie, but Poppy was all me. From the blonde hair to her bright eyes, she was my spitting image since we both took after our mom, something we both paid dearly for. She peered up at me, eyes drooping with lethargy. "I'm nearly done."

It was a lie, both of us knew it. There were still too many subjects for her to catch up on, too many to finish in one night. And she had the entire weekend ahead of her.

"You know, you don't have to complete everything. Your teacher said—"

"I want to," she cut me off, fixated on the book in her frail hands. I could smell it on her. *Desperation.* She was shaking from the cold and I plucked the blanket up from the couch before draping it over her.

"I don't want a free pass." Not wanting to offend her, I lazily moved the books out of her reach, turning her papers away. "Nyxie—"

"You're tired, Poppy," I told her, watching as her hands shook. "You're *tired* and you need to *rest.*" My eyes flitted across her exposed arms, at the tiny freckles forming constellations there. "We all understand if you're a little behind on school," I eased her worries. "And if anybody has a problem with that, they can deal with me."

She knew exactly who I was talking about. With a tremulous sigh, Poppy begged, "Is Annie mad at me?"

I smiled grimly. What was it about kids that made them care about everything around them? Then again, Annie and I were forced to grow up quickly. We'd been a pair of worrying little people for years.

I sat down on the old couch and it whined under my weight. "Come here," I said, opening my arms and she clambered into them, still shuddering. My grip around her tightened as I pressed my nose to her head, inhaling her familiar sweet scent. I hated that I was shaking as well. "Why would you think that?"

Poppy sniffled, clutching my white shirt, part of my uniform at the grocery store. "Because she had to take another job," she confided, voice cracking with the weight of her words. I closed my eyes, feeling them blaze. Annie worked the morning shift at the local grocery store and I worked the afternoon shift. But today, she'd started at the cafe as well. "And she's already so tired. I hear her crying at night."

"She doesn't hate you." I didn't know how else to reply.

Annie and I tried our best to not burden the girls with our financial problems. Living inside a bubble was better for them. Poppy said nothing else. She just let her eyes flutter closed. If Annie was here, she'd scold me. Poppy was getting too big to fall asleep with us because she was afraid of the dark. There was a nightlight in the room she shared with Indigo, but she refused to fall asleep there. I didn't have the heart to tell her to go to bed. Instead, I held her tighter, rocking side to side, just like I'd done when she was younger.

As she drifted off, my thoughts meandered to Beckham and his friends. I could never conclude whether I truly hated him. My animosity stemmed from the fact that *he hated me.* And he had a somewhat good reason to, especially after what I'd done. The part that hurt me the most was that he hadn't come back to ask why I'd done what I did. I thought he'd known me better than that, but I was wrong.

Nothing could describe the fear in my heart when I'd seen Indigo sitting with them. I kept my home life separate from my school life. Seeing a morsel of that life so close to Beckham had made fear distort my vision. I'd trusted somebody once before with that part of my life and look what happened; I got fucking sued, Annie was now working two jobs and the rent was heaping up. Hopefully, that problem would be ironed out very soon.

I'd received the emails from Benson and my jaw had dropped with how much they were going to pay me. My wallet already felt full, opposing how dusty it usually was. It meant I no longer had to work at the grocery store and I could pay off our debts to the landlord. We were struggling, we really were.

I had too much pride to ask anyone for help. Once, last year, I'd been on the verge of telling Beckham about what my life was like. I'd trusted him. But that trust wasn't reciprocal and looking back at it, I was glad I hadn't told him anything. I'd already made the mistake of confiding in the wrong people, in weak people. They would find a way to use your weaknesses against you to overlook their own.

My annoyance at myself grew because my thoughts were

stilled plagued with Beckham and our two interactions today. The thought of him pushed me in the direction of Beth, somebody I'd never met before. A fairly tall girl with smooth dark skin and big eyes. Pretty. Beth was so pretty. And she was also protective of Beckham, that much I could tell. There were strong feelings on her part, but I couldn't put my finger on the meaning behind those feelings.

As much as I hated Beckham, I couldn't deny that I could read him like a book. He didn't like Beth, at least not romantically. Either Beth was oblivious or she held out hope his feelings would change. That was enough to make me pity her and I felt nauseated at the thought that I had humiliated her.

The common cause of catfights among women was men. I had no reason to hate Beth, my actions fuelled by the desire to one-up Beckham, unconsciously hurting Beth in the process. It seemed to be a common occurrence with me, focusing on my end goal without comprehending that I could hurt people on my way there.

Beth didn't have a reason to hate me either, fuelled by whatever Beckham had told her. And there was the problem: *Beckham*. I scoffed quietly, hating that I let him get to me. *Again*.

The door to the house opened and in shuffled Annie, exhaustion clear in her posture and expression. She leaned against the wall, dropping her bag beside her. It was obvious; she'd taken on another few extra hours. I watched her with a heavy heart, hating that her usually warm brown eyes looked lifeless. They were drooping as if her eyelashes had anchors attached to them. She said nothing, just shoved away from the wall and escaped into the bathroom.

And then the crying came.

Swallowing roughly, I picked up Poppy, groaning at her weight in my arms. I had to remember she wasn't a baby anymore; she was turning thirteen soon. I carried her into her room, depositing her onto the bed she shared with Indigo. The latter rolled over in her sleep, binding her arms around her big sister. Poppy snuggled into her hold, snoring lightly.

On my way out, I flicked the nightlight on, knowing that Poppy would have a heart attack if she woke up in the dark. Annie was still sobbing when I halted outside the bathroom door. Her sobs were like a fork grinding against a stainless steel pot. I felt it in my teeth, in my entire body, and I hated it. This was the one part of the routine that I abhorred. For a few hours, I could forget whilst I attended classes, surrounded by carefree students, taunting people, and enjoying myself.

But Annie was working her ass off, worrying, crying. Pushing the door open, I spotted her sitting on the dirty tiles, reminding me I needed to scrub them. Annie glanced up when I entered, face red and wet with tears. A choking sound escaped her as she rubbed her nose. And following the routine, I sat down next to her. She dropped her head onto my shoulder.

"I'm sorry." She always apologised, even though she didn't need to. We were all doing our best to survive. "I've just—I've had a rough day."

Gently rubbing her shaking hands, I asked, "What happened?"

She sniffled, trying to wipe away her tears. "Nothing, it's

silly. I just have to get used to working for Donovan. He has a habit of yelling at his employees."

I sighed. Annie didn't react well to being yelled at, she never did. We had our asshole of a dad to thank for that. "He yelled at you?"

Another sniffle left her and she forced a laugh as she nodded. "I mean, it's my first day. I'm bound to mess up because I'm still learning the dynamics of the place." She shook her head. "I messed up so many times, Nyxie. I'd be surprised if I still have that job tomorrow." Her words shook with the fear of losing a source of income. A source we needed.

Anger grew inside of me. "As you said, it's your first day. He can't expect you to be perfect."

"I'll do better," she assured me, sounding a little more confident. I believed her fully. She'd hopped from job to job and she always worked to the best of her ability. "But it's the yelling I have to get used to." Her eyes filled with shame. "When he yelled at me for dropping this one customer's cappuccino, I had to run to the back before anybody could see me cry. Do you know how embarrassing that is? Who still cries when they're being yelled at—"

"*Lots* of people," I interjected, not wanting her to belittle herself. And she wasn't just *any* person either. She was the daughter of Matthew Taylor; a man who believed violence and anger was the answer to everything. Being raised by him came with side effects.

That was a euphemism for trauma.

Annie was quiet for a second, wiping away the last of her tears. "I have to text Beth and thank her." I raised a brow. "She followed me out when she saw I was about to burst into tears."

The guilt was back. "Did she help?"

My sister nodded. "Did exactly what you're doing right now. She just sat with me, although in silence. Gave me her number in case I ever needed a friend to talk to."

Annie never really had friends, and I could hear shy happiness creep into her tone when she uttered that Beth could be a friend. I sighed. When I saw Beth again, I had to apologise to her.

"I hope she makes working for Donovan a little better," I added, completely sincere. Annie smiled, her previous sadness gone from her expression. Moving on from the topic of Beth and Donovan, I took my phone out and handed it to Annie, where the emails from Benson were opened. I'd been staring at it for a while, unable to believe my eyes.

"What's this?" she asked.

Running a hand through her short brown hair, I answered, "My new job. Quit my one at the grocery store today." Annie's dark brows banged together in confusion. "This one will pay much more. Look." I gestured to the phone again.

Her mouth dropped open in shock, and I nearly laughed at the comical sight. "Nyxie," she spoke in an airy voice, one that hinted her mind wasn't in sync with her actions. "This– how—" She paused, shaking her head. "No, this *can't* interfere with your studies—"

"It *won't*," I assured her, scrolling through the email and pointing at a sentence. "If anything, it'll *help* with my studies. Annie, this is a dream come true. I can put my skills to use and perhaps this could even give me a jump start for when I graduate."

Since I was a sports business and management major, this internship could do wonders for my career. Helping the Trojans during the duration of the Crosstown Cup could mean getting noticed by influential people in the sports industry. Loads of them attended the matches between USC and UCLA. Going into public relations sounded ideal. I'd love to work for a team and do marketing, damage control and things like that.

And that's what I'd be dealing with in the coming months of my life, depending on how spread out the hockey matches were. Special extra points were given to sports divisions for fundraisers held in the community or even regular events to boost morale and get more people to support; because the Crosstown Cup wasn't just about competing and building skills—it was also about bringing a community split by a rivalry closer together.

And it just so happened that event management was part of my courses. Pair that with the notes that I'd compiled about the team for the past year; this role was made for me. And not only was I going to help the team win, but I'd be bringing in much-needed money for my family.

Annie stared at the digits of my payment, phone shaking in her hands. The email stated that I'd be paid every week a match and fundraiser are held.

"This is," she choked on an incredulous laugh, "this is going to help us *so much*." Raising a tremulous hand, she rubbed her red nose.

"We can't tell him," I stated firmly, and Annie froze, looking terrified. "With my job at the grocery store gone, I don't have my half of the payments for him. Quit one of your jobs and pay him what you can."

"But Poppy's physiotherapy bills—"

I cut her off. "Will fall to me now. You've done as much as you can, it's time for me to help more." I hated that this was Annie's life. Four years older than my nineteen years of age, Annie already had the weight of the world on her shoulders. She cared for us, worked two jobs and gave up her dream of furthering her education. It was high time I paid her back.

She sighed, the worry leaving with her breath. "Okay. I'll continue making the payments, but I'll set some more money aside for groceries and rent." I went to intervene, but she spoke again, "*Until* Poppy's bills are paid off. Then you can pay rent." I smiled at that and she threw an arm around me.

Poppy's physiotherapy sessions had ended a week ago and we were still behind on payment. By a lot. She'd twisted her ankle terribly and could barely walk. At first, I'd thought it was a silly twist, like when you stepped wrong, but Poppy had been in constant pain. Physiotherapy was our only option—and the reason for Annie's second job.

Luckily for us, public school was free so we didn't have to worry about Poppy and Indigo's fees. The school provided them with everything they needed. Indigo's preschool was on the same premises so we didn't have to drive too far out.

"You should get some sleep," Annie murmured through a yawn and I laughed softly. Her eyes were filled with exhaustion. Growing up, I was always jealous of those eyes. And her hair. And her facial features. Because she wasn't burdened with our mom's looks like Poppy and I were, but I'd gotten over that jealousy in a matter of days. We were in the same boat. There was no need to push anyone overboard in jealousy or anger. Not like our mom had pushed our grandma overboard, and now they were both gone.

"You're right," I whispered but made no move to get up. She didn't either, just placed her head back on my shoulder.

"Do you remember the forts Uncle Robbie used to build us in the bathroom when we lived with Grandma?" she asked suddenly, no doubt wishing she had one of those as she struggled to find comfort on the tiles.

Hearing the nostalgia in her voice filled my body with lead. All these years, and she was still trying.

"You know I don't, Annie."

According to stories from Annie, Uncle Robbie had been our mom's best friend and looked after us whenever he could. A young Annie even believed that he'd had something going on with our mom whilst our parents had been separated. He'd died months before our mom had gone back to our dad, devastating Annie. She was the only one who sometimes spoke of him, albeit in secret, considering our dad had hated him.

Annie tried to keep the memory of him alive, but it never triggered anything. Days after I'd turned seven, Uncle Robbie had gotten into a car wreck with me in the backseat. He'd died on impact. My grandma said I'd gotten off lucky. A concussion that left me with retrograde amnesia.

I couldn't remember a single fucking thing from before the accident. Unfortunately, Uncle Robbie was part of those memories. Every smile, every joke and tear shed. Gone. As if he hadn't once been loved by me.

But even when nobody wanted to talk about Uncle Robbie, Annie continued to tell me stories of the man that had loved us when our dad hadn't wanted to. She believed that I'd remember someday. So I let her speak of him whenever she wanted to. And speak she did. I shifted slightly on the cold tile, listening to her relay story after story.

And that's where we fell asleep, on the cold tile of the bathroom floor. Just like when we were kids; hiding.

The first thing I noticed was the agonising pain in my neck, courtesy of sleeping on the ground. The second thing I noticed was that there was a fluffy blanket draped over me. And the third thing I noticed was that a tiny person was lying on my chest. At first, terrible memories returned, violating my thoughts. I was sure that when I opened that bathroom door, when I opened my eyes, I'd be met with misery. I was so sure that when I left the bathroom, my dad would yell at me.

It was routine and so far, all the boxes were ticked; I'd slept in that bathroom with only a blanket and I held a tiny girl to my chest. Said chest began throbbing with fear, but then I recalled last night, putting Indigo and Poppy to bed, sitting with Annie—and I realised I was safe.

I groaned in pain as I lifted my head. "Indie, what are you doing in here?"

Her arms were wrapped around me, but she wasn't asleep, merely staring at the wall opposite her. "You and Annie had a sleepover without me," she pouted and I snickered slightly, trying to crack my neck.

Indigo stood up, lifting the blanket with her. My laughter died down when I realised she associated the bathroom with a cheerful place, a place where she had frequent sleepovers with her sisters. She didn't see it the way we did; a hiding place. I hoped it always stayed that way.

"Where's Annie?" I inquired, standing up and stretching. Bones cracked and I let out a loud yawn. I was going to be in a lot of pain today.

"Making breakfast," she countered, kissing my knuckle before scurrying to the kitchen, blanket dragging behind her.

I smiled at that and headed towards my room. There were two beds belonging to me and Annie, respectively. Both were untouched since we'd slept on the floor. I stalked over to my dresser and placed a fresh pair of clothes on my bed, deciding to shower after I had breakfast.

On my way to the kitchen, I found Poppy leaning against the door to her room, placing her right foot on the ground and lifting it repeatedly. She was grinning to herself, probably thrilled about being able to go back to school. Her teacher was kind enough to agree that she stay home for the duration of her physiotherapy and sent her work over. But I knew she secretly pitied us. With money having to be put towards the physiotherapy bills, there was barely any for transport and I didn't want to bother Georgia more than I needed to.

Poppy looked up when I passed her. "Dad come home last night?" I questioned, slipping my hand into hers and guiding her to the kitchen. She shook her head and I let out a sigh of relief. I didn't want to take my chances and go check his room. Knowing Poppy, she'd been up early already and peeked through the keyhole of his room. She'd always hated him. "Good."

"Morning, my lovely sisters!" Annie greeted, depositing a few eggs onto plates. There was an apron wrapped around her. It was worn out, one that Poppy and I bought her a while back. In white font, it read: *world's best mommy.* "I've got eggs and bacon galore!"

Indigo clapped excitedly, laughing when her breakfast was put together in the shape of a smiley face. Poppy stabbed a folk through the egg, making it weep yolk, and Indigo screamed at her for murdering the egg. She demanded we host a tiny funeral and Poppy egged her on, pun intended, by demanding we bury the slain where it belonged—in Poppy's ravenous tummy.

The blonde roared like a monster, gobbling the egg, yolk dripping from her mouth. She chewed dramatically, causing Indigo to giggle like a lunatic. I beamed, moving past Annie to get to the fridge. She nudged my hip as I took out a carton of orange juice, lining up three glass cups and one plastic *Barbie* one. The cups were mismatched, having lost their siblings time and time again when Indigo tried to reach for high cabinets and dropped things.

Whilst pouring the juice, I stared at a screaming Indigo who tried to lean out of the way when Poppy threatened to smear yolk all over her precious face. Annie scolded the two, but the smile on her face never wavered. She looked healthier; like she had a good sleep, which was weird considering we'd slept on cold tiles the entire night.

I wondered how my mom could leave this behind. I

wondered how she could leave without looking back, without thinking of Indigo's melodious laugh, Poppy's sweet smile and Annie's abundant love for her family. A separate space of hatred inside me was reserved just for my mom. She'd never been a good mother, but her faults had been eased by the presence of my grandma and Uncle Robbie—probably the only two people who loved us.

Even after Uncle Robbie's death and our mom running back to our dad, we still had our grandma. But Eliza Taylor just *had* to ruin that too, jealous that we loved her mom more than our own. She'd gotten a restraining order against my grandma on the grounds of stalking and harassment, her case fuelled by the fact that my grandma had planned to file for custody of us. Although I was probably only fourteen at the time, I still understood the complex feelings of heartbreak my grandma had gone through during the process. When she'd been asked to leave our lives, my sisters and I felt her absence. And then my mom left. So what was the fucking point? She should've let my grandma take us when she had the chance if she was just planning to leave anyway. I'd never forgive her for that.

My phone began ringing noisily and I wondered who was calling me this early. It was on the coffee table. Annie must've placed it there when she'd woken up. Indigo hopped off the chair, dashing for my phone and bringing it to me. I kissed her head, taking the phone from her and seeing that it was Nailea.

I frowned, answering it as Annie shushed the girls when Poppy flicked egg yolk at Indigo. "Nyxie's Pecan Farm, which nut would you like to speak to?"

"Dude, guess what?!" Nailea screamed, prompting me to

hold the phone at a distance. When she was done squealing, I brought it back to my ear. I'd learnt to never guess when Nailea asked me to. She never gave you enough time because her excitement propelled her to just blurt the news. "There's a party tonight!"

Taking a bite of bacon, I chewed before stating, "There's a party *every* weekend. I don't see how this concerns me." If this was one of those times Nailea implored me to tag along with her and her friends, then she was going to be painfully disheartened, as usual.

She squealed again and I cringed at the deafening noise. "But ask me who's throwing it!" Not even a second later, she spoke again. "The hockey boys!" I hummed, my interest peaking. "I heard a lot of members from other sports divisions are gonna be there to show their support. You know, since the hockey boys are finally joining the cup after *ages*."

"And who did you hear this from?" I inquired, taking another morsel of bacon, only for Poppy to whack my hand because I was eating from her plate. "Because last time you heard there was a party at a barn, but when you got there, a farmer made you clean up cow—"

"That's only because the girl that told me about the party hated me because she thought her boyfriend cheated on her with me—which wasn't true!" Nailea justified and I smirked to myself, recalling how her perfect hair had smelt like cow shit for days. "But I have an excellent source this time. Sebastian told me about the party."

A crease must've formed between my brows in confusion because, as Annie shuffled past me, she gently smoothed the line.

"Sebastian invited you? Sebastian Hayes? The guy that's almost as unpleasant as the guy whose feet he worships? The guy that hates you almost as much as his captain hates me?"

Indigo raised her head at the mention of the blonde man, murmuring to Poppy that he had the looks of Prince Charming with the personality of Lord Farquaad. I nearly laughed at the accuracy.

Nailea was silent for a beat and I knew there was a catch. "Well, he didn't *exactly* invite me. He said, and I quote: don't you dare show up." I snorted. Nailea was known to show up at every party. Sebastian had only succeeded in motivating her to attend by saying that. "He was using reverse psychology." Of course that's what she concluded. "So?"

"So what?" I returned.

"We're going tonight, right?" she probed, her tone pleading. Without even having to be in her presence, I knew her lips were in a pout and she was doing that puppy thing with her eyes.

I sighed, peering at my now cold egg. "Nailea, I can't." Annie frowned at me and I turned away. "I'm booked today—gimme a sec," I added when I spotted my older sister trying to catch my attention. Muting the call, I urged Annie, "What?"

"Go tonight, enjoy yourself—"

I was already shaking my head. "No, I'm not leaving you alone tonight." Annie placed her hands on her hips, looking like an offended mother.

"I won't be alone. I have these two little devils. Besides, when was the last time you went to a party?" At my silence, she grinned. "Exactly. Now, *tell* Nailea you're going."

Huffing, I unmuted the call, informing Nailea I'd be attending. She screeched so powerfully that I was certain my eardrums exploded. I hung up after she promised to pick me up. She was the only other person who knew about my sisters, which was why she frequently helped with transport or babysitting. I was grateful for her, truly.

As I sat down, eating my cold egg, I realised I could use this party to my advantage since all the hockey boys would be there—*especially* Beckham. Knowing how the team could be, I knew it would be troublesome to get them to behave, solely because I was a girl. I could deal with their attitudes, but the flirtation, sexist remarks, teasing and even the bullying would be hell. And that's when I set my plan for tonight in motion.

Chapter 4

Beckham

I'd always known Nailea was a popular one. Her beauty alone demanded an invitation to every party. She was a frequent name thrown around the locker room, although none of the boys had ever been given a sliver of her attention. I could see the appeal, but I'd always found her beauty a little unnerving. Nobody could look that perfect; it was impossible. I'd expected to see her at my party, alone even, considering sometimes she would arrive without her supposed friends. But I swallowed my tongue when I walked downstairs, seeing Nailea dancing on top of a table, swinging her jacket above her head. Although, my attention wasn't on her. It was the girl next to her.

Nyx fucking Taylor was dancing on the table I ate at every morning, barely wearing anything and drunk out of her mind. She was laughing with Nailea and the sight was so foreign that I had to blink a few times. Wearing a barely-there tank top and tiny jean shorts, she looked like something out of every frat boy's fantasy. Her hair was loose, bouncing all over the place with each sway of her hips.

Nyx had the personality of a robot whose default setting was to be a bitch, but this was something entirely new. I'd never seen her at a party before as she tended to avoid them. It was suspicious that she'd showed up at *my* party, at *my* house. The music grew louder as people cheered the two girls on. I couldn't believe what I was seeing and it appeared many others felt the same way.

A carefree Nyx Taylor was a sight to behold.

Nailea wrapped her arm around Nyx's bare waist, pulling her back to her front. To my surprise, Nyx was grinding against the short girl, eyes closed as she held her arms up, swaying her head to the music. I scowled when a guy shoved past me, trying to get a closer look. My annoyance grew when he began tossing money at the two, but they weren't paying attention to him or any of the other guys.

More people were climbing on sofas and counters, trying to get some of the attention Nyx and Nailea were receiving. The latter tossed her head back, eyes rolling to the back of her head as she spun, sending the crowd of horny guys into a screaming fit.

"I don't know if I should be turned on or disgusted by myself," Sebastian said over the music as he stopped next to me, a red cup of beer in his hands. I raised a brow at the look in his clear eyes and he laughed, the sound lost among the noise. "Chill, I'm talking about the tiny demon, not your girl."

The smirk stayed on his lips when I glowered at the implication of his words. He must've seen that I was on the verge of punching him so he pushed away, laughing the entire time as he disappeared into the kitchen. Since he never enjoyed being surrounded by too many people, he always ate the night away. I scoffed, turning my head to find Grayson.

And that's when Nyx's eyes caught mine.

I froze, unable to move from my spot against the wall. The smirk that tugged at her full lips was my undoing. She ran her hands up her bare stomach, dragging the material up a little as she brushed over her breasts before disappearing into her hair, hips swaying all the time. Tossing her head back, she ran her tongue over her teeth, winking at me. My fists clenched and my eyes narrowed, making her grin widen.

If possible, the music became even louder, causing the ground to tremble. I'd have angry neighbours knocking soon. Nyx held her hands out in front of her in fists. Keeping eye contact with me, she twisted both hands, showing me two middle fingers paired with a wink.

Unable to help myself, I chuckled.

She smiled at that, twirling on the spot and tilting forward slightly. The group that was standing behind her went ballistic. She raised her head, flipping her hair behind her, reminding me of a mermaid—or perhaps a siren, luring men to their deaths. Her hands were running over her body, and many of her audience followed her actions with eager eyes. I realised with a scowl that the majority of the hockey team was part of that audience.

Surprising nobody, seeing as Nailea was a touchy and overly affectionate drunk, the latter stepped forward, gripping the material of Nyx's top in her hands and yanking her forward. And then their lips met. The crowd of horny students screamed.

Another chuckle left me as I watched them make out. It didn't look very enjoyable because both of them were trying to dance while kissing, so it was all over the place. Nyx pulled away and not even a second later, she burst into a fit of giggles.

Nailea did the same, dramatically wiping her mouth with the back of her hand as she yelled, "That was fucking disgusting! I'm pretty sure I've got saliva up my nose!"

Nyx could barely speak through her laughter and nodded her head, eyes clenched shut and hands pressed to her probably aching stomach.

Sebastian appeared again, holding a bag of chips. "What did I miss?"

Deciding to torture him, I responded, "They made out."

His eyes expanded in shock, pupils dilating. "Who made out?" I didn't respond. His head turned to stare at the two girls as they climbed off the table. "Them?" I still didn't respond and Sebastian swore. "Tell me."

Patting his shoulder, I walked away. Pushing my way through the crowd, I found everybody turning back to their dancing. Pride filled me at the thought of everyone enjoying themselves. I wanted my team to have fun. The only member who wasn't present tonight was Jai, the right-winger. He was disappointed he couldn't make it, but everyone had promised to drink on his behalf. And they were keeping that promise, considering how they were drunkenly floundering around.

I was stopped by a delicate hand being placed on my chest and I nearly rolled my eyes, not in the mood to be seduced by a puck bunny. The term was used to describe fans of ice hockey whose interest in the sport was mostly due to their sexual attraction to the players instead of the actual sport. They were fun to have at a party, I had to admit, but could get annoying quickly.

However, I was surprised. I followed the smooth skin of the hand, finding Nyx standing in front of me. She was staring up at me with wide, innocent eyes. This was a ploy. Nyx was the furthest thing from innocent. She was a fucking minx.

"Yes?" I raised a brow, waiting for her to remove her hand, but she merely trailed the length of my shoulder, hand slipping into my hair and both my brows rose.

And something else.

I was a man and a hot woman was touching me. The only downside was that it was Nyx eliciting these reactions from me. She smiled drunkenly, reminding me she was intoxicated and that if she wasn't—she wouldn't be this close to me. Not after what had happened.

"I'm surprised," she mumbled, causing me to have to lipread when I asked her to repeat herself. "Your party doesn't suck as much as I thought it would've. Did you invite Nate?"

There was an amused glint in her eyes, telling me she was enjoying seeing the way my features scrunched up in anger. It was as if she was reminding me of what she'd done, of how she'd helped the bastard that was my previous captain. And it was a good thing. I *needed* to be reminded. Even drunk, she knew how to pull my strings. I raised a hand, gripping her arm and moving her away from me slightly. She laughed, stepping closer again and binding my arms around her waist.

When she began swaying, I stood there, glaring down at her. "Step the fuck away from me," I grumbled. My tone was sharp, but she barely reacted.

Nyx looked up at me. "Make me."

Before I could speak, she twirled around, pressing herself against me and placing my hands on her bare stomach, her own hands lifting to go to my hair. She rolled her hips against mine and I curbed a groan. Over her head, I saw Sebastian watching me with a smirk as he chewed on a doughnut. Other members of my team were watching me as well, grinning at the girl pressed against me.

Ignoring them, I dragged my right hand up her body before locking it around her throat and she froze. I leaned down, lips brushing her ear as I interrogated in a rough tone, "What the fuck are you doing here, Taylor?"

"So *cynical*," she mused and I could hear the mirth in her voice. "Poor baby Hunt, so distrusting of others." She turned back around, driving my hand to slip to her nape before she proceeded, "And for good reason too." Her lips tipped at the corners, a smile that a devil would give its victim. "People these days, motivated purely by self-interest."

She snickered at my obvious displeasure, glancing away from me, swaying on the spot. The hand that was at her nape moved into her hair and I yanked at the blonde strands, forcing her to tilt her head back and look up at me. "Did Nate send you?"

Nobody had heard from that fucker since he'd lost the captaincy and left the school. But Nyx would keep in contact with him and she was probably his ticket into whatever gossip he was missing out on at USC.

She laughed, eyes lighting up. "As if Nate would concern

himself with you or me." My grip on her hair tightened, only making her smile grow. Her words were bait, trying to taunt me. And I fell for it every fucking time. "He left you behind when he left the school, sweetheart. Don't be conceited, you're not that important—"

"So you're lonely then?" I intervened. "Because I'm starting to think you have a thing for throwing yourself at hockey players."

Nyx laughed softly at that, revealing two dimples on either side of her cheeks. She rarely smiled wide enough to reveal them and the sight of it had me thinking that it didn't fit her personality. It was like giving a lion an adorable smile.

"You like to flatter yourself, don't you, Hunt?" She glimpsed to the side, spotting a few of my teammates, and she winked. "Perhaps it's just the *hockey players* who have a thing for me."

Swearing softly, I stepped back, dragging Nyx behind me. If she was at the party to fuck with my head, then she needed to leave—*after* I interrogated her. The Nyx I knew hated my guts. Either she was a confident drunk, even more than her sober self, or she wanted something, something for Nate. That asshole seemed like somebody who couldn't let go of the past, get over his loss. If there was one person I hated more than Nyx, it was Nathan Wyatt.

I guided her past the theatre room where couples were making out and others were watching music videos on the large screen. Oliver, one of the defencemen, stood in the corner, his arms around a girl. He raised a brow at seeing me with Nyx, nudging Jasper and the two grinned at me. I didn't know how it happened, but it went from me dragging her, to her slipping past me and pulling me along.

She grinned at the other drunken occupants of the house before stomping up the stairs, making her way past grinding couples and into my room. I stared at the back of her head as her eyes scanned the area, no doubt being hit with a flood of memories. It took a few seconds for her to compose herself and then she spun around with the beginning of a smirk appearing on her lips.

Sensing that she was about to start one of her mind games, I spoke before she had the chance to. "What are you doing here, Taylor?" I questioned, leaning against the now shut door.

Still smirking, she shrugged. "I wanted to talk, you know, it's been a while." Her head tilted to the side and she watched me carefully, her smirk turning into a grin once she saw that she had unnerved me with her icy stare.

Growing frustrated with her obvious taunting, I sauntered towards my bed and muttered, "If this is some sort of ploy to help—"

"Nate," Nyx finished with a thoughtful look and my jaw clenched. "Nathan Wyatt," she murmured, no doubt feeling the weight of his name. It was like a boulder placed on your chest, stripping you of all air. "Did you know that you always mention him around me?"

The question was rhetorical so I overlooked it and reiterated my initial question. "What are you doing here?" She stepped closer, pushing me down onto the bed. With a smirk, she straddled my lap, yanking me closer.

"Fine, I came to talk," she spoke airily, running her nose up my jaw to speak into my ear.

"You could speak to me without touching me," I hissed through gritted teeth, still not trusting her presence.

On their own accord, my hands framed her hips. I told myself it was to stop her from moving because she began rocking to the beat of the music coming from downstairs. When she rolled against me again, I smothered another groan. This proved I needed to fucking get laid.

Pouting dramatically, she urged, "Where's the fun in that?" I scowled and she snickered. "I came to tell you I start on Monday since you're that curious."

"And let me guess," I began, tilting my head and realising why she'd led me to my room, why she was throwing herself at me. "You came to beg me to keep the guys in check." The corner of her lips tilted, but she didn't speak. "We both know they hate you and you think that by doing this," I gestured to where her hips were moving against me, "I'll help you."

She paused, speaking in the most condescending tone ever. "Oh, baby, that's not it at all." My eye twitched in irritation. Leaning forward, she pulled my earlobe between her teeth, and this time, I didn't have enough time to disguise my groan. "I'm getting sick of you comparing me to Nate all the time, you know?" she murmured, fiery breath hitting my ear. "You're obsessed with him, just admit it."

There was a teasing smile on her face, hinting that she knew something I didn't. This was all a game to her. I wasn't going to take the bait, not this time. "Fuck you, Taylor."

Her lips quirked as she stretched back. "Are you offering, Hunt?"

My hand cupped the back of her neck and I wrenched her

forward, catching her by surprise and making her squeak. Our noses were touching as I informed her, "I'm not gonna play your games. We need you, I'll admit that. You've got a better shot at helping us with the fundraisers than Benson does. But I want you to stop whatever you're doing." And to hurt her, I added, "Plus, I don't take Nate's sloppy seconds."

Pain flickered through her eyes and momentarily, I felt bad. But it was gone in a second, the same as the emotion she'd just displayed.

Indignantly, she pushed off me, smirking at the prominent bulge in my jeans. "Do yourself a favour and get laid."

I placed a hand over it. "You offering your famous services?"

Without responding, she twisted on her heel, checking the time before leaving my room, and I didn't know whether to laugh or throttle her. When I went downstairs, Oliver winked at me, making obscene gestures with his hands after witnessing us appear from upstairs, before pointing in the direction Nyx had gone.

Rolling my eyes at his childish antics, I traced the path she'd taken, only to see a guy from the football team cornering her. Adam, I think his name was. His team had won three of the five football matches against UCLA thus far.

And the hockey team hadn't even played one match yet. I grimaced at the reminder.

Not a few feet away stood a girl glowering at Nyx. I recognised her as one of the many foreign exchange students. Although I knew she was from Japan, I couldn't seem to put my finger on her name. She was tall with sleek black hair, dressed to the nines in a skin-tight black dress. Her catlike eyes had been on Adam, but the latter's eyes were all for Nyx.

Couldn't blame him, to be honest.

"You wanna test some of those moves out on me?" Adam asked Nyx jokingly, referencing the performance she and Nailea had given everyone.

It was then that I noticed the easy air between them and I realised he'd probably only approached her because she was familiar. Nyx glanced to the side, pinpointing the upset girl, and beamed. For a second, I thought she was going to antagonise her.

Yet, she replied, "Adam, this is my friend..." She gestured to the girl, clearly not knowing her name.

Sensing what Nyx was doing, the girl supplied with a bright smile as she stepped closer, "Emiko." Her husky accented voice was nearly swallowed by the music.

Nyx nodded, grinning when she saw Adam almost shyly glance at Emiko. "My friend, *Emiko*, over here," she began, wrapping an arm around Emiko's waist, "taught me all the moves I know."

I smirked when Adam's eyes became hooded. He wasn't even looking at Nyx anymore, but rather at the raven-haired girl by her side. "Did she now?" he sought teasingly, voice deep. Emiko flushed red and nodded. "Well, would you like to have a drink with me?" He smiled lightly before turning around, gesturing for her to follow him.

Emiko glanced to Nyx, probably bewildered as to why she'd done that. But the minx just tapped Emiko's ass and declared, "Go get your man." The taller girl sent Nyx a grateful smile before rushing after Adam.

"Do my eyes deceive me or do you have a heart?" I inquired, shoving my hands into my pockets as I made my way to her. She rolled her eyes when she saw me approaching and I stifled a laugh.

"Of course they deceive you. It's the only reasonable explanation considering you once thought skinny jeans were a good look on you."

Shrugging, I countered, "Steph seemed to have opposing views to you."

Without missing a beat, she quipped, "Steph Coleman also petitioned for the school to allow her to wear t-shirts and bras with holes in them because they were imprisoning her nipples." I turned my head to the side, hiding my smile. "Does the slogan *free the nipples sound familiar to you?*"

She just had an answer for everything. "What happened to girls supporting girls? You'd shit on her idea?"

"If you wanna see my nipples, just ask," she mused. "No need to beat around the bush." My eyes dropped to her chest momentarily before raising back to her eyes, eyes that were twinkling with mischief. She was fucking with me again, as always.

"Pass," I snorted, making her feign a pout. "But I'm sure Nate will take you up on that offer," I added, mocking her previous words of me always bringing him up around her.

All playfulness left her expression. Even though the air was stuffy inside the house, the air around Nyx and me went ice cold. I felt a shudder slither down my spine. Her eyes were glaciers as she glared at me, hostility fuelling her words. I felt like a passenger on the Titanic, heading straight for the iceberg that would cause me to sink. And her words were the frigid waters that would freeze my blood.

"You just can't move on, can you?" I said nothing. "At least his daddy didn't have to pay for his captaincy."

That was a low blow. I didn't like being reminded of my dad's offer to pay Coach Ford to make me captain. No money was exchanged and I'd earned my position with hard work. But people still talked about it; people like Nyx. Rage built in my chest, like fire ready to disintegrate the ice shards she was flinging with the intention to impale me.

Making it evident that I was examining her from head to toe, I stated, "But he had to pay for something else, didn't he?"

There were two sides to the rumour that'd spread about her last year. The one side made more sense and I believed it; that she was being paid to help Nate with his events and marketing strategy. The other side was plain stupid; that he was paying her to sleep with him, but students were greedy for gossip and word-of-mouth twisted information. The meaning behind my words was clear as day.

I was going with the second rumour.

Her lips parted, but no words came out. She shut her mouth, nodding to herself as if seeing me in a new light. I didn't like that look. Then she left and I didn't follow her. I stood there, staring at the spot she previously occupied. There was an uneasy feeling in my chest, one telling me to go after her.

I knew I brought Nate up a lot, but I did it to remind myself of what Nyx had done, to remind her and hope that she'd feel some sense of fucking guilt for aiding the man that had put us through hell. But she never did. So why the fuck should I?

A tap on my shoulder broke me out of my stupor. It was Grayson. "Beth's headed your way, just a heads up."

My mind was still reeling from my conversation with Nyx and I spluttered, "*What?* Who invited her?"

"I did," Grayson retorted innocently, although he knew I didn't want to see her until I could place us firmly in the friendzone. "Stop stringing her along, man. Now's your chance. It'll make things easier, trust me. The longer you go without explaining things to her, the more time you give her mom to try and set you two up." I grimaced at his words.

With an encouraging smile, his tall frame shuffled away, disappearing into the crowd as he beckoned for Jasper to join him outside for a game of beer pong. I wasn't in the mood to talk to anybody, not at that moment. But it seemed the world wasn't on my side because, a second later, I was staring into the kind eyes of Beth.

"Hi!" she greeted me over the loud music, moving a little closer so I could hear her. "I've been looking for you since I first got here." She was wearing a pair of jeans with a cropped sweater, her braids now decorated with beads that matched the blue of her sweater.

"Hey," I greeted warily, not knowing how to behave around her after she'd stormed off at the café. I considered Beth one of my close friends and hurting her feelings didn't exactly sit well with me, not when I'd seen her go through the worst. So I mustered up my pride and said, "About what happened—"

"You're cool, no worries," she cut me off, probably sensing that I was about to apologise for not telling her the full truth.

"*I* should be the one apologising, seeing as the situation didn't even involve me." There was a sheepish look in her eyes and she wouldn't meet my gaze, too embarrassed.

When somebody jostled her again, I placed a hand on her upper back and guided her towards the kitchen where it was less rowdy. Subconsciously, I kept my eyes peeled for Nyx, trying to spot her in the crowd. Sebastian was in the kitchen when we got there, eating a bag of chips. When he saw Beth, he offered her an attempt at a smile, which was more of a grimace, before leaving.

"I'm glad we sorted that out," Beth spoke again, allowing Sebastian's rudeness to float by her, as she usually did. "I'll admit, the little girl inside of me was upset because you're one of my best friends, but when I got home, my mom spoke some sense into me."

I tensed at the mention of Vivian Braswell. "Your mom?" I asked gently, pouring us two cups of soda. One more cup of beer and I was bound to throw up.

Beth nodded, thanking me as she took the cup. "She said I can't expect every guy I meet to not have a past. That'd be unfair, you know?" I nodded, even though I didn't fully understand what was going on. She took a sip of her drink before speaking again. "Nyx and you have history, so what? Things happened, but it's in the past."

"In the past," I repeated, trying to read between the lines. Beth's face was moist due to the heat in the house and she coughed when she took another sip from the cup in her hands.

"I mean, I don't exactly like what she did to you and the team, but that's *your* problem, right? It has nothing to do with me. I just wanna say that I'm on your side, no matter what."

She gave me an awkward thumbs-up, one that had me cracking a small smile. Before I knew it, I was pulling her into my arms for a hug, not missing the way she sank into my embrace. "We're good, Beth. No worries."

A sigh of relief left her. "Thank goodness. Thought I was gonna have to fly solo at the brunch—"

And here was God's way of fucking with me again. Beth was interrupted, and I was thankful because I didn't want to go to the brunch, especially one planned by her meddlesome mom.

But the interruption came in the form of a grinning Nyx, who stumbled into the kitchen with Nailea. The two girls were laughing, both trying to keep the other upright. Beth tensed when she noticed them, her grip around her cup tightening in apprehension.

"God, he's so fucking hot and for what?" Nailea questioned Nyx in exasperation, moving to the fridge to get two bottles of water. "Too bad he's a dick."

Nyx snorted, grabbing the beverage from her friend. "I know exactly how you feel, Nai, trust me." She raised the bottle to her lips, eyes finding me. The easiness in her posture disappeared in an instant.

Surprisingly, it was Beth that spoke first. "Nyx, is it? I just wanted to apologise for the other day—"

"There's no need, trust me," Nyx stopped her, a tiny smile tugging at her lips and I frowned, wondering what was up with the sudden change in attitude towards Beth. "I was in a bad mood and if I said anything to offend you, I'm sorry." She didn't offer anything else, but she sounded genuine. "I should also thank you, for helping my sister when Donovan yelled at her."

Beth's eyes swelled with surprise. "Annie's your sister?" Nyx was grinning as she nodded. "Wow, um, I didn't know she was your sister. But she's super nice."

Nyx smirked. "Unlike me?" That managed to make Beth laugh. "Seriously though, I appreciate you being there for her." Beth only smiled shyly, looking away when Nyx's gaze became too much. I was so invested in their conversation that I'd forgotten there was another person present.

Nailea was eying my proximity to Beth and I prayed she didn't press on it. My prayers went unanswered. "Since when have you got a girl, Hunt?" She shared a glance with her blonde friend, the latter staring blankly at me.

I cursed inwardly. There was no way to answer her question without hurting Beth in the process. Beth laughed into her hand. Nyx saved me from having to answer. "I gotta call Annie. You coming, Nai?"

In the blink of an eye, the two were gone, leaving me alone with Beth. We fell into a comfortable conversation and I listened to her talk about her new job at the café. However, my attention wasn't fully on her, part of my brain still hung up on a question that'd been nagging me since Nyx had left.

Did she save me from labelling my relationship with Beth, or did she leave because she didn't want to hear the answer?

Chapter 5

Nyx

My sports media law and ethics class dragged on for what felt like hours. The chair was hurting my ass and the lecturer's voice was blander than the tea Indigo once made me. It was agonising. Perhaps class would've been better if Nailea was there, but she was absent because she'd drank so much on Saturday that the hangover was still with her.

Or maybe she was just lazy.

I'd gotten used to the seat next to me being vacant. The only times it was filled were during the classes I shared with Nailea. She was majoring in sports journalism, so we had some classes in common. She was the only one who bothered to speak to me, probably because I didn't exactly look friendly. And even more so today.

The cut in the corner of my mouth was red, even though I'd received it in the early hours of Sunday morning when I'd arrived home. At least the bruise on my cheekbone was fading, but I'd still covered it with some makeup to be safe. When my lecturer announced class was over, I nearly leapt out of my seat. Shoving my notes into my bag, I rushed out of the classroom.

It was a fifteen-minute walk to the edge of campus where the rink was. USC hadn't always had their own ice rink. Instead, they'd trained and hosted games at Lakewood Ice and Anaheim Ice. Our rink was a somewhat new renovation, one that I was thankful for.

Carrying two bags, one filled with files and the other with clothes; my shoulders were hurting. I was sweating by the time I arrived and had already removed my jacket, but I knew I'd be freezing soon. Entering the building, I passed the rink; still vacant. Loud laughter was coming from the locker room and I rolled my eyes. Passing the door, I headed to Benson's office.

I found him seated behind his desk. Last night, I'd decided that the two of us weren't enemies. We were both working towards the same thing; the team's success. So I no longer had to be stingy with my knowledge. And he could do much more with that knowledge than I could, seeing as he was the coach. Dropping my gym bag onto the floor and the other onto his desk, I startled him and he looked up with irritation in his eyes. Ignoring him, I rummaged through my bag, taking out a thick file and handing it to him.

"My notes," I told him, gesturing for him to take them. He took it hesitantly, seemingly perplexed. "You and I both know that majority of Coach Ford's plans stayed where they originated—in his head."

Benson opened the file, shock replacing the irritation. "Miss Taylor—"

"He'd make physical copies of the drafts but once he added

his revisions and finalisations, the drafts went into the trash and his mind absorbed his new idea," I continued, taking out another file and thinking back to how Ford was like a sponge. "My plan for this year was to help Coach Ford, before he left, of course. I knew he was protective of his team and unwilling to let just any stranger close to them. I had to gain his trust and respect before he'd let me close to his boys. So I did what I do best; I studied my ass off."

The older man in front of me nodded as he flipped through the first file. "I'm impressed," he said mindlessly, engrossed in my notes. It wasn't a compliment, more like a statement of astonishment, as if he didn't expect something like this from me. If it was truly a compliment, I would've thanked him.

Suppressing my annoyance, I added, "With a degree in sports management, there're many routes I could take. Then, I was settled on becoming a sports agent, and I wanted to impress Coach Ford with my abilities in studying a team." Taking out the third file, the last one, I planted it next to the others. "I attended every game they played, sat in the audience with a notebook and pen."

And sometimes a very hyper Indigo, but I didn't add that.

Benson froze, looking up at me. There was genuine respect in his eyes and I knew that if he wasn't as proud as he was, he would've complimented me—for real this time. I had the satisfaction of seeing him come to the realisation. "So, you're telling me—"

I ran a hand over the files. "These files contain every single one of Coach Ford's plans, his line combinations, his lists of each player's strengths and weaknesses, and many more." I leaned closer. "Only, I didn't ask him a *thing*. I absorbed what I witnessed at the games. A good sports agent needs to negotiate contracts and endorsement deals to maximise value for their clients. And to do this, you must know your clients like the back of your hand."

And I knew all twenty players of the USC ice hockey team. That information was immortalised in my files. Benson sent me what was supposed to be an appreciative smile.

"Miss Taylor, you have no idea how much you've helped us."

Smirking, I crossed my arms. "Oh, believe me, I know." He scowled at my words and my smirk grew into a grin. "But we're on the same team. Do what you want with my notes, study them and learn everything you can about the team that's now trusting you to lead them to victory."

"And what will you do?"

"What you hired me to do—marketing, event planning," I answered easily before continuing. "People tend to underestimate the role this plays in the cup."

Benson nodded, seeing where I was going. "So if we have enough wins against UCLA and pair that with the points gained from events—we could beat them by a landslide." I clapped condescendingly, but his smile didn't waver. "You know your stuff, Miss Taylor."

My lips twitched. "It's my job."

He shook my hand in his rough one before asking, "What do you think, Hunt?" Benson's head twisted and I had to hide my surprise at seeing Beckham seated on the couch in the office's corner. I hadn't noticed him when I'd walked in, too focused on Benson. "Did she pass the test?"

Beckham's stormy gaze met mine, flicking momentarily to the cut at the corner of my mouth before his jaw clenched. I hadn't seen him since the party on Saturday. My pride wouldn't allow me to face him. It disgusted me. He believed I'd *slept* with Nate for money. I knew his opinion of me was low, but that was an all-new low.

The edge of his lip tilted. "With flying colours."

Crossing my arms, I stood taller, although it did nothing. "Thank you for the seal of approval I didn't need." Shifting my attention back to Benson, I inquired, "So, what are we starting with?"

"You have any of Ford's training programs in here?" He gestured to my files and I nodded. "I think the first line should work out, I'll take the rest to the ice."

There were twenty active players on the team, consisting of twelve forwards, six defencemen and two goalies. Only six of them went onto the ice during a game; three forwards, two defensemen and one goalie. This was known as the first team or first line, the one that got the most ice time.

I clasped my hand together. "I'll take the first team."

After I'd handed Benson all of my notes, I considered that part of my job done. I'd given him all the resources he needed to make the most of his new team and all I had to do was focus on the marketing and events aspect of things. But I changed my mind at the last minute; for one reason.

And that reason suddenly stood to his full height, glaring at me. "You'll *what?*"

I rolled my eyes. "I won't repeat myself when you've heard

me. Wastes valuable time, bro."

Beckham growled, trying to get the attention of Benson. "Are you seriously going to let her train us? As the captain, shouldn't that responsibility fall to me?"

Benson carefully placed the files in his draw, probably planning on coming back to them later to study. Even though I didn't necessarily like him, I was glad that I could help with his part of the job.

"Hunt, if you've forgotten, you're *part* of that first team. She won't train you, she'll *oversee* the training. I can't exactly be in two places at once."

And thank the Lord for that. Two Coach Bensons would be a nightmare. I could barely stand the one.

Realisation dawned on Beckham like a kick to the head. He glowered at me and I grinned in return, angering him further. "You're doing this just to annoy me. Tell me, are you that desperate for attention?"

Lips curving, I retaliated, "Tell me, does female authority scare you that much?" Benson snorted, probably glad that somebody else was at the receiving end of my taunting. "Go get your boys and meet in the locker room."

He didn't move from his spot until Benson snapped at him. I watched him leave with a smile.

"Good luck." Benson nodded at me.

Picking up my gym bag, I waved at him. "*You're* going to need it more." I left his office, going to the public bathrooms that were used when games were held at the rink.

I discarded my jeans and sweater, replacing them with spandex shorts and a sports bra. My outfit was important, a tactic I needed to see if my plan on Saturday had worked. Grabbing a hair tie, I pulled my hair into a bun to keep it out of the way. I wasn't initially planning on training with the guys. But I knew that they'd find some sort of loophole by saying that girls liked to boss them around without doing anything for themselves—which was why I was going to do every exercise with them.

Back in middle school, we all had that gym coach who never got off their ass but kept calling us lazy, making us run laps. I hated that coach because he had no idea what we were going through as he just sat there eating. So I could relate to Beckham's boys. They'd be more than willing to listen to me if I was working with them and not just barking orders. The only downside was the makeup I wore that I'd no doubt sweat off and reveal the bruise on my cheek. But I'd cross that bridge once I got there.

Passing Benson's office, I noted the door was closed, but I could hear the chatter. He probably had the other groups in there with him and was discussing his plans for them. Like a proper damn coach. My lips quirked.

When I arrived at the locker room, I found five scowling men. And I nearly burst into laughter. The only one who wasn't glaring at me was Grayson. I hadn't seen him since the party at their place. The house was shared between him, Sebastian and Beckham. Grayson was the friendliest of the three. It was weird. Nobody could be *that* friendly.

The locker room stank of sweat and there were clothes everywhere. If you got past the smell of sweat, you were blasted with an obnoxious amount of cologne. Skates were lined up against one wall and some jerseys belonging to past players were framed.

One had the last name Hunt; Beckham's dad.

"Well, aren't you all just adorable," I mused, tossing my bag onto the floor and placing my hands on my hips. "Up and at 'em! Ten laps around the rink." Nobody moved, staring at me with incredulity.

"I thought you were joking," Jai muttered to Beckham, running a hand through his inky hair. Beckham said nothing, standing with crossed arms and staring at me. His turbulent eyes dragged across my outfit before he looked away. "She can't coach us." He turned to me, appreciation in his eyes. "But maybe she can be motivation."

I hummed to myself, scanning him from head to toe. Jairaj Mahajan; USC's very own star. Except, he wasn't famous, at least, not outside of campus. As the resident fuckboy, he was used to girls falling into his lap—which was probably why he was staring at me like that. As if I was a piece of meat being dangled in front of a dog. I nearly scoffed at his audacity.

Grayson glared at him. "Jai, don't"

No, please, Jai. Go ahead.

Involuntarily, a smile grew on my lips, tugging harshly at the cut there. I realised Jai hadn't been at the party on Saturday. If he'd attended, then he wouldn't have dared to speak to me the way he was. But now I had to deal with him my way. Fortunately, he didn't listen to Grayson, standing up from the metal bench and swaggering over to me.

I didn't move. "Laps, now," I stated firmly.

He shook his head. "Sweetheart, the only lap you need

to concern yourself with is mine. You can sit on it while—*holy mother of fuck*!" He yelled further obscenities in what sounded like Hindi, bending over in pain as I held his right index finger in my hand, twisting it. Howls of pain left his lips. "You fucking psycho!" He dropped to his knees and I leaned forward, dropping his hand.

Beckham watched me, irritation flickering in his eyes. "Did you just break his finger?"

"Sprained it." I rolled my eyes, spotting Oliver laughing to himself at Jai's pain. "Try rice, bro."

Jai looked up at me. His anger grew when some of his teammates laughed at him. "You want me to put my finger in *rice*?"

"Get up," I scoffed, seeing as he was still kneeling in front of me. "As much as I love guys going down on me, this isn't it. And no, you can't put it in *rice*. Unless your finger is an electronic contraption?" Jai glowered at me, standing up. I spoke slower this time. "Rest. Ice. Compress. Elevate."

People managed to forget one of my courses last year was sports medicine and injuries. I could break every bone in his body whilst naming it and explaining how it needed to be healed.

Jai cradled his hand to his chest. "Fuck you."

I smiled. "Cute." Turning to Grayson, the only one I knew would listen to me, I said, "Go get Aiden. He'll be our first line right-winger for the two weeks it takes for Jai's poor finger to heal."

Grayson nodded. "Yes, Ma'am." He dragged a swearing Jai out of the locker room. I turned back to the remaining four men and wrinkled my nose. Sebastian was smirking as he got up, leaving the room to run laps. Jasper stood up next, a delighted laugh escaping him, followed by Oliver and leaving me alone with Beckham.

I thought of Annie's words this morning whilst I was getting dressed. She'd told me to assert dominance. It was hilarious coming from somebody as soft-hearted as her, but her advice did the trick.

The asshole interrupted my thoughts with his voice. "You can't just sprain my player's finger, Taylor." He didn't sound angry. If I squinted, I could detect a hint of amusement.

"He was annoying me." I shrugged, noting the clean smell he carried as he stepped closer.

For a moment, I was taken back in time. It was my first year of college and my first time attending an ice hockey game. I'd stayed behind, wanting to talk to Coach Ford about shadowing him. The celebrations were usually held in the locker room. However, all of his boys were crammed into his office with him and I'd figured it out once I found the locker room empty.

Empty, except one. It was the second time I'd laid eyes on Beckham Hunt. He was smiling at me. *"First game, Tinkerbell?"* His words were teasing, even though I'd watched him get bulldozed on the ice.

"Considering how you just played, I should be asking you that, Annika."

I'd given him a nickname of my own, one I hadn't been able to explain to him yet. Standing in the locker room with him brought me back to the moment we'd first spoken. So much had changed since then.

"And you sprain fingers when you're annoyed?" Beckham's voice brought me back to the present.

Ah, I'd *almost* forgotten that we hated each other.

I shook my head, scanning him just like he did me at the party before he'd delivered that stinging blow. "No. I sprain appendages." My gaze stayed on the front of his sweatpants and I tilted my head. "Want me to try it out on you?" Surprisingly, he chuckled, trailing me as I left the locker room, heading to the ice. I could feel his gaze on me. "Stop staring at my ass—"

"Says the girl currently talking about my dick," Beckham cut me off, easily catching up to me because of his long legs. I didn't respond, smiling to myself when seeing Jai sitting on the bench with a first aid kit next to him, hastily trying to wrap his finger. "And you wonder why I think you're a sociopath."

"Huh?"

Beckham wasn't looking at me when he spoke again. "You sprained his finger. The guy's in pain and you're smiling. Sociopath."

I watched Grayson and Aiden join the other three for laps. "Just because I enjoy watching vile men suffer, doesn't mean I'm a sociopath." His mouth quirked. "Go run laps," I demanded, sick of his presence next to me. The arguing felt way too similar to the banter I was used to with him and I didn't want any reminders of it.

Benson walked past with the thirteen other players and their eyes strayed to me as they passed. But they looked away immediately when they saw who I was standing with. They skated onto the ice, following orders—unlike the man next to me.

And that was the problem. He was still next to me and not running laps. "And you're still here because?"

Overlooking my question, he sought, "What happened to your lip?" The concern in his voice was obvious.

I knew he'd ask me, eventually. The ass was always shoving his nose where it didn't belong. "Nailea got a little too rough last night," I shot back. "*Laps.*" He stood there for a second, trying to determine if I was telling the truth or not. "Is there a reason why you're still here—"

"I wanted to apologise," he muttered, not looking at me but rather at the ice. There was a tense silence as I let his words sink in. There was no way he was apologising.

No fucking way.

I blinked in confusion. "Did you hit your head?" When his lips quirked upwards in amusement, my brows furrowed. He was smiling at me. "*My God*, you hit your head." My heart started rattling inside my chest when he let out a small laugh, causing me to panic. "What's going on with you, you absolute freak?"

Beckham only chuckled and I wanted to die. I *hated* not knowing what was going on. "I'm apologising for what I said at the party," he said smoothly, like he was speaking to a child and enjoying unravelling my control like a ball of yarn. What made it worse was that he wasn't even looking at me, no, he was watching his teammates and talking to me as if we were best friends that had a small spat.

Without thinking, I gripped his arm and tugged him so that he was facing me. "Are you high right now?" I whispered, checking his eyes for any hint of red.

He leaned down with a smirk, nose nearly brushing mine. “No. Are you?”

“No. But I *am* wondering why you’re apologising to me. You have a motive or something?” I asked with an elevated brow, trying to figure out if this conversation had a purpose.

Beckham grinned. “You saying you don’t want me to apologise?”

I snorted. “I’m sorry if I gave you the impression that I care what you think—”

“You seemed to care the moment I said it,” he spoke over me and I wanted to scream at the fact that he’d caught that split second of weakness.

“Well, then I guess the wind blew away all of my fucks on the walk over to the rink, fortunately for us all,” I shot back, tilting my head to the side as he stared down at me.

I nearly thought I had the final say when he spoke again, eyes trained on the cut by my mouth. “Who hurt you?”

My jaw dropped at his straightforward question, pulling at the cut that had his attention. Fumbling for words, I ended up saying, “Did you apologise so that you could fish for information?”

Brief disappointment churned in my stomach but soon turned into satisfaction at the fact that I could turn the situation on him.

He looked over my shoulder before glancing back at me, lowering his voice to a whisper. “I apologised because I felt bad,” he said firmly, his tone making me question my entire existence. “Hurting women is not part of my hobbies, despite my treatment of you and what you think of me, Nyx.”

“Go run laps,” I blurted, but he didn’t move. My tongue felt heavy, no words forming in my throat. There was genuine concern in his eyes, and I didn’t know what to do with that information. In the end, I swallowed roughly and said, “Nobody hurt me.”

Beckham looked at me a moment longer. “For his sake, you better be telling the truth.”

Then he did as I asked him, surprisingly. Watching him walk away, I felt my heart rate pick up speed. *I* usually controlled how our conversations went, and I did it as a way to protect myself. That was the first time in so long that I’d relinquished control and let the conversation stray where he wanted it to, albeit unwillingly. I didn’t like it one bit.

Biting my lip, I scanned my surroundings. Jai was still struggling with his finger and rummaging through the kit. Sociopath. Beckham’s words affected me more than they should’ve after our conversation. And I hated it.

He was an asshole who stuck his busybody ass into situations where he didn’t belong and came to inaccurate conclusions. He only ever looked at me to judge, it’s what he always did. Yet, even I had to admit that I may have taken it a little too far. I tried to justify myself by saying that Jai was disrespectful. Even so, guilt developed in my chest. There were other ways to discipline somebody; the cut by my mouth said enough. My eyes stung.

With a sigh, I sauntered towards Jai and he looked up when he heard my footsteps. He didn’t look too happy. I sat next to him, taking the tape out of the kit and grabbing his right hand. His features twisted into an expression of confusion as I taped his index and middle fingers together. After I was done, I made a sling out of a bandage and enclosed it around his wrist before securing it around his neck.

"Rest; limit the use of this finger for a few days," I began gently, keeping my voice resolute. "Ice; apply ice for no longer than fifteen minutes. Compress; that's what the buddy tape is for." I gestured to his taped fingers. "Elevate; keep finger raised at a level above the heart. That's what the sling is for."

I stood up again, ready to run my own set of laps, but Jai's voice stopped me. "Thank you. And I'm sorry." Judging by his embarrassed frown, it took a lot for him to say that.

"I'm sorry too," I responded with genuine guilt. He offered me a smile and I backtracked. Twisting around, I spotted Beckham leaning in front of us, done with his laps.

He eyed Jai's taped fingers before looking back at me. I didn't like what I saw in his eyes, didn't like that he'd witnessed me going soft. It was a side I hid well, only exposing it when I was with my family. And I didn't want Beckham anywhere close to that, especially after our most recent conversation.

Chapter 6

Beckham

I was running late for practice today, courtesy of Professor Martin, who'd held back the entire class. It wasn't my fault that some students didn't hand in their assignments, yet everybody was punished. It pissed me off because that was such a high school teacher move to pull.

I had to bite my tongue to prevent myself from voicing my thoughts. If I'd spoken back, then I'd be sent to Dean Waverly's office, which would've wasted even more time. So I shut up. Listening to Professor Martin speak about the principles of quantum mechanics could be interesting—when I didn't have somewhere to be.

The team was probably halfway through practice by now, and I was still stuck in class. Benson would let it slide, but it was Nyx who'd be up my ass about arriving late. I was still stumped on what exactly her plan was at the party and I promised myself I'd figure it out. Then there was the case of her cut lip. She stayed on my mind throughout the rest of class, until I climbed in my car and drove to the rink. There were only five minutes left of practice. Grabbing my gym bag, I left my car and headed to the entrance.

There wasn't anybody on the ice and I groaned, knowing that I'd missed quite a deal of training. Some players were on the benches, ready to leave and joking around. I walked past the locker room, wanting to speak to Benson first and apologise for missing practice. As captain, I needed to set a good example.

That meant not missing fucking practice.

"How's the finger?"

I halted when hearing Jasper's voice. He was leaning against the wall, watching as Jai fidgeted with his taped fingers. The two hadn't spotted me as a corner hid me from their view. I stayed silent, wanting to hear if Jai was in any pain. For fear of disappointing me, they were never really honest about minor injuries.

That was Nate's doing. He'd expected perfection from every member, although he was heavily flawed. I remembered the lectures, him breaking down our confidence and trying to force us into mindless members of his team. I remembered the gaslighting, him making us feel as if we imagined the chokehold he had us all in.

Jai laughed to himself, sending Jasper a pinched look as he flexed his right hand. "It's already getting better." The playboy wasn't moist with sweat like Jasper, making me conclude he hadn't joined practice. "Hurt like a bitch at that moment, though. Thought my fucking finger was detached from my hand."

Satisfied that my player was okay, I turned on my heel, continuing my journey to Benson. Jasper snorted. "Can't blame anyone but yourself. Although, I'm surprised it wasn't Beck who broke your damn finger."

There was a hint of scolding in his tone and I stopped again, backtracking. I'd never intentionally hurt my players and I was ready to make my presence known and question Jasper about what the fuck he was implying.

But Jai spoke for me, confusion apparent in his words. "What the hell does that mean?"

"Fuck, I forgot you weren't at the party," Jasper answered, slapping Jai on the back as he laughed at his confusion. "She's Beck's girl, man." At that point, Jai could've been a mirror because our features were scrunching the same way. "Something's going on between them again and I don't think you wanna get yourself stuck in an awkward place. They were all over each other on Saturday, even disappeared to his room for a while."

Realisation dawned on me and I shook my head, but I couldn't stop the grin that forced its way onto my mouth. Images of Nyx dancing against me, wrapping her arms around me flashed through my mind. She was smart, I'd give her that. I pushed away from the wall, dead-set on finding the minx to confront her. I'd had it all wrong. Nyx had been at that party for a reason; to make a statement. I was merely a pawn in her little game of chess. She had me believe I was in control when in reality—it was *her* calling the shots.

I found her standing with Grayson, explaining something to him. The latter saw me approaching and smiled before focusing back on the girl in front of him. Dropping my bag on a bench, I slipped one arm around Nyx's waist, pulling her back to my chest. She made no sound of surprise. Although she was standing next to the ice, she wasn't cold. Her skin was warm and had a red tint to it, like that of sunburn. Just like yesterday, she'd probably joined in on the training.

"Grayson," I acknowledged the smiling man. "Mind if I had a word with my girl for a second?" His green eyes darted between the two of us. I couldn't see Nyx's expression, but judging by the amusement Grayson was radiating, I knew she was scowling.

"She's all yours." He saluted.

"She sure is," I mumbled, watching him walk away. As stubborn as she was, Nyx didn't turn around or even acknowledge my presence. She just stood there, pretending like I didn't exist. My frustration grew and I leaned down, murmuring, "Do you enjoy using people?" She scoffed. "There was a method to your madness, after all, you little sociopath."

Like a damn genius, she'd killed two birds with one stone. Not only did she put me on edge, and make me paranoid about what her plans were—but she'd also completed the task she'd set for herself. My irritation was just a bonus point for her.

"I saw an opportunity and took it. It's not my fault you're not the sharpest tool in the shed." Finally, she twisted in my hold. "Men can be disgusting. Just look at what happened with Jai. He saw me as a piece of meat rather than an authoritative figure here to help him."

Her actions began weaving together, tied closely by her words and I couldn't blame her, not really, not when it was obvious what she was doing.

"He wasn't at the party," I murmured in realisation. And

he hadn't witnessed what happened between Nyx and me. He saw a beautiful woman and went for it.

"Exactly, but the rest of your team was there. They respect you enough to—"

"To not touch what's mine," I finished, nodding to myself and looking down at her. "I get it." I understood what she was saying, but I didn't like it. Sure, she pissed me off beyond comprehension, but that didn't mean I liked the fact that she felt uneasy in a room full of men. Sighing, I let go of her. "You know, you could've just asked me for help. I would've spoken to them—"

"I don't necessarily enjoy being painted as the damsel in distress, Hunt. I solve my own problems," Nyx interjected, crossing her arms over her chest. "And don't kid yourself, you wouldn't have helped me."

I'd never felt more like an asshole than I did at that moment. Because there was truth to her statement. *No*, I wouldn't have helped her. I was already angry about her being recruited; I hated that it was her of all people so I definitely wouldn't have agreed to help her with anything. And knowing her, she wouldn't have specified what she needed help with. She was too proud for that.

"Taylor," but she was already walking away, ponytail swishing behind her. And then she was gone.

It was almost as if she had the entire interaction prepared, saying only what she'd planned to. I swore softly, running a hand through my hair and debating if I should go after her.

Deciding against it, I grabbed my bag and went to Benson, apologising for missing practice but promising to train on my own anyway. He looked annoyed with me, but I wasn't in the mood to argue with him. When I finished changing, I jogged around the rink a few times to warm up. After that, I sauntered into the gym. It was empty, but I didn't mind. There was something pinned against the wall and I found a chart there. In neat handwriting was a training program.

"She knows what she's doing." Sebastian's voice sailed into the gym as he appeared, still wearing his training shorts. "All the plans, it's the same as the ones Ford did with us. Only, she made some minor adjustments, made them better."

Nyx must've made an impression on them today if Sebastian was complimenting her. I didn't respond, reading the first thing on the list and moving to where crates were stacked above each other, three feet high.

Plyometric training was annoying, but it was important. Jumping made the muscles exert maximum force in brief intervals and helped to increase power, after all, it was what made us explosive on the ice. Taking in a deep breath, I hopped onto the crate, holding the position for a second before jumping down again. Repeating it ten times, I followed the instructions and took a five-minute break.

Sebastian took a seat on a bench and I noted he was eating a bag of chips. "Trouble in paradise?" he taunted and I scoffed, standing up to continue my next set of jumps. The blonde laughed.

I didn't want to think of Nyx. There was an unexplainable feeling in my chest and I couldn't name it. I'd never felt less like a man before. Nyx may have detested me and vice versa, but she was still a woman who felt uneasy in the presence of twenty young men, hesitant about helping them because she was panicked they'd leer at her and tease her. Yet, she couldn't ask me to help because she knew I'd refuse, torment her. *So she helped herself.*

With a heavy groan, I realised that the scorching sensation inside me was self-loathing.

Taking my third break, I rubbed the sweat from my forehead and stated, "You knew."

It wasn't a question.

"Obviously," Sebastian scoffed, looking offended that I hadn't come to the realisation sooner. He was a people-watcher, after all, but the rivalry was between Nyx and me. Surely, I would've noticed something about her before him? Understanding where my thoughts were headed, he articulated again. "The first hint was that she showed up at the party. That was just weird."

I grunted in agreement, doing my last set of jumps. "I thought Nate sent her."

Chewing on another chip, Sebastian rolled his eyes. "Why am I not surprised?" he queried rhetorically and I glowered at him, trying to regulate my breathing. "Second hint was the fucking fact that she was all over you. And she wasn't doing it to snoop, the giveaway was that she kept making sure one of your team members was in sight. She wanted us all to think you guys were back together—"

"She was drunk—"

"She was *scheming*," he pointed out. "But you're so caught up in your hatred for her you couldn't see past it. And she used that to her advantage. She was *betting* on you being an asshole.

And I don't even need to ask whether she taunted you with talk of Nate. Do you know why? Because she probably did. Nothing like mentioning your enemy to light a fire under your ass and make you forget about everything else."

Not in the mood for a conversation involving Nyx, I ignored Sebastian and focused on finishing my workout. It was just us and Benson left at the rink, everybody already having left. They were probably getting ready to do something fun. I couldn't even rest. Once I got home, I had a fucking assignment to do.

An hour must've passed before I spoke again. Guilt had weighed me down ever since Saturday. And I couldn't refrain from asking, "Did you believe the rumour?" Sebastian had dozed off on a foam mattress and his head jerked when he heard my voice. "About Nate and Taylor."

He knew what I was referring to, the disgusting side of the rumour. With a heavy sigh, he responded, "Yes." I swallowed around the lump in my throat. He looked ashamed of himself, that he'd thought so low of her, someone who was now helping his team. "Did you?"

"No." I could tell Sebastian knew the answer but asked anyway. Out of everyone on the team, it was probably just Grayson and me that didn't believe the rumour when it had first sprung up. "She was with me, wasn't she?" I questioned rhetorically and Sebastian frowned. It was also what propelled me to apologise to her for what I'd said at the party. "I trusted her."

Sebastian found a comfortable position on the mattress before he questioned, "Then why'd you go along with it?"

I shrugged. "How would *you* feel if your girl was scheming with your enemy?"

"Like absolute fucking shit."

"Exactly," I finished, feeling my chest tighten with guilt at the fact that I'd pretended to believe the rumour. And I couldn't forget the effect it had on her either. Closing my eyes, I sank onto the floor. It was a memory I often tried to forget. Last year, close to the end of the spring quarter and during final exams, I'd been looking for an empty classroom to sit in and study.

But somebody had beat me to the abandoned art room I ordinarily used. Muffled cries had been coming from inside. When I'd peeked through the keyhole, I'd seen Nyx crumpled on the ground, sobbing into her hand as she spoke to whoever was on the other end of the phone. I couldn't be sure if it had been Nailea or somebody else, because she'd never mentioned a name. All I knew was that she'd been heartbroken that people believed she was sleeping with Nate for money and that they were slut-shaming her. I never spoke of that moment.

Because the next day, Nyx had been her robotic self again, leaving no evidence of her previous tears. Even after summer break, when she'd returned for her second year; she'd shown no sign of weakness.

I snapped out of my daze when Benson wandered in, bag over his shoulder and keys in his hand. He tossed them to me and I caught them. "You leaving?"

He nodded, glancing momentarily at Sebastian. "Lock up when you guys leave." I placed the keys by my sweatshirt. "You can keep those in case you ever wanna train late. I've got another set."

"Thanks, Coach," I responded, wondering why he was lingering at the entrance. Sebastian must've been thinking the same thing because he scrunched his face in confusion. "Anything else?"

Benson's face suddenly went serious, mouth turning into a thin line as his eyes glazed over in displeasure. "Yes, there's one more thing." My brow curved. "I'd like for you to behave professionally. As Captain, you're supposed to be setting an example."

I stood up, feeling my earlier anger return. "What's that supposed to mean?" This just wasn't my fucking day, was it?

"Miss Taylor is officially part of the staff, is what I mean," he shot back, raspy voice growing louder and Sebastian watched the two of us apprehensively. Benson and I hadn't gotten along when he first arrived, but I thought we were improving. "That means you *treat* her like part of the staff."

It was obvious he'd learnt of what had happened with Jai, but that wasn't my fault so he had no right to be yelling at me.

But his next words stopped me.

"So stop *groping and touching* her!"

My heart dropped to my stomach at the implication of his words. "Excuse me?"

Benson crossed his beefy arms over his chest. "You heard me. Do you think I didn't see you earlier with your arms around her? I'm old, not stupid, Hunt."

Nyx was always the one touching *me* first, to *taunt* me. There was never any meaning behind her touches, like at the party. My hatred for her usually curbed any desire to speak to or touch her. So I wondered what the fuck Coach was talking about if Nyx was always willingly stepping into my arms or teasing me.

But then I thought back to earlier; when I put my arms around Nyx and she didn't look too enthusiastic. She'd fucking *known* Coach was watching. From his perspective, he probably saw me making advances on a girl who wasn't interested. It was uncharacteristic of her because usually, she'd resort to teasing.

Ready to explain to him it was a misunderstanding, I opened my mouth. "Coach—"

"You'll stay away from her during training," Benson cut me off, tone leaving no room for argument. "I'll be having a meeting with the rest of the boys as well. Each one of you *will* respect her. She may get on my nerves like hell, but she's still a girl dealing with a bunch of idiots, myself included." He glowered at Sebastian and me. "Understand?"

Unable to say anything, we nodded. With one last glare, he left. The moment he disappeared, Sebastian let out a bark of laughter, clutching his abdomen as he fell back onto the foam mattress.

For the first time, I realised why people refused to get caught up in the web of Nyx Taylor. She made you think you had control, made you think you could easily free yourself from her web. But once you're ensnared, like a black widow spider, she bound you in silk, in soft touches, before puncturing you with her fangs.

Just like her arachnid counterpart, she did all the work herself whilst using those trapped in her web.

First, she'd solved the problem of the guys flirting with her by making it seem as if she was with me. Second, not only did she get revenge on me for what I'd said at the party, but she'd also got me in trouble with Benson. Lastly, she no longer had to pretend there was anything between us to keep the guys away because she had Benson on my case after he'd seen us earlier.

Nyx had solved all her problems by using the gullible men around her. And she did so without even having to ask them a thing.

Chapter 7

Nyx

"The fight for the Crosstown Cup has officially begun!" Benson's voice boomed across the locker room. I snickered because it had started in November already, during the fall quarter. We were probably the last sports division to join in, others having won and lost matches already—as well as having hosted some of their fundraisers.

"Well," Benson added with an embarrassed grin when he noticed my amusement, "it's officially starting for *us*." The hockey boys had been given leave from classes today, just because it was their first day of proper training. They needed to get into the swing of things seeing as they were delayed as fuck.

Twenty men sat before Benson, each one listening intently. I leaned against the wall, eying everyone. They were all serious, dead-set on winning this year to make up for their last loss. I hadn't necessarily had high hopes at first, but after last week and watching Benson interacting with his team, I'd decided they had a pretty good chance.

Benson had dropped his egotistical attitude slightly and was constantly reading from the files I'd given him. The boys were on their best behaviour around me and I knew it was because Benson had spoken to them. Beckham hadn't spoken to me in the past week unless necessary—and I wasn't complaining. My only focus right now was helping this team win. I owed it to the school because it was because of this job that I could pay off my family's debts and perhaps finally make that big move.

The other day, still not believing my luck, I'd curiously asked Benson why they chose me for the job. Many of the other coaches had assistants that helped them with events, but Coach Ford had done everything on his own. When he'd left, I wondered why they didn't just hire an assistant for Benson. He'd said that it was one of my professors who had recommended me to Dean Waverly. She'd argued that it would be a waste to spend money on a stranger when they had somebody perfectly worthy of the position on campus. I was forever grateful for the school. Which was why I needed to do my best.

"We have our first match on Sunday at our very own rink," Benson continued. A home game. It made it easier for our supporters to surround us. "Dean Waverly informed me there are three other matches this week, including the volleyball, football and baseball teams taking place on Wednesday, Thursday and Saturday, respectively." He turned to me. "Any word on their fundraisers?"

I nodded, feeling everyone's eyes on me—except Beckham's. "The volleyball girls hosted a car wash last week. The football team is hosting a karaoke night tonight, and the baseball team has a drive-in movie night planned for Friday," I stated, reading from the mental list I'd made. "With our first match on Sunday, I say we host our fundraiser on Saturday, seeing as the baseball game is an away game. Only some students will leave to support and we'll have everyone else here."

Benson nodded. "Okay, there are ten points available to win within our division. We need at least six and we have to keep the matches going. Can't let them accumulate points so early on."

"If we, by chance, win early on and there's no need for further matches," I added, "Dean Waverly said the fundraisers will continue, allowing us to stack up on the points missed from the unneeded matches."

In my opinion, it was a smart idea. If perhaps, one of the teams took home the wins of the first six matches, they'd win by a landslide and leave four points uselessly floating around. That left it up for grabs when it came to events, and I planned to snatch them regardless.

Benson thought about it for a second. His eyes found mine, a wary look present there. "For now, let's prepare for ten matches in case it's a difficult battle with us needing to go until the tenth round. That means ten fundraisers, Taylor. Can you handle it?"

"We have ten matches, Benson, which means being prepared for ten matches. Can you handle it?" I shot back and he released an amused chuckle.

The sound of shuffling feet met my ears and I watched Benson lead the team towards the ice. I sat in the front row, placing my backpack next to me as I took out my notepad. Ten fundraisers was a lot. Dean Waverly had given me a budget, as she did with the coaches of the other teams too. The challenge was to throw amazing fundraisers, raise money for charities, build hype for matches and ensure everyone had a great time. I had my work cut out for me. But I always loved a challenge.

With the first fundraiser only four days away, I needed to hurry on my finalisations. The invitations were completed, having been designed by myself and Poppy. I was hoping to send it to every student and encourage them to bring friends and family. I aimed my first fundraiser solely at teenagers and young adults. I wanted to start with a bang, making everybody excited for what was to come.

Opening my laptop, given to me by the school courtesy of my scholarship, I stared at the invitation with its gold decorations and font. In large letters at the bottom stood the names of five homeless shelters in the community that the money would be going towards. It was attention-grabbing because I wanted to people know that the hefty sum they paid for a ticket was going to be put to good use.

Satisfied, I emailed the invitation to Nailea, knowing she'd send it to every student and print out some physical copies to give to random people. I glanced up from my laptop, watching Beckham command his first line. He looked more muscular than he usually did because of the padding that he wore.

The uniform was in the official USC colours; cardinal and gold. As captain, there was a letter "C" on Beckham's jersey. He was watching his teammates do some drills, yelling out commands as Benson stood at the other end of the rink, speaking to the other boys. It always ruffled me how deep

Beckham's voice was. He wasn't one to speak a lot, except during training and it was like his voice took a brief nap and had that rough edge to it whenever he decided to use it, making him constantly sound like he'd just woken up.

The same went for his physical appearance. The guy needed minimal effort to look good. His hair was in its usual messy state, some strands dangling in his eyes. Beckham hadn't spoken to me since last week when he'd arrived late for practice. That day, I'd known Benson was watching us, known that he saw Beckham's arms around me and I'd been counting on it. Which was why I hadn't teased him or flirted. All of my plans had been leading up to that moment.

Beckham was right when he'd said I came to his party with a motive. He'd just guessed wrong, thinking I was there on behalf of Nate. I'd been there for myself. He may have guessed wrong, but he was still right about the motive. So, I didn't get why he was upset. My laptop dinged as Nailea's response came through, stating that she'd send the emails through tonight.

When I looked up again, Beckham was watching me. A chill ran down my spine and it wasn't because of the ice. All traces of teasing and playfulness were gone from his expression. His gaze was pure hostility. His ego must've taken a beating when he'd realised I'd used him. Poor baby probably thought I was still interested in him. I could never be interested in somebody who thought me to be a slut. I had standards and wouldn't let him sit at his table, tossing me crumbs. It also helped to get him off my back about my dad having slapped me after that party when I'd arrived home drunk. Beckham didn't need to know anything.

He didn't *deserve* to know anything.

The asshole didn't break eye contact and I chose to look away first, not because I was intimidated, but because the rest of his team was gawking at us. I'd figured it was going to be awkward, given our history together. They were probably used to seeing their captain, previously an alternative captain, all over me last year. Then there was the split after the Crosstown Cup had ended last May. And now we were back in each other's spaces after eight months of trying our best to avoid each other.

Forced proximity at its finest.

Or maybe that was a euphemism for entertainment to everybody but the two of us.

Clearing my throat, I organised my plans for the rest of the fundraisers. I made neat little folders containing invite templates, the contact information of small businesses and a list of charities in our community. After I was done with that, I read over a few pages of the pdf version of my sociology of sports textbook to prepare for the test in two days. By the time I was done, it was only noon.

I was just reading through the money we still owed Poppy's physiotherapist when a hockey stick slammed onto the ground next to me. My eyes trailed the black stick, passing gloved hands before travelling up to meet narrowed eyes. Beckham's thick brows were scrunched, a sign that he was annoyed. He looked slightly surprised that I hadn't flinched at the loud sound of the stick.

My heart had been scared worse before.

"Yes?" I drawled, trying to look past his humongous form and seeing that the boys were leaving the ice, waddling towards

Benson's office like penguins. I nearly laughed.

Beckham didn't look too happy about being the one sent over to me. It was obvious by his expression and tone. "Emergency meeting. Benson got a call." The bright light of my phone caught my attention and I saw five missed calls from Annie. I hadn't even realised that I'd put the device on silent. "Let's go."

Just as I was about to respond to Annie that I'll call her back soon, a message came through from her. And my blood ran cold. *It's Indigo.* My bones felt like rusted metal, creaking as I reached for the device.

"Go on without me," I told Beckham, clicking on Annie's contact details and waving him away.

He looked pissed off, ready to argue, but I was already walking away, leaving all my things on the bench. The sound of the ringing was like a ticking bomb. There was a lump the size of a tennis ball in my throat. I knew this day would come eventually, but no matter how much I prepared myself, I knew I'd never be ready. I stupidly hoped that Annie and I would've had things under control before this happened.

Stupid, silly, naïve me.

Annie picked up after a few seconds and I slipped into the janitor's closet. The lump in my throat made it difficult to speak and I could feel the pace of my breathing increase to the point where it felt like I was running a marathon with little hydration in the blazing heat of the sun.

"Nyxie," my older sister choked out. I could hear cries in the background, the sound like shards of glass stabbing holes all over my body, all my strength seeping out like a crimson liquid. "I— what— I don't know what to do or say to her— fuck— I can't do this—"

"*Annie.*" I kept my tone steady, gentle. She was beating herself up about this, just like when it had happened with Poppy. Annie was somebody who couldn't stand to see anyone hurt. If you cried, you could bet she'd cry with you. Because of her big heart, it was difficult for her to be the tough one, to speak words of comfort because she'd be feeling half, if not all, of your pain. "What happened?"

There were sniffles and I sat down on a crate. Annie took in a deep breath. "He wasn't supposed to be home, but he needed a change of clothes and Indie didn't go to school today because she was sick—"

I closed my eyes, realising that they both were in a rough spot. He hadn't expected anybody to be home. Annie was supposed to be at work, and the rest of us at school, but Indigo had woken with a cold this morning and Annie had taken the day off. That meant no money paid to her that day and Indigo missed out on schoolwork. He definitely wouldn't be happy about that.

"Did he pick a fight with you?" I urged, voice weak with exhaustion.

Annie hiccupped. "Yes, but nothing I couldn't handle. The thing is, I gave Indie some medicine, so she was fast asleep in her room. He didn't *know* she was there. Everything was going fine until he started yelling at me—"

I groaned. He rarely hit Annie, but he always went after her with his words. It was one of the reasons she was so soft-spoken, almost afraid of the world. It was why she'd reacted so strongly to Donovan. “Annie—”

“I nodded obediently and took the verbal beatings. All he had to do was take his clothes and leave.” She subdued a whimper, voice pitching higher as she broke down. “But then Indie came out of the room.” I pressed a hand to my head, feeling a migraine coming on. “She tried to stand up for me, said I was only at home to care for her and it wasn’t my fault.”

That sounded like Indigo. My mouth had landed me in hot spots more times than I could count. I could fully admit that I never knew when to shut up. Indigo was exactly like me. And she would pay the price that I constantly did.

The knot in my throat grew bigger. I could scarcely speak. “Where?” The million-dollar question that I never thought I’d propose regarding Indigo. The silence was tense. When I tasted something salty, I realised I was silently crying.

Annie was mute for a beat, perceiving how much this question meant. “Butt and back,” she uttered.

Part of me was relieved that it wasn’t in a conspicuous area. He was more careless with me, as seen by the bruise and cut I’d sported last week.

Other people would argue that spanking kids to discipline them was normal. Other people would call me dramatic, but they didn’t live with us. My nose was burning and I rubbed a hand over it. Annie knew what I was going to ask next. It was a routine since we were little girls. Starting with us and moving down to Poppy. And now Indigo.

“Hand,” I paused, a sob clawing up my swollen throat, “or wooden spoon?”

Her response was like a knife being plunged into the

beating organ in my chest. The only reason that organ was beating was because of the three girls that shared my blood.

In a small voice, Annie countered, "Wooden spoon."

The air left my lungs and I sagged back against the wall, uncaring that the crate was hurting my ass. If anything, I wanted the pain. I wanted to feel what Indigo was feeling. Matthew Taylor didn't spank, that was the first thing that needed to be pointed out.

He beat.

"Put her on the phone," I managed to speak through my awkward breathing.

I could hear Annie walking to Indigo's room. The closer she got, the rowdier the cries in the background became. Another noise reached my ears and I pulled the phone away momentarily. Shouts were coming from outside the janitor's closet and I wondered if the boys were arguing. I could deal with that shit later.

"Nyxie?" a shaky voice piped up and I pressed the phone back to my ear.

"Indie," I muttered, feeling fury build inside me at the defeat in her voice. She began crying the moment I said her name. I never wanted her to cry again. I wanted that sassy smile on her face, the bright glow in her warm eyes. Annie and Indigo had the same eyes, but Annie's had lost their glow a long time ago and I wasn't going to let that happen to Indigo.

Indigo hiccupped violently, emphasising how long she'd been crying. The guilt pushed down on my shoulders like an invisible pressure. I felt like Atlas; the titan cursed to carry the weight of the world on his shoulders. Except mine was guilt.

"It hurts, Nyxie."

Knowing just how bad it was to be beaten with a wooden spoon, I could easily sympathise with her. It was her first time. He must've lost his temper to lay a hand on her. Hurting Indigo and Poppy was something he restrained himself from doing, knowing that he could get in a shit load of trouble for hurting kids. Annie and I were an entirely different story. Two adults, willingly staying with him for one reason only—our sisters.

"I know, sweetheart," I whispered. I repeated the same things I'd told Poppy when she was first hit by an enraged Matthew Taylor, the same things I wished somebody had told me. "Listen to me, Indie, you did nothing wrong—"

She stopped me, sounding petrified. "Daddy said I was disrespectful. And I was, Nyxie! I told him I'm sorry. I'm *very* sorry." Her words collapsed into tears again. I could hear Annie crying as well. The soft murmurs told me that the latter had dragged Indigo into her arms. "Daddy said naughty girls should be disciplined. I don't wanna be naughty." I could barely grasp what she was saying through the tears.

The same things he'd told us. It was manipulation at its finest. It wasn't Indigo's fault. The fault was with him; a cowardly man.

"Indie," I pleaded over her cries, needing to drill some words into her head. He could force his words into her mind with just a few beatings, but I couldn't do that. They said actions spoke louder than words. Yet, for once, I hoped it wasn't like that. I hoped my words were discernible through the pain she'd suffered. I hoped my words slithered through the cracks that he'd made in her tough armour. I hoped it injected itself into her bloodstream, following the pathway to that beating organ. I hoped my words replenished the love that he fought to take.

Not the love for him though. I couldn't give a fuck if Indigo ceased loving him for what he'd done.

I wanted to replenish the love she felt for herself. The fresh fear that he'd instilled in her would mature into a rage, but that rage wouldn't be aimed at him. It would be directed at herself, she'd feel undeserving of love because some pathetic asshole had told her she was an undisciplined little girl. I would know.

I felt that same rage towards myself every day.

"We love you just the way you are, Indie." I cleaned my tears, sitting straighter. I heard Annie mumble her agreement. "Every girl is strong in her own way. Some are silently strong, like Annie, and some are loud. *You* are loud, Indie. Don't be silenced by him, I'm begging you. You stood up for Annie and I'm *so damn proud of you.*"

"But Daddy—"

I cut her off. "Men like him are gonna tell you things. It doesn't mean you have to listen. You know what happened the first time I was beaten with that ugly spoon?"

Indigo sounded curious through her stuffy nose. "What?"

"I stared at it and I told myself that this is nothing but an *object*. He used that to make me scared. Do you know why? Because *my words scared him. Your* words scare him, Indie. Don't let anybody silence you. He's a little bitch. I mean, who even hits girls?" Striving to lighten the mood, I added, "Say it, Indie. What is he?"

She giggled and I sighed in relief. "He's a little bitch." The arguments grew louder and I wondered what the fuck had the team so riled up.

“Exactly,” I told her, a smile growing on my lips, being watered by Indigo’s innocent laughter. “Now, ask Annie to run a hot bath for you later. I’ll leave early and pick up some bubble bath on the way home, okay?”

“Okay. Bye, Nyxie.”

Annie took the phone from her. “Thanks, Nyx. I don’t know how you do that.” I heard her tell Indigo to go get her bathing suit, seeing as she liked to swim in the bathtub.

“Keep her away from him,” I suggested once I was sure Indigo was out of hearing distance. “I don’t want her in that position ever again. It’s not like he cares enough to want to speak to them. Let’s just keep them both out of his way. Accident my fucking ass,” I hissed in frustration, “I don’t know how much longer I can put up with his shit, Annie.”

She hummed in agreement, mumbling something to Indigo before turning her attention back to me. “I’ve been eyeing some apartments ever since you got that new position. If we aim for the cheaper ones, we can be out of his clutches sooner than expected.”

I pondered her words, wondering whether we should save up to afford a nice place or jump at the cheapest one that opened up. “Once we have enough, we take the girls and we’re gone, okay? Remember the plan?”

“Leave a note with a threat that if he ever comes to find us, we’ll go to the police,” she murmured. Not that we would go to the police, not until we both had stable jobs. If we didn’t, we’d be found unfit to care for Indigo and Poppy.

“Good, I’ll—”

Annie cut me off. "But what about Mom?" Her question was asked hesitantly, unsure how to approach the topic with me.

My brows scrunched in obvious confusion, wondering what she had to do with anything. "What about her?"

"What if she decides to return?" my sister continued, only furthering my bewilderment. The last time we'd seen her, she was addicted to cocaine and sleeping away the hours. "She's in rehab, Nyxie. We have to consider her when it comes to our plan because knowing her, she'll mess it all up—"

My lips parted in surprise, jaw going slack at the revelation. "What? Who told you she was in rehab?"

The door to the janitor's closet flew open and I jolted to my feet. Beckham stood there, rage emitting from him like heat from a fire. It was obvious that he'd switched gears, going from the captain to a predator who anticipated a threat. His eyes were indifferent and that was a warning, the same as a sword being drawn. He ambled inside, closing the door and trapping the two of us inside.

"Annie, I'll call you back," I muttered, hanging up and shoving my phone in my pocket, trying to overcome the disorientation at my sister's words. Beckham was furious. I'd experienced his anger before. It was blazing, trailing you like a dragon ready to incinerate and destroy, but this was different. This was a fit of icy anger, making the temperature in the closet drop. "Can I help you?"

His figure was tense. The skates were gone, replaced with socks, and his helmet was off, exposing the fluffy hair. Venom dripped from his words.

"No. But you're helping someone else, aren't you?" I didn't react, not in the mood for his tantrum. I had a family to get home to. "When were you going to tell us that Nate now plays for the UCLA ice hockey team?"

I froze, the information like a bucket of ice water over me. It felt like I was drowning; the water forming a burning sensation in my lungs. For the second time, the same surprised words escaped me. "What?"

No, no, *no*. That couldn't be right. If Nate was on the team it meant that all of my efforts had been for nothing, all of the hurt had been for nothing—I got *sued* for fucking nothing.

A sarcastic laugh trickled from Beckham's throat and he shook his head. "You're good, Taylor, I'll give you that." He stepped even closer, eyes momentarily flitting to the dried tears on my face. "Tell me, were you going to feed him information? Help his team win against us?"

I glowered at him, feeling a torrent of outrage surge from deep within me. "How *dare* you, asshole? This is the first time I'm hearing of this!"

If anything, I would've expected to hear the news from Nate himself. We didn't talk, but Nathan Wyatt wasn't an idiot. The moment he'd arrived at UCLA, he would've figured out why I'd done what I did and he wouldn't step foot onto the ice again. Which was why Beckham's words made no sense.

He barely reacted. "Nice try. You probably thought you could go on with this plan of yours for the whole year. But, Benson has a friend who works at UCLA and he recognised Nate on campus." His eyes narrowed to slits. "You got caught out."

The accusations caused the pounding in my head to intensify. I hadn't heard from Nate since before he fucking left the school but deep down, I *knew* that he wouldn't ever play hockey again. He fucking hated the sport.

"Did you hit your head or something? I have no idea what you're talking about."

Beckham continued speaking, leaving no trace of the guy that had apologised to me just the other day. "You'd go against your school for him? But then again, wouldn't expect anything less from Nate's submissive bitch."

The words pierced my skin, but I fought to not blanch. *He's hurt*, I told myself. *People say things they don't mean when they're hurt*, I tried comforting myself. Usually, I'd fight fire with fire. But Beckham was all ice this time. His words were cruel and calculated. He was aiming to hurt me.

So I'd do the same because I was hurt too.

"I see you're still jealous that I chose Nate over you."

That stopped him in his tracks. Then his mouth twisted into a sinister smirk, a chuckle escaping him. "Baby, I never wanted you. I'll admit, you had my attention for a good time" he explained, running a hand through his hair. "The thing is, you had Nate's attention too. But here's the difference between him and me; I wouldn't pay for something I could get for free."

I couldn't help it. I flinched. My eyes stung and the lump was still in my throat. I didn't have a witty comeback. I didn't know what to say.

And it fuelled Beckham's angry satisfaction.

"You don't deserve an explanation from me," I hissed through clenched teeth. "You didn't even *ask* for one. You just labelled me as Nate's slut. And whether it's true or not," I continued, traitorous tears in my eyes, "it's still better than being labelled your girlfriend."

His eyes flashed with anger but a begrudging laugh escaped him. "Oh? And who says I even fucking *wanted* you to be my girlfriend?" His words had an edge to them and I felt it in my teeth.

"I don't know," I spoke sarcastically. "Because I remember you giving me your jersey. Or how about the *many* times you'd ask me to stay after practice?" His jaw was clenched now as I used his past actions against him. "Let's not forget my favourite, the time you called me in the middle of a party that was thrown in *your* honour to wish *me* a happy birthday."

There was silence for a few seconds, too long because it made my mind linger on the words I'd just uttered. Beckham and I had an unspoken agreement that we'd forget those six months when we teetered on the border between friendship and something more.

After Nate, nothing was the same. But no matter how much I detested Beckham, I couldn't just forget about what could've been, how much he'd helped me. I'd always abhorred my birthday and his phone call had brightened that day a little.

Beckham seemed to snap back to reality. "I remember that day," he mused. "It was the night I fucked Avery Malcolm." The pain must've shown on my face because his amused expression faltered momentarily. I blinked quickly, feeling a rebellious tear scramble down my cheek. The anger that controlled him wavered. "Shit, wait—"

I pushed past him, opening the door and practically

scampering away. His hand was suddenly around my wrist and I yanked it back as if his touch was fire, cradling my wrist against my chest like an injured baby. The tenderness in his eyes made me want to bawl.

"I hate you," I declared, hearing the despair in my voice, "I hate you. But I'm human enough to acknowledge the fact that I *liked* you, Beckham." He gulped and I took another step back as a bland laugh left me. "And the height of those feelings I had for you was probably on my birthday. So thanks for ruining the *one* good memory I had of you."

Beckham's brows furrowed in distress. "Nyx, wait—"

"Did Nate even *tell* you I was still in contact with him?" I inquired as I tilted my head and wiped my face. "The team didn't mention me, did they? Not even Benson?" His jaw clenched. I laughed incredulously, running a hand over my face. "You just *assumed* that I had something to do with it even after I *told* you Nate left this school and team in his fucking past! And that includes me!"

"You've worked with him once before," he retaliated in defence, looking slightly defeated as he stepped closer, gaze trained on the fresh tear tracks on my face as if he couldn't believe he was the reason for them.

"You're pathetic. Pretending to care about some silly little cut on my mouth as you claim to not hurt women. Apparently, that doesn't apply to me. Because based on all of the insults you've flung my way since what happened between us, it seems like I'm the golden exception."

Beckham was quick to shake his head. "Don't act as if you're some sort of angel—"

"I *know* I'm not an angel. I've been called a bitch more times than I can count and there's no counterargument because I *am* a bitch," I spoke over him. "But I aim to tease, to get under your skin because your mere proximity pisses me the fuck off." I pointed a finger at him and sneered, "*You* are the one that seems to take satisfaction in playing a role in my hurt." Swallowing my pride, I continued, "And yes, I'm *man* enough to admit that some of the things you say hurt me, Beckham, that I cry sometimes. So how come *you* can't admit that you were hurt by me helping Nate instead of playing this *stupid* game of thinking my every breath has something to do with him?"

My voice was burned out, completely dog-tired of the back and forth. "You knew how Nate was treating us," he said in an equally tired voice.

I nodded slowly, taking note of his hunched shoulders, and the vacant look in his eyes. I'd seen it in myself many times before.

"He emotionally abused you guys," I said, watching Beckham fight the urge to flinch. Nate constantly threatened his team members and made them feel inadequate, and anxious which resulted in over-compliance, shame for not being able to do anything and guilt for not living up to expectations.

"And yet you still helped him," Beckham stated as if all the answers were in that simple sentence, the reason for every action and word.

"Despite your history with him, Nate cared about me," Beckham's jaw clenched, "I helped a friend that wasn't willing to be helped," I spoke slowly. "Anybody with eyes could see

Nate wasn't going to win the captaincy, not with his opponent being you. But I helped him because he was alone. *Knowing* that he would lose I *still* helped him because he needed at least one person to soothe that loss. *You* chose to see it as a betrayal, all because you were jealous; something you still can't admit to."

Still wanting to get the last say, Beckham spoke, "You could've told me, you know?" We both knew that was a lie. He never would've listened if I planned to help the guy he hated. The outcome was always going to be the same. "You could've told me instead of—or did you not trust me?" he asked suddenly, looking somewhat pained.

There was no humour in my smirk. "Who did I lose my virginity to?" His face dropped and he looked regretful, for once, like he shouldn't have stormed into the janitor's closet and blamed me for every little thing that went wrong. "There's my trust. Now tell me, where's yours? I suppose it's somewhere between Avery Malcolm's legs, isn't it? A rare treasure seemingly only visible on my nineteenth birthday."

Slipping past him, I collected my things. I ignored Benson when he called for me, rushing out of the rink. It took me a half-hour to walk from University Park (where the campus was situated) to Skid Row; my neighbourhood. There was also the extra ten minutes to pick up the bubble bath for Indigo, but I needed the air. I was quiet when I got home, not wanting to burden Annie with my problems. Indigo was better, smiling the entire time as she was surrounded by us. My dad didn't come home and I was thankful. There was no telling what I'd do in an act of anger.

Indigo and Poppy took a bubble bath once the latter got home from school. Later that night, I lay in bed, listening to Annie's soft snores. Beckham's eyes wouldn't leave my mind, no matter how hard I pushed the image away. I saw the anger there, the pain. I could sympathise slightly. His team was like his family and he saw me as a threat, but that didn't give him the right to hurt me.

Nobody had the right to hurt me. Never again.

Just as I was about to doze off, my phone shone with a new notification. I reached for it, seeing tons of missed calls from Nailea. The earliest one was from a few hours ago. With a disappointed groan, I realised my phone had been on silent again. Making sure Annie was asleep, I slipped out of our room and headed to the kitchen before calling Nailea back. She answered on the first ring, as always.

"Nyx," she greeted. "You had me worried sick. I went to pick you up at the rink and Benson said you *walked* home? *Estúpido*. Weren't you telling me just last week that some guy was shot in the street next to yours?"

I gasped, completely forgetting that Nailea was going to pick me up. I'd been so hasty to get home that I hadn't messaged her. "I'm so sorry, Nai. I should've called you to let you know. I'm sorry if I wasted your time—"

"That's not my point, Nyx," she insisted, sounding frustrated. "You walked home alone. Anything could've happened to you." I didn't hold it against her, but people from privileged neighbourhoods always thought the worst of ours, believing that somebody was shot, kidnapped or beaten every passing minute. I knew nothing would've happened to me.

The people in Skid Row knew each other well.

"Nothing happened," I assured her. "I'm home and I'm safe—"

"Would you let me be worried for just a minute?" Nailea interjected heatedly. "Don't downplay what could've happened. I'm glad you're safe but *please*, don't do that again. If you need a ride somewhere, I'll be there, Nyx. No matter where I am, okay? Just *call* me."

I didn't know how to respond to her and I felt my nose begin to burn. Regardless of her saying that I could call her, I still felt like a burden. Nailea drove all the way from her dorm on campus to my place so that I could get to class every morning. If that wasn't a burden, then I didn't know what was. Still, she constantly insisted that she didn't mind.

Angrily, I remembered my dad was the cause of this. He was the cause of me struggling to accept that somebody cared. Even as Nailea waited for my response, I couldn't figure out what to do. Should I thank her? Should I apologise for making her stressed? The latter was something I was leaning towards.

In the end, I chose to say, "Okay."

She hummed. "I'm picking you up early tomorrow. Be ready. Don't do anything stupid again." I smiled, promising her that I'd stay safe until she saw me again. Then she hung up, but not before blowing obnoxious kisses into the speaker. I climbed back into bed, Nailea's obvious affection for me still shaking my soul. And for the next few minutes, I whispered to myself that I deserved that affection.

Chapter 8

Beckham

"To be honest, I think you're an idiot."

Those were *not* the words I wanted to hear, especially from my mother of all people. She was supposed to be on my side, to understand my dilemma. Instead, she was tossing me frowns whilst she moved around, grating chocolate and checking on the batch of cookies in the oven. There was flour all over her apron and dough stuck in the slowly greying brunette strands of her hair. Merely looking at her brought comfort like no other, and comfort was something I was desperately in need of. So after practice, I dropped my things at my place before driving to my childhood home.

My mom was in the middle of mixing cupcakes when I entered, the radio blaring music as she danced around the large kitchen. That was one of the things she'd begged for when she married my dad—as she always reminded people when they visited her. The kitchen was heaven for her and she spent all of her time there so it was no surprise when I found her head buried in a bowl of flour.

"Thanks for that, Mom, truly. It's just what I needed to hear," I spoke sarcastically as I held the piping bag in my hand, gently icing the cupcakes for my mom's second-grade class.

The woman in question stopped in front of the counter, crossing her arms and tutting. I knew a lecture was coming. "Are you telling me I raised you to be an asshole?" The question was simple but simultaneously lethal. "Since when do you insult girls you like—"

I groaned. "*Mom—*"

"No, you listen to me, young man," she said, wagging a dough-covered finger in my face as her hazel eyes flared with disappointment. "I've heard you moan and groan about that girl since the day you met her," I felt my face heat up, "I didn't question you when your words of admiration turned to words of hatred, *no*, I let you be because your father believes in letting you figure things out for yourself, no matter how much of a dumbass you are."

Squeezing more icing onto the next cupcake, I muttered, "Again, thanks."

But my mom pretended like she didn't hear my biting rejoinder, furiously grating chocolate as she spoke. "All you ever do is come home to complain about her, but let me ask you, Beckham Rigel Hunt—"

I nearly swore in embarrassment. "Not the middle name—
"

"—What did *you* do?" she asked with an expectant look, dropping the last piece of chocolate onto the counter. I stayed silent, not knowing how to answer her question. She already knew what I'd done, seeing as I came home and told her about the altercation I'd had with Nyx in the janitor's closet. Her question made it obvious that she expected *me* to think about what I'd done.

When I still didn't speak, my mom continued. "You knew Nate as a captain and only a captain. Judging by what you told me, this Nyx knew him as a friend. Maybe he was different with friends—and I'm not justifying the shit he put your team through—I'm just saying that you have to look at things from her perspective as well, why she helped him."

I pondered on what she was saying, finding truth in them and annoyance at myself for always jumping to conclusions. It was on the tip of my tongue, to argue that Nyx could've told me about it, but I knew it was useless. I would've still gotten upset, unwilling to see things from her perspective because of the person I knew Nate to be.

A groan left me and I ended up squeezing too much icing, watching as it drowned the cupcake. "He left and still manages to torment my life."

My mom rolled her eyes, using her hand to wipe up the excess sugary sweetness. "Only because you're letting him. And I agree with Bash about Nyx bringing up Nate because she knows it'll throw you off. And she probably knows this because *you* are the one who tries to use him against her," she said softly, cleaning her hands before stepping forward to cup my cheek. "It's *so* like you to focus on the action and not the reason; you're like your father in that sense. You're thinking of the fact that she keeps allowing the mention of Nate to build, whether you bring him up or her. But have you ever thought about why?"

I grinned, trying not to be nauseated at myself. "Other than to piss me off?" My mom jokingly slapped my cheek. I shrugged, genuinely not knowing the answer.

"I'm gonna take a wild guess and assume that it's because she's scared." My brows furrowed at the thought of Nyx being frightened of me, at the thought of that cut she'd had, but my mom proceeded, probably sensing my panic. "Not *of* you, but rather being hurt by you," she murmured, "*again*, might I add. If you stay mad at her for helping Nate, there's no way of you getting close enough to break her heart. *Again*," she added with narrowed eyes.

The oven dinged and my mom scurried to get her cookies before they burnt. She laughed happily as the smell of chocolate chips wafted through the air, eagerly grabbing her phone to take pictures of it, no doubt to tease my dad whilst he worked a long shift. I glanced away from her, my entire body feeling heavy after our discussion. Coming to visit her, I'd expected to be comforted, but maybe a good lecture was what I needed.

Once five minutes had passed, I muttered, "You've never even met her." It was the truth. Nyx and I had never dated, we'd never met each other's families. It was her that had held back and I let her because I knew she had her reasons. But then the little flames between us had been extinguished before they had a chance to flourish. Two strangers trying to be more.

Hazel eyes twinkled with laughter. "I didn't need to. I've heard enough to visualise this entire relationship—if you can even call it that, seeing as you're too much of a coward to ask her out," she laughed at the pinched expression I wore. "You boys need to stop underestimating me, I know a lot more than you think."

Elated that the topic was no longer a tense one that suffocated me with guilt, I chuckled. "Yeah? Like what?"

"Like the fact that Gray's been in love with our baby River since they were kids," she began teasingly and my jaw dropped, mind going to the clumsy redhead that had the misfortune of being Sebastian's little sister.

Jaw still slack, I coughed out, "What?"

She raised a mocking eyebrow that still had flour on it. "A mother always knows," she said with utter confidence, not hiding the fact that she considered herself Grayson's mother. "I know a lot of things, even when you all try to hide it from me. Want to be impressed some more?"

I grabbed the bowl of grated chocolate and began sprinkling it over the iced cupcakes. "Go for it."

She hummed. "I also know that River returns his affections." I glanced at her, pulling a weird face at the thought of the two of them together and my mom laughed. "Take Beth even. She has nothing to be shy about but I know she's gay—" I froze, nearly dropping the glass bowl, "—Beck! *Careful* with that."

Slowly placing the bowl down, I turned to look at her. "What did you just say?"

As shameless as she was, for once, Helen Hunt looked embarrassed. "I know it's not my place, she probably only told a few of you that she trusts, but it's rather obvious. Do you know how much restraint it takes not to punch Vivian Braswell in the tits every time I see her?" she rambled. "Gosh, what kind of a mother forces her daughter to date boys when—"

I zoned out, feeling a ringing sensation in my ears as my mom went on and on about what a terrible mother Vivian was. Part of me wanted to scold her for assuming somebody's sexuality, but I couldn't get myself to do so. It was probably because deep down I *knew*. Everything suddenly clicked inside my head; why Vivian was so deadest on the idea of me and Beth together, why she controlled her daughter so much, why Beth had such a deep love for—

"—River," my mom was still speaking. "I always used to wonder if it'll be a little love triangle between them and Grayson, but I guess when Vivian stopped allowing River to come over on the basis that the Hayes' were problematic, Beth outgrew her crush. I think Bash knew she was crushing on River at some point."

"No wonder she's always so awkward around him," I mumbled to myself. Sebastian had probably been the first to know. He'd known for years and that terrified Beth because she hadn't told anybody yet. But I knew Sebastian. He wouldn't say a thing.

My mom's eyes met mine, looking sheepish. "Please don't tell Beth that I know. I don't want her to be uncomfortable when she visits. And I *adore* her visits."

It took a moment for me to find my voice. "I won't." She smiled in relief as I stood up, having no idea that she'd just caused me to have an existential crisis. Before I could leave to get some fresh air, my mom called me back. "Yeah?" I hoped she didn't have another bomb to drop on me because I was still reeling from the previous one.

“I know one more thing,” she began gently, popping a piece of chocolate into her mouth. “I know you’re hiding something big from me, something that’s got your insides all twisted up because you don’t know what to do.”

She stared at me in the way that all mothers do. I wondered whether my dad’s investigative skills had rubbed off on her, and I didn’t know whether to love it or hate it. Still a little woozy about the discovery of what Beth’s mom was putting her through, I found myself admitting, “I think somebody’s hurting Nyx.”

Once the sentence was out there, it felt like reality and not just some silly assumption I had. My mom visibly shuddered, gripping the counter and clearly not having expected that admission.

“Well, then,” she murmured, “what you do next depends on what kind of man I’ve raised you to be.”

I swallowed my guilt. “She’d never trust me. And I don’t blame her either.”

My mom pursed her lips. “She trusted you once, didn’t she? Before you let that green monster take over and dictate your every move. You might not realise it, but that same monster still influences you; that’s why you supposedly hate her so much.”

“You know, she said something similar to me in the janitor’s closet,” I muttered. She’d claimed I couldn’t admit that I was jealous of Nate for having her on his side. “But even if we hated each other or not, this isn’t something I can overlook.” My mom wore a look of sympathy. “You can’t tell Dad.”

As much as I trusted him, he was also a lieutenant at the Los Angeles Police Department. If I even mentioned it to him, he would feel obligated to do something. Nyx hadn't sought help yet, which told me she had a good reason to endure whatever she was going through. Throwing her life out of sorts by reporting anything would only make her hate me more.

"I trust that you'll do what's right," the words were soothing. "You're a good man, Beck. But even the most perfect man would lose his mind when it comes to the woman he lo—"

"Don't even finish that sentence," I cut her off, ignoring her laughter. She just grinned at my annoyed look. "Now I just have to figure out how to get the girl that hates me," I paused, groaning, "to trust me again."

People always reminded us that it was a blessing to wake up in the morning. Somewhere out there, somebody didn't get the chance to open their eyes. But, in all honesty, I would choose a peaceful death in my sleep over waking up to the sounds of grunts and moans. I turned over on the small sofa, squeezing the pillow against my head to drown out the sounds, but it was no use. Of all days Sebastian decided to bring a girl home.

Thursdays were the worst, an unnecessary bridge between the middle of the week and the weekend. Sometimes I woke up on a Thursday fully expecting it to be Friday—only to be heavily disappointed. This Thursday, in particular, was even worse, considering that I could hear Sebastian's headboard banging mercilessly against the wall that our rooms shared.

Maxine screeched his name like a banshee, uncaring that he shared the house with two other people. Grayson was probably trying to burrow into a hole and die there. I'd planned to sleep in, seeing as morning classes were cancelled so students and professors could go and support our football team at the game against UCLA, but Sebastian had put a major dent in my plans by deciding to make a dent in the wall our rooms shared.

I sat up, groaning as my bones whined in pain; a side effect of sleeping on a damn sofa all night, a sofa that was too small. However, it was the gentlemanly thing to do seeing as Melissa was laying in my bed, body wrapped in my blankets. The latter was the twin sister to Maxine and Sebastian had brought them both home last night. However, he appeared to have a preference for the bustier of the two, which had upset Melissa who'd then found her way to my room in the middle of the night.

The girl had been drunk and begun undressing before plopping onto my bed. I'd hopped out of it as if it was on fire. She'd spent an hour crying about how people always chose Maxine over her, even though they had the same face. I'd held my tongue to keep from telling her it wasn't the face Sebastian was interested in. She didn't deserve to be let down even further.

After trying to make out with me, unsuccessfully, she'd passed out, naked as the day she was born. My covers needed to be washed, I reminded myself as I stood up, stretching and yawning loudly. A loud shriek cracked through the air, confirming that Maxine had orgasmed wildly.

What a beautiful Thursday morning.

Sense the sarcasm. I halted next to my bed, covering Melissa's naked chest that must've exposed itself when she'd tossed and turned. Once she was safely covered, I ambled into my bathroom. The hot water was alleviation to my aching joints and I wished I could stand there for longer. Lathering some soap onto my body, I heard a loud and impassioned yell. I recognised the voice as Sebastian's and he didn't sound too cheerful. That was odd, knowing the man just had a good fuck on this fine Thursday morning. There was the slamming of doors and loud stomps coming from the stairs.

"The fuck is going on," I grumbled. Quickly rinsing myself and stepping out of the shower, I grabbed a towel and dried myself before wrapping it around my hips. When I entered my room, I saw Melissa pushing up into a sitting position, blankets swathed around her waist and exposing her tits to the cold air.

Without a word, she stood up and entered my bathroom; the door shutting behind her. Just as I was about to knock and ask her to leave my room once she was done, my door swung open and an annoyed figure strolled in.

Of course Nyx fucking Taylor would be at my house on a Thursday morning and proceed to disturb everyone. We weren't on good terms at the moment. Well, there'd always been something *off* between us for the last eight months—but it was worse now, the hostility heightening after I'd accused her of working with Nate.

And the height of those feelings I had for you was probably on my birthday. So thanks for ruining the one good memory I had of you.

I'd gone to bed with her words in my head. I didn't expect to feel that constricting sensation in my chest, but I did. I supposed I deserved it, especially after what I'd said to her. Nyx rarely showed any emotion, yet, I could still hear it in her voice.

And the height of those feelings I had for you was probably on my birthday.

I blamed the conversation with my mom. Because of her, I was looking way too deeply into everything that was happening around me, including any interaction with Nyx and what I said. But the more I thought about it, the more painful the feeling in my chest became—so I elected not to think about it, not *now* at least.

For now, my main concern was that there was a very good possibility that Nyx was being hurt by somebody. That didn't sit well with me at all, whether I hated her or not.

Nyx strolled in as if she owned the fucking place; as if she hadn't used our past against me the last time we'd spoken. Her black jeans looked pasted onto her, the zipper ending just beneath her belly button. A cropped white sweater adorned her upper half. I smirked internally as I watched her locate me, bright eyes narrowing and hands going to rest on her hips.

"The fuck you doing here, Taylor?" I sought, feigning indifference as I strode over to my dresser and felt her gaze rake over me. "I don't remember hiring a—"

She didn't let me finish, holding up a hand to shush me. "Okay, enough with your prostitute comments," Nyx said, her nose twitching in displeasure. "Yes, I get it. You think people pay to fuck me." I stayed silent, taking a pair of boxers out of the drawer. "I'll fuck your mom for free, though," she declared and I froze. "Your dad too. Maybe your grandparents and friends as well. I'll fuck everyone for free. Except you. You can go fuck yourself, asshole."

Unable to stop myself, I chuckled, although I didn't look at her and kept my gaze trained on the dresser. Without turning around, I inquired, "What are you doing at my house, Taylor?"

Although it was the second time now, it was eery having her back here, knowing that back when she used to visit—we'd been something else, something neither of us had had the chance to label before everything went to shit.

It's still better than being labelled your girlfriend.

Her words hurt me more than they should've; because I was supposed to be over that shit and I was beginning to think I'd never really gotten over it in the first place, just suppressed it.

Nyx scoffed, the sound dripping with irritability. "Some captain you are. I emailed you last night—"

"I hate checking my emails."

It was a lie, but I wanted to piss her off, regardless of my plan of getting her to trust me. It seemed I had a long way to go. I'd seen her email come through last night. Seeing her name had made that weird feeling materialise again. I hated it, so I hadn't opened the damn email.

"I don't give a fuck about what you hate doing," Nyx fired back as I slid my boxers on underneath my towel. "I email you information that needs to be read. You *will* read it and you will take note of things. I know you have no idea how to read—"

An affronted grunt left me as I reeled around to face her. "I fucking know how to read."

Where she heard something as preposterous as that, I had no idea. Her features contorted into one of gentle surprise, plump lips parting and brows raising into a delicate curve.

"Oh?" she jeered, crossing her arms over her chest. "Well, then *read* between the lines, dumbass. I don't give a fuck about your hatred for me. What's important here is the damn team. You'd truly ignore important emails just because you don't like me?"

My jaw clenched and so did my fists. I never expected Nyx to be somebody who'd take the high road. And I didn't need to be painted out as a poor captain.

"I don't need a lecture, especially from you." I tossed my towel into the hamper, glowering at the blonde in front of me. She didn't look too happy. But, then again, she never did around me, not for a long time.

"Would you prefer one from Dean Waverley? Because I can make that happen once she finds out the boxes for Saturday weren't prepared because you were too much of an *idiot* to open my emails."

Slowly, I stalked towards her and she didn't move an inch. "Are you threatening me?"

"Why, does it turn you on?" Nyx mocked, eyes briefly flitting to the tented front of my boxers. If she wasn't entertained before, she was now.

I rolled my eyes, taking another step. She still didn't move. "There's this thing called morning wood. Don't flatter yourself, sweetheart."

"There's also this thing called a liar and I'm looking at one right now," she mused in a bored tone.

I hooked my fingers through the loops of her jeans and yanked her to me. Satisfaction coursed through me at the surprised yelp she let out. Few people managed to surprise

Nyx Taylor. Her hands came to rest on my bare shoulders to stabilise herself.

"Tell me what your email said."

The fire in her eyes died down slightly when she apprehended I wasn't going to quarrel with her. I wasn't stupid. There was only a certain amount of her bitchiness one could handle.

Her lips pursed, drawing my gaze to them. "No. If you were interested you would've read the fucking email."

"Didn't God rain kindness down on his people?" I urged, aggravated at the fact that she wouldn't tell me what the email had said.

She shrugged. "I was standing under an umbrella that day."

My left hand detached itself from her loops and slid to her bare lower back, pressing her against me. The smell of strawberries invaded my senses.

"*Nyx*," I grunted, frustration seeping from my words. And it was the reaction she wanted. "Tell me." If the email was what had gotten her so angry then we could just sort it out by her revealing its content to me.

She shifted her weight, brushing against my dick and she smirked. "I'll recite the entire thing from memory for you," she murmured with a charming grin. "*If* you pay extra."

My restraint snapping, I shifted her against the wall, right hand finding her delicate throat and gently framing it, careful not to startle her. "You think you're funny?"

"I think I'm fucking hilarious," she shot back with a smile, blinking innocently. "You have my trauma to thank for that."

I dipped my head lower, unsure whether I wanted to laugh

or scream. Nyx knew exactly what buttons to push. She was angry with me and came for payback, and boy, she was getting it. I could hear the tiny breaths leaving her and feel the air hitting my chest.

"Tell me what the email said," I reiterated, hoping she'd listen this time.

She smiled. "I don't want to."

My eyes narrowed, only amusing her further. I let a small silence pass between us as I contemplated what to do. She was definitely in control of this conversation, as she'd probably planned. Perhaps I needed to throw her off again, and it gave me the perfect opportunity to voice the words I'd been restraining since the conversation with my mom, words that had been grating my throat.

When Nyx raised a brow, I muttered, "You know, hurting you is not something I take satisfaction in." The fire in her eyes died down, slowly being replaced by panic. "And I *have* hurt you, so I don't blame you for bitching on me all the time, now included."

She shifted on her feet. "Okay, Dr Phil. You done now?"

My mouth quirked. "I'm done once you agree to a truce," she scowled, "at least for the duration of the Crosstown Cup. After all, we're going to be seeing a lot of each other." The words left me before I could even rethink them.

A truce sounded perfect. I wouldn't hold what happened with Nate against her and she wouldn't go out of her way to piss me off, to use our past against us. Being civil could lead to helping her if she truly needed it, if somebody was hurting her.

"And what do I get out of this?" she taunted. "Free sex?

Wow, I can't even remember the last time I had sex without any money being involved."

I scoffed at the fact that she wasn't taking me seriously. "Don't fuck with me, Nyx. I'm serious."

"Oh really?"

"Just listen to me—"

"I'd listen if you made sense for once," she voiced, eyes gleaming with delight.

I bottled the impulse to smile. "Nyx, please."

Her teeth took hold of her lower lip before she muttered, "I really do love it when men beg." My eyes still hadn't left that lower lip, now red and slightly puffy after being held captive by her teeth. A pink tongue slid over it. "Will you do it again?"

Humouring the minx, I quipped, "Depends on if I'll gain your cooperation."

All she had to do was agree to the truce. And she needed to do it fast before I did something utterly foolish. I was on the threshold of my restraint, and she knew it. There was something off about her breathing as she peered up at me, her games catching up to her. Mirth danced between the blue flecks in her wide eyes. The minx always got a thrill out of fucking with my mind. She always did. I waited patiently for her voice to reach my ears, even dipped my head lower; as if we were sharing a secret.

But it never came.

When I raised my gaze back to hers, I found her peeking around my arm, eyes colder than ice. Letting go of her, I turned around, seeing Melissa standing by the bathroom door, wrapped in a towel and looking confused.

An uncomfortable feeling tugged in the centre of my abdomen, multiplying and firing its siblings down my every nerve. My blood felt thick with the sensation. Melissa was eying the proximity between Nyx and me, eyes gleaming with surprise. I'd forgotten about her completely, so caught up in my banter with Nyx.

Nyx.

I twisted my head, scrutinising the blonde. The sprightliness was gone. Her face was inscrutable as she needled Melissa, "Didn't I just kick you out of Sebastian's room?"

So that was the commotion I'd heard whilst in the shower. Melissa tucked a wild strand of brown hair behind her ear before responding in an awkward tone, "Um, that was my sister. Maxine. I'm Melissa."

Nyx swallowed roughly, stepping away from me. "Twins. Cute."

Melissa's gaze darted between us. "So, Nyx Taylor, right? We're in the same journalism class—" The brunette stopped speaking because Nyx straight up left the room. She didn't look back. "That was rude," Melissa huffed, looking at me. "But then again, that's Nyx for you."

I grabbed a pair of sweatpants and slipped them on, wanting to hurry and find Nyx. We weren't done talking yet. "What's that supposed to mean?"

"Everybody on campus knows she's a bitch," Melissa replied. "Don't even get me started on the rumours—"

"Get out," I ordered, stepping towards my door. "When I come back, I want your clothes and yourself gone." I didn't stay to hear what she had to say next because I was already rushing down the stairs.

Grayson was in the living room, surrounded by cardboard boxes still sealed in plastic. He looked up when I entered, busy cutting through the plastic seals with a knife.

"What's happening?" I asked him.

He ripped open a box, pulling out bags of flour. When I looked closer, I saw the logo of the local grocery store plastered on each of the boxes.

"We need to make box sets," he responded, pointing to another corner of the room where there was a heap of glittery black boxes.

"So we're unboxing only to box again?" I inquired in annoyance, not seeing the point. Grayson chuckled, moving onto a fresh box that contained packs of instant jelly.

"The grocery store delivered these and we have to fill those," he pointed to the black boxes, "with a few of each." I pulled a face, still not understanding and he groaned in mock vexation. "Didn't you read the email Taylor sent?"

Guiltily, I scratched the back of my head. "I can't remember."

"Fuck off," he snickered. "We have to make box sets filled with fruits, puddings, jams, and all that shit. It's for our fundraiser on Saturday. At the entrance, guests will hand in a ticket that they paid for and in return, they'll receive one of these." He gestured to an empty black box. When I looked closer, I saw the team name there in a fancy white font.

I was regretting not reading the email because I was beyond lost. I didn't even know what the fundraiser was about or what I was supposed to do. Seeing my probably constipated expression, Grayson snatched a white card from the coffee table and handed it to me. It was an invitation and very eye-catching.

Join the USC ice hockey team for a legendary dinner and food fight, and don't fret; the foods used in the fight are those that have passed their sell-by date and were donated by restaurants and stores. All proceeds will go to our phenomenal community's homeless shelters, listed below. Prizes will be up for grabs as well.

Please note that each shelter has an amazing programme to adopt a child for a day. This is a lovely time to step up and take some children to the upcoming hockey game against UCLA. Allow them to experience this fun time. If wanting to do extra donations or to find out more about the 'adopt a child' programme, contact Nyx Taylor to be put in connection with the homeless shelter of your choice.

Fight on, Trojans!

Once I was done reading, I glanced up and Grayson was peering at me with a smirk. I could tell he was waiting for me to praise Nyx. Being one of my housemates, Grayson had fallen victim many times to one of my infamous rants about her. I didn't give him the satisfaction of letting him know how good I thought her idea was.

But I knew he knew because he spoke again. "You should see the community hall." I raised a brow, placing the card back onto the table. "That's where the rest of the guys are, setting up the place. Taylor got all the decorations, dessert and food at a discount because she's promoting small businesses in the community."

Eying the smile he wore as he unpacked more boxes, I added, "You sound like her number one fan."

Grayson's green eyes crinkled at the sides with the force of his smile. "Number one? Nah," he shook his head, curls swaying. "Probably number two. The top spot obviously belongs to you." I grimaced and he laughed louder.

"Where's Sebastian?" I ignored his previous comment, wanting to know where my blonde housemate was.

"Went to pick up the last of the boxes at the store." Grayson sounded amused. "You should've seen it, man. Taylor kicked Maxine out of his room and told him to go to the store like she asked him to or else she'd shave his hairy ass while he slept."

"She's a scary thing," Maxine added as she entered the room, wearing one of Sebastian's shirts, and a glass of apple juice in her hand. It was easy to tell the difference between the twins. Maxine's hair was longer and she had bangs.

Grayson went back to unpacking and I smothered a snort. He had no idea how to look Maxine in the eye after listening to her moan all morning. She, however, had no problem with sitting down on the couch as if she did this every day. Deciding to annoy him, I left him alone with Maxine and went to look for Nyx. I found her outside, standing next to a car. Nailea was in the driver's seat, eyes closed.

Nyx was leaning against the passenger door, phone pressed to her ear and a dimpled smile on her face. She hung up with a quiet laugh and that's when I moved closer. I wore no shoes and no shirt, but I needed to speak to her. About what? I didn't know. Grayson had already filled me in on the fundraiser. But something inside me pushed my feet to move towards her. When she dragged her gaze from her phone, she looked up to the second floor of the house. Whatever she saw there made her smile drop.

"Taylor," I called out, catching her attention.

Her glare made my feet stop their journey. She opened the passenger door, startling a dozing-off Nailea. "I'll be back for the boxes," she said in a flat tone before hopping into the car. With that, Nailea started the car and then they were off.

I sighed, running a hand over my face. Feeling eyes on me, I shifted slightly, looking towards the window of my room. And there stood Melissa, wearing nothing but my jersey. When she noticed me staring, she smirked, establishing that she knew exactly what she was doing. I narrowed my eyes, feeling anger build inside me at her audacity after I'd told her to leave.

The front door opened and Grayson stepped out, complaining about how awkward he was around Maxine. He then questioned why I was standing outside in nothing but sweatpants. I said nothing, merely pointed to my window where we could see Melissa parading around my room.

Grayson chuckled darkly. "Fuck, I wouldn't wanna be her." Melissa stopped at the window to wave at us. "She won't be wearing that smile much longer."

It nearly sounded like a threat and I wondered what he was hinting at. "I'm not going to hurt her," I told him in a tired tone. It was too early for this shit.

The man next to me smirked. "*You* won't." He clapped me on the back. "But your girl will."

I tilted my head to stare back at my room window. Melissa

seemed to be making herself comfortable. *God*, Nyx would skin her alive and not even blink twice. But as much as my pride ached to admit, Nyx's anger had almost nothing to do with me, at least not all of it. I could read her like a book and her reaction was solely because Melissa had taunted her—something *she* usually did to others.

I didn't even want to imagine what was coming Melissa's way.

Chapter 9

Nyx

"Why are you even so worked up?" Nailea asked through a giggle as she stopped the car. A mother and her kids crossed the street, sending Nailea a grateful smile because the previous car had ignored the red light. I sat in the passenger seat, gripping the seatbelt and seething, only fuelling Nailea's laughter.

I huffed, trying to rid Melissa's stare from my mind. "You should've *seen* her, Nai, the way she looked at me." My fists clenched. "I hated it because it's the way *I* look at people." Her eyes flashed through my mind and I groaned, becoming frustrated with myself for concerning myself with her. *I* was the one who frustrated people, not the other way around. "She was *taunting* me."

Nailea nodded, stepping on the gas. In a light tone, she proposed, "So, this has nothing to do with her having slept with Beckham?" I knew I shouldn't have added that fact when relaying the story. It was irrelevant. If I had laser vision, the curly-haired woman in the driver's seat would've been nothing but a pile of ash. She caught my death glare and choked on another laugh. "It's a *genuine* question!"

"Why should I care who he sticks his dick in?" I challenged, struggling to get a grip on my displeasure. It was like trying to catch air; completely futile. "He can stick his dick in whatever he wants until his dick catches a disease, shrivels up and falls off. Then, the only place his dick will be in is a jar because they'll have to cut it off and he'll be dickless—"

"Can you *stop* saying the word dick!" Nailea blurted, eyes wide as she lurched around an old lady. She yelled an apology through the window and the old lady raised her middle finger in response. Nailea ignored her, already focused on the road again. "Every time you say it your voice goes a little higher and you make me jump. One more time and we'll crash into a tree."

Her face was red and she peered at the rear-view mirror, fully expecting us to be chased by a cop or something. I apologised smoothly, rolling my eyes as I realised my argument didn't even make sense. And that irked me. Because my arguments always made sense. It was the reason I'd been on the debate team in both middle and high school. An inhumane groan left me and I sank my head into my hands.

"I really couldn't give a fuck about who Beckham sleeps with, Nai," I informed her, my words filled with ¾ sincerity, and she nodded, eyes flitting to the rear-view mirror. She knew things would never be the same between us again. "It's Melissa that's the problem. She thought she achieved something by tossing their activities in my face all because she knew of our history. She taunted me."

Taking a second to peek at me, Nailea's stare was dripping

with sympathy. To taunt me was to trigger something deep within me. I didn't like being painted as a fool. I outsmarted others. I taunted others. I'd been on the receiving end of humiliation before, put there by someone who wanted me to suffer. The taunting was torturous, highlighting that I was outsmarted. I had much more to lose than just popularity and friends. That was when I realised people sought to step on others and use their backs as a ladder to their destination. I wasn't anybody's ladder. And I wouldn't be put down. Melissa's stare sought to make me feel small. Her stare triggered memories, a stare exploding with satisfaction.

A stare almost identical to my dad's.

"You know you can talk to me, right?" Nailea said when she saw me drowning in my thoughts, still concentrated on the road. But that was the thing; I knew I could talk to her. The problem was doing it without feeling like I was weighing her down with problems she had no need to worry about. "I know we're not best friends or anything, but I just want you to know that I care, okay? You can come to me."

Self-loathing filled me when I noticed the implicit sadness in her countenance. I thought of every time she'd offered to drive me somewhere. I thought of when she'd asked me to go to parties with her, knowing that I would refuse. And that's when I allowed myself to sense the desperation around her, the same scent that lingered on me. Nailea may have had lots of friends and was invited to every raging party because the entire campus wanted to be in the range of somebody so ethereal—but I knew none of them were close friends. They were only around for the image or to use her in one way or another.

This friendship thing was new to her almost as much as it was for me. She was alone. Something in that loneliness, something in that desperation called me to her.

Which was why I chose to say, "It's my dad. He's not a very good person and he's played a huge role in why I am the way I am today."

Nailea risked swerving off the road to place a quick hand on mine. "I figured something was wrong a while ago already. Whatever you need me to do, I'll do it." She took in a deep breath, looking jittery. "Can I just ask, does he hurt you?" After a few seconds of deliberation, I gave her a single nod. "*Hijo de puta*," she swore. "Is there nowhere else you can go?"

Taking note of her restrained anger, I shook my head. "We had my grandma once. If she was still around, she would've taken us in without blinking twice. But my mom," I sighed, "she was fucked up. When she found out my grandma was gonna file for custody, she got a restraining order against her. My grandma was forced to leave."

I had no idea where the sweet woman was now. If I was her, I wouldn't come back at all too, even after the termination date of the restraining order had passed. Eliza only ever brought pain into the lives of those around her. I didn't blame my grandma for not having the heart to come back. I only wished that I had some sort of way to contact her, to tell her that my mom wasn't around, tell her that we needed her.

But that was just that; wishful thinking. Annie and I were adults now and we needed to deal with our problems.

Nailea's grip on the steering wheel became firmer. "And where's your mom now?"

"Annie says she's in rehab," I mumbled, turning to stare at passing cars. "She could've left us with my grandma. I mean, if she was always planning on leaving, she could've at least left us with somebody who cared." Not our dad. Our lives would've been so different if my grandma had kept us.

For the rest of the drive, I explained to Nailea the plan Annie and I had, and how we were going to leave once we had enough money. I waited for that feeling of regret to materialise after you comprehended that you'd overshared. I waited for that fear because I'd just let somebody else in after I'd promised myself to never put my family at risk again. But it never came. All that arrived was an intense feeling of gratitude when Nailea said she had an older brother that was trying to sell his apartment.

"I don't talk to him much," she admitted, "but I'm his baby sister so he'll be forced to give me a discount on it, right?" I smiled, trying not to bawl. "Just leave it to me." Another squeeze to my hand.

She drove us to Daisy's Delicacies where I was supposed to meet Annie. She'd taken on some extra shifts and Donovan wasn't objecting. He'd claimed to be losing staff members and emptied his soul to Annie one day, whining about how he didn't want to run his mom's business into the ground. Annie had comforted him the best way that she could; by listening.

But it was obvious why his employees were quitting—because he was an asshole.

When we pulled up outside, I hopped out of the car and strolled inside. The cafe wasn't very busy as it was still early morning. There were a few regulars, I assumed, sitting around and drinking coffee as if they did it every morning.

A couple sat at one table eating breakfast. They looked to be slightly older than my dad. For a split second, I wondered if that was what my parents' relationship would've been like if they were still together. Going out for breakfast whilst the kids were at school, cuddling on the couch, taking us to the park, and attending school functions and sports events.

Perhaps they would've been at my debates, Annie's bake-off, Poppy's volleyball matches, or even the recital Indigo's ballet class would be hosting soon. My eyes prickled at the thought. I must've been staring at the couple for quite some time because the woman looked up, eyes meeting mine.

My cheeks flamed at being caught gawking, but the woman offered me a kind smile paired with a little wave. She nudged her husband, who I only then realised was attired in a police officer's uniform, and he indulged his grinning wife by waving at me as well. I awkwardly returned their waves whilst wondering if I reminded them of their daughter or something.

Because most people weren't that friendly.

If somebody had waved at my dad whilst he was having breakfast, he'd probably snarl like a rampaging bear. With red cheeks, I ducked my head and pushed through the staff doors. I found Annie in the break room, a tired Indigo seated on her lap.

The girl still wasn't feeling well. Just yesterday, we'd taken her to the doctor and they'd diagnosed her with a common cold but still put her off for the rest of the week. It made our schedules slightly more difficult since Annie worked and Poppy and I had school. But my morning classes were cancelled so I could take Indigo for a bit whilst sorting out the boxes.

"How's she doing?" I urged Annie, proceeding to take Indigo.

Annie gently placed her in my arms and her face nuzzled its way into my neck. "Sleepy. She just had breakfast and I gave her the meds the doctor prescribed."

"And Pops?"

"Julie's mom picked her up earlier this morning, right after you left."

Julie was a new girl in Poppy's class and her mom, Georgia, was such a blessing because she solved all of our transport problems. She'd offered to drive the girls to and from school since it was on her way. I'd insisted on paying for gas money, but she refused each time.

When I shivered, I discerned that the air conditioner was on full blast. It wasn't healthy for a sick child to sit in a room as cold as this. But, once again, Donovan was an asshole. When I quizzed Annie, she told me that he'd cautioned her he was already allowing her to keep Indigo at work, so she didn't have the right to complain about his air conditioner.

Beth popped her head into the room. "Annie, you've got a new customer at one of your tables." She spotted me, a smile appearing on her lips as Annie shyly mumbled that she'd be right there. "Hey, Nyx. You good?"

I nodded and winked at her. "I'm always good, Macbeth." She laughed before leaving again. The sound made me smile, glad that there were no hard feelings between us.

Annie stared at me awkwardly and I raised a brow. "Do you happen to have plans tonight?" she questioned gently, busying herself by checking the time.

My lips quirked upwards. "Not that I know of. Why? Do *you* have plans, Ms Taylor?" She'd been acting different for some time, no longer coming home from work and starting her daily crying session in the bathroom. I was glad, but also curious as to what had made her happier as of late.

She flushed as I shifted Indigo in my hold. "Shut up. A few of us from the café are planning a little something tonight."

I couldn't help myself, I smirked. And if my arms were free, I would've poked Annie's flaming cheeks. "And I'm assuming that a special someone will be attending?" Annie didn't say anything, just attempted a glare but failed miserably because she was the same shade as a tomato. "Okay fine, I won't tease. Tell me about them?"

She smiled slightly, smoothing down her dress. "No."

Feigning a gasp, I begged, "At least give me a hint."

"If I give you a hint, you'll figure it out immediately."

Still grinning, I asked, "A small hint? Please?"

Annie sighed, rubbing her temples. She was the worst at giving hints, honestly. She always ended up giving everything away. Which was why I wanted her to give me a hint. After some thinking, she said, "Fine, a skull."

There was pride in the grin she wore, believing that I couldn't figure it out. What a shame. I let five seconds of silence pass to give her the impression that she had me stumped.

I waited until she was about to laugh at me, then said, "It's Beth."

Her mouth, which was previously opened to laugh, produced a gasp of astonishment. "What? How did you get to *that* conclusion?"

"Indie and I call her Macbeth, a character from a play by Shakespeare. Another play by Shakespeare is Hamlet, and the most prominent symbol for that play is the skull of Yorick," I grinned. "Did I get that right?"

She looked ready to either cry or laugh. "You're a bitch."

"You shouldn't have given me a hint," I said through laughter, watching her turn red again. "You think she likes you too?"

Annie shrugged. "I mean, I think so? She's always there when I feel a little overwhelmed. She's overly affectionate and touchy with me. But I think she's confused about what she wants. It's scary, I know that."

I couldn't speak from experience, but having been there when Annie had begun questioning her sexuality, I knew it was scary. She'd been eighteen years old with no mom to turn to and a sister who hadn't even had her first kiss yet.

"And her mom's not helping either," Annie proceeded to ramble.

"Her mom?" I echoed.

Annie's face screwed up. "She's pressuring her to start dating somebody." A wary glance was tossed my way. "Preferably Beckham."

Smiling sadly at her attempt to protect my feelings, I voiced, "I don't think he likes her like that."

"But that's the thing; Beth *knows.* She just doesn't wanna disappoint her mom." Annie ran a hand over her face. "The last thing I want is to scare her away with my feelings when she hasn't even figured her own out yet. My goodness, I hope

I'm not imagining this attraction." She turned around, her eyes closed as she tried to ease her nerves.

I heard heavy breathing on the other side of the door and I frowned. Bouncing Indigo when she stirred, I told Annie, "I'm gonna give you a moment."

I slowly backtracked, stepping out of the staffroom—only to bump into Beth.

The taller girl awkwardly tried to make it seems as if she'd just arrived, but by the way that I'd knocked the door into her, I knew she'd been leaning against it. We stared at one another like two idiots. No words passed between us. She gave me a small grin and then entered the staffroom, the door shutting behind her.

Despite the bitch in me wanting to eavesdrop, I moved to wait by the counter. I turned around to sit and was met with one half of the couple, the woman.

I froze at the welcoming smile she wore and the look of absolute glee in her hazel eyes, the colour reminding me of Nailea. "I'm sorry," she apologised, still smiling, "but I've been trying to figure out why you look so familiar and then it clicked. You were almost at every USC hockey game last year."

Striving for a smile of my own, I responded, "Yeah, are you a fan of the team?"

A thought formed in the back of my mind. I could use this woman's love for hockey to encourage her to bring friends and families to matches and fundraisers.

When she grinned again, I knew I had her.

"My son's on the team," she ended up saying and I gaped in surprise. "Do you think they have a shot at winning this year?"

Her question was straightforward, emphasising that she was *definitely* the mother of a player.

Blinking hastily, I tried to get my mind back into the present moment. "Um, well I think they're fully capable of winning. I've been helping the new coach with some things—"

The woman cut me off, her astonishment obviously fake and I frowned at her terrible display of acting. She had a hand on her heart and everything.

"Wait, you're Nyx, aren't you? I'm Helen." She didn't let me speak, continuing her ramble. Part of me wanted to smile at her enthusiasm. "My son has told me *so* much about you and you're doing a great job thus far, from what I know," she paused, "say, what do you think of the new captain?"

I ran a hand over Indigo's back, raising an eyebrow at Helen's grin. "Beckham Hunt?" She nodded eagerly. "He's great," I informed her, "really knows his team and what he wants." When I realised there was truth to my words, I couldn't help but feel slightly annoyed. If possible, Helen's smile grew ten times in size.

"I was a little worried," she admitted with a sheepish smile, "a new captain doesn't always take well to the team as quickly as he did." I could only nod, completely forgetting that I was trying to get this woman to buy tickets to everything. Her husband called her over, looking mildly disturbed. "It was nice meeting you, Nyx."

And then she was walking back to her husband, the latter staring at her incredulously and appearing to scold her. She only shrugged in response. I was still standing in a bubble of confusion when Annie appeared. Once again, her face was aflame.

"I'll tell you tonight," she mumbled and I smiled. She trailed me to Nailea's car where she greeted the girl with a bright smile.

"Anna Banana!" Nailea blew her kisses as I fought to forget my weird interaction with Helen. "Good to see you. Wanna explain why you're so red?" I laughed at the question then laughed harder as Annie shyly hid her face behind her hands.

The two spoke whilst I wondered what role my dad would play if Annie finally got into a healthy relationship. There was no other answer. He would ruin it, most definitely. I didn't want that to happen. He would want to control her relationship just like he fought to control us with his stupid rules.

Matthew Taylor was a stickler for those rules. Growing up an only child, he'd been spoilt rotten but remained top of his class, captain of the football team and his parents' pride and joy. His parents had had this rulebook that he was supposed to follow and he'd memorised that shit.

Never raise your voice, Matty. Never disrespect your elders, Matty. Always take responsibility for your actions, Matty. Always behave yourself, Matty.

But that rulebook was tossed into the fire once he'd gotten my mom pregnant during their senior year in high school. His parents had been appalled by his actions and cut him off, wanting nothing to do with him. *Always take responsibility for your actions, Matty.* My mom, Eliza, was young and immature, but she'd wanted to have that baby.

Nine months later, Anabeth Taylor had been born; Beth after my mom and Ana after our grandma, Anabelle. When he'd knocked my mom up almost four years later, he hadn't even stayed to see me be born. Because of the wreck, I didn't remember anything from before seven, but Annie had said we'd lived at our grandma's place whilst our dad flitted in and out of our lives when he wanted to.

They'd only gotten married and moved in together when my mom had fallen pregnant with Poppy. Theirs was a fucked up relationship and I would've been glad if they hadn't gotten together after their initial separation. But that would mean no Poppy and Indigo. So in a way, I had a reason to be thankful that my mom had gone back to an abusive asshole like him.

I knew the story of my parents because of my grandma. She'd told it to Annie and me back when we were still allowed to see her. She'd never really liked my dad and made her distaste for him obvious, warning my mom away from him. But to no avail. As I'd told Nailea, she was the only one who had seemed to care. And my mom was a coward. Once they were both out of our lives, there was nobody to curb my dad. He was still a stickler for the rules, obsessed with the idea of perfect daughters.

The rules had changed to fit us.

Never raise your voice, Annie. Never disrespect your elders, Nyxie. Always take responsibility for your actions, Poppy. Always behave yourself, Indie.

I never liked when people taunted me because, for many years, it was what my dad had done to me, still to this day. He taunted me because he knew I couldn't always speak back, and couldn't raise my voice. I hated it. To him, what he was doing wasn't abuse. In his own words, he was disciplining us. Somewhere in his fucked up mind, he believed this wholeheartedly. Sometimes, when he'd hit me, he'd call me Eliza.

Because I looked like the woman who'd left him with four kids.

Poppy and I had it the worst because of our resemblance to her. My dad was the reason Poppy needed physiotherapy. He'd pushed her a little too hard during one of his drunken tantrums and she'd tripped over a loose floorboard, landing at a bad angle. I could tell he felt bad, horrified at what he'd done, but not enough to apologise. His anger outweighed the little love he had for us.

He would disappear for a while whenever he accidentally hurt Poppy. The same happened when he'd hit Indigo for the first time. It was like he was appalled by his actions, but was still the same person when he returned. I didn't see the point. Sometimes he'd even apologise to Annie for yelling at her. Me? He never cared about me. I could take a fist to the eye and see him at the breakfast table the next morning, smiling. It had been that way since I was a young girl.

There'd been times when I had to go stay with my grandma for a while, just because my mom didn't trust my dad not to hurt me. That had been just after the wedding when my dad was still getting used to us all living with him. He couldn't take his constant anger out on my mom, not when she was pregnant.

And I looked like her.

He hadn't laid a hand on me then. But there'd still been a possibility, especially when he looked at me with that familiar rage in his gaze. The very thought that he'd beat a child was nauseating.

Shaking my head to rid myself of the memories, I strapped Indigo into the backseat, placing her fluffy blanket over her. Annie passed me her backpack, filled with extra clothes and her meds. The flush in her cheeks was gone now, but a smile still lingered in her eyes.

Plus, her lips were fucking swollen.

She pecked Indigo on the head before doing the same to me. I smiled, sinking into her embrace. Annie laughed, squeezing me to her chest. "What's with you?" she teased, kissing my head again. Annie was the closest thing we had to a mom. The four-year age gap between us may as well have been twenty years.

"I love you," I whispered, momentarily forgetting that Nailea was witnessing all of this. People at school constantly joked that I was a robot. I'd heard people speaking about it before. They had no idea what I'd do for my sisters, though.

My big sister's brows sank into a soothing furrow as she grinned. "I love you too, sweetheart," she murmured, running a hand over my back before pulling away slightly. "By the way, it completely slipped my mind," her eyes drifted to Nailea before she lowered her voice to a whisper, "but you asked me about rehab."

It hit me that I'd meant to ask her about it after that day in the janitor's closet but I never did. "Shit, yes. I wanted to know how you knew she was there."

Nailea was too busy on her phone to even pay attention to us, but she already knew everything, and I made this clear to Annie by speaking in a normal tone.

My sister stared at me flatly. "She told me, obviously. It was around a month or so ago when she called me out of nowhere," Annie explained, looking pained. "She tried to call you too but you wouldn't answer. Then she asked me to talk to you, ask you to give her a chance to explain. But I knew you took her leaving the worst, and I wasn't going to force you to do anything you didn't want *or* mention it if it was going to upset you."

I offered her an apologetic smile, wanting to argue but knowing that I couldn't. "You're right, it would've upset me." And probably thrown me off course.

"See," she rolled her eyes, but she was grinning. "I'm open to all questions, but only if you're ready. Now, get going." With one last hug, I climbed back into the car as Nailea started it.

Annie waved as we drove off. Indigo was already completely passed out, her meds taking effect. My dad hadn't been home since the day he hit her. I was thankful he hadn't returned yet. The thought made me wonder if my mom would decide to return. It didn't surprise me that Annie had spoken to her. She was too good of a person to ignore her, even after she'd left us with a piece of shit father. It soothed me slightly to know that Annie knew more than she let on. One of us had to be mature when it came to our mom, after all, and I was glad it was her. God alone knew what I would've told my mom if I'd answered her calls.

Probably to fuck off like she'd always wanted to.

Nailea drove us back to Beckham's house. I was a little hesitant about having Indigo around the guys since I'd always kept my family separate from my school life. But I had no other choice. In my relationship with the hockey team, *I* wore the pants, which meant I'd take no bullshit. This was nothing like last year and Nate was long gone. The vulnerable side of me prayed that he was the only rotten apple in the basket.

"I might miss classes later," I told Nailea, gesturing to my sister. "I have her until Annie's done with her shift, which isn't until later this evening. Can you get me some extra notes?"

"Sure thing. Consider it thanks for making notes for me last week when I missed classes." A sly smirk pulled at her full lips. "You know, when I was hungover."

I laughed. "You mean when you were too lazy to get out of bed." She shrugged, prompting my laughter to grow louder. I shrugged Indigo's bag onto my back before unstrapping her. She was still fast asleep and I gently placed her head on my shoulder as Nailea threw the blanket over her. "See you later," I greeted.

"See you later, babe. Call me if you need anything." Nailea blew kisses before driving off.

I watched her disappear down the street before turning around. Subconsciously, my eyes drifted to Beckham's room window. The curtains were drawn, but I could still feel Melissa's stare, even though she was probably gone. I cursed inwardly and trudged towards the door. Without knocking, I shoved it open and made my way to the living room—where I was entirely blown away.

Oliver, with his bright red hair, was standing with a scissor in his hands, expertly cutting through the tape. Jasper was helping him. They took out the contents of the plain brown boxes and passed them to the next person, Jai. The latter's fingers had healed quicker than expected and he was now neatly placing foods into the black boxes that I'd ordered a few days ago.

Sebastian stood next to him, helping to lid the boxes. Once they were closed, the boxes were passed to Grayson, who snipped through golden ribbons. The ribbons had been Poppy's idea and seeing them now; I was glad I'd listened to her. After the ribbons were cut, Grayson draped them around the box and pushed it towards Beckham, where he tied little bows. I couldn't believe my eyes. The idiots were actually following orders. The entire first team was there to help box. I thought I'd have to send a few more heated emails to get them to cooperate.

Stepping further into the room, I mused, "Seems like Nyx's little helpers are making progress. I have to say, I'm surprised." Grayson laughed whereas Beckham looked up and scowled. "Would you like for me to get you little hats? With little bells on them and everything?"

Jasper scratched the top of his recently shaved head. "Wouldn't mind, honestly. Head's been kinda cold without my hair."

"Nobody told you to get gum stuck in your hair," Jai added, raising his head and dark eyes flashing to me in greeting. I nodded.

Sweat beaded on Oliver's forehead and he rubbed it away, cutting through more tape. "It's a good look for you." The defenceman chuckled when Jasper glowered at him for the use of his sarcastic words. "Kinda reminds me of an egg."

Sebastian nodded in agreement and I laughed before stating, "We should start a business." In the time that I was gone, they'd managed to get far. Grayson raised an eyebrow as if asking what business. I acknowledged his unvoiced inquiry. "A box packing business, if that's a thing. We'd make so much money." I walked to the couch and settled Indigo there. She sank back into the throw pillow, still asleep. "But, I'm already making enough money."

"From your paid internship?" Beckham spoke up with a scowl. But it didn't look as intimidating as he expected because he was currently tying another bow. Jasper mimed the motion of tossing money around.

I put Indigo's bag on the floor next to the couch and peered straight at Beckham. "That too. But, I was talking about my *oh-so*-famous prostitution services." They all froze. Beckham's lips twitched as his teammates waited for me to explain. I sauntered towards their captain. "You know, if you want, you could tuck some money into my thong."

Oliver choked on air but Beckham didn't waver. "You'd like that, wouldn't you," he murmured, eyes narrowing.

I stepped around him and let out a small laugh as I scrutinized their work. "Silly me, I forgot I had to be wearing one for that to happen." The implication was obvious and five pairs of eyes dropped to my jeans as I sashayed away. Grayson was looking at the opposite wall, face red. "I'm helping myself to whatever's in your fridge."

My stomach was close to eating itself. Thankfully, the boys had some grapes in the fridge and I hopped onto a barstool, chewing in satisfaction. Hushed murmurs came from the living room and I snickered into my hand. Ten minutes must've passed before Jasper stumbled into the kitchen, pouring himself a glass of juice. He didn't meet my gaze and I smiled down at my grapes. He was a handsome fellow, but I doubted that he'd like it if I told him he reminded me of Diego, Dora's cousin. But the resemblance was uncanny. He was just missing the hair. Jasper, along with Oliver, was a defenceman and they both had the muscle to speak for it.

Childlike giggles met my ears and the sound brightened my mood. Indigo was awake. Jasper leaned against the sink, sipping from his juice as he gestured towards the doorway.

"Got knocked up on one of your jobs?"

A loud laugh bubbled in my throat and Jasper grinned in victory as I threw him with a grape. It bounced from his chest. "Fuck you, asshole. She's my sister."

He shrugged, still smiling. "I figured."

I threw another grape, but he caught it in his mouth; pride emanating from him and I rolled my eyes. I peeked out the doorway and saw Grayson seated next to Indigo, muttering something that made her giggle like crazy.

"I didn't know you had a sister," Jasper expressed again, placing his empty glass in the sink.

I smiled grimly. "Few people do."

Indigo's laughter abruptly turned into wild cries. My heart nearly stopped beating as Jasper and I scrambled into the living room. I found her contorted into a ball on the floor, arms wrapped around her legs as she wailed into her knees.

"What happened?" I yelled, picking up Indigo as she continued to sob like a hysterical person.

Grayson was pale, eyes wide as he sputtered. "I don't—I didn't—" I rubbed Indigo's back, heart shattering when she hiccupped. Oliver and Jai stopped their work, watching in bafflement. "Beck tossed me the roll of ribbon. I was gonna make her a bow." His eyes went to my sister and I watched his brows crinkle. "He tossed it and I raised my hand to catch—"

I didn't hear the rest of his words. I didn't need to. My shoulders slumped as I realised what had happened.

Grayson had raised his hand. Just like my dad had raised his hand on Indigo a few days ago.

I held her tighter, burying my nose in her hair as Grayson apologised, even though he didn't know what he'd done. Jasper disappeared into the kitchen to get Indigo some water. Grayson plopped onto the couch, head dropping into his hands. I wanted to comfort him because Indigo's pain-filled sobs were enough to dismay anyone, especially Grayson, who thought he'd caused it. But I had to comfort *her* first. Oliver was freaking out, asking if he should call the ambulance. Sebastian led him outside to have a breather with Jai following behind.

But I wasn't concerned about them. I was concerned about Beckham. Or maybe it was the other way around. His grey eyes were churning with questions as he gazed at me. He tilted his head slightly. No words were exchanged between us but, for some reason, I could grasp what he was trying to tell me. His brows drew together as he thought back to what he'd just witnessed when he'd tossed the ribbon to Grayson.

No, no, no.

He looked to my lips next, where I'd previously sported a cut. Then he looked at my face. *I wore makeup.* There was *no way* he could've seen the bruise. But I'd also trained with them that day, which meant that I'd been sweating.

No, no, no.

"She's easily frightened," I explained to Grayson, taking the water that Jasper offered and encouraging Indigo to take small sips. She was still sniffling like crazy and Grayson apologised again. "New people and all."

Grayson nodded, still looking dazed. Beckham didn't look convinced. If anything, he looked furious. His fists were clenched at his sides and I glanced away. When Jasper pointed me in the bathroom's direction—although I knew where it was—I twisted on my heel. I set Indigo down on the closed toilet. She gripped the glass in shaking hands.

Indigo may have had a mouth that was way older than she was, but she was still a baby. Five years old, just a little away from turning six. It was easy to forget her age when she was such a smart cookie, but it was obvious as I watched her cry.

"I feel so bad, Nyxie," she hiccupped. "I made Grayson panic—but—I," she wiped her face with one hand, trying to stop the tears. "I thought he was gonna—"

"It's okay, sweetheart," I told her, not wanting her to feel guilty. She'd done nothing wrong. The entire situation reminded me of when I'd been younger and the same thing would happen to me. But I no longer flinched. I wouldn't give anybody the satisfaction. "Do you wanna go home? Because we can—"

Indigo cut me off, shaking her head. "My blanket."

I nodded, "I'll go get your blanket, honey." Nearly tripping over my feet, I hurried out of the bathroom, rounding a corner and stumbling into a chest. I would've landed on my ass if it wasn't for the arm that went around my waist. The tattoos were a dead giveaway as to who was holding me. "Beckham—"

His voice was a low rumble, anger twisting his words into shards, ready to pierce through skin. I expected him to taunt me because I paraded around campus acting like this powerful woman, but the moment I went home; I was a helpless little girl. The moment my baby sister cried, I dissolved into a state of panic—nothing like the composed woman he knew.

But three words left his mouth and I stopped struggling in his hold.

"Somebody's hurting you."

Nothing else. Just a statement. The last time, he'd *asked* me if somebody had hurt me.

It wasn't a question this time.

My mouth opened and closed like a fish, shocked that he'd thrown it out there like that. There was no way for me to work around it and that was probably his intention. My mind was a mess, all over the place so I said the first thing that popped up in my brain. "I don't know what you're—"

One hand gently cupped the side of my face and I shuddered, staring up at him because he didn't let me look away, keeping my gaze.

"Nyx," his voice was a guttural whisper. "Who's hurting you?"

Chapter 10

Beckham

Nyx blundered out of my hold like a bar of soap the moment the question left my lips. I barely had a second to comprehend what was happening before she twisted around me, disappearing into the living room. She returned a beat after with a blanket in her hands, going into the bathroom once again, the door shutting behind her. I sighed, leaning against the opposite wall. Nyx's voice was hushed through the door, sounding as if she was trapped underwater. Her words were incoherent and I gave up on trying to eavesdrop. My mind reeled back to what had happened a few minutes ago. One second, Indigo had been giggling at the jokes Grayson was making; Grayson who wouldn't hurt a fly. The next second, I'd tossed him the roll of ribbon, and suddenly Indigo was bawling.

But I saw what happened.

Grayson had been looking at me to catch the ribbon, but *I* had been looking in his direction, which meant Indigo was in my view. I'd watched her flinch the moment Grayson had raised his hand. And it hadn't just been any flinch like Nyx had tried to pass off as her being easily frightened. A scare like that would've made her jump.

But the little girl had recoiled, eyes focused on Grayson's hand. She'd shrank back as if expecting to be hit. The memory tormented my thoughts, even though it had happened recently. Seeing the fear in Indigo's eyes had awakened something in my chest.

Seeking to control my burgeoning rage, I left the house, heading to the backyard. The last thing we needed was for me to go on a rampage, demanding to know why Indigo was scared. The pool glistened underneath the sunlight and I contemplated taking a dip. It would help cool me down.

I heard the sound of ripping cardboard and assumed Oliver, Jai, Jasper and Sebastian went back to work. The last time I'd seen Grayson, he was pacing the hallway. I knew he had a soft spot for Indigo as she reminded him of somebody. And the thought of hurting her was killing him.

"Fuck, fuck, *fuck*," Nyx cursed as she elbowed through the backdoor and, on instinct, I moved to hide behind the wall. She was running her hands through her hair in turmoil, the blonde strands becoming messy. "You shouldn't have brought her here, you stupid *bitch!*" There was nobody else around and it was quite clear she was speaking to herself.

She ambled towards the edge of the pool and sank to her knees, angrily splashing at the water with her hands. I would've laughed if the situation wasn't severe.

I stepped out of my hiding place and said, "You and Nailea didn't sleep together, did you?" Nyx was smart and I knew she'd catch onto what I was implying.

Judging by the way her eyes narrowed as she pushed to her feet, I knew I had her. "Why?" She angled her head to the side, reminding me of a puppy. "Were you expecting an invitation?" Her chest was rising and falling at a rapid pace and I suspected her thoughts were running wild.

"The other day," I proceeded, glancing towards the trees as I strolled towards her. "At the rink, you told me that Nailea got a little too rough with you." Her little nose crinkled in barely subdued fury.

Nyx crossed her arms, stance becoming defensive. "Oh, I remember that day. It was when I hurt your feelings." Her plump lips formed a pout and her eyelashes fluttered in mock consolation. "You thought I was interested in *you*, of all people, but I was only using you to get what I want. How did that feel, bigshot?"

Her words were like water down my back; I knew she was only spitting venom because she was scared. That wasn't a word I ever thought I'd associate with Nyx Taylor. But here we were.

"You said she got too rough with you," I reiterated and she grimaced. "But you *lied*." I halted in front of her and she didn't move away. Slowly raising a hand, I settled my thumb at the corner of her mouth. "You had a cut. Right here."

Her reply was flat. "Fine, you caught me. One of my clients had a huge dick. Could barely wrap my mouth around it when I gave him head. Split the corner of my lip in the process." Her nose twitched again. "But the pay made everything worth it."

I ignored her attempts at trying to deflect my probing—because that's what I was doing. I was *probing*, interrogating her even though I had no right to.

But this wasn't just something you overlooked, as I'd told my mom. This wasn't me passing a child who had dropped their ice cream as they cried. I could overlook that. This wasn't a petty fight between my friends, one I didn't have to intervene because they'd sort it out on their own. This was potential abuse. And no matter how much Nyx got on my nerves, abuse wasn't a joke.

My thumb moved from her mouth, brushing her delicate cheekbone. Momentarily, she leaned into my touch, my palm framing the side of her face just like it had a few minutes ago.

"And you had a bruise, right here." The skin was smooth now, dotted with light freckles and slightly red because of her displeasure.

"My client was also into impact play," she quipped, eyes sparkling the same colour as the water we stood next to. "He had some whips and things got a little out of hand. But, once again, the pay made everything worth it."

Irritation scratched the back of my throat and I itched to yell at her because she never took me seriously. She had a way of dancing circles around you. Her words put you in a trance and by the time you woke up, you could no longer remember what you were talking about. The look she was giving me was similar to the one she nearly obliterated me with when I'd cornered her in the janitor's closet. And suddenly, it was difficult to breathe. I'd cornered her that day, allowed my indignation to take the front seat and drive me down a street of unnecessary argument.

My voice was just above a whisper. "You were crying."

And I wasn't just talking about her crying before I'd

entered the closet. I was referring to the tears she'd shed whilst speaking with me too; when I'd ruined the one good memory she had of me. Guilt festered from deep within me.

Nyx chose that moment to recoil and she pushed me away, hands shoving at my chest. Panic. I could feel it leaving her body in waves as if she was the sun and I was somebody to whom she was trying to give sunburn.

"What the fuck are you talking about?"

I shook my head, trying to gather my thoughts. "When you were on the phone, you were crying." Her lips parted, but no words left her. Muttering a curse, I realised she was thinking of the time I'd caught her crying about the rumours spreading around campus, rumours regarding her and Nate.

But she didn't know I caught her. And that wasn't a door I wanted to open right now, so I clarified, "The janitor's closet."

Some panic left her features, but she was still on edge. "You mean when you accosted me and accused me of working with Nate. What a lovely day that was."

She probably didn't expect me to feel bad, but I did. And after Nyx had left earlier this morning, I'd finally gone through my emails; one of them was from Benson. According to his friend at UCLA, Nate's transfer and reregistration had been a last-minute decision and wasn't decided upon until a few days ago. Which meant there was no way he could've gotten onto the team on such short notice.

"About that," I groaned, nervously scratching the back of my neck and she huffed, waiting for my response. "I'm sorry."

The words were like swallowing razors because this was my third apology to her in the time span of a week. It highlighted the way I treated her, leaving it out in the open for me to see, for me to analyse—and I didn't like what I saw. This was a girl I'd essentially worshipped before and now I was treating her like shit. My mom was right.

Neither of us spoke for a few seconds and I got the impression that she was processing my words. Through all the insults, we had never apologised to each other and it was clear by the frown she wore that she was taking this apology and the past two instances into consideration.

"Do you think I'm stupid?"

That was *not* the response I was expecting. I had to blink a few times because I thought I was imagining her sudden outburst. Yet, I wasn't.

"What?" I urged stupidly.

Nyx shoved my chest again and let out an annoyed huff when I didn't move. "Do you think that by saying sorry I'll suddenly spill my deepest, darkest secrets?" she challenged, still trying to shove me. "This whole apology thing only started after you saw the cut on my mouth. That's low, even for you, Beckham."

Okay. I couldn't blame her for thinking that was my motive. "I mean it, Taylor. I'm sorry. Benson sent—"

"An email to the entire team, yes, I know," she intervened, breathing thickly because of her efforts of trying to push me. "I helped him compose the fucking email." I grimaced and she nodded, enjoying my astonishment. "That same day you *accused* me of working with Nate, Benson called me later to explain the situation. Because, if you've forgotten, I'm part of the staff."

If it was possible, my guilt grew heavier. All this time, I'd been seething, shaming her and giving her the cold shoulder when she had nothing to do with Nate. And she knew the truth all along, but didn't try to clear her name with me.

Because she didn't care.

She couldn't care less about what I thought of her. I was like dirt under her shoe and the last person she'd run to for help—if the situation at the party proved anything. I didn't know how to feel about that. Although they were mostly filled with anger and confusion, my thoughts still heavily circled her.

And she couldn't even care less about my existence.

"Taylor—"

"Stay out of my business." She took a step back. "My life is none of your concern. And don't you *dare* pretend to care," the words left her in an angry hiss. "If you truly cared about me, you would've asked me for my version of what went down with Nate, but you didn't. So don't try and shove yourself back into my life now that you think you can be the knight in shining armour."

There were so many things I wanted to say, but I couldn't. We stood staring at each other for a few tense seconds, Nyx's chest rising and falling with her heavy breaths. She was right, she was completely right, as always. I had no right to propel my way into her life when I was the one who had decided it wasn't worth staying.

Nyx may have been the one to cause the rift but it had been *me* that hadn't tried to shut it. I allowed it to grow bigger until we were on opposite sides of what could've been. With one last withering glance that made my balls want to shrivel and crawl up into my ass for security, Nyx went back into the house.

I was late for fucking practice again. If Professor Martin was going to keep this shit up, I'd have no choice but to report her to Dean Waverly. Our first match of the season was on Sunday and today was our last practice. Thankfully, it wasn't as bad as last time, just by a few minutes. Parking my car, I hopped out and rushed into the building. The foyer was empty, the opposite of what it would look like on Sunday.

I enjoyed game days. The place was always filled to the brim and the air clogged with cheers and yells, the sound of skates on ice, and the sound of the hockey stick knocking the puck. A crowd decked in our colours whilst chanting our names. It was absolute bliss. I passed the rink and saw the first and second teams on the ice. Maddox, the centreman from the second line, replaced me for the time being, and Kayden, the centreman from the third line, took Maddox's spot.

Sebastian stepped into the role of the captain and it was always an impressive sight to witness. He was colder than me when it came to supervising his team. His instructions were clipped and he never spoke more than he needed to. But he was fucking great at it which was why he was the alternative captain for the USC Trojans. His position was made clear by the "AC" on his jersey.

Whenever I was close to the ice, a thrill shot through my veins, as if my body knew where it needed to be. Like any college student, there were rumours around campus regarding me. Many seemed to believe that my position and captaincy were because of my dad's influence. I didn't have the energy to contend with every single person who gossiped about this. My team knew the truth and that was all I needed. I'd climbed my way to the top, like any other determined person. There had been no pressure from my dad where he'd made me attend hockey classes growing up. He hadn't placed me in a box and decided to live vicariously through me now that he was older. No, my dad had rarely spoken to me about hockey as a boy. I'd learned to love the spot by witnessing how much *he loved it.*

My success as a hockey player stemmed from the fact that I enjoyed doing what I did.

Sebastian nodded at me as I passed the rink. From the corner of my eye, I saw Indigo resting in the bleachers. From what I remembered Grayson telling me yesterday, the girl had a cold and was booked off from school for the week. She was bundled in a thick pink jacket and matching pants, a fluffy hat on her head with kitten ears and gloves on her hands. When she caught me looking, she hid beneath the seat and I laughed. Nyx probably didn't know she was sitting there. Knowing the blonde, she'd seemingly advised the little girl to stay in Benson's office; where it was warmer.

Once I got to the locker room, I hurriedly stripped out of my clothes and put on the uniform that felt like a second skin to me. The padding had been exasperating at first, but I'd gotten used to it. I grabbed my skates and slipped them on. Keeping my skate guards on—a hard plastic covering for the blades—I left the locker room in search of Benson's office.

I had a late slip, one that Professor Martin had condescendingly written for me when I'd told her I was late for practice. Benson was on the ice so I'd just leave it on his desk. The slip held zero importance and Professor Martin knew that. She just wanted to piss me off. Without knocking, I opened the door and an ear-shattering shriek embraced me. There was a resounding *thump* and I froze. I wondered if Nyx had caught Indigo in the time I was dressing and sent her back to the office.

Benson's desk was buried in drawings, crayons, and some storybooks. The chair was pushed to the back and I guessed Indigo had flung herself to the floor. After what had happened with Grayson, I needed to caution myself around her. And here I was barging into the room like an idiot. I strolled around the desk to help her up, only to be confounded.

Tucked away underneath the desk was a small figure, arms wrapped around her knees. But there was no fear in her expression like I'd expected; there was excitement. Her cheeks were flushed and her eyes shut in expectation.

Like Indigo, she was dressed in thick clothes, a blue bomber jacket and grey sweatpants. But she wasn't wearing a hat, her long blonde curls tumbling down her hunched shoulders. Shyly, she peeked one eye open.

And suddenly I was looking at a replica of Nyx.

Now that the girl's features weren't scrunched in anticipation, it dissolved into a face I knew all too well. She had the little nose, the wide blue eyes and the full lips. I may not have known Nyx when she was younger, but I'd bet good money that this was what she'd looked like at that age.

Was this God's way of fucking with me for hurting Nyx? Was he sending the ghost of her past to taunt me? Her present self was already ignoring me since yesterday at my house. She'd give all the training programs to Grayson who would then relay them to me, even the information regarding tomorrow's fundraiser.

"Who are you?" a delicate voice spoke up and my attention veered back to the blonde underneath the table. She sounded puzzled and she tilted her head in the same way that Nyx did.

Something burned in my chest. She had three siblings that I didn't know about. Even when we were on good terms, I had no idea about them.

I blinked to rid myself of the stupor I was trapped in and held out a hand. "Beckham." She gingerly placed her hand in mine and I helped her up. "And you are?"

For my sanity's sake, I hoped I wasn't talking to a ghost. Her hand felt real enough.

"Poppy," she countered, looking marginally dumbfounded as she peeked at the door.

I placed my late slip on the desk, gathering the drawings into a stack so that Benson would easily find my slip. "What were you doing under the desk, Poppy?"

Poppy angled to face me, shaking her head as if just remembering that I was there. "Hiding." My hands halted their actions of organising Benson's desk. "We're playing hide and go seek."

Remembering the sound she emitted when I'd entered the office, I sought, "Do you always scream when you play hide and go seek?" Poppy's entire face turned red. "That's kinda a direct lead to find you."

She crossed her arms over her chest, jutting out her hip and I contained a smile. This was definitely a little Nyx. "For your information, Mr Beckham," I raised a brow, "you caught me off guard as I've been hiding for some time."

"Who's seeking?" I inquired, already having a feeling about who the answer would be.

Poppy confirmed my suspicions by saying, "My sister, Indigo."

I chuckled heartily, running a hand over my face. "Indigo's watching practice."

"I figured," Poppy shrugged, taking a seat at the desk and reaching for her abandoned book next to her schoolbag. "I'd watch practice too but it'll only make me miss volleyball."

"You play volleyball?"

The little blonde beamed at my interest in the sport. "Yep! But I haven't been playing for the last few weeks and I was looking forward to it, but Coach put me off for another *two weeks*." She lifted her legs and shook her boot-covered feet. "I had a sprained foot. Needed physiotherapy and everything."

"A coach's concern would always be their players. They want to be sure you're healed," I explained to her, acknowledging that she was disappointed. Coaches would be even more sceptical if that injury was sustained during practice or a game. "Did you sprain your foot playing volleyball?"

And there it was. Fear meandered along the boundaries of her iris, weaving with the luminous blue colour, eclipsing it slightly.

Her voice came out delicately. "No. I fell. At home." I nodded, deciding not to question her further. She looked dismayed enough. Abruptly, her tone changed to one of weariness as she pointed to my jersey. "Hey, you're the captain that made my sister cry."

My spine went stiff at her words. "I think you've got me confused with Grayson—"

Poppy was adamant that she was correct. "No. Turn around." Another hint that she was a miniature version of Nyx. Sighing, I twisted around as she read the back of my jersey. "You're Hunt, the captain that made my sister cry." Perplexed, I turned to face her again. Seeing my confusion, she spoke again. "Don't even bother asking what she said. Annie says I'm not supposed to use words like that."

Nyx. I made Nyx cry. *Again*.

Before I could say anything else, Nyx entered the room, Indigo in her arms. They were yet to notice us. Indigo was pouting as Nyx admonished her. Seemed like she got caught hiding in the bleachers.

"You're supposed to be sick, Indie," Nyx groaned, standing strong against the puppy eyes her baby sister was giving her. "Sitting in the cold won't help which is why I asked you to *stay here*."

Seeing Nyx and Poppy in the same room made the resemblance more obvious. The latter chose that moment to speak. "We were playing hide and go seek. I was seeking and Indie was hiding." Nyx's features softened but immediately hardened upon locating me. "So please, don't be angry at her."

Nyx placed Indigo down on the ground and the girl happily barrelled into Poppy, whispering her thanks.

"A word." Nyx left the office and I followed, closing the door behind me. The thud that sounded right after was confirmation that Indigo and Poppy were pressed against the door, eavesdropping. "Listen—"

"Whatever you're thinking, don't," I cut her off, already backtracking. "I know your opinion of me is low, but not even I would use *kids* to get what I want." I wasn't even angry about her assumptions. I had no right to be. "Three siblings. I never would've guessed."

She curled her lip into a grimace. "And what's that supposed to mean?"

I shrugged. "It just seems like something you'd mention on the first date. Or the second. Maybe even the third."

Her lips pursed. "We never dated, Hunt. I didn't owe you anything."

I nodded, agreeing with her before saying, "But that's only because we agreed not to label what we were." Her nose scrunched in irritation and I smirked. "If there'd been labels, you definitely would've been my fucking girlfriend, Taylor."

"That's rich coming from you," she retorted promptly, crossing her arms. "Weren't you reminding me the other day that you didn't want me to be your girlfriend?" I grimaced at the memory of how I'd approached that encounter in the janitor's closet. "It's *so* like you to commit only when it'll benefit you. Use our past against me if you want but I'm not telling you a fucking thing."

"I'm not—"

She wasn't finished. "You wanna know why I never told you I had any siblings? Let you be any closer than what I needed you to be? Well, I guess, deep down, I knew you weren't going to stay." Her tone was flat, her stance completely casual. But I could see right through it, could see the dismay she endeavoured to repress.

I didn't say anything, mostly because I didn't know how to reply to that. She was waiting for me to say something, anticipating an argument. But I knew better now, knew that arguments were her way of changing the subject and throwing me off. Choosing my battles wisely, I walked away. Nyx watched me until I rounded the corner, heading for the ice. I didn't talk to her throughout practice, letting her anger simmer down.

And once she was calmer, I would try again.

Chapter 11

Nyx

Indigo couldn't stop bouncing with excitement as I buttoned up her sparkly coat. I could barely slip the buttons through the little stitched slits. The bed creaked with each jump and I let out a sigh of relief when I finished the last button. She hopped off and dashed towards where her bag was. Just as she was about to scamper out of the room, I tucked my finger into the hat of her coat and dragged her back. She giggled as I pulled her back into my arms.

I spun her around, poking her tiny nose. "Not so fast, little monster. You promise me you're feeling okay?" She nodded, squirming in my hold. "And you're not just saying that because you wanna go with Pops?" She shook her head.

Annie and I were reluctant about sending her along with Poppy tonight. She was still recovering from her cold and earlier when she'd watched the hockey boys practise without me knowing, I thought for sure the ice had worsened her cold.

"I promise, Nyxie," she lifted a hand, her pinkie jutting out. I beamed, hooking mine with hers. "Pinkie promise." Just as I was about to step around Indigo, it was her that pulled me back, her small hand gripping the bottom of my sweater. "Are *you* okay?"

I frowned, staring down at the concerned look on her adorable features. "What are you talking about?" I questioned with a laugh, trying to pass it off as a joke. But Indigo didn't budge, her warm eyes narrowing.

She hopped onto the bed and patted the spot next to her. "Have a seat." Snorting into my hand, I followed her request and sat down, her hand suddenly on my own. "I hate seeing you cry, Nyxie." I went to intervene but she persisted. "You never cry and when you do—it's because of Beckham."

This was coming from an almost six-year-old.

"Indie," I began in a soothing voice. "Don't you worry your pretty little head about anything, okay? I'm completely fine." A lie. But Indigo was five, she didn't need to stress about my problems.

Her eyes narrowed again. "Nyxie, you're my sister—"

"I didn't notice—"

"And I *know you*—"

"I'm glad you do—"

Indigo huffed. "But you act a little stonier than usual around Beckham," she informed me, her words assembling a lisp with her two missing front teeth. "You do the same thing around Daddy—"

My chest tightened at the mention of our dad. "Indigo, I'm—"

"And I *know* it's because you're scared and sad," she finished, looking older than she was. "You tell all of us to come to you," she pouted, "but who do you go to when you're feeling sad?"

Her eyes were moist with unshed tears and I sighed, pulling her into a hug. Indigo was a child. I hadn't expected her to be as observant as she was. No wonder she'd been rude to Beckham the first time they'd met at the cafe. I hadn't allowed her to meet him before, even when she would attend games with me. When I'd started gaining attention from the rest of the team, Annie would take her and they'd sit separately.

"Do you want me to come to you when I'm sad?" I asked quietly.

Indigo shook her head. "Not me, maybe Annie. She's better with words than me. I just want you to talk to somebody." I weighed the little girl's words, recalling how I usually bottled everything inside.

Stonier.

She said I was stonier around Beckham. If I admitted it to myself, I'd always been stony with Beckham, from the very beginning. Perhaps that was why I'd never told him about my family. Maybe Indigo was right. Maybe I *was* scared. I'd been able to tell Nailea because I could sense some desperation around her. She needed a friend as badly as I did. But there was no desperation around Beckham, no weaknesses.

And that's what made him so scary.

People that powerful and self-assured were destructive to people like us; people still trying to find their footing.

"Indie!" Annie yelled from the living room. Indigo looked up at me, silently asking if I was okay. I nodded, allowing her to dash out of the room before following. Annie was standing at the table, brushing Poppy's hair into a neat ponytail. The latter grinned widely as the front door opened and Georgia walked in with her daughter, Julie, next to her.

Georgia was a single mother who had recently moved to California. Despite being new, she was always volunteering and helping whenever she could. Alongside all of that, she even baked occasionally and I was using some of her cakes at the fundraiser tomorrow. The allowance that each coach had been given to cover event planning was over enough and I'd begged Georgia to let me pay her for her hard work. As expected, she'd refused, but let me pay for half the ingredients.

Julie had inherited her mother's good looks and I had no doubt she'd be a popular girl in high school with her looks and intelligence. She screeched in excitement and flung herself into Poppy's arms just as Annie finished her hair. I was glad Poppy was making friends. Kids could be harsh and Julie was like a light arriving at the perfect time.

"Aunty Georgia!" Indigo squealed, her short legs carrying her to the older woman who threw her in the air before snuggling her. I beamed at the sight and greeted Julie by hugging her.

Annie handed Poppy's bags to her and kissed her head. "Thanks again for inviting them, Georgia."

"It's no problem." Georgia waved her hand. "Julie's been begging for a sleepover since Poppy hurt her foot." I laughed at the embarrassed smile Julie wore at her mom's words. "They've got the entire night planned out."

Poppy nodded, hooking her arm through her best friend's. "Manis and pedis, followed by a skincare routine." I raised an impressed brow. "We're gonna do each other's hair and watch *all the Harry Potter films.*"

Indigo pulled a face and I knew it was because she was terrified of Voldemort. Georgia spoke up next. "And this little monster and I are going to have a Barbie marathon." Indigo squealed.

Barbie. Why the fuck did everything remind me of Beckham? He still hadn't figured out why I'd nicknamed him Annika. And I doubted I would ever explain why.

Georgia placed Indigo down on the floor and looked at her daughter. "Why don't you put the bags in the car."

Annie grinned gratefully. "Thanks again, Georgia." The older woman gestured to our room and Annie followed, asking me to help the girls to the car.

I frowned at that, wondering what the two of them had to discuss. Opening the door, I led the girls to the driveway where Georgia's car was parked. Julie unlocked the trunk and I helped stack the bags. With one last kiss on each of their heads, I pivoted to make my way back inside, a bizarre feeling in my stomach.

"Therapy working?" I could hear Georgia's husky voice through the open room door. My frown was back. Annie murmured her response. Therapy? Was Annie going to therapy? That couldn't be right. She scarcely had time for herself. "I know it's difficult, cupcake, but things will get better."

I couldn't hear Annie's retort. She's always had a faint voice so she sure as fuck knew how to whisper. Georgia sighed before articulating again. "I know she's not the best person, but better late than never. She's attempting to do something now." My first thought was that they were talking about our mom and my blood ran cold.

My ears were ringing. Did Georgia know what our home life was like? The very idea made a lump form in my throat. No wonder she'd been offering to help out so much. She *pitied us*.

"I just feel so tired." That was Annie, speaking slightly louder this time because of the emotion coating her words. "It's like this weight on my shoulders, Georgia, and I *have* to shoulder it on my own until all of this works out. I wouldn't dare try and pass some of it to Nyx. You know how she feels about the whole thing and the last thing I want to do is upset her when she has to focus on her studies."

Georgia seemed to be consoling her because I heard shuffling. They were definitely talking about our mom, it was the only topic Annie never brought up with me. I could talk about anything else, except that. One of Annie's greatest qualities was her big heart. She could forgive and forget.

That, however, was something I struggled with. I felt slightly guilty that she was shouldering whatever it is that she was, but what could I do? She'd always been the mother in this household and I knew she didn't take challenging decisions lightly. I trusted her, I always would, and I reminded myself to ask her if everything was okay. If it wasn't, then I would help bear whatever she was carrying. It was the least I could do whether I despised our mom or not.

Hating her didn't permit me to hurt Annie in the process, however indirectly that may be. Georgia and Annie spoke for a few more minutes and I occupied myself by going to the bathroom. I didn't want to snoop any more than I already had. By the time I was done, the two women were waiting in the living room.

"So what do you two pretty girlies have planned for tonight," Georgia asked casually and I froze, quickly telling myself to act normal. Annie still looked frazzled. "Don't look at me like that. C'mon, it's a Friday night. I'm sure there are lots to do."

Annie's eyes drifted to me and I shrugged. "I have a fundraiser tomorrow so I'll probably just get some rest."

Annie nodded. "And I've had a *long day*."

Georgia scoffed. "*Boring*. You girls should have a night out." Annie and I shared an edgy glance, one Georgia didn't miss. "Think about it. You both deserve to do something fun."

She shuffled both of us into a hug before leaving. Annie shut the door behind her, leaning against it with her eyes closed. The more immature part of me wanted to needle her about her confidential exchange with Georgia. But she looked depleted, so I didn't.

The house was peaceful without Poppy and Indigo. The two were always racing around, making noise as if they were trees and the loud sounds they produced were oxygen. My dad still hadn't returned and he'd texted Annie earlier, telling her she shouldn't bother cooking for him since he wasn't coming home. It was the only reason we'd agreed to let Poppy and Indigo leave with Georgia. If my dad returned and found them missing, he'd lose his mind, certain that people were out to hurt his daughters.

It was ironic, honestly.

I looked back at Annie. In just over a month, she'd be turning twenty-four. Back when we were in middle school, she would do odd jobs for neighbours to make extra money.

During our high school years, she'd worked part-time jobs and then immediately after graduating, she had jumped straight into full-time hours. All for us. It was obvious that Annie had never gotten the chance to be young. She'd been an adult for years; a mother, a father. She deserved a night out.

"You know," I began, unsure of how to approach this. Annie's eyes opened. "Our football team beat UCLA yesterday." I didn't necessarily like speaking about school, afraid that I'd unintentionally hurt her feelings.

She grinned, eyes lighting up. Ever since I could remember, Annie had fed off the happiness of others. If you were happy, it was guaranteed to bring a smile to her face. "That's great! First win?"

I shook my head. "I think it's their fourth win so far. Our volleyball girls also won on Wednesday." The baseball team would play tomorrow morning and then the hockey boys would take the ice on Sunday for their first match. "They're celebrating tonight. At Pulse."

Nailea had subtly dropped the name of the club a few times. At least, she *thought* she was being subtle. But it was clear what she'd been trying to accomplish. Maybe Beth would even be there, seeing as she was friends with some Trojans. They'd decided to take things slow because of Beth's mom, from what Annie had told me, but I knew she was dying to see her outside of a work setting again.

Annie nodded, not taking the bait. "Is that a hospital?"

I grinned at the bewildered frown she wore. "No, Annie. It's a club." Smiling, I added, "And I'm inviting you." Her eyes widened. "Why do you look so surprised?"

She laughed fumblingly, moving away from the door to pace. "Well, you've never invited me before. I always assumed you were embarrassed by me—"

My lips parted in shock. "Annie—"

"If not that, then it's because of what happened with Nate last year," she pressed on, shaking her head as her feet hit the floor, wandering in a little circle. I called her name and she looked up, chagrin in her eyes. "I mean, I wouldn't blame you. What happened was my fault—"

"Anabeth!" I blurted, intent on stopping her running mind. Whenever she got like that, it was difficult to get through to her. "You know what happened wasn't your fault, it was mine. I got us into that mess the second I decided to help Nate." I moved towards her, clutching her chilly hands in mine. I felt rotten about my thoughts earlier, questioning her conversation with Georgia even though I *knew* I had to bear the burden of our mom too. "And I don't want us to dwell on the past, okay?" She nodded, breathing unevenly. "Plus, I could *never* be embarrassed by you. It's clear you're the hotter sister."

Annie couldn't fight the grin that threatened to appear. "You sure you want me to tag along?"

"Always."

"I can't believe we didn't think this through," Annie grumbled as we stood in line outside of the club. A bouncer remained right at the front, checking IDs. And I was underaged. "They won't let you in. And I *obviously* won't go in without you."

It'd taken us an hour to get ready. Annie had worked so hard on her appearance—in case she ran into Beth—and was dressed in a light blue cropped cardigan with a matching fluffy miniskirt. For the first time in years, she'd applied a little make-up, and she wore a pair of silver heels.

I wouldn't let this night end in a disaster, not when my sister looked this hot.

The line grew shorter and so did Annie's calm facade. We both had our IDs with us since we always carried them, but I doubted the bouncer would be swayed by a nineteen-year-old and her sweet older sister.

"What if I just briefly wave it in front of his face?" I proposed, becoming desperate as we grew closer to the bouncer.

Annie flicked my arm. "And have him briefly toss you off the side of the building?" The bouncer was big enough to carry both of us in each hand. Annie pouted as the people behind us jostled us. "I wore my nicest panties tonight."

"Anabeth Taylor, are you planning on getting laid tonight?" I mockingly scolded, deepening her pout. It seemed like she had the same thoughts as me and hoped Beth would be at the club.

"Don't full-name me," she scowled, watching as I dug into my purse and pulled out my ID. "What are you—oh my, are you *actually* going to wave it past his face?" I nodded, eying the bouncer who was just a few feet away. "Good luck being tossed off the building."

We stopped in front of the large man and I grinned flirtatiously. His lips never jerked and my smile dropped somewhat.

"ID?" he sought in a rough voice. Annie trembled anxiously, gripping my hand as I held my ID in the other.

Before I could say anything, another person spoke up. "They're with me, Buffy."

I shifted to see Beckham leaning against the wall, dropping a cigarette and stepping on it. If I didn't hate him so much, I certainly would've jumped him. He wore dark jeans and a tight white shirt, his tattoos visible through it.

Without a word, the bouncer let us pass.

Annie, however, stopped, grinning at the man. "Buffy? Like Buffy the Vampire Slayer?"

He glared at her but she didn't move from his beefy side, proceeding to tell him all about how people often mentioned Annabeth from the *Percy Jackson* series when she introduced herself, which was why she went by Annie. All this with a huge smile. Buffy overlooked her, continuing to check IDs, but my sister babbled on.

More people shoved past me and I dropped my ID. "Fuck," I cursed, stooping down to look for it. But there were so many people entering the club, plus it was dim. A whistle sounded through the air and I withheld the urge to lecture whoever it was, focusing on hunting for the tiny card.

I felt a sudden hand on my ass, tugging down my dress that probably rose when I'd bent. On reflex, I straightened with a gasp. An arm went around my waist, pressing me against a hard chest and I let out a small sound.

"Let go of me," I commanded.

Swiftly, I was spun around and I tipped my head back to

peer into Beckham's eyes, still squeezed against him. He lifted his other hand, the little card imprisoned between his long fingers.

"Looking for this?" He bent lower, lips brushing against my ear as he whispered, "*Kennedy.*"

Fuck. He was smirking at me, overjoyed with the information he'd just discovered. He was practically beaming with this new knowledge and I felt dread fill my lungs.

"Step away from me."

He did as requested, still smirking. "Whatever you say, Kennedy."

"It's *Nyx*," I hissed, feeling warmth build in my cheeks.

My mom had selected the name Nyx for me, after the goddess of the night. At least, that's what she'd told me when I had asked. My dad didn't think it was an appropriate first name by the time I had to get my ID. So he and my mom had compromised on my second name, Kennedy, being switched to my first.

But Nyx had always stuck.

"This seems to say otherwise." Beckham flashed the little card and I wrenched it from him, shoving it back into my purse as he chuckled in amusement.

I planned to evade his annoying ass. Beckham Hunt seemed to think that he had a right to know what went on in my life. After being an asshole for *months*, it pissed me off to know that he thought he could just switch up and I'd trust him.

My home life was something that I kept locked up. If I wanted you to know, if I trusted you, I'd give you the key. But my fear was justifiable. There were dreadful people out there; if last year was anything to go by. Instead of waiting for the key, some people would crash through the wall with a fucking car, causing irreparable damage.

Ignoring him, I reached for Annie's arm and towed her away from Buffy. I could tell she sensed something was wrong with me, but she didn't probe, allowing me to lead her to the bar where we ordered shots. Nailea soon joined us, dressed in a skin-tight red jumpsuit that complimented her skin tone. With her added spirit, Annie and I drank more, considering that Nailea was already past drunk.

After what felt like an hour, Nailea yanked me to the dancefloor since Annie declined, urging us to have fun. She promised to watch our purses and slapped our asses as we moved along. My mind was murky because of the liquor and I was thankful. Sometimes it was better to not think. Annie must've felt the same because when I glimpsed at the bar, she was ordering more shots.

I twisted around, allowing my body to sway in sync with Nailea. Her arms wrapped around me and we giggled drunkenly. The music was deafening and I could feel the ground shaking. Strobe lights were flickering, making me see an assemblage of colours each time I blinked. It probably wasn't a good idea to get drunk the night before the fundraiser.

"Damn, look at Beckham!" Nailea screeched in my ear, making me recoil.

I whirled to where she was pointing and spotted Beckham seated at a booth, a girl straddling him as they made out. Her hands roamed underneath his shirt as his own skimmed to her ass, groping to his heart's content. He yanked her hair, exposing her throat so that he could suckle the soft skin. I swallowed roughly, still swaying with Nailea.

I refused to acknowledge the painful feeling in my chest.

Opposite Beckham sat a very crestfallen-looking Jasper, attired in blue jeans and a hoodie. He stared ahead at something, arms crossed and slumped low in his seat. It looked like he wanted to be anywhere but where he currently was. By the time I pivoted back around, Nailea was already grinding against somebody I was sure was on the football team. The guy was flabbergasted by the attention he was receiving from the beautiful girl.

I marched away, fully equipped to head back to my sister, only to find that she was engaged in a deep conversation with Beth, the latter dressed in jeans and a cropped shirt. The two were laughing together, sharing drinks. I'd only be a party pooper if I were to join their conference. Four out of the five people I knew were blissfully occupied.

That left one person.

Straightening my dress, I sauntered towards an unamused Jasper. He was still scowling ahead, but I couldn't tell at what exactly. When he saw me advancing, his brows soared and his frown turned upside down.

"Little goddess!" he exclaimed. Okay, so he was wasted as well. His dreary character had me anxious for a second.

The bellowing of his speech grabbed the attention of Beckham, who drew away from who I just recognised was Melissa, the taunting twin. The latter sucked at the skin of his neck as his grey eyes found mine. He looked suddenly uncomfortable and whispered something in Melissa's ear that had her grimacing in anger.

Annoyance bubbled within me because Melissa, somebody I hated, was essentially making out with my fucking ex. He had the absolute audacity to claim that he cared when he could fondle a bitch like Melissa.

I snubbed them, thumping down next to Jasper as he enveloped a brawny arm around my shoulders and dragged me to his broad chest. A musky scent embraced my nose and I moaned drunkenly. Nothing was better than a man who smelt the way he looked—hot as fuck.

"Where's the rest of your team?" I questioned, laying a hand on his chest.

He shrugged. "It's just Beck and me tonight. He was *supposed* to be my wingman. Clearly, he's occupied." The man in question peeked at us, transferring Melissa so that she sat next to him. She pouted, looking disturbed. "Didn't expect to see you here," Jasper murmured, looking somewhat apologetic for Beckham's actions. I always forgot that his entire team knew what went on between us.

"Last minute decision," I responded, ignoring the fact that Melissa was trying to crawl back into Beckham's lap.

I must've been doing a pretty shit job at concealing my thoughts because Jasper was cupping my jaw, gently turning me to face him. "Hey," he mumbled, tucking some hair behind my ear, "ignore them, okay?"

The uneasy feeling grew.

"I'm unbothered," I replied with a forced smirk and Jasper sent me a flat look. "If anyone here is bothered, it's you," I persisted, discerning that his eyes gravitated to the dancefloor again, transforming into that familiar glare. I followed his stare, locating a couple dancing intimately. The girl was unfamiliar but I knew Stefan; a member of the football team. His bright blue hair made him easy to spot. "Which one are you pining for?"

Without missing a beat, Jasper replied, "Him." I watched Stefan drag his hands down the girl's front, swaying with her. "He invited me, seeing as his team won, to celebrate." Jasper scoffed, placing his hand over mine and rubbing circles. If I wasn't as tipsy as I was then I wouldn't have been so open to his touch.

Unbeknownst to Jasper, Stefan had glimpsed over while he was talking. I raised a brow, cupping Jasper's jaw and turning him to face me. I pressed a kiss to his cheek, disregarding his bewildered laugh and momentarily peeping to the side. Stefan had floundered for a second before promptly swaying with the girl again.

I rolled my eyes, comprehension dawning on me. "Men are *so* childish," I grumbled, flinging my leg over Jasper's lap and straddling him. His hands went to my hips, confusion in his eyes. "He's trying to make you jealous. And by the looks of your attitude for the past few minutes—it's *working*."

One of the first steps of flirting was to never look *too* interested. Your significant other would use it to their benefit. And Jasper was one of my own. There was no way I'd let him be at a disadvantage.

Jasper's astonishment was obvious and I rolled my eyes again. "Really?" He tried to peek around me, but I yanked him back. "What was that for?" he urged, rubbing the back of his neck.

"Don't be an idiot," I admonished. "Let me handle this. If he's going to treat you like an option, show him you have options too." I dragged my nose across his jaw and he shuddered. "Is this okay?" He nodded. "Now, I'm going to kiss your neck and you're gonna be a good boy and stare Stefan in the eye. Okay?"

He nodded again and I dipped my head forward, placing small kisses on his neck, easing towards his jaw. Sucking gently, I heard him groan and I elevated my gaze, seeing him gazing ahead. Upping my game, I propelled my hips forward, grinding against his crotch and he let out a deep moan, eyes rolling to the back of his head.

I tilted my head back, finding Stefan frowning at us, his girl long gone. From the corner of my eye, I could see another hormonal man observing us with a scowl; Beckham. Seemed like his girl had left him, too. I smirked at him, running my tongue over my teeth and smiled as Jasper nipped my collar bone. Beckham's gaze dropped to where my hips were moving against his friend. His jaw clenched and I stifled a laugh. Jasper's hand caught my nape and he drew me forward, pressing his lips to mine.

We were both intoxicated which made things all the more fun. I nipped at his bottom lip and he groaned, trying to slide his tongue into my mouth, but I wouldn't grant him access. He yanked my hair and I gasped, providing him with an opportunity to brush his tongue against mine. My hips didn't stop moving and it was plain how much Jasper was enjoying our make-out session.

My hands went to his stubbly head, working across the

short strands and he chuckled against my lips before stating, "Sorry, darling, you have nothing to grab onto."

I pulled away slightly, feeling giggles develop in my throat. "How about I go to the toilet and get a plunger?" Jasper exploded into a frenzy of laughter and I accompanied him, tears leaking out of my eyes. An ache settled in my stomach the longer I laughed and Jasper tugged me close when I nearly tumbled off his lap.

A throat cleared; I shifted to see Stefan there, looking awkward. "Hey, you wanna go grab a drink?" he urged Jasper, who was drying his teary eyes. The latter peeped at me and I simpered, sliding off his lap.

He stood up, peering back at me as if I was his mentor or something. I snorted. "Go ahead, darling. Once you're done, meet me in the toilet," I smirked. "You know what'll be waiting for you." I ran an innocent hand over my head and Jasper pulled a constipated face, striving to restrain his laughter as he marched away. "Go! Diego! Go!" I hollered after him, snorting when he raised his middle finger before leaving with Stefan.

Beckham was still looking at me, but I avoided his stare. My eyes were trained on Melissa as she stood sulking with her friends, no doubt upset that Beckham was no longer paying attention to her. Two birds with one stone. Jasper had gotten the attention of Stefan *and* I'd pissed off Melissa.

Maybe even three birds with one stone because Beckham looked angry as fuck.

Melissa stomped her foot as she explained something to her friends and they all glowered at me. I lifted a hand and wiggled my fingers in an innocent wave.

"They don't even know me, but they hate me because Melissa does," I mused and leaned back in my seat, knowing that Beckham was listening. "I love it when they play follow the leader with me. Fan behaviour right there." I wobbled onto my heels, straightening my dress for the umptieth time.

Almost tauntingly, I sashayed towards Beckham. He didn't move as I tipped forward, giving him an eyeful of cleavage whilst my hand slipped into his jeans pocket. When I pulled out a scrunched twenty-dollar bill, he raised a brow. "You didn't think I gave shows for free, did you?"

I shoved the money into my bra and turned on my heel, feeling his eyes on me the entire way to my sister.

Chapter 12

Beckham

For some reason, I *knew* I shouldn't have shown up at the club tonight. It was a gut feeling, but when everyone else claimed to be busy, I knew I couldn't disappoint Jasper. He'd been pining for Stefan for months now and this was his opening. So I agreed. And now I regretted my decision.

"Sorry!" Nailea drunkenly blurted, both hands pressed to her mouth as she gawked at the humongous beer stain on my *white* shirt. An acting career was out of the question for her because she was sniggering whilst simultaneously trying to look remorseful. "I tripped."

The lie was evident and I cursed, pulling at the now sticky material of my shirt. This was payback at its finest. She was doing it for Nyx.

"You threw it at me," I informed her, making her laugh louder. Just a few seconds ago, I'd watched Nailea dash towards me before she flung the entire cup, snickering as it spilt on my shirt. I didn't have a spare one and I was somewhat glad that

Nailea gave me an excuse to go home. As I was about to step away from her, I halted. "How are you getting home?"

She was unmistakably drunk out of her mind and in no state to drive. Her intoxicated state paired with the fact that she was somebody many students regularly lusted after was dangerous. There were some sick fucks out there.

"Hitching a ride back to the dorms," she countered, sulking because I probably didn't give her the pissed-off reaction she was anticipating. She'd done me a favour.

I nodded, turning on my heel and shifting through the crowd to get to the toilet. Once I was there, I hauled off the shirt, groaning as the beer dribbled from it. With an annoyed sigh, I hurled the entire shirt into the trashcan. Tipping over the counter, I splattered my face with some water, soaking a paper towel into it to wipe at my sticky chest. Beer trickled from my tattoos and I wiped it away. After I was done, I made my way to the exit, reminding myself to text Jasper that I was leaving. The latter had spent the past few hours with Stefan, so he certainly didn't need me around.

The cheers grew more vulgar and I frowned, inwardly questioning who decided to get naked this time. Just earlier, some guy had shed his clothes like a snake and flashed everyone his dick. He'd gotten thrown out and ran away without his clothes. I wouldn't be surprised if he ended up getting arrested. I faltered slightly when somebody fell on me.

Before I could force them away, Jasper stated, "Man, it's Melissa."

A scowl emerged on my face without me even trying. I hadn't expected her to be at the club tonight, but there she was.

She'd wanted attention from me and I'd hoped that if I gave her the ten seconds of having the upper hand on Nyx that she so desperately wanted—she'd fuck off.

But to no avail.

"And I'm supposed to care why?" I queried rhetorically as I trailed the path to the exit. People were gawking at my bare chest, probably expecting to get a second naked show. Well, they were going to be severely disappointed—because I was leaving.

Jasper tugged at my pants and I swore, spinning around to jostle him back, but he looked concerned. "She's arguing with Nyx."

Elbowing him out of the way, I altered my route. "Why the fuck didn't you start with that?" As if I could give a fuck about what happened to Melissa. I was wondering how long it would take for the two of them to clash. There was so much tension between them, you could cut it with a knife—and Nyx would use that knife to slit Melissa's throat.

Jasper directed me to the bar where a crowd was appearing around Nyx and Melissa. I noticed Annie standing behind her sister with Beth, a glowering Nailea by their side. Maxine appeared neutral, not standing behind her twin sister, but not standing behind Nyx, either. However, it didn't matter, because Melissa was backed up by her friends; Lisa and Pippa.

After Nyx had made out with Jasper and stolen twenty dollars from me, she overlooked me as usual. She'd danced around with her sister, Beth and Nailea, drinking together and laughing at people's dance moves before laughing at their own dance moves. Until now, Melissa and Nyx didn't cross paths again. Things were about to get ugly.

"You walk around campus as if you own the place," Melissa snarled, eyes flaring with irritation. Her face was turning an odd shade. I couldn't tell if it was because of the alcohol or because of her rage. "And people are stupid enough to worship you."

"*Ooh*," Nyx pulled a scrunched face, turning slightly as she caught my eye. Her gaze faltered on my chest. "You hear that, Beck? She just called you stupid."

I scowled at Jasper when he snickered, but Melissa quickly retorted again, standing taller. She had her height over Nyx.

"You're there on *scholarship*." Nyx's eye twitched, but she remained gazing at the brunette. I glimpsed at Melissa, wondering how she knew that. Not even I knew that.

"And?" Nyx shot back. "All you've achieved by saying that is proving my intelligence." Melissa stepped closer, and Nyx grinned. "Listen, if you've got beef with me—I promise you it's one-sided. I couldn't give a fuck about you, honestly."

The blonde turned, grabbing her purse from Annie and looking ready to leave. Nailea hooked her arm through hers as Melissa watched on, face becoming redder. I knew the feeling well. I went through the same thing whenever Nyx had the last say in an argument, which was regularly.

Melissa's eyes found mine. I saw her plan before it happened. She wanted to use that supposed upper hand she had.

Me.

She looked back at Nyx before stating, "You're just jealous!"

Nyx let out a genuine laugh, showcasing the dimples she

buried so well with her perpetual scowl. "Bless your delusional heart," she returned, scanning Melissa up and down. "I didn't even know Maxine had a twin. Until the other day, I thought you guys were one person."

Even *I* winced at Nyx's response. That was the worst thing she could've said to somebody as self-absorbed as Melissa. Jasper cackled without a care in the world and Stefan, whom I didn't even notice, was laughing too. Melissa fumed, yanking her arm away from Maxine who tried to lure her sister away.

"You little bitch!" Melissa roared, taking three steps forward, seizing Nyx's bicep and twisting her around. Before Nyx could even act, Melissa had elevated her hand, palm landing on Nyx's cheeks with a resounding slap.

The crowd went silent. Even the volume of the music lowered. The air went soundless, waiting for Nyx to pounce, for her rage to spill over. Nailea was floundering, grappling to come to terms with what had happened and Annie gazed at her sister in concern, a frowning Beth gripping her hand.

Nyx stood paralysed, looking at Melissa as if she was an alien. Slowly, she hoisted a hand to her red cheek, full lips separating in shock. People hollered for her to fight back. But she didn't. From where I was standing, I could see her eyes begin to flood and I cursed, pushing away from Jasper.

"Don't bark if you can't fucking bite," Melissa smirked, stepping back triumphantly. Her friends clapped her on the back. Mutely, Nyx shoved her purse at a gaping Annie and dashed off towards the toilet.

A second later, Nailea reacquired her footing and lurched herself at Melissa, tackling her to the ground. The girl had her claws out and scraped at her face, yelling obscenities I was sure weren't English.

Annie looked ready to run after her sister, but I stopped her. She twirled, confusion in her moist eyes as I inquired, "How did you guys get here?"

"Booked a ride," she sputtered out, Beth staring at both of us in concern.

I nodded, removing my keys from my pocket and delivering them to her. "I'll drive you home. Go to my car. Black jeep with a sticker of the team logo on the back. I'll go get Nyx." Annie nodded, still in a trance. I didn't stay to see two bouncers pull Nailea off from Melissa, focused on my destination.

The hallways were void, seeing as everyone had heard about the catfight taking place and I used that to my advantage, jogging instead of having to elbow people out of the way. My hand was just about to pull on the door handle when a woman walked out and blundered into me.

In her inebriated daze, her hands ran over the exposed skin she found. I cleared my throat and she looked up, seeing the anxiety in my features. "She's a mess."

And that's all it took for me to weave around her and push open the door. What I witnessed made my heart drop out of my ass.

Nyx stood arched over by the counter, wheezing. She was muttering something and a hiccup followed each word. But she wasn't crying. Annoyed, she jerked at the edges of her hair, a habit of hers. A dry sob left her, followed by another. Then another. And then she was panicking, hands going to claw at her throat.

Shut up. Shut up. Shut up. Shut up. She was mumbling it to herself. It was almost as if she didn't want herself to cry, wouldn't allow that vulnerability to flash through.

She gagged, speeding towards a stall and throwing herself to her knees. My feet propelled me forward and I followed her into the stall, squatting next to her and holding her hair back. But there was no vomit. She was just dry heaving.

Gently, I smoothed some baby hair away from her flushed face. She groaned in agony and I knew it was because her abdomen was clenching with the intensity of her heaving. I slipped an arm around her, squeezing my hand to the soft satin material covering her stomach as I proceeded to rub little circles.

"Get away!" she shrieked, discerning I was there with her. Rubbing her face, she sought to shove me away from her, looking ashamed. All she succeeded in doing was pushing me onto my ass and I slumped back against the wall. "Get away," she chanted, holding back tears as she scratched at my chest.

Of all people she had to cry in front of, it had to be me. I could just imagine the inner turbulence she was going through. In a swift move, I cupped her nape, dragged her forward and she collapsed into my lap. My arms went around her, preventing her from escaping. She fought and fought, cursing me out.

Then she gave in.

My facial muscles tightened as I listened to her breakdown, raucous sobs leaving her mouth, body trembling with the force of it. It was a ghastly sight, seeing her cry. She was always the most composed person in the room, reluctant to let anyone get to her. Her tears streamed down my chest, but I didn't mind. I peeped down to see her eyes closed, face scrunched in distress. Her cheek was still red, some areas welting because of the rings Melissa wore on her hand. The sight of it made rage blister inside me.

Nyx hiccupped repeatedly, nestled in my familiar hold. I couldn't even linger on the fact that it had been so fucking long since I'd last held her in my arms. All I could concentrate on were the cries of distress leaving her lips. I wiped her tears, pressing my nose to her hair as she whimpered.

"We need to leave," I muttered when her cries died down and her eyes shot open, alarm gleaming within the blue hues. She shook her head, mumbling her disagreement in a diminutive voice. "Nyx—"

"I *can't* go back out there," she forced out.

It was an effort to stand up with Nyx clinging to me. The thought pierced my insides because Nyx never clung to anybody.

"We'll take the back," I informed her, sighing in relief when she didn't dispute. I tucked her into my arms as I steered us towards the back door. When we arrived at the doors, I spoke, "I need to do something real quick. Could you wait here—"

"No," she shook her head furiously, echoing the word as tears swelled her eyes again. "Please, don't leave. *Please.*"

She was *begging* me. I swore underneath my breath and pulled her back to me, taking my phone out of my jeans. "I'm not going anywhere, baby." With Nyx trembling in my hold, I clicked on Jasper's contact. The phone rang for five beats before I heard his voice. "Jas," I began, looking down to Nyx as her eyes scanned the area in terror. "Can you do me a favour?" He hummed in response. "Find Melissa." Nyx froze at my words and I ran a gentle hand down her side. "With direct orders from me, neither she nor her friends are allowed at *any* of our hockey games or *any* of our events. Understand?"

"Gotcha," Jasper acknowledged, sounding enthusiastic about presenting the news. It would no doubt break their hearts, seeing as Melissa and her friends were puck bunnies to the core. I hung up and escorted Nyx towards the parking lot where my car was.

I opened the back door to set Nyx there, frowning when I saw Annie in the driver's seat. "What are you doing?" I questioned her.

"I'm driving. Don't worry, I'm sober. Stopped drinking two hours ago," Annie replied, inserting the keys and I watched dumbfounded. "What's your address?" she queried absentmindedly, taking out her phone and opening Google Maps. When I didn't answer, she looked up at me, quirking a brow. "Hello?"

Nyx climbed into the car but wouldn't let me close the door, sticking her leg out. She was still in a stupor, refusing to speak.

"Why do you need my address?" It was supposed to be the other way around. *I* needed *their* address so I could take them home.

Annie pulled a face, momentarily glancing at her sister as she reached for me again. "Um, duh. We're going to your place. Now get your ass in the car."

Were all Taylor women like this?

"And why are we going to my place?" I pressed, trying to close the backdoor but Nyx still wouldn't let me.

The brunette gazed at Nyx, eyes softening and losing their luminosity. She then turned to me. "Same reason I'm driving. She's not gonna let go of you." I apprehended then that Nyx wasn't being stubborn by refusing to let me close the door. She wanted me next to her and wouldn't let me close the door until I climbed in. Annie must've seen the puzzle in my eyes because she mumbled uneasily, "She associates you with safety right now. There's no way she's letting you go."

Her words made frost form in my veins. She uttered them with knowledge as if she'd been in my position before. "You say that like it's a frequent thing."

I could easily tell the difference between Nyx and her sisters. They wore their emotions for the entire world to see. *Fear.* The same emotion I'd seen in Poppy before when I'd questioned her about her foot. The same emotion I'd seen in Indigo when Grayson had raised his hands. And the same emotion I could see in Annie's eyes right now.

So instead of questioning her further, I climbed in, drawing Nyx to my side as I shut the door. Annie nodded shakily, starting the car. I gave her my address and let her drive us to my house. Grayson was probably asleep by now, but Sebastian would still be awake, watching a movie in bed. The drive lulled Nyx to sleep and after a few minutes, her head dropped to my chest.

"I'm sorry for the inconvenience," Annie whispered, eyes levelled on the road and I frowned, unconsciously running my fingers through Nyx's hair. "My mind was all over the place and I shouldn't have let you go after her. Usually, I'm in your position when she gets like that. I should've known better than to let somebody else take over."

I swallowed roughly, looking at the sleeping girl as Annie practically screamed the answer to the question that had been plaguing me.

"Does somebody *usually* hurt her?" Annie's lips quivered and my hold on Nyx stiffened. "Her low tolerance for men," I spoke slowly, allowing myself to voice my assumptions. "It's a man hurting her." Annie didn't reply, but she didn't need to. I'd been right in my assumptions after all.

Annie's phone rang and I listened to her assure Beth that they were okay. The concern in my childhood friend's voice made me think back to what my mom had told me. The realisation quickened when I saw the small blush Annie sported when Beth made her promise to call her in the morning. It took a lot of convincing, but Beth eventually hung up. The rest of the ride was hushed and Annie turned off the car when we pulled up outside. I slid out of the car, hoisting Nyx and holding her sleeping form to me as I marched to the front door.

"Pocket," I told Annie and she removed my house keys, unlocking the door. It was dark inside, but I knew the area like the back of my hand. I trudged up the stairs, stopping in front of one of the guest rooms that the team sometimes piled into.

I kicked open the door and flicked on the light. "Bathroom's through there." I pointed to a door. "Careful, though. You share it with Grayson. His room is on the other side." Annie nodded, dropping their purses on the bed. "There should be some shirts in those drawers. The boys always leave their shit behind. You'll maybe even find some shorts or sweats. Extra blankets are in the basket over there. I think Beth even left clothes here before."

"Thank you," Annie muttered, gratitude dripping from her words and tone. I nodded stiffly, still holding Nyx in one arm as I pointed to random spots in the room. Annie tugged at a strand of her sister's hair, features scrunching in pity. "She's gonna have to stay with you tonight. I mean it when I say she clings." It irked me that Annie spoke with such familiarity.

How many times did they go through this that Nyx was *conditioned* to cling to somebody? It must've happened numerous times for her brain to switch off and focus on one person, for it to become an uncontrollable habit. My throat burned with the hateful words I wanted to utter.

Before I whirled around, I urged, "For how many years have you been in my position?" Annie's throat bobbed, lips pursing. "I won't ask any more questions," I assured her, striving to ease her mind. "But, at least give me that." Even I could hear the desperation in my voice. It was obvious.

I nearly left because of how long Annie stayed silent. But at the last minute, she mumbled, "Twelve years."

And there came that surge of guilt that should've appeared after every bad thing I did to Nyx. When I'd bullied her, fed into the rumours although I hadn't believed in them. That guilt should've arrived as a trickle after each action. But now, after piling up, it was a tsunami. I nearly staggered as my knees buckled.

Annie wouldn't look me in the eye and for both of our sakes, I turned on my heel and left for my room. It was dark and I flicked on the light. My bedsheets were changed since that night Melissa had slept here and I'd changed my curtains as well, wanting no memory of the girl in my room. I settled Nyx on the bed before going over to my closet. Swapping my jeans for grey sweatpants, I seized a shirt for Nyx.

Even asleep, she looked to be in discomfort.

"Nyx," I shook her shoulder gently. After a few seconds, her eyes fluttered open. I expected her to panic at the sight of me, yet she didn't. However, she did look annoyed at being woken up. "You need to change into something more comfortable." I tossed her the shirt and she barely caught it.

I entered my bathroom and Nyx followed, presumably not wanting to be alone. Whilst I wet a clean cloth, Nyx attempted to change out of her dress. With a small smile, I unzipped it for her and she mumbled a quiet thanks. I handed her a new toothbrush and when we were done getting ready for bed; I held up the damp cloth.

"C'mere," I murmured, tugging her forward and setting her on the counter. Stepping between her legs, I held the cold cloth against her cheek and she flinched. "Sorry," I muttered. Once most of the red was gone, I rubbed some ointment onto the welts to help with the inflammation. Melissa's rings had done a number on her. I cupped her uninjured cheek and she favoured into my touch. "You're not gonna believe it when I tell you tomorrow that you willingly let me touch you."

Nyx stunned me by laying a hand over my own. "I'm aware of what's happening, Beck," she whispered, sounding embarrassed. "It's not two separate people you're dealing with. I'm still me." Her words were small. She offered me a smile. "I still hate you, asshole."

But her subconscious associated me with safety and there was nothing she could do about it. Satan could've been the one to help her and Nyx could do nothing but cling to him.

To her, I probably was Satan.

I chuckled, taking her in my arms and she pressed her face into my neck. I could see myself in the mirror above the counter, see the way she was drowning in my embrace. My grip tightened.

"I missed this," she mumbled tiredly, sounding in a reverie.

That weird feeling inside me returned. "Missed me holding you?" I felt her nod and I gulped. I'd missed it too. My hand cupped the back of her head, holding her close. "Who's hurting you, Nyx?" I asked, hating that it was a question relating to her in the first place.

She tensed, clinging a little tighter to me. "Beckham, please," her words were a mumble against my neck.

I moved away slightly, framing her face in my hands so she couldn't look away. Her eyes were swollen, the blue tone rimmed with red.

"Whether it was one time or a thousand, he laid a fucking hand on you. He's gonna pay, Nyx, trust me on that." She stayed staring up at me, her features pained as she let me lean my forehead against hers. "Do you believe me?"

Any closer and her lips would've caressed mine with her next words. "I believe you."

With a satisfied nod, I slid her off the counter and carried her into my room where I placed her on the bed. She tugged back the blankets, practically drowning in my shirt. I watched as she stretched back and a second later; she pulled off a black bra. She tossed it at me and I caught it, locating my twenty dollars tucked into the lace of it. An amused laugh left me and Nyx gave me a little smile, slipping under the covers.

"I think I prefer soft Nyx, she speaks less," I told her whilst she reached a hand out to me. Taking Annie's words into consideration, I hopped into bed, putting some distance between us. It took three seconds for Nyx to obliterate that space by throwing her bare leg over me, hand finding the right side of my chest. "You're gonna hate me in the morning again, aren't you?"

Nyx was quiet for a beat. "I don't think I ever hated you," she said eventually, not elaborating at all.

It felt like my heart stopped beating. I glanced down to see her tracing patterns on my chest with her index finger. The words wouldn't leave my mind, too much weight attached to them and I didn't know whether I was strong enough to unpack them, to make sense of her whispered statement.

After a few minutes, when Nyx struggled to fall asleep, I spoke again. "Somebody who uses their fists in an argument is weak." Nyx blinked but said nothing. She focused on the beating of my heart and I placed my hand over hers, watching as she drifted to sleep.

Chapter 13

Nyx

I felt that prickling sensation on my skin and I knew somebody was staring at me. I could *feel* it. There was a soft touch sweeping against my cheek, the very cheek that Melissa had slapped. Memories of last night infiltrated my thoughts and I repressed a shudder. I could still see the amusement in her eyes when she'd apprehended I wouldn't retaliate. And for a second, for a split second, I was being admonished by my dad again.

It was an out-of-body experience. With one tiny slap, Melissa had unearthed a tsunami of buried emotions. Each time my dad raised his hands, I never reacted, took that fear and buried it six feet under the ground. And I trampled on it every day, refusing to be a victim. Never again would I flinch, never again would I cry at the hands of a monster, a bully.

The last time I'd flinched at my father's brutal touch, I was ten years old.

Now I was nineteen, and all that emotions were hurrying back, dead-set on asphyxiating me to make up for lost time.

A feeling of fear built in my chest. I loathed it, didn't want it. Fear had no right to be inside of me. I felt violated by it. But it was there, nonetheless. I could feel myself disintegrating, the stray pieces being fashioned into that scared little girl with the blonde pigtails and sparkling blue eyes. My closed eyelids acted as a screen and my memories played out before me.

I could see that blonde little girl fleeing to the bathroom to hide. I could see Annie hastening after her, a three-year-old Poppy wailing in her arms. I watched them cluster on the tile, a blanket swathed around them.

Seconds later, a frail woman fell through the door, skin bruised and eyes swollen. She looked like me. And I hated it. I watched her fall to the floor with her three daughters, thin arms binding around them in a makeshift fortress. But it couldn't stop the inebriated man that blundered into the bathroom next. He was yelling, face red, and a bottle of whiskey in his hands. The bottle tumbled to the floor and he prowled forward, yanking at the pigtails belonging to little Nyx.

Annie screeched until her throat was raw, holding Poppy to her chest as Eliza shouted at her husband, urging him to let little Nyx go. Eliza launched to her feet, ready to battle the man for her daughter, but he jostled her back and her head banged against the bathtub. And she was out cold. Annie implored him to leave her sister alone, Poppy still clutched to her chest. But he didn't.

He was furious and I knew why, could remember that day so clearly. Little Nyx had emptied all of his alcohol down the drain. She'd thought that if she got rid of the liquor that turned her dad into the monster that maltreated them, he'd be restored. But she was so naïve. Because it wasn't the liquor that made him a monster.

He just was.

The intoxicated man hauled her to the kitchen by her hair and she cried for her mommy, for her sisters. But they couldn't go after her because he'd locked them in the bathroom. Little Nyx was frightened. Her dad filled the sink with ice-cold water and settled her on a broken stool.

Daddy, please, she pleaded, tears gushing down her chubby face. But her daddy was long gone, substituted with a void of a human being. He clawed his hand into her hair, cupping the back of her head. *Daddy, please*, she whispered, eyes glowing with tears.

Matthew Taylor glowered at her and pushed her face forward into the water, keeping her there as she screamed, bubbles accumulating. He kept her there for a few seconds and she was trying to shove away, but he was more powerful than her. He yanked her out, stared down at her red face as she convulsed from the lack of oxygen.

Daddy, please! Her words were a scream this time, fear suffocating her. She didn't want to drown. With another scowl, he pushed her back into the water, barely allowing her to take a deep breath.

Her lungs were burning, a fire churning there. She clawed at his arms, but it was futile. If she hadn't been submerged in the water, she would've heard her big sister's anguished shrieks as she pounded against the locked bathroom door, clawed against the worn wood until her nails were splitting and bleeding.

Matthew lifted little Nyx again and she heaved for air,

sobbing hysterically. She was choking, eyes bloodshot and head pulsating. Her dad swore at her, blustering about respecting him but she could barely hear him over the ringing in her ears. She breathed in deeply before she was pressed into the water again.

When he pulled her out after a few seconds, she wasn't crying. She didn't scream. She didn't beg him. She didn't look at him. Because she realised then that it wasn't her disrespect that was the problem.

It was the monster that held her in his clawed hands.

For the last time, he jostled her back into the water. Her arms dangled limply at her sides, eyes closed as if she was resting. Her lungs were blazing again but she welcomed the sensation. It told her she was still alive, that he hadn't broken her yet. There was a raucous, continuous crash. For the first few seconds, Matthew overlooked it. But then he let go of little Nyx to investigate, telling her he hoped she'd learnt her lesson.

Slowly, she laid her shaking hands on the counter and pulled her face from the water. Her hair was sopping, face a bright red shade, matching her eyes. Her chest moved up and down at a rapid pace, striving to get back the oxygen her lungs had been deprived of. In the background, she could hear screaming. In a stupor, she climbed down from the stool and followed the shrieks.

She discovered Annie in the hallway, her hand pressed to her bruised cheek as Matthew stood over her, yelling. That's when little Nyx saw the foundation of his anger. There was a humongous hole in the bathroom door, made by Annie with the hammer she'd found in the cabinet. She'd obliterated the wood in an attempt to get to little Nyx. Even in her groggy state, little Nyx propelled herself to Annie's side, gripping her. Angrily, Matthew raised his hand.

But little Nyx didn't flinch. And she never would again.

"Nyx!" I felt myself being rocked vigorously and my eyes flew open, meeting the stare of Beckham. I was panting and his eyes were wide. He let out a loud sigh when he saw I was okay and dropped back onto the bed. "I thought you were having a fucking seizure."

Not a seizure. Just a nightmare. I keened, feeling the sunlight hit my puffed eyes. "Why the fuck are your curtains open? Some of us are vampires, bitch."

"And she's back," Beckham mused with a smirk, rising out of bed and stretching. His grey sweatpants hung low on his hips, exposing a rather prominent v-line. The muscles in his arms bulged as he yawned and I felt my mouth water.

No, Nyx. I internally berated myself.

I pushed out of bed, doing my own set of stretching and feeling Beckham's eyes roaming over me. "Are you staring at me or did you have a stroke?"

Beckham scoffed, trudging to open his windows. "I think I'd prefer the stroke over you." I grinned, trying to tame my hair. He wasn't being awkward about what had happened last night, thankfully, but I knew he had questions. After a silent five minutes of him making up the bed and me brushing my teeth, he urged, "You okay?"

"Ah," I sighed as he passed. "The age-old question. Sorry, Bucko, but the answer is one of the world's anomalies."

Beckham scowled at me, leaning down to wash his face.

The stream of water made me freeze which was why I'd wiped my face with a cloth. I didn't want to lean over the sink, not when that memory was so fresh.

Beckham discerned my expression and I twisted away.

"No, I'm not," I confessed.

He followed me back into the room, frowning. "Look, I've been doing some thinking." I tensed and he instantly appended, "And I've realised that you must have a good reason if you're enduring the abuse. You're right, I can't just force myself into your life and demand to know what's happening. But I meant what I said last night." He shook his head, tugging anxiously at his hair.

I watched him pace and other memories came rushing back. I remembered the distress in his eyes, and the rage in his voice as he asked Jasper to confront Melissa. I remembered his delicate touch as he stroked my hair during the car ride. I remembered how tenderly he had carried me, cleaned my face, and held me as I fell asleep. My memories took me even further back, to before Nate. Beckham had been gentle with me even then. A man had never touched me so softly before; as if I was a glass rose.

And of all people, it was Beckham.

I never hated him, I had to admit that *one* truth that I'd shielded with lies in an effort to protect myself.

I never hated him. How could I when, subconsciously, I knew he was the first man I'd ever let myself trust—no matter what came afterwards.

My words were a whisper. "Thank you." I wasn't looking at him, afraid that I'd cry. And we didn't need cry-baby Nyx returning. This moment between us was territory we hadn't stepped foot on in a very long time and I could tell he felt the same way because he nodded tensely, scratching the back of his neck. To ease the tension, I stated, "Your dick is hard," and pointed to the bulge at his front. "I'll accept it as morning wood, *this time*."

Beckham grinned. "That would be a lie." He didn't offer any explanation, but I didn't need one. I checked the time, deciding to go home before heading to the hall to set up for tonight's charity event. "Are you gonna go back to being a bitch to me again?" He was smirking and I laughed, deciding not to bring up his mention of a truce.

"Of course, can't have people thinking we're going soft on each other," I countered smoothly, picking up my bra and dress.

"I'm anything but soft right now, baby," he retorted and I glimpsed at him, lips twitching. "I'll let you change and send your sister in." He winked, heading for the door.

It was as if he knew just what I needed; for the situation to be made light of. Because if I focused too much on it, it would drag me down.

Just as he left, I yelled out, "Not your baby!"

His laughter wafted through the air and I shook my head, sitting down on the bed and trying to rid myself of my nightmare. I refused to allow those memories to take over. They were memories for a reason. Whilst I waited for Annie to arrive, I planned out my revenge on Melissa.

All because she was an insecure little bitch, she'd unearthed *years* of trauma for me. I wouldn't let that slide.

After what felt like forever, Annie tumbled into the room,

throwing herself at me. "Oh my God!" she exclaimed, pressing my face to her chest as she hugged me like a concerned mother. "Nyxie, I'm so sorry. *God*, I knew it was a bad idea to go out last night—"

"Annie," I tried to calm her down, pushing away slightly and gripping her trembling arms. "I'm okay, I promise." I offered her a smile. "Nothing I haven't already experienced." That was the wrong thing to say because Annie burst into tears. "Annie, *please*."

My sister sniffled, ugly crying with snot and everything. "You shouldn't have to be used to things like this, Nyxie. I shouldn't have to explain to Beckham the process you go through because there shouldn't be a process in the first place." She hiccupped violently, her whole body jolting. "And I couldn't sleep last night because my mind was working so hard—"

"You didn't sleep?" I interrupted. "Please tell me you got some rest?"

Her hand raised to wipe her nose as she nodded. "Yes, Beckham warmed me some milk last night—"

I gaped. "What? When was this?"

Annie sniffled again. "You were out cold and I found Beckham in the kitchen, pacing." She paused, taking a moment to gauge my reaction. "He cares about you, you know? He always has. At least, that's what Grayson told me—"

"Whoa, whoa, *whoa*," I cut her off, again, mostly because what she was saying was scaring me. "And when exactly did you have the chance to talk to Grayson about my non-existent relationship with Beckham?"

She blinked owlishly at me. "Before I went to get milk, I

needed to pee but when I went into the bathroom, Grayson was already peeing. After he got over his initial shock of me being in his house, let alone his bathroom, we had a conversation—but that's not the point!" She cut herself off this time, a frustrated noise leaving her. "The point is that I feel even *worse* because Beckham cares for you and I ruined it all by allowing you to do what you did for me and now you're lonely and sad and it's all my fault," she cried, making zero sense at all. But I let her cry, let her get rid of the unnecessary guilt she carried.

"Annie," I called softly, helping to wipe away her tears, but she wouldn't listen.

"That was the first time I had a proper conversation with him and I'd have to be blind to miss the fact that he cares about you *so* much," she continued, shaking her head in anguish.

"Annie—"

"I can't protect you from Dad and then I ruin your relationship with the one man who actually cares for you," she beat herself up, eyes wide.

I shook my head. "I *chose* to help Nate, okay?" I accentuated firmly, hating that she felt that way. "And Beckham," I sighed, "well, he chose to believe what he did. That has *nothing* to do with you, you hear me?" She nodded, my words probably going in one ear and out the other. So I pulled her into a hug.

"I had a nightmare," I whispered, moving on from the subject.

Annie didn't even need me to explain. "*God*, what if they all start coming back? You've worked so hard to be rid of them."

Shrugging, I replied, "Maybe it was futile. I'll never be able to forget. Do you still think about the first time Dad hit you?"

She slumped. "Not all the time. But no matter how much time passes since I've last thought of it, it's still so vivid."

I'd heard this story before. Annie had been nine years old when our dad first raised his hand to her. On one of the rare occasions that our dad had visited whilst he and our mom were separated, Annie had gotten in trouble for referring to Uncle Robbie as her dad. From what she'd told me, I didn't blame her.

Seven years. He'd needed *seven years* before deciding his daughters were worth his time. *All* of his time and not just random visits when he'd felt like it.

Anybody was better than Matthew Taylor and my heart ached for a young Annie who attempted to seek fatherly love from somebody else. It wasn't a wonder why he wouldn't permit her to talk about Uncle Robbie.

"We're gonna get away from him," I declared, leaving no room for doubts.

"I know that," she smiled sadly. "I just wished it didn't come at the expense of losing others along the way."

Uncle Robbie dying. Our Aunt Indigo dying. Our grandma disappearing. And our mom running off. All of them had once been balms that soothed the sting of being the daughter of Matthew Taylor.

But it was our turn to leave him now; a possibility he probably didn't acknowledge. I acknowledged it though. It had been a possibility since the moment he'd slid that ring onto my mom's finger. A way out. I'd already been thinking of ways out—whether I'd realised it or not.

And that opening was fast approaching.

The white jumpsuit I was wearing didn't have a blemish on it and that was an accomplishment considering we were in the middle of a food fight. The event was halfway through and already a massive smash. I hadn't expected so many people to show up, but we were raising tons of funds. The first part of the event had been a dinner followed by an hour break to wander the gardens whilst the boys and I removed the tables and brought out the forts, setting up for the food fight.

I dipped just as an expired cake went soaring over my head. The desert ended up hitting Sebastian smack dab in the face. He had a green ribbon around his wrist, implying his position on the green team. Their members were being knocked out fast. My ribbon was red. I sped off before someone had the chance to take me out.

Annie rushed past me, red ribbon around her head as she dashed forward, pie in her hands. Beth turned around and the pie descended on her face. Annie was snickering. It was good to see her beaming after the conversation we'd had this morning. She was concerned about me, and rightfully so. But I'd promised her I'd be okay. We had to focus on our big plan, getting out of my dad's clutches.

Beckham was right when he'd said I had to have a good reason. If we were to report my dad, Poppy and Indigo would get taken away from us. We had no other family besides our grandma and mom. Annie didn't have a solid job and her salary wasn't enough to cover two kids. I was still in school and I didn't have a job. Our girls would be placed in a home and there was no guarantee that they wouldn't get adopted.

Poppy and Indigo had *bawled* when Annie and I weighed the pros and cons of them being taken. So we endured the pain a little while longer. After my internship ended, we'd have over enough money to break free from my dad and get a restraining order against him.

I was snapped back into reality when Annie shouted, "Duck!" A glob of jelly sailed over my head and I saw a guest rushing away, a blue ribbon around their ankle.

I giggled, following Annie as we zigzagged through the hallways, ducking behind the shields that the boys had created out of old desks. Jonas, a defenceman from the second line, sped past us and we dropped, muffling our laughter. It was a weird feeling, having this much fun.

My heart ached at the fact that Annie and I had never had this. We hadn't had these wholesome games and laughter when we were younger. Growing up, we'd constantly been terrified, unsure if our laughter would cause our dad to have an episode. I wished we'd had that, had the chance to be kids. But we'd try to give Poppy and Indigo that. They didn't deserve to grow up as fast as we had.

Abruptly, a pie descended from the top, landing on Annie's head. She groaned, apprehending she was out and had no choice but to head to the foyer. Nailea had been one of the first people to be caught because she'd accidentally dropped soda on herself. One flutter of her long lashes had persuaded half the hockey team to give her a second chance and stay in the game.

But Sebastian was having none of it and had demanded

that she stay out of the rest of the game, regardless of whether the soda stain was an accident or not.

I sprinted away from Annie, not wanting to be jumped by whoever had gotten her. A mouldy cheesecake narrowly missed my face as I ran, thrown by Wesley, the right-winger from the third line. I flipped him the bird and rounded the corner, hearing his deep chuckles. I found a tray of old pies stored under a desk and grabbed one. When Jasper flew past my hiding spot, I launched the pie, watching as it missed him and I swore.

My eyes widened when I saw he had a milkshake in his hand. He smirked, adjusting his route and heading for me. I squealed through laughter as he pursued me. He was faster, but I spun around obstacles and hallways.

"Come on!" I hollered, eluding him. "I helped you make Stefan jealous!" It was low of me but I didn't care. I wanted to win. "You owe me," I continued with a small pout, only making him laugh harder.

Jasper countered with, "And I helped you make Beck jealous. We owe each other nothing." He cackled evilly and my jaw dropped. There'd been no intentions of making Beckham jealous. *Maybe.*

Just as Jasper was about to hurl the content of the cup at me, a rotten banana splattered against his face. We both froze, shifting to see Nailea standing there with a banana peel in her hands.

I burst out laughing as Jasper barked, "That's cheating, Nai. You're out!"

She dropped the peel and crossed her arms over the white

playsuit she wore. "Nailea Rubio doesn't play by no rules, motherfucker!"

Somebody had definitely spiked the punch because she was clearly wasted. Jasper groaned and stomped off. I thanked Nailea and was about to run off when an angry voice rang out.

"Rubio!" Sebastian bellowed furiously, a blue bandana around his head as he stalked towards us. "Your ass is supposed to be on that fucking bench because you're *out*."

There was a large pink stain on his white shirt that looked a lot like a strawberry smoothie. When he stopped next to us, I got a whiff of said strawberries. *Fresh* strawberries.

Nailea's forehead creased as she swayed drunkenly. "My *ass* has nothing to do with you, Halo."

I jerked when I thought somebody had snuck up on me and glanced around quickly.

"It's *Hayes* and you know it, you little—"

"I don't like you," she stated with a pout.

Before Sebastian could yell at her, I interjected, "Aren't you supposed to smell like sour yoghurt?" The foods used during the fight were most definitely *not* fresh.

Sebastian only grew angrier. "That's because this troublemaker over here," Nailea waved at me with an adorable grin, "drove to the fucking store after I said she was out, bought a strawberry smoothie, drove all the way back, *searched* for me during the game and fucking *threw* the smoothie at me."

I felt a laugh crawl up my throat. Sebastian looked pissed as hell but Nailea was smiling as she said, "It was an accident."

I hid behind Sebastian's tall frame just as somebody ran past. "Accident my fucking ass," he riposted, muscles clenched.

Nailea smiled. "You have a thing for asses, don't you?"

Sebastian growled, his glass-like eyes narrowing. "If you wanted revenge, you've gotten it, Rubio. But you can't fucking interfere with the game. Bench. *Now.*"

I watched the two, finding the entire thing hilarious. Sebastian stood at a whopping height of six feet and five inches whereas Nailea was only five feet tall. Her thick eyebrows were literally in line with his nipples. But she glared back as if her height rivalled his.

"Who the hell is Rubio?" Nailea questioned. "I have no idea who that is." I snorted. "My name's Susan and I don't know who you are."

The giant of a blonde swore. "I swear to fuck I'm gonna drag you by the—"

"Is it because I'm Spanish?" Nailea inquired innocently, fluttering her lashes.

"I thought your name was Susan?" I asked with a grin, seeing as Sebastian was on the verge of a meltdown.

Nailea blinked at me. "Who the hell is Susan?"

Sebastian let out a string of curses and tipped forward, his arm wrapping around Nailea's small waist. She produced a mousy squeak as he effortlessly tossed her over his shoulder. I watched her squirm, fighting to get out of his hold.

"Stay still unless you want my handprint on your ass, Rubio," Sebastian grumbled.

Nailea stayed still.

I was still smirking as they disappeared. Over the intercom, I could hear Jai's voice as he named everybody who was out. Each time someone entered the foyer, he would call out their name before marking it off the list and stating how many members of each team were left.

There was one blue person, one red person and one green person.

I needed to be cautious. Just as I turned another corner, I slammed into a chest. When I pulled back, I saw it was Beckham and silently cursed. He was wearing black jeans and a white shirt—the same as Sebastian. Just as he had predicted, we'd gone back to being normal, as if nothing had changed.

He smirked at me, a peeled rotten banana in his hand, probably planning on crushing it against my face. There was a blue ribbon around his wrist.

"Beck," I nodded, smiling and eying the banana. He said nothing, stepping closer. "It doesn't have to end like this." He squinted and I nearly snorted. "You don't have to do this."

He shrugged. "I dunno, kinda like the idea of winning, Tink." Of all people to be left in the fucking game. He lifted his hand to smash the banana against me but wavered.

And there it was, the true reason it would never be completely normal between us. Because he was afraid of scaring or hurting me. No matter how hard he tried, he wouldn't be able to do it.

"Do it," I told him, staring him in the eye, trying to taunt him and distract him. Perhaps I could get the banana from him and turn the tables. "Here's your chance to win at something. Unless you're a pussy." He swore and I lifted a brow, shuddering at the deep curse. "I know being an idiot is a personality trait, but for once, don't be an idiot. Please—"

A banana being crushed against my face cut me off. My

stomach twisted with revulsion. I *hated* bananas. And now a rotten one was all over my fucking face. I wiped away the mush that was covering my eyes as Beckham grinned down at me, rubbing more banana on my neck.

"Sorry, but I like the sound of winning a lot more than the sound of you begging, baby."

"I wasn't *begging*," I groaned, trying to clean my face. "And just for that—" I gripped his arms and spun him around.

And then a pie slapped Beckham's face.

The tinfoil plopped to the ground and I could barely see Beckham's face through all the cream. He tried to wipe it away but only worsened it. I helped by rubbing cream all over his neck, chest and jeans.

I located Benson standing with a green ribbon around his head, grinning at the fact that he took Beckham out.

"I like the sound of you losing more than I like the sound of me winning. *Baby*." With a triumphant Benson next to me, I sauntered back to the foyer.

And as usual, I could feel Beckham's eyes on me.

Chapter 14

Beckham

"Teenagers are fucking scary," Sebastian grumbled to me, watching as a group of teenage girls scampered past, tittering and waving at us. Each girl was ornamented in USC merchandise and I discerned Grayson's last name on one of their t-shirts. Three of them wore mine and two wore Sebastian's. A student had started a small business selling merchandise to support the different USC sports divisions. The weirdest thing I'd seen so far was a bikini with Sebastian's face on the ass. But at least the little store was making money.

I took another puff of my cigarette, casting the girls a glower in hopes that they'd leave. The match against UCLA wasn't due to start for another six hours. But there were always early birds, those that wanted to watch us during our last practice. Instead of scampering away, the girls leaned against the wall a few feet away from us. Sebastian scowled and I groaned, disposing of my cigarette before heading for the rink.

Benson was on the ice with Levi and Aiden, the wingers

on the second team, running through some last-minute things seeing as they would substitute for Sebastian and Jai at some point through the game. Nyx stood to the side, yelling something at a noncooperative and moody Levi. She was dressed in black tights with a matching sports bra and an oversized grey jacket.

"You're not keeping up with Aidan!" she howled, marching along the outside of the rink, blue eyes never leaving Levi, much to his obvious displeasure. "Keep up!" At her voice, Levi blundered slightly and sent the puck flying. He whirled on his skates, glowering at the blonde. "What?" she snapped. "Got a problem?"

He skated closer and I tensed, noticing Sebastian stiffen beside me. Levi had anger issues and I didn't like the thought of him taking that rage out on Nyx.

"*You're* my fucking problem!" he bellowed, jabbing a finger at her and Benson sighed, calling Danny and Jonas onto the ice, the defencemen from the second team. Like Levi and Aidan, they needed to be prepared for when they had to substitute for Oliver and Jasper.

Nyx didn't bat an eye. "*No*. Your problem is that you skate like you've got an anchor chained to your balls." Levi bristled at her words, but she wasn't done. "If you keep skating like that, you're gonna drag Aiden behind. I've seen you play before, you used to be better. Explain to me why Aiden's improving, but you're slacking?"

She definitely wasn't beating around the bush. This had been a dilemma with Levi since last year. When Nate had been captain, he played favourites. He had favoured Levi over Aiden and constantly hounded the latter to practice until his legs felt like they were going to fall off. Thus, Levi became lazy because he sat on his ass all the time whilst Aiden improved.

I'd been planning on having a chat with Levi but had no idea how to admonish him without bringing up Nate. It was a tough subject for all of us. But Nyx just solved that problem. And like many other men, Levi didn't take too kindly to being reprimanded by a woman.

"I don't have to explain shit to you," he hissed, becoming frustrated. "You're not my fucking coach so back the fuck off."

Her nose wrinkled. "I know I'm not your coach, dumbass. But I don't have to be your coach to see that you've got the ego of a king who thinks he can do no wrong."

"That's ironic coming from Nate's slut," Levi retorted and I felt my fists clench; the urge to beat the fuck out of him taking over.

But Nyx didn't let him ruffle her. "Even more ironic coming from Nate's little bitch." Levi's glare hardened. "Seems I wasn't the only one kissing ass to stay on his good side." A slow smile took form on her lips. "Yes, I know all about the favouritism and the effects it's had on you—"

"You know nothing—"

"You're *lazy*," she enunciated slowly as if she was speaking to a child. "It's like you expect Aidan to carry all the weight, but that's not how it works. Work *together*." Without looking away from him, she commanded, "Sebastian! Jai! On the ice!" The blonde next to me wore a curious expression but moved to put on his skates, nonetheless. Jai obeyed, grabbing his hockey stick and stationing himself next to Sebastian. "Oliver and Jasper, go defend Gray," she pointed to the goalie. "You two," she pointed at Sebastian and Jai, "try to get the puck past them."

Piqued, I watched everything unfold. Like two beings that shared one brain, Sebastian and Jai steadily worked together, passing the puck to each other as they skated circles around the defencemen that tried to hinder them. Sebastian knocked the puck towards Jai and the latter blasted it forward. It skidded right past Oliver and Jasper before being caught in Grayson's hand; effortlessly.

And that was why he was our goalie.

Our team clapped, but Levi wasn't dazzled. He turned to Nyx with a jaded look. "They didn't even score."

She raised a brow. "Are you deaf?" He grimaced. "I didn't tell them to score. I said to get the puck past the defencemen. And they did. They worked *together*, not separately. Learn to do so before you're replaced." Levi's fists clenched at the apparent threat. "And before you come at me for not being a coach, those are Benson's words, not mine."

"What?" Levi looked to Benson for confirmation and received a grimace paired with a slight nod.

"He was waiting until you pissed us off before he spoke to you. Unfortunately, I have a lower tolerance for hormonal men than he does so you've gotten your reprimand early." Nyx stared at him, no unnecessary emotion in her character.

Benson sighed. "Why did I even hope that you'd soften the blow?" Nyx smiled at him. "Soothing voice of a woman, my ass."

Levi didn't get to add his two cents because Nyx's phone

rang. Benson skated towards Sebastian and Jai, clapping them both on the back. Aiden stood woodenly, watching his partner, Levi, scowl at Nyx as she spoke on the phone.

I scanned her for any injuries. She appeared fine, but that didn't ease my nerves. Nyx didn't seem too upset with my new knowledge of her home life, but that could change in a heartbeat if I tried to intervene. I could tell she was trying to deviate things back to how they were before. But I wouldn't allow that.

No matter how hard I tried, I couldn't forget how she'd been whimpering during her nightmare. Her features had been scrunched in horror and she'd ben pleading underneath her breath. I'd had no choice but to wake her. Having her quarrel with me was better than watching her be in distress. A lot of things made sense now, why she didn't speak about her family, why she never spoke about herself, even when I was on the verge of asking her to be my girlfriend.

Yes; I would've asked her.

"*Fuck him*," Nyx seethed and I was snapped back to reality. Her face was crimsoned with anger as she conversed with the person on the other end of the call. "They're having a great weekend with Julie. Why do you have to pick them up, Annie?" She nodded as her sister articulated. "What the fuck does he mean he doesn't *trust* Georgia with his daughters?" Nyx pinched the bridge of her nose. "As if he even cares. The girls are gonna be heartbroken that he cut their weekend short. Keep them with you, take them to the park or something. Dad can choke on his dick for all I care."

Dad.

I stood straighter at the allusion to the man in her life. It *had* to be him hurting them. It was the only male who had access to all the Taylor girls.

A dad that hurt his kids.

My blood churned inside my veins. A dad was supposed to protect his kids. I warned myself to calm down in case I was jumping to conclusions. She could've had uncles, an older brother I didn't know about. I'd only agitate her if I came to my own conclusions.

After another few seconds, Nyx hung up and swung around, finding Levi observing her. I didn't even notice him paying attention to her, too caught up in my thoughts.

Wearing an entertained smirk, he urged, "Daddy issues?" She didn't respond, gaze narrowing. "No wonder you're such a bitter bitch."

If it was possible, her face became even redder. She didn't bother to respond to him, storming away. Levi chortled before skating back to the centre of the rink where Aiden was waiting with a disapproving frown. Benson caught my eye and tilted his head, gesturing for me to go check on Nyx. I was going to anyway. I nodded, following the path she took.

On the way, I passed the group of teenage girls. They were gallivanting around, praising the team pictures. Disregarding them, I opened Benson's office, knowing that this was a safe haven for Nyx, a place where she could unwind away from us. Benson didn't allow the team here unless he invited us.

"Go away, Beckham," she snapped, gazing out the window. Her arms were crossed and shoulders stiff. The jacket she previously wore was flung onto the couch and judging by her red-tinged skin, she was getting hot.

I closed the door behind me and sauntered towards her. It was evident she was unsettled about more than just Levi. The phone call from Annie visibly perturbed her. Stiffly, I cleared my throat.

"Wanna talk about it?" She whirled around to face me, thoroughly confounded and I had to refrain from laughing. Catching her off-guard was my new favourite thing. "I can't help with whatever's going on at home, but I'm Levi's captain. Let me help with this."

Nyx gazed at me for a few seconds and I took a seat on Benson's desk, grinning at all of his notes. The team was getting somewhere, thanks to the girl in front of me.

"Daddy issues," she muttered with a scoff and shook her head. "I hate what it means."

"Do you though?" I questioned, attempting to alleviate the mood with a little teasing. If she wanted things to be normal between us, I'd *try*. "Have daddy issues, that is."

Her eyes bore into my soul as she spoke. "*I* don't have any issues. My dad is the one with issues." She ran a hand over her face, stepping closer.

And her dad was my central suspect once again. No matter how much she tried to hide it, despondency trickled from every word. My temper was back and I forced it down, not wanting to go into a fit of ferocity. It was the wrong time.

"Levi's an idiot." An idiot that I was going to deal with very soon. His ass was benched at the next game. It had been coming for a long time, his attitude only pissing off his fellow teammates.

Nyx nodded, agreeing with me. "I don't care, honestly. I stopped caring a long time ago. I'm just tired of dealing with idiots like Levi. When Benson first got the boys off my case, I told him that he shouldn't interfere when they proceeded to disrespect me. I wanted to deal with it myself in case they thought I was cowering behind Benson, but I know that he secretly reprimands them."

"He just wants to help," I proposed, acknowledging that Benson truly cared about her. But I also knew that Nyx didn't enjoy accepting help.

"Even when they try to help, they go about it all wrong," Nyx huffed. "I overheard him once, telling you all to respect me because I just as easily could've been your sister or daughter or mother and they wouldn't like it if I was disrespected." She took another few steps closer to me. "I *deserve* respect, *not* because I'm a woman. Because I'm a human being. Benson should reinforce that." She stopped between my spread legs and I sat straighter.

I planted my hands on her hips, tugging her to me and she heaved a brow. I smiled. "On behalf of all men that's ever underestimated you, I'm sorry."

She pinched my nose. "You're one of them, asshole."

"Okay, I'll admit. I wasn't the nicest person to you." She scowled and I chuckled before pulling her even closer. "But—"

The door opened and Grayson poked his head inside. He eyed our proximity before stating, "Benson wants everyone on the ice."

Nyx smiled at him and stepped away from me. It was a good thing because I had no idea how the rest of my sentence was going to play out. But what? What had evolved? I still held some animosity towards her for what had happened with Nate, but I was finding it difficult to hold on to that anger when I knew she'd never truly hated me.

I don't think I ever hated you.

That seemed to be the only thing I could cling to. With one last look at her, I followed Grayson back to the rink.

I could feel the sweat dripping down my back, the cheers of the crowd nearly deafening me. The mouthguard was beginning to feel uncomfortable because of how long I'd had it in. We were in the last few minutes of the third period of the match with the Bruins having scored two goals and us Trojans four. The sound of skates on ice eased the tension building in my body. All around me were players decked in their school colours. Every time I blinked there was a flash of red and gold that the Trojans wore. Scattered in between were the signature blue and gold colours of the Bruins.

Sebastian was skating towards me, easily guiding the puck as two Bruin defencemen readied themselves for the approach. He shot it to me just as I was ringed by opposing players. I tried to skate around them as they fought for the puck and I managed to shoot it towards Jai. The right-winger caught it effortlessly—only to be rammed into the plexiglass like a spoonful of jelly. By the time he pushed to his feet, the puck was already with a Bruin defenceman who passed it to their centreman. The latter skated with the intention of scoring, teammates flanking him in defence.

Knowing what was about to happen, I prepared myself. Just as the centreman hit the puck to their left-winger, it was intercepted by Oliver; our right defenceman. The redhead immediately hit the puck to an awaiting Jai who skirted around the players that tried to block him. Finding his chance, he shot it to me. I caught it with my stick, my heart in my throat as I skated towards the net. The defencemen tried to tackle it from me but I feigned a hit to Sebastian before taking my shot. I watched the puck barely slide past the goalie's stick.

Then the buzzer went.

Next thing I knew, I was being tackled by my teammates, my vision distorted by a sea of red and gold. Screams erupted from all over as the final minute ticked by.

"Trojans! Trojans! Trojans! Fight on!" It was a repetitive chant that carried through the rink, one that my team joined in on as we huddled together. Grayson was slapping me on the back, his hockey stick held up in victory. He'd done a great job, blocking four out of six of the Bruins' attempted goals.

The UCLA team congratulated us before skating off the ice, their heads held high as they thanked their supporters. Benson was celebrating with other faculty members, his expression filled with a mixture of disbelief and pride. My eyes drifted to the front row, seeing Nyx cheering alongside Nailea. The two were shaking each other wildly, thrilled with our first win. I could see my teammates saluting each other and I felt exactly what this win meant. It was our first win after so long. Our first win since Nate and our first win without him. The cheers continued all the way to the locker room; the boys still completely euphoric because of the atmosphere.

"Well done, team!" I whooped with a grin, seeing Oliver and Jai excitedly pushing each other around. Jasper began banging on his locker just as Benson entered.

He looked at us, seemingly at a loss for words. He ended up saying, "Bring it in, boys." We practically tackled him, each one howling something different. Benson basked in the attention and I chuckled, muttering that he could attend our party if he wanted.

Once we were all dressed, there were still many supporters around that congratulated us on the win. By the time we arrived back at my place, the party was already in full swing. The walls of the house were vibrating with the intensity of the music.

The guys had obtained an entire DJ booth and Aiden was currently managing it, taking advantage of his position and making the music as loud as possible. Streamers were everywhere, a disco ball hung from the ceiling and strobe lights were blinding me. It looked nothing like my living room. Even though it was a last-minute party, almost everybody was present.

It seemed Benson had taken me up on the invitation because he was at the party, in the kitchen and cramming his face with food. He deserved to celebrate with us. It was thanks to him and Nyx that we were doing better. After Coach Ford had left, I'd thought we were done for. I was a new captain, Ford was gone and Nate had left our team a jumble.

But then came Benson, which wasn't much, but paired with Nyx—they were a power duo despite being oil and water.

"Beckham!" A light voice called and I spun around, eyes

landing on a smiling Beth.

She looked happier these days, a fact that I had to acknowledge considering who her mother was. Although we were frequently around each other, I was yet to talk to her since seeing her at the club that fateful night. And honestly, I wanted her to come to me. It would feel wrong to make the first move and ask how things were going with her mom after mine had told me what she'd done.

"Hey, Beth," I greeted when she flung herself at me with a hug. Noting that she was very much drunk, I squeezed her shoulders affectionately before allowing her to step back. "How've you been?"

She beamed, blinking rapidly and I chuckled. "*Great*, actually. I'm loving working at the café *and* I've made some new friends. Did you know Nyx has a sister named Annie?" She pulled a face at her own words, momentarily forgetting I was there the day she'd found out. "Yeah, I was surprised too. But Annie's cool."

I was smiling at her rambling, thinking of the way Annie had blushed when speaking to Beth. "That's great—"

"Is she here tonight?" Beth cut me off, eagerly peering around the crowd and making her inebriated state clear with her wobbling. "I only saw Nyx—holy shit, did you see the bikini she's wearing? To *die* for." Whether she was talking about Nyx or the bikini, I didn't know. But I was amused, nonetheless. "She's kinda cool, I guess. Annie talks very highly of her." I only nodded. "Did you know both Annie and I have the name Beth in our full names? Weird right? Oh my *God*, this is my song!"

Before I could respond, she was already sprinting away when Aiden changed the song to something she apparently liked. Watching her disappear, I couldn't help but feel happy for her. She was swaying on the dancefloor, encouraging the people around her to join in. Nailea was amongst the group, easily being pulled into the circle.

Once I was sure Beth would be okay, I left through the backdoor, discovering tons of people splattering around in the pool. With it being winter, our heated pool came in handy. Fairy lights were strung up all over the backyard and a bonfire was glowing, my team lounging around the fire. Oliver was warming himself, dripping wet from being flung into the pool by Jai. There was a makeshift rope around that area of the yard and I chuckled at my team's attempt at making a VIP area. But it was serving, because nobody dared cross that line, appreciating that they were invited in the first place.

The wind stroked my bare chest as I wandered towards them. They hollered like idiots when I approached and I thumped down next to Jai, taking the cigarette that he passed me.

"An impressive start, boys!" Oliver yelled, turning his ass towards the fire.

"Let's hope we keep it going like this," Jasper chimed in, leaning back on the cushioned bench. "And move away before your ass catches fire." Oliver scowled at him but moved away from the fire when Sebastian pretended to lurch and push him. "Cheers to us, motherfuckers!"

Those that had bottles of beer in their hands raised them whereas Jai and I raised our cigarettes. I took a deep puff, letting the smoke supply my lungs before releasing it.

"Why'd you invite everyone if we're going to sit all the way over here?" Grayson sought, sipping on his drink as he watched the party-goers.

Jai smirked, waving at a group of girls that were splashing in the pool. "Because we need people to cheer for us. Besides, we're the main characters."

"Keep dreaming," Nyx scoffed, approaching us in nothing but a thin black bikini. *Beth was right*, that was all I could think. Her hair was tied up in a knot at the top of her head and she kicked legs out of the way to get to Jasper where she dropped into his arms. She tripped slightly, making her intoxication known. "Everybody knows I'm the main character."

I took another puff of my cigarette, gazing at her. She'd known what she was doing when she'd put on that bikini. The bottoms were barely there and one wrong move would expose her breast. But the minx still hopped around as if she was wearing a fucking hazmat suit.

Jai leered at her swimsuit before saying, "You're a *hazard*, that's what you are." I hummed in agreement. Jasper pressed an obnoxious kiss to the side of her head. I must've been scowling because Sebastian nudged me. I had a feeling Jasper was doing it on purpose.

"Can I just say," Nyx began, taking a swig of Jasper's drink, "that I'm thoroughly surprised that you boys won?" My team fell into a torrent of grievances and she elevated a hand, hushing them. "Only because it was the first game and I was doubtful of how ready you were. *But*," she grinned drunkenly, "I'm one proud mama."

Oliver coughed out a laugh. "If you're our mama, does that make Benson our papa?"

She shrugged. "Depends on how big his dick is." Oliver gagged and she giggled maniacally. I smiled at the sight. "But it's obvious who the real papa is."

Jasper held her closer. "It's me, right?"

Snubbing them, I inhaled more vapour, closing my eyes as I let the sensation take place. When I opened my eyes, Nyx was in front of me, an ominous smirk on her face. Nothing good could come from that inebriated shimmer in her eyes. She thudded onto my lap, pressing her lips to mine. The guys exploded into cheers and I froze as she sheathed her arms around my neck, dragging me closer to her. She slipped her tongue into my mouth and I had no choice but to exhale the smoke I was withholding.

Nyx pulled away with a triumphant grin, blowing the smoke towards a gaping Jai.

I stared at the minx on my lap, unable to come to terms with what just happened. Drunk. She was quite certainly wasted. After a few seconds, I installed my cigarette between my lips again. Not even a heartbeat later, it was seized from my mouth and between Nyx's lips. She slanted back against my chest, smoking happily. I groaned, encompassing an arm around her waist.

"I'm confident in our abilities," I articulated after clearing my throat and Jasper laughed. Many of the guys seemed to be enjoying my predicament. "This is only the start of an amazing year, trust me. If we keep working like this, we can win every game. Of course, points don't come from wins alone."

I peeped down at the girl in my arms and she puffed smoke into my face. When I didn't react, she grinned stupidly. I had to bite my tongue to stop myself from smiling in return.

"No sir, they don't," Nyx provided. "Which is why you have me. You see, this plan has *always* made sense. But you all couldn't stand the fact that a girl would help you. Now look, y'all won the match and our first fundraiser was a success. Say thank you, Nyx."

Oliver winked at her. "Thank you, mama."

"My pleasure, son," she bowed her head. Jai stood up when he saw some girls waving him over. Wearing a cocksure smirk, he dashed towards the large pool and plunged in. Sebastian soon followed his teammate and Oliver trailed them as well.

"Hey, isn't that Stefan?" Nyx inquired absentmindedly, pointing towards the backdoor.

It was Stefan; his blue hair was hardly discreet. He examined the area, looking for Jasper. The latter perked up. "He actually came?"

A snort escaped Nyx as she mumbled into my neck. "If the night goes well, they'll both be coming." I couldn't stop my smile.

Jasper frowned at her and stood up, grabbing the attention of Stefan. The two gazed at one another like lovesick doves. I had to throw a water bottle at Jasper to get him to move. He faltered slightly and then he was prowling towards Stefan.

"Go bestie!" Nyx hollered and Jasper blew her a kiss. I shook my head.

"How come Annie's not here?" Grayson caught my attention and I glanced at him. I forgot he was there, seeing as he was so still.

Nyx breathed more smoke. "Babysitting. She insisted I celebrate with you guys or else I would've been with her."

Grayson nodded. "You know, Indie was really bummed that she couldn't watch the game. A phone call from you could do the trick."

Nyx honest to God *sang* Annie's phone number and Grayson grappled to save it to his phone. Once he had it, he thanked her and hastened towards the house, looking for a tranquil place. That would be difficult.

The way Aiden was playing music, the roof would soon cave in. And then it was just the two of us in the supposed VIP area. Nyx moved in my lap, kneeing my dick and I bit back a profanity.

She was grinning like an idiot, showcasing those dimples of hers. "How do you make a pool table laugh?"

Pulling a face, I asked, "*What*?" I'd never seen her this intoxicated before. Part of me believed this to be dangerous. Sober Nyx would stab you if you pissed her off.

Drunk Nyx would straight-up murder you.

Nyx giggled, nearly suffocating from her laughter. "You tickle its balls!" I wasn't laughing at the joke, I was laughing at her. She was practically crying, her face almost crimson. "What do you get when you jingle Santa's balls?" She could barely get the words out. "A white Christmas!"

"You're disgusting," I whispered, still smiling. Drunk Nyx wasn't as shielded as sober Nyx. It was refreshing; like I received VIP access to her personality. I'd missed it, having her in my arms and so carefree. "Where did you hear all of these?"

I wiped a tear from her cheek as she responded, "I used to waitress back in high school. You'd be surprised at the shit people come up with. Here's another one. What kind of bees produce milk?" She gave the cigarette to me before cupping her boobs. "*Boo-bees.*"

Deciding to humour her, I took a puff of smoke and replied, "Suddenly, I'm no longer lactose intolerant." She practically howled with laughter and I grinned, taking delight in her smile.

"You know," she said, sitting straighter so she could wrap her arms around my neck. Her eyes inspected my features before she smiled drunkenly. "I've always found you *very* attractive." A laugh followed her words and she shook her head. "But your ugly makes you actions." She paused, frowning. *"Huh?"*

I chuckled, flicking her nose. "Somebody had a little too much to drink."

Nyx shifted again, chaotically moving her other leg around me so that she was straddling my lap. I raised an inquisitive brow, but she wasn't fazed, a concentrated look pasted onto her features. I took another puff of the cigarette as she interlaced her fingers at my nape.

"Annie told me that you care about me," she blurted, eyes wide with wonder.

My spine straightened in suspense. "Did she now?" I tossed a question against her own, not wanting to talk myself into a predicament.

Annie and I hadn't talked long. Our conversation had mainly consisted of our worries about Nyx. I supposed it was weird for her to witness me stressing about the very girl whose guts I supposedly hated. And it had been my first proper fucking conversation with her.

Nyx nodded. "And I thought about it. But, if you cared, you would've stayed, you know." I stared at her, at the look she was wearing. She laughed suddenly. "Of course, I'm not angry about that anymore. Maybe it was the right thing. I hurt Annie and maybe I deserved the hurt in return—"

"What are you talking about?" I interrupted her inebriated ramblings, knowing she wouldn't be speaking about her feelings if she wasn't intoxicated. If Nyx wanted to discuss what had happened between us, it was best to do it sober because I wanted her to remember what we spoke about.

But she didn't stop, looking too concentrated. "We could've been friends." Her eyes met mine. "That would've been cool, right? We got along and I really liked you." My attention focused on her use of the past tense. "We didn't work out, so what? I got over it." *Fucking ouch.* "But you still hate me." She frowned. "So I pretend to hate you in return even though you just annoy me. And that's for the best, right?"

I didn't know how to respond to that, so I focused on something else she said. "I wouldn't be able to be your friend, Nyx."

Her smile was wistful. "I know." It was silent between us whilst we passed the cigarette around. After about ten minutes, she yawned. "Is it nap time yet?" It was currently 10 pm but she'd been on her feet all day so I knew she was exhausted. The buzz was beginning to wear off. "I'm gonna go nap," she mumbled tiredly.

"My room," I told her and she nodded, climbing off my

lap and stumbling away. I shamelessly watched her walk away and found many other guys watching. When they caught my eye, they hurriedly looked away. I tossed away the last of the cigarette just as Grayson approached, looking perplexed. "What?"

He sat down next to me. "She wants to speak to you." He handed me the phone and I frowned, wondering why Indigo would want to speak to me. As far as I knew, she despised both me and Sebastian.

I took the phone. "What?"

"Beckham." It was Annie's voice that welcomed me. "I was so worried. Nyxie hasn't been answering her phone—"

"She probably left it inside. And she went to take a nap now," I cut her off. "She's fine, don't worry." I could hear how badly she was freaking out.

Annie didn't drop the hysterical pitch in her voice. "She can't come home tonight." I tried to interrupt but she rambled further. "Listen to me, Beckham. She *can't* come home, alright? Just trust me."

Overlooking Grayson, I stood up, following the path at the side of the house and moving to the sidewalk. Suddenly, I felt completely sober. "The person who's hurting you all, is he there right now? Your dad?" She stayed soundless. *"Annie."*

"Yes," she whimpered. "But he's in a good mood, got paid today and it needs to stay that way. Nyx can't come home at this time of the night, completely drunk. He'll lose his mind."

"Isn't he going to question where she is?"

"No, as far as he's concerned, Nyx is at her literature camp. One of our many excuses in case of situations like this," Annie returned. "I'll call her tomorrow and fill her in so she's up to speed."

I nodded, but then apprehended she couldn't see me. "Alright. Thanks for informing me."

It must've been challenging to relay such information to me; an outsider when it came to their family. Annie bid me goodnight before hanging up. I stared back at my raging house and decided I was done for tonight, returning Grayson's phone and treading up towards my room.

Nyx was sprawled out in my bed, wearing one of my shirts. When I shut the door, her eyes fluttered open. "I have fifteen missed calls and twenty text messages from Annie," she muttered. "Guess I'm camping out here, huh?"

For a second, I wondered how many times she had to stay away from her own home.

Gone was the spirited twinkle in her eyes. I didn't like that. "Why can't you hear bunnies having sex?" I asked and her brows met in thought. "Because they have cotton balls."

She snickered, turning her face into the pillow before laughing again. It was the last thing I heard as I entered the bathroom to take a shower, her laughter.

Chapter 15

Nyx

I adjusted the straps of my floral sundress as I stared at myself in the mirror. It was Tuesday and my first day back at classes. I'd taken yesterday off because I was hungover and also to do some damage control back home. By the time I had reached back at the house, my dad was long gone, thankfully. Annie wasn't fibbing when she'd said he was in a great mood. He hadn't yelled at any of them, hadn't raised a hand, and hadn't gotten upset with my vacancy. Annie, bless her heart, thought that he was getting better. But I wasn't the same. It was all very peculiar.

There was no way Matthew Taylor could just wake up one morning and decide to stop being a monster. I would sometimes wonder if he loved us, but that didn't stop him from hurting us. It was his way of controlling us. And if he was anything, he was a control freak. He wouldn't just let go of that in the blink of an eye. When Annie had picked me up from the guys' place, I was astonished to find her unhurt. The same went for my other sisters.

But I wasn't complaining, just suspicious.

The bathroom was empty, everyone probably having their lunch. I'd arrived late today since I'd attended a parent-teacher meeting with Annie in regards to Poppy. Like I knew she would, the blonde was at the top of her game, catching up on all the work she'd missed out on. Her teacher had been very dazzled, though she had a few personal questions she'd voiced once Poppy was told to go play with the other kids.

Things like Poppy's random bruises or how quiet she was, why she never raised her voice or why she never stood up for herself.

Annie had countered placidly that Poppy was very bashful and we were working on it. As for the bruises, volleyball practice easily covered that. Poppy was always diving for saves, banging into the ground. Her teacher was still a little sceptical but took our answers to heart. Like I'd expected, it hurt to lie about our situation.

It always did.

So far, I'd missed my sports event management class as well as my sociology of sport class. I couldn't ask Nailea for notes since she didn't share those classes with me but I knew my professors trusted me to get up to speed. I wasn't a top student just for shits and giggles, and they knew that.

I tipped over, tugging at the velvet material of my knee-high black platform boots. My dress was short in order to show off my pretty little boots. I only hoped I wouldn't run into Professor Coleman. The man made it his duty to concern himself with our outfits, trying to implement a dress code.

At fucking college.

Since it was my first day back after the whole club fiasco, I needed to make an impression. Reaching into my bag, I pulled out the blood-red lipstick, applying it sleekly. I checked the time and realised this was when Nailea usually made her way to the cafeteria for lunch.

Content with my appearance, I left the bathroom. Rumours must've spread about what had happened at the club because some students were watching me. I cast them smiles and held my head high. A stroke of air alerted me that Nailea materialised at my side. She didn't look at me and vice versa, facing forward and walking down the hallway, destination in mind.

"Those are your neck-stepping boots," Nailea reflected with a tiny smile, knowing exactly where we were headed. "Things are about to get *crazy*."

I grinned, turning a corner. We found Melissa in the cafeteria, her sister missing and Nailea notified me that she had an extra class that ran through lunch. That made things easier. I spotted some of the hockey boys at their own table; Oliver, Grayson and Jai missing. Jasper smirked at me and I winked. Beckham noticed my destination and sat straighter.

When Melissa noticed me advancing, she stood up, smiling in amusement. "Look who came back for more!" she exclaimed, crossing her arms over her chest. Her friends snickered and I rolled my eyes. Her vehement tone bagged the attention of almost all students in the cafeteria. Just like she wanted. "Missed you yesterday," she mused, still smiling. "Too scared to face me?"

That was the thing about violence. It made people think

they were suddenly superior and everyone was supposed to be frightened of them. As if I was scared of Melissa.

"Had a gynaecologist appointment," I told her, waving a flippant hand. "Quite the hassle that was. Your daddy got his dentures stuck in my pussy when he ate it Saturday night." Melissa's smile dropped and Nailea laughed loudly. "I'm in the mood to make you my stepdaughter. How do you feel about that, sweetheart?"

Her fists tightened, looking like they wanted a replay of what she'd done on Friday. "You've got a lot of nerve running your mouth like that when we all know what a coward you are." There were murmurs of assent and I tilted my head imperceptibly to see that we had quite the audience.

I beamed. "Is that any way to speak to your mama?" Melissa straight-up growled. My eyes gravitated to the long scab on her forehead, one she'd tried to cover with foundation. "Nai, baby, did you have fun picking Melissa's skin from underneath your acrylics."

Nailea scrunched her face up in a gorgeous smile. "*So much fun.*"

One of Melissa's friends, Pippa, spoke up in her defence. She was stunning, truly, the twin of Snow White with her pale skin and dark hair. If only her personality wasn't so repulsive. And she was smart too, sharing many of my writing classes plus—she wrote for the school magazine. Where I would write about the hockey team, she wrote about the drama students and their performances. I'd heard she wanted to write plays someday. In another life, we could've been friends.

I loved ambitious women.

She wore a thin brace on her right hand due to her carpal tunnel syndrome, a reminder that she spent too much time behind her laptop, typing.

"You couldn't even take Melissa on your own," Pippa interjected, glowering at me and then Nailea. "You had to let your rabid dog loose on her. That's a coward if I ever heard one—"

"Oh, shut up. Your name directly translates to hand job in Italian," I cut her off and she froze, mouth dropping open in shock. Lazily, I pointed to her right hand. "Repetitive motions or any wrist movements that are done continuously are usually the causes of carpal tunnel syndrome. Living up to your name I see." Nailea choked on the snort that she tried to restrain.

Google was my best friend when it came to pulling off today's plan. Lisa, the other friend, hauled Pippa back, seeing as she was on the brink of lurching for me. Melissa scowled when a few students snickered. "Once again, you're all bark but no bite."

Nailea glanced at the scab on Melissa's forehead. "Sorry about the mess I left behind. I was trying to find your other three eyes."

I nearly broke character and laughed but I tried my hardest to hold a straight face. Melissa, however, appeared to be losing her mind. She glimpsed towards Pippa and Lisa before looking back at Nailea. "What the fuck are you talking about?"

"Bees have five eyes," I supplied in a blasé tone and Melissa's jaw shuddered in exasperation. "Melissa means honeybee," I apprised her.

Provoked, she snapped, "That doesn't mean I'm a fucking

bee! What the fuck are you trying to—"

"My name is of Arabic origin and means amazing and strong," Nailea articulated over her with no trouble and I nearly peed myself. She was so good at this, I may just have to employ her in the future. "And just like Pippa, I live up to my name. Ain't that right, Nyxie?"

I poked her cheek. "One hundred per cent, baby."

Melissa's eyebrows were shivering and it looked like she was about to have a stroke. I noticed Beckham standing close by and he was grinning at me. He knew what I was doing since he'd been in Melissa's position infinite times. I was taunting her, fucking with her mind.

It was one of my best skills—to be an absolute pain in the ass.

Nailea recommenced speaking. "But you know who has the most interesting name here?" The question was rhetorical. "My girl Nyx. It's the name of the Greek goddess of the night.

I shrugged. "Or it can just mean night. Like night-night."

Melissa pulled a face. "Night-night?"

Grinning evilly, I moved closer. "That's right, darling. *Night-night*." Before she could even blink, I twisted my arm back and hurled a forceful punch to her nose. I felt something crack beneath my fist.

She plunged back onto the table as cheers and gasps broke out around us. I shook my now bruised hand and stepped back, smiling at Lisa and Pippa as they endeavoured to revive their queen bee. Literally. She was sprawled on top of the table, out cold.

"Violence is never the answer, kids!" I yelled at the

encompassing students. "But it can sometimes be a *very* good solution." Nailea flung an arm around my shoulders, laughing.

Lisa turned to me, infuriated. "You're gonna get in trouble for this."

I smiled. "No, I won't." Drifting closer, I murmured something to her. When I pulled back, she was pale. "Understand?" She nodded. "Inform your friend," I tilted my head in the direction of Pippa.

With that, I spun on my heel, leaving the cafeteria. Jasper made quite the commotion by bowing and shrieking my name. Sebastian just stared at Nailea, but I could tell his lips were quirked. At the doors, Nailea and I separated.

I needed to run my hand under cold water and Nailea was going to inform Maxine about what happened, warranting that there'd be no more upheavals from her twin. It was obvious Maxine was drained by her sister's antics.

Pushing through the bathroom doors, I grimaced when I noticed my split knuckles. "Fuck," I mumbled, finding my fingers already blistering. They stung even worse when the water hit them. The door opened again. "That was fast," I mumbled, thinking it was Nailea.

"What did you tell them?" Beckham demanded, going to take my fist in his hand. "To keep them silent?"

I winced when he wet a paper towel and dabbed at my wound. "Lisa has never once written her own essay for class. I doubt she's in the mood to get expelled." When I winced again, Beckham sent me an apologetic glimpse. "And Pippa sucked the drama assistant's dick so she could write the script for next month's play."

Impressed, Beckham nodded. "And how exactly do you know that?"

"I know things."

My response was vague on purpose, to irritate him. I hopped onto the counter whilst he disposed of the bloodied paper towel. He retrieved a fresh one, raising a brow at my position. Slowly, I spread my legs, ensuring my panties were covered.

He stepped between them and I smiled. "If you wanted to get between my legs, you could've just asked. You're always throwing yourself at me."

He rolled his eyes. "Says the girl who kissed me on Sunday." My lips sealed at his words. Never before in my life had I been too timid to address a subject. And it certainly wasn't my first time kissing someone or even kissing Beckham. I wasn't a virgin by any means, either. But Beckham could turn me into a fucking schoolgirl. "Are you *blushing*?"

He stopped his act of cleaning my hand to gawk at me and I felt my cheeks crimson further. They were traitors, my cheeks. Beckham seemed unimpressed by our kiss but I wasn't going to lie, it kept replaying in my mind. It was scarcely even a kiss since the idiot had sat like a cucumber. I didn't understand. It was the first time since we'd declared each other rivals. Surely, he would've felt *something*, right? A memory, at least.

I couldn't be the only one tormented by the flesh memories.

"Shut up," I mumbled, keeping my eyes on my hand. When he smirked at me, I scowled. "I hate you." He laughed in rejoinder, going back to cleaning my knuckles.

His movement was slower, tenderly clearing away the blood.

A drop of water trickled from the paper towel, settling on my uncovered thigh. It was something so trifling, but it made me shudder. The corner of Beckham's lips tilted up slightly. I was surprised steam wasn't emerging where the droplet had landed. Because my skin felt on fire.

After a while, he muttered, "You'll need some ointment." I nodded, waiting for him to step away. But he didn't. He studied my outfit, eyes lingering on the boots and he swallowed roughly. His voice was guttural when he stated, "You look gorgeous."

I didn't react. "Is this your way of trying to manipulate me?" I trusted my voice didn't divulge the mess that was occurring behind my ribcage. It had been so fucking long since Beckham Hunt had complimented me. I wanted to throw up in anxiety.

His eyes snapped to mine, the usual storm caught up in his irises. "Accept the fucking compliment." Unlikely. The guys I knew only complimented me when they wanted something.

"Accept the compliment," I purred. "And then what do I do after that? Die?"

Beckham's brows banged together. "What?" he grunted. "You're relentless, *Jesus*. It was just a compliment."

"And since when do you compliment me?" I investigated, overcoming a shiver when he planted his hands on either side of me on the counter. "I thought you wanted nothing to do with Nate's sloppy seconds—"

"Don't think I don't know what you're trying to do," he whispered, hauling me closer. My ass skidded on the counter until I was held against him. I settled my hands on his shoulders in an attempt to keep some distance. "You mention Nate to piss me off, so I'd leave."

I shrugged. "Then leave."

He chuckled darkly. "Nice try." I scowled. "You wanna know what I think? Nate is a defence mechanism for you, to get me away from you before you do something stupid—like kissing me. There's a fine line between love and hate, baby," he tantalised with a smirk.

"I'm gonna kill you."

"Cute." He palmed my nape and dragged me forward. "You kissed me. It's my turn." I could barely process his words before his lips were pressed against mine.

There was no aggression in my body, not like I'd expected. After every dispute between Beckham and me, I would feel my anger boil until I was sure my veins would explode. Whenever I saw him, I wanted nothing but to stab him in the fucking eye in annoyance. But as his arm bandaged around my waist and the other drifted to my hair—I dissolved in his arms, like a missing puzzle piece finally finding its way back to the fucking puzzle.

The girl that spent her days ridiculing men vanished into thin air. She was nowhere to be found as I sheathed my arms around Beckham's neck, trying to get closer even though there was no space between us. We were pressed completely against each other. I sucked eagerly at his bottom lip, hearing him groan against my mouth. His tongue probed at my lips, seeking admittance. It was like I was an entirely different person because I granted him access without a battle. Which was nothing like my usual self. And that was why being with Beckham scared me so much.

His hand possessively splayed itself on my bare thigh

before slowly trailing upwards. I yanked his hair and he growled, causing me to smile softly. I lifted my ass slightly so that he could bunch my dress at my waist. A squeal escaped me when he pulled the band of my underwear, letting it snap back against my skin.

"Look at that," he grumbled with a smirk, leaning away slightly to place kisses on my jaw. "Eight fucking months later and you're still my girl."

I let out a small moan when he sucked at the skin of my neck. "I'm not yours."

Annoyed that he was no longer paying attention to my lips, I lured him back. His hands were everywhere at once, leaving warmth in their wake. It felt entirely too stuffy in the bathroom. He nipped at my neck and I shuddered. A sound outside the door startled us both and we pulled away, glimpsing at the door. But there was no one there. When I looked back at Beckham, he was already staring at me.

His lips were red and inflated. Mine probably looked the same. Due to my tugging, his hair was pointing in all directions. I didn't look any better with my dress at my waist. We stared at one another as if we couldn't believe we'd just let that happen. I didn't know what was going on in his mind but I was internally berating myself for enjoying kissing him again. The first time, I could blame it on the alcohol.

Now what?

A singular touch from him seemed to set my skin ablaze. *Always*. I'd been with others after him and never had they been able to drag such a reaction from me. *I* controlled how the kiss went. Not with Beckham though. Never with him. And that shit scared me. The space in the bathroom was suddenly too small. It felt like I was suffocating. I hopped off the counter and Beckham hauled me to his chest.

"Hey," he said softly, tilting my chin to look up at him. He looked just as perplexed. The man had hated my guts for the past year and was suddenly ready to devour me in the bathroom. It was weird. For both of us. "Calm down."

Calm down? I'd just made out with my supposed rival, the guy who'd been an absolute dick towards me. And I fucking *enjoyed* it, *wanted more.* That was definitely not normal, especially with our past.

"I—"

"I know, baby," he cut in, glancing at my lips for a beat.

He'd kissed me to get back at me for what I'd done on Sunday. By his reaction, it was plain it hadn't been his intention to make out with me. I hadn't planned to fucking *melt* in his arms either. If I became too dependent on this asshole again, it was going to be a shitshow. He already knew what was going on in my family. Letting him closer than before only meant trouble.

Shaking my head, I stated, "I have an idea about the next fundraiser."

Beckham scowled. "Nyx—"

"A fashion show," I continued and he sighed, pinching the bridge of his nose. Unfortunately, he didn't poke a fight with me—which was what I *wanted.* I *wanted* him to get upset and yell like he usually did. I wanted things to go back to normal before everything complicated had happened. "The design students are all for the idea."

He blinked at me. "I'm listening." He still didn't look annoyed. It was like he became immune all of a sudden. *Fuck.*

"They'll design the clothes that people will model. At the end of the show, the attendees will get the opportunity to bid on the outfits. The money will go towards the designers and the money that's made from ticket sales will go towards feeding schemes."

I wasn't lying when I'd said I had an idea. That actually was my plan for the next fundraiser. I was just using it to throw him off too. Not that it was working, though.

"Sounds good," he responded, clearing his throat. I nodded, grabbing my bag from the counter. Before I could march away, he articulated again. "You know, you can't just forget that happened."

I crossed my arms, cringing at the burning sensation as my knuckles brushed against my arm. "And why's that?" I ridiculed.

Beckham took a predatory step forward, yanking me towards him and kissing me again. And just like before, unable to help myself, I melted. Like an eager child, I was on my toes, trying to get closer to him. No matter how much I told myself to step away, my body didn't want to. My desires steered me forward, taking control. His hand was underneath my dress, palming my ass and my hands were tugging fruitlessly at his shirt.

Suddenly, my feet were no longer on the ground, legs wrapped around his waist. I yanked at his hair as we kissed. It was him who drew away, eyes glimmering with desire.

"That's why," he murmured. I stayed silent, panting slightly and still trying to figure out how he pulled a reaction like that out of me. When I couldn't come to a conclusion, I panicked.

"I have to go," I mumbled and he let me down.

I didn't look back, slipping out of the bathroom. On the way to my next class, I passed a group of philosophy students handing out flyers for people to join their spiritual club where they probably spoke about the meaning of life or some shit.

One student danced in front of me and I froze, narrowly missing an elbow to the nose. "Join our club if you want all things good to come your way." I tried to shuffle around him but he was resolute, even when I claimed to be late for class. "With positive thoughts, you'll attract positive results!"

"No, thank you," I grinned and kept walking.

Beckham and I were over; and I was fine with that. I didn't need him back, not at all. The kiss only complicated our already complicated relationship. *Beckham left*, I had to remind myself, *and I drove him away*. What I felt for him may have been vague anger and disappointment disguised as hatred, but he very much hated me.

The philosophy student forced himself in front of me again, swinging the flyer. "Like attracts like. It can be thoughts or even people. At our next meeting, we go into depth about this topic. You should join." This was the universe's way of laughing in my face. *Like attracts like?* Was this supposed to allude to Beckham and me? As if. "Will I see you there?"

Just to get him off my case, I nodded and he beamed, handing me the brightly coloured sheet. He then hopped into the path of the next person as I studied the flyer.

In bright letters at the top, it said: *Law of Attraction, what's meant for you will find you.*

"Oh fuck," I murmured.

Chapter 16

Beckham

"What did you do to her?"

Okay, so when Benson had summoned me to his office, I hadn't foreseen those words leaving his mouth. His face was sour and his brows drew together into an irate furrow. Pestered was his typical appearance but after our win on Sunday and him being invited to the afterparty, I thought our relationship had progressed.

Clearly, I was scammed. If Benson had laser eyes, I would've been nothing but a pile of ash by now.

"What do you mean?" I elected to take the ignorant route and have him reveal to me exactly what the predicament was.

Benson's face turned a weird mixture of red and green. I had to refrain from questioning if he needed to see a doctor because that vein in his forehead looked seconds away from popping. His eyes narrowed, reminding me of a snake on the verge of attacking. I didn't like the thought of being bitten, figuratively, and needed to turn away his anger.

"Taylor," he hissed, highlighting his likeliness to a snake. All he was missing was some scales. Although, if he proceeded to neglect to moisturise his face, he'd be donning some scales very soon. *"Are you even listening to me?"*

No, I honestly wasn't.

I was finding it troublesome to pay attention to anything because somebody had been tormenting my thoughts for the past day. Nyx Taylor was in a mood. And when Nyx Taylor was in a mood, everybody steered clear. She'd been a ball of rage throughout practice earlier, getting frustrated with the littlest thing. The moment practice had ended, she'd stormed out of the building as if her ass was on fire and hopped into Nailea's car.

At first, I'd thought it had something to do with our kiss yesterday. I mean, it sure as fuck had been playing in my head on repeat. How could I forget something like that? Nyx Taylor had fucking *melted* in my arms, after all this fucking time. The memory of her sinking into my touch, moaning for me was stamped in my brain. I could still feel the creamy skin of her thigh underneath my hand, feel the material of her underwear as I tugged at it.

If it hadn't been for the sound outside the bathroom that had startled us, I was sure we would've taken it further. Neither of us had seemed to be in our right minds. She'd avoided me ever since but that didn't stop me from jerking off to the thought of her. Not my finest moment but come on, it was Nyx Taylor. If I didn't stop thinking about her, I'd be sporting a boner soon and that wasn't something I wanted Benson in my presence for.

I cleared my throat, adjusting my sweatpants slightly.

"Why do you automatically assume it has something to do with me? If you haven't noticed, she's been pissed off with *everyone*."

Benson snarled. "Yes, I can see that—"

"Then it could just as well be anybody else's fault—"

"But as much as she's pissed at *everyone*, you're the only person she hasn't snapped at," Benson cut me off, brows hiked as he tilted back against his desk. "You wanna explain that to me? I thought your throat would be the first she went for but you've been safe from her anger this entire time."

I fabricated a grin, shrugging dramatically. "Gee, Coach, I dunno. Maybe she has a crush on me?" I shook my head when his glare hardened. "Are you sure you're angry because she's pissed? Or is it maybe because you're afraid that I did something that made her wanna quit? You and I both know that she's been pulling both her own *and* your weight. If it weren't for her files that you used to train us, we wouldn't have won Sunday's much."

He stood to his full height, aiming a finger at me. "*Don't* test me, boy. Just because you're the son of this and that doesn't mean you get to speak to me how you want. You may be the captain but I'm still your coach," he bit out gruffly and I tensed, no longer amused with the circumstances. "I know I'm not what you boys had in mind for a coach, but I'm trying my best, *yes*, with the help of Taylor. The point is, I'm *trying*. And you don't get to treat me like shit just because of who your parents are. Don't think I haven't heard the rumours flying around about—"

"My dad *didn't* buy me the position of captain," I spoke through clenched teeth, wrath covering every single word.

Fucking sick and tired was what I was of those fucking rumours that somebody sprouted out of their fucking ass. "That rumour was started by Nate Wyatt after he realised he was being threatened as the captain."

Amusement flickered through Benson's eyes and I clenched my fists. "So your dad didn't offer to buy you the captaincy?"

If this was his way of fishing for information then he was going about it the wrong way. If he wanted to know the truth he should've just asked. I didn't mind explaining the situation to those who wished to know the truth. If people wanted to know the truth, it meant they cared enough to not believe ridiculous rumours and reach out to me. What I minded was people who egged the rumour on.

"I didn't take you for a gossip girl, Benson," I jeered, relaxing somewhat when I apprehended he was just an idiot who didn't know how to address delicate topics. "Yes, my dad offered to buy me the captaincy. *But*," I said when seeing his mouth open to bicker, "it was only an option if the team became desperate."

The older man's face scrunched in confusion. It made me think of Nyx and the way her tiny nose scrunched up whenever she was taken by surprise, or when she didn't understand something. I instantly shook the thought away and concealed it because I did *not* want to associate the girl I fantasised about with the man standing in front of me.

Benson voiced his inquiry. "If the team became desperate?"

I nodded. "Contrary to what everyone else believes, Coach, it wasn't just about me. It was about the whole team. We were desperate enough to have my dad pay the school to make me captain—if Nate didn't step down."

"I've heard some things about that fellow," Benson appended, looking lost in his thoughts. He was presumably rearranging everything he thought he knew about the situation and substituting them with what I was narrating to him now. "Was he really that bad?"

A laugh thrust its way out of my throat as I shifted back against the door. It was a sceptical sound rather than an amused one because *bad* wasn't a good enough word to express Nate's position as captain.

"You don't even know the half of it." I groaned. "Nate played favourites all the time. Each week he had a new top three from each team." His name left an astringent taste in my mouth, making it feel as if I'd just barfed.

"Isn't that good?" Benson sought. "I mean, doesn't that motivate other players to do better?"

I shook my head. "Not the way you're thinking. It made everybody so competitive to the point where the entire team became toxic. Nobody trusted each other, we didn't work together. Each player played for themselves instead of their team."

Benson grimaced. "No wonder you lost almost every match last year."

My smile was sombre as I nodded. "After the Crosstown Cup ended, we had a meeting without Nate. We all knew that he had to be replaced. As the alternative captain, I was next in line, but Nate wouldn't step down."

"Why didn't you just tell Coach Ford or Dean Waverly?"

I hauled my gaze to his genuinely disconcerted expression.

"Because *physically*, there was nothing wrong with us. Nate trained us properly. As far as anybody else could see, he did his job as a captain. Everybody condemned the team for just being shit at playing. But *mentally*," I pointed to my head, "we weren't doing the best. By putting each member against the other, Nate fucked with our minds. He gaslit us, making us feel like we were imagining it all. And unfortunately, adults tend to disregard the importance of mental health."

Benson swallowed, looking at me with sympathy. "So he played the part of a qualified captain and nobody could fault him."

"We could fault him for the mind games, but nobody of authority here cared. He was a good captain and he had the proof. Each player was physically perfect, could skate circles around opponents, block and score with their eyes closed. But that was the problem, we were perfect on our own. Not as a *team*."

I could see comprehension dawn on him. "And when they test the strength of the team, they do individual evaluations because you're each part of a whole."

"Exactly," I grunted.

Whenever we'd lost a match, Coach Ford would do individual evaluations to see who the problem was. But that was what was wrong, nobody had been the problem because when tested on our own—we were perfect. Nate had made us lose trust in each other and that was what provoked our losses. It didn't matter how foolproof Coach Ford's plans were when we could no longer execute them.

"And how did you get him to step down?" Benson shuffled

around his desk to take a seat.

"He didn't step down. Not exactly," I continued explaining, recalling all that had happened last year. "He knew exactly how to mould us, make us opponents. There was no way we'd confide in each other when each of us was trying to be the favourite; the best. What he didn't count on was us coming together."

It was Grayson who'd first proposed the idea of us all coming together. He could see how Nate's captaincy was affecting us all mentally, the only one who could acknowledge the fact that it was emotional abuse; having been through it before.

Many had been prepared to quit ice hockey because it was beginning to influence their studies. All three teams and the spares had met up at my house where we'd presented our anxieties. At first, we all hadn't been in agreement. Some had been outraged that we'd dare go against our captain. It had taken a full week of reflecting for everyone to realise that we'd been manipulated.

Benson was fascinated. "So you spoke up against him?"

We'd done exactly that. "Nate's dad's a lawyer and we didn't want to make claims yet, so our main goal was to get rid of him as a captain by explaining that he wasn't what we needed. My dad paying for the position was only a last resort if Nate didn't agree to step down. We were afraid he'd try and convince Coach Ford that we were just bitter about losing in our division during the Crosstown Cup. But he came up with something else. He wanted us to compete for the title."

I hadn't wanted to compete. Nate always excelled in

everything he did because he always got what he wanted in the end. My throat became tight at the next part of the story. I didn't like to speak about it. Benson was obviously curious so I chose to hastily explain it if he asked. And he did.

"How did you compete?"

"Ford had us each take turns to coach the team before a match." I remembered having to play against community teams. "He wanted to see who the better captain was. Obviously, the team played better with me guiding them because I made it a rule to always play together. As a team, we shared one brain on the ice, not six." Benson nodded. "But Nate thought he could score points in the last test, seeing as people loved him. We were observed in a relaxed setting in order to see which captain they were more comfortable with, and not only them but other students as well. Students had to vote for who they thought was the better captain. A good captain keeps his team and community together. In easier words," I cleared my throat, "we had to host events."

Events weren't my most powerful skill. Grayson regularly planned our parties and Sebastian took care of the food and guest list. Benson perked up, his eyes losing that serious look and being supplanted with one of wonder.

His lips tilted and he tossed me a huge grin. I shuddered. "Do my senses deceive me or did our best girl Taylor play a part in this section of the story." I glowered at him and he chuckled. "Alright, tough subject. I see."

A lump was in my throat. Nyx Taylor. Shit, what I would've done for that girl. She'd been at every game, cheering us on. There hadn't been a moment she wasn't on my mind. *Tinkerbell*,

I remembered I'd first called her. School was everything for me and so was hockey.

But then suddenly there was *her*.

Everything about her was mysterious, only intriguing me further. We'd never labelled what we were, but I knew the team discreetly referred to her as my ex. Maybe she was. It sure felt like it because we'd been 'together' for six months before things had gone to shit. And maybe that was why I was more hesitant to listen to her. Because it felt like a betrayal.

She'd been mine.

And then suddenly she wasn't.

"Now you know," I mumbled as I moved from the door and stretched. My back was hurting from sagging back against the wood. "I trust you'll keep your comments to yourself now that you know the full story?"

He nodded. "But you still haven't answered my initial question." I frowned and he rolled his eyes. "What did you do to Taylor?" Again with that question. He should've asked what I *didn't* do to her. I sure as fuck didn't treat her like I usually did.

I shrugged. "Nothing."

Besides shoving my tongue in her mouth. But I wasn't going to tell him that. He gazed at me for a few seconds, like a snake. Then he let me leave, thanking me for trusting him. I also apologised for insulting his coaching skills, to which he responded with a dramatic roll of his eyes. I shook my head before travelling back to the locker room to collect my bag. Everybody was gone by now. I shoved my clothes into my bag and left the rink, hopping into my car. Sebastian and Grayson had probably left when they realised Benson was keeping me behind me for a while.

The air felt good on my slightly moistened skin as I drove with the windows down. It was nearly eight in the evening since practice had ran late so I stopped to pick up some doughnuts at Daisy's Delicacies, a tired Beth greeting me behind the counter. She spoke to me for a while as Donovan began to lock up for the night.

"She was pissed that I skipped the brunch," Beth said in reference to her mom. "I think what upset her, even more, was the fact that I didn't care. When that angry text came through, I literally couldn't have given less of a fuck. I've been trying to avoid her, even though we live in the same damn house."

I sipped from the free coffee she gave me. "You know, the boys and I have always thought that your mom was a little—"

"Too controlling?" she finished with a faint smile, nodding her head slightly. "Yeah, I just figured it's because I'm her only kid, you know? Her marriage didn't work out, Dad ended up fleeing back to South Africa to get away from her, and her life just didn't go the way she planned it to. Part of me pitied her so I obeyed. But I'm tired of that shit now, Beck."

All I could do was nod and sip my hot drink as she spoke about her family, something she rarely ever did. I knew Beth's parents had only been married for a year before her birth, hastily tying the knot after Vivian Braswell and Khumalo Makeba had supposedly fallen in love. Their divorce had already been finalised before Vivian even realised she was pregnant, at least that was what Beth had once said.

Although I'd never seen her dad in person before—because

she usually visited him in his home country—it was obvious Beth took after him. Where her mom was a petite brunette with slightly tanned skin, Beth was tall with skin the same shade as the chocolate trapped in her irises.

"Dad said I could come and stay with him for a while," she continued, "just in case things get out of hand with Mom. I'm willing to try though, which is why I said I'd attend the stupid dinner she's hosting for her cousin." An amused smirk was sent my way. "She asked if you'd be joining, but I said I already had a date."

Grinning, I needled, "Annie?" She nodded, her smirk dissolving into a bashful smile. But her shoulders were somewhat tense. I placed a hand on hers. "I'm happy for you, Beth."

And that was all she needed for the discomfort to leave her body. She didn't need to explain anything, didn't need to say anything else. I understood.

"At least you'll no longer be forced to hang out with me to please my mom," she quipped teasingly as I checked the time.

I leaned over the counter to kiss her cheek. "You know I love hanging out with you, Beth. But I gotta run right now, have to visit my dad. Call me when you get home safely, okay?"

She nodded, shooing me away with a smile. "And please remind Lieutenant Hunt that he needs to stop eating all the brownies your mom makes. I still haven't received any."

"He eats them as soon as it comes out of the oven so if you want some, you have to be in the kitchen while my mom's baking." She only laughed at my advice.

With my purchase ready, I was back on the road and

headed towards Glendale. The ride took me ten minutes and eventually, I parked my car in the visitor's area of the Northeast Station of the Los Angeles Police Department. I seized my visitor's badge from the glove compartment and reached for the box of doughnuts.

I locked my car and sauntered towards the main doors. Greeting the receptionist, Linda, I went straight through. I crossed the open space filled with cubicles and twisted around a corner, grinning at those who waved. And then I saw something that made me stop in my tracks.

The door to one of the interrogation rooms was open. And handcuffed to the table was none other than Nyx fucking Taylor.

I blinked a few times, convinced that I was imagining things. But she didn't disappear. She sat there, gazing at the wall with a stagnant look in her eyes. It hadn't even been an hour since practice had ended. How the fuck did she get *arrested*? She still wore her gym shorts and a loose sweater, hair pulled into a bun.

"Nyx?" I promptly thought of the worst; that she'd stupidly gone and murdered someone.

Her eyes snapped to mine and I saw they were bloodshot, inflated. She'd been crying. There were dried tear tracks on her face and I marked that there were bandages around her hands. My concern skyrocketed.

A dry laugh shook her and I winced. "Of course!" she bellowed, standing up but was hauled down instantly because she was cuffed to the table. Her eyes filled with tears. "Of course you're here! Come to see me break down a little more?

Do you take joy in it or something? Seeing me hurt and crying? Because you're *always* fucking there to witness it!"

She looked far from happy to see me. I didn't respond to what she was saying. It was plain to see that something had happened and she wasn't thinking clearly.

"What are you doing here?" I questioned, becoming worried the longer she gazed at me like a wounded animal.

"Apparently, I'm fucking crazy!" Nyx shot back, seething. Just then, a woman I identified as Officer Davies slid past me, moving to stand in front of the table. Nyx glowered at her, seeming to forget about my presence. "Come back to get your ass chewed out by me again?"

I knew what she was doing, I'd witnessed it before. She was taunting a fucking *cop*. Davies took no note of her. "You're lucky he didn't press charges or you'd be sitting comfortably in a cell, Ms Taylor."

Nyx scoffed. Davies barely reacted. "Why? Is he sad because I kicked his brand new car?"

Car? Davies stared her down. "You did more than just kick his car, Ms Taylor. According to witnesses, you shattered his windows with your fists, stabbed his tires and spraypainted crude words on the doors."

I glimpsed at her bandaged fists. She quaked at the older woman's words, lips shaking. I was finding it hard to believe that she'd done all of that. I mean, I knew she was pissed but not pissed enough to obliterate somebody's car and get arrested within the time span of an hour. And where the fuck had Nailea dropped her off for this to have happened?

The blonde minx smirked. "And I enjoyed *every second of*

it."

Davies offered her a scowl in return. "You're free to go."

If my eyes weren't misleading me, I detected that same terrified look in Nyx's eyes as Davies uncuffed her. The latter acknowledged me with a nod as she led Nyx towards the lobby where a tall man stood waiting. Nyx resembled a child trying to dig their heels into the ground. The man had deep brown eyes, nearly black, and even darker hair. He was the spitting image of Annie and Indigo.

Their dad.

They'd called her dad to come and collect her.

My grip on the box of doughnuts tensed. This was the man that hurt her. This was the man responsible for that bruise and cut she'd donned. I eyed him from afar, disgust and anger burning within my chest.

"Sorry about the inconvenience," the man told Davies with a courteous smile, the same smile that Annie wore when she served customers. "My daughter was always one for the dramatics."

He peeped at Nyx and she looked towards me. I kept her gaze, wordlessly pleading for her to clarify what was going on. A layer of tears settled over her eyes and she blinked it away.

Linda watched from her spot behind her desk.

Davies nodded, probably used to dealing with rebellious teenagers. "Have a good evening."

And then she marched away. I still stood quite a distance from the father-daughter duo but I could see Nyx's dad glaring at her. With one last look at me, Nyx followed him to the parking lot.

But something wasn't right. My gut told me that I shouldn't let her leave with that man. Anybody with eyes could see that he was concealing his anger. Once they were alone, he'd channel all of it towards her. I mean, what dad enjoyed picking their daughter up from the police station? I understood why Nyx was taunting Davies.

She *wanted* to be placed in a holding cell. She didn't want to go home. So I followed them, seeing them stop next to the truck Annie always drove.

"Nyx!" I yelled out. She halted, slowly turning around. Her dad did too, not fretting to conceal his scowl. She glimpsed uneasily from me to her dad. I'd never seen her so frightened before. My fists itched to trounce the man's face in. "We've got literature camp in half an hour," I informed her and her nose wrinkled. I forced a chuckle. "Don't tell me you forgot. We're reading *Pride and Prejudice* tonight. Our essay on it counts for half of our grade."

Acting wasn't a talent of mine, regrettably. Nyx's voice was weak as she countered softly, "I completely forgot." She stared at her dad then at me. "I'm sorry, but I'll be missing camp tonight—"

"What happens if she misses it?" her dad spoke directly to me, probably trying to figure out my relationship with his daughter.

I looked like an idiot, wearing sweaty gym clothes, a visitor's badge and holding a box of doughnuts. He forced a look of concern, pretending to care about her academics.

My mind nearly shut down as I tried to think of a rejoinder. "She fails." It was the first thing I could think of. Her dad didn't look convinced, turning to climb into the truck and gesturing for Nyx to follow. I thought back to something that Melissa had once used against Nyx. And then I spoke, "She'll lose her scholarship."

And that fucking got his attention.

He was speechless for a minute as Nyx stared at the ground. "Nyx," he said in a harsh voice. "I thought I taught you better than to neglect your studies. Why does this young man have to remind you about important things like this? That's *your* job." She murmured an apology and he sighed. "You better get going. If you fail that class you can bet you're going to pay your own tuition fees."

"Yes, Dad," she returned and my throat constricted at the sight of her. This wasn't the girl I knew. I wanted the strong Nyx back, the one that teased me and made me smile.

Not the shell of her.

The Taylor man glowered at her. "I won't be home tonight. Inform your sisters that they need not leave dinner out for you and me. I have to go clean up the mess you made."

She nodded again, shuffling towards me and I encircled an arm around her waist; possessively. No matter what happened in the past, this was *my* girl, and I wasn't going to let him hurt her.

Instead of leaving, he shifted his attention to me. "Thank you for reminding my daughter…" He let the sentence dangle in the air, anticipating me to give him my name.

"Beckham Hunt," I finished the sentence, grip around a shaking Nyx tightening. "Surely, you've heard of my dad. Lieutenant Hunt." I tipped my head in the direction of the building. "He runs this place. Probably for the past ten years."

It was a veiled threat. And the man in front of me caught it. I was the wrong person to make an enemy of. One wrong move and I'd have the entire Los Angeles Police Department up his ass.

His attitude changed and he was suddenly very gentle. "Well, thank you again, Mr Hunt." He nodded at his daughter. "And remember what we talked about, Nyxie," he reminded her and cast me a long glance, making it obvious that he was warning his daughter about sex. "We don't need any surprises."

Although she was shaking, although her voice was weak, she still found the strength to say, "Ironic considering you have two of those running around."

That triggered her dad. What she said must've really pissed him off because it seemed like he forgot I was there. To him, it was just the two of them. It felt like it happened in slow motion. His right hand clenched—the hint I picked up—before he peeled his arm back. Nyx stood still as his fist barrelled towards her face.

But it didn't touch her.

In a split second, I let go of her, dropping my box of doughnuts before catching her dad's fist in my right hand; right in front of Nyx's pale face. His brown eyes met my gaze as he quickly veiled his fury with feigned shock. But I'd seen enough and the rage burning through me needed an outlet.

I squeezed his fist in my hand, watching him wince as his knuckles cracked. "Were you about to hit her, Mr Taylor?" I asked, voice adorned in the anger I was feeling.

He looked torn between playing the victim and yelling at

me. He chose the former.

"I would do no such thing. I merely wanted to hug my daughter goodbye when you *attacked* me." His eyes scanned the parking lot, looking for an audience that would act as a witness to his absurd claims. "Release my hand at once, Mr Hunt."

My grip tightened and he cringed, feeling his pinkie separate from the rest of his fingers. "Respectfully, I think the fuck not."

I shoved him back and he stumbled over his feet. He didn't get far though because I stepped forward and grabbed him by the throat, pressing him against the door of Annie's truck. When he tried clawing at my chest, I tightened my grip and flexed my arm, his feet coming off the ground.

"Nyxie," he called for his daughter, nails scratching at the hand around his throat. "Tell him to stop." He could barely get the words out.

I glanced over my shoulder, seeing the blonde slowly picking up my box of doughnuts. When her dad called her name again, she looked up, meeting my eyes.

"You're about to be disappointed, Dad," she hummed, red eyes filled with loathing as she stared at the struggling man. "Beckham doesn't listen to me."

Her dad tried to say something but I squeezed his windpipe. "How does it feel to be the smaller one in an argument for once?" I questioned, listening to him whimper. He turned away, trying to catch Nyx's gaze but I used my free hand to yank his head back. "Look at me when I'm fucking talking to you."

"Let go of me," he begged. I dropped him and stepped

back. He heaved, trying to get air to his lungs. Running a hand over his face, his gaze darted from me to Nyx. He glared at me. "I will *not* stand for this—"

My fist met his jaw and he toppled over. I turned to look at Nyx as I shook my hand. "His name?"

"Matthew," she murmured, watching me carefully.

When he stood up, blood dripping from his mouth, I yanked him by his shirt. "Matthew Taylor," I muttered, making sure to convey my disgust. "If you *ever* lay a hand on my girl again, LAPD will be the least of your problems."

He spat blood at my face and Nyx scoffed. "Fuck you, Hunt. How I discipline my daughters is none of your business." He chuckled as his bloody saliva dripped from my face.

I held the neckline of his shirt and pulled, hearing a satisfying *rip* as I tore the obviously expensive material from his body. I pushed his form to the ground and used his shirt to clean my face. Once I was done, I tossed it at him.

"No, it's not my business," I agreed. "What *is* my business, however, is you *beating* girls that can't fight back. There's a jail cell with your name on it, Matthew. Don't make me be the one to drag your pathetic ass there."

And that's where I left him. I wrapped an arm around Nyx and led her to my car, far away from her dad. She didn't say anything, but there was a satisfied gleam in her eyes. I could tell she hadn't expected me to intervene—and neither had I. But witnessing it had pushed me past my breaking point.

Matthew Taylor had tried to hit her.

Not merely hit, he'd tried to *punch* her. And she'd only uttered one sentence to trigger him. The girls probably had to walk on eggshells around somebody with a temper as bad as his. He was the predator in their household and he thrived off it, that much was obvious. However, each predator had their own habitat, and the fucker had just stepped into mine.

Now that I knew what I was up against, I wasn't going to let that man lay a single finger on the Taylor girls again.

Chapter 17

Nyx

Sometimes I hated myself. I hated myself, and it was all my dad's fault. In his mind, everyone was the problem except him. Every scowl hurled my way, I questioned what I did to warrant that. What had I done to bother him? Was there a way to make things better? I'd spent hours crying because I wanted to make my dad happy. But I could never do anything right. I always felt as if there was a tube shoved into my chest, gradually bleeding me of my worth. I hated myself more with every passing day.

Every time my dad raised his hand or voice, I'd feel another piece of myself begin to break. I didn't think there was anything left of me to break anymore. He'd trampled my confidence for years until I was nothing but his puppet, his good little girl. He carved words of disgust into my skin each time he articulated. No amount of scrubbing could free my skin, I'd tried.

Foolishly, I'd placed my dad on a pedestal. To me, he was this judge who determined my worthiness. And I was never worthy. Thinking back on it, it irked me that I ever wanted his admiration. It meant nothing. He'd spent his entire life seeking approval from his parents and he demanded us to be the same.

Sometimes I hated that I remembered things so precisely. Instead of it replaying in my mind, it felt like I was reliving everything again. It was the worst. I remembered the first time my dad had hit me, at least, it was the earliest memory I had of being hit. I'd been around eight years old, almost a year after my parents had gotten married.

My dad had cuffed me to the window bar in my room. He'd cuffed me because I'd spoken back to him. Annie couldn't unlock me because she hadn't had the key. But she'd kept me company the entire day whilst my dad went to work. My mom had left earlier with baby Poppy, before the commotion, and I'd like to think she didn't know what happened. Or else she'd have done something.

I'd whined to be let loose, screamed my throat raw. Annie had sat next to me, running her fingers through my hair. My pants had been moistened with piss and shit because I couldn't go to the bathroom. There'd been vomit all over my clothes because I'd suffocated on my cries and threw up what little breakfast I'd eaten. Annie had laid on her bed, crying. My dad had gotten home first, and he hadn't been thrilled with the mess I'd made. He'd slapped me, right across the face. One of my baby teeth had fallen out, blood trickling from my mouth. My mom had bathed me that night, muttering apologies in my ear as I sobbed in her arms.

Over the noise of the shower, I'd been able to hear my dad commending Annie for being a good girl for two whole days.

He'd given her two dollars like she was a dog needing a treat. I'd waited with my mom after that, not wanting to be around him. Annie wouldn't look me in the eye. I'd thought my dad finally turned her against me. She'd stayed by his side during dinner. When my mom had put me to bed, I'd stammered a quick prayer and settled my tooth under my pillow. When I woke up the next morning, the tooth had been missing.

And in its place—two dollars.

Annie was my whole world. She'd clung to my side since I was born. I loved her with every cell I was made up of. I may have resented my dad, but at least he'd done something right. He'd given me her. He'd given me somebody to cling to in my time of need; when I couldn't go to my parents. Annie had sacrificed everything for us. She didn't go to college and put what money she'd saved for school towards us. And yet my dad still took that money. He took from us, monthly. We paid him, and he always insisted it was to take care of him.

Apparently, he'd cared for us and now it was time to be switched.

He had a job, I knew that, I just didn't know what he did. Nor did I know what he did with the money. Until this morning. *Fuck.* I could feel my eyes begin to prickle as I leaned back against the bed. Beckham's bed. Somehow I always found myself here. And I hated it.

Beckham wandered into the room with two steaming mugs of hot chocolate and he planted them on the dresser. He'd changed out of his gym clothes and now wore loose grey sweatpants with a t-shirt. I wanted to hate him, I really did. I wanted to hate that he pulled these absurd feelings from me, wanted to hate that he always saw me at my worst, wanted to hate that he tried to protect me.

He was always there.

I tried my hardest not to think about him because if I thought about him, I'd be reminded of what we could've had. That wasn't something I needed right now. Needed at all.

"I wish I could hate you," I muttered, tugging at the shorts I wore.

I wouldn't meet his eyes because I hated the pity that I saw there. I hated that he'd witnessed what was a normal occurrence for me. I hated that I *loved* what he'd done for me, that he'd stood up for me against my dad.

After my dad had driven away, Beckham had escorted me to his car. I'd waited there as he went to meet his dad and then we left. His dad; a fucking lieutenant. There was another reason to stay away from him.

He sighed, sagging against the wall. There was so much sincerity in my voice. Because I meant it. And he could see it.

"I know," he countered distressingly. "But that doesn't mean I'm not gonna help you, Nyx."

I visibly bridled and clenched my fists as I pushed to my feet. I tried to keep my voice muffled because Sebastian and Grayson were downstairs. They probably thought something was going on between the two of us again.

"I don't *need* your help." The hitch in my voice told me that I was lying. Acknowledging the fact that I needed his help was easier than admitting it aloud. I didn't want to be weak.

I didn't want to be like my mom.

Beckham stared at me, his gaze calculating, sizing me up.

I wanted to hate it. I wanted to hate that his stare alone could make me feel so exposed as if I wore all of my emotions on my sleeve.

"Being strong doesn't mean that asking for help or admitting that you're in pain is weak."

My bottom lip shivered. "I wish I could hate you," I stammered again, sensing my body heat up with emotions I couldn't explain. "I don't understand why you're *everywhere*." My hands were trembling now. "After what happened, you were nowhere to be found and when we *did* run into each other, you could never hide your hatred for me." He stiffened in trepidation. "Now tell me, where is that hatred, Beckham?"

"Nyx—"

Shaking my head, I walked closer. "No. Where is that hatred?" He didn't answer me because there wasn't a fitting answer. "Did your fortress of anger get ruined by this sudden wave of pity that you feel for me? Is that it, huh?" I hated that I was on the verge of tears. "You found no reason to stay when you *assumed* that I was sexually involved with Nate. You ignored me for the rest of the time, essentially *bullied* me and now you're suddenly back? Just tell me you pity me and be done with it."

There was a reason why I never told people. I didn't want them to view me differently. I didn't want them to *pity* me. If Beckham didn't know I was being abused, I was pretty sure he would've stayed hating me.

And that hurt more than it should've.

His eyes became turbulent with rage. "I *don't* pity you, Nyx."

I scoffed. "So you still hate me? Is this your way of revenge, huh? Every time I'm about to lose my fucking mind, you're there. And I *hate* it. I fucking hate it." I wiped my nose with the back of my hand and sniffled. "If that's the case, laugh," I seethed. "The *oh-so independent* and *strong-willed* Nyx Taylor is an absolute fucking *mess*."

He attempted to move closer but I stepped away, refusing to let him touch me. His glower sank but he was still pissed off. "What is it with you and thinking that I'm trying to use you? Can't I be a decent fucking person?"

"Where was that decency last year?" I shot back, catching my voice cracking. "Where was that decency when you constantly berated me, when you walked away without hearing my side of the story? Where was that *so-called* decency, Beck?" My hands were quivering again and I folded them into fists, scorning the stinging of my cuts.

It looked like he was battling with himself over there, wanting to say something but fighting against it. "Nyx, I'm so sorry," he whispered, his voice guttural. "I just want to help."

"I've heard that before." My gaze gravitated to my feet, and lingered there. "Props to you though. You're more original than Nate was." I gave a supercilious clap that made my cuts burn, and glanced up, seeing him grimacing. "Kissing me. Pretending to care again, as if you even cared in the first place. *What* do you want from me? *How* is this going to benefit you?"

It was an explanation I required more than my next breath. Because I could see the thin thread tying me together being hauled on each day. It terrified me to death. I'd spent years being strong for my sisters, and barely shed a tear. And suddenly I always found myself crying about what my life had become instead of doing something. I was becoming like my mom. And I hated it.

Beckham groaned, moving closer. "Why do I have to benefit from it?" He looked genuinely disconcerted and it prompted my chest to tighten, my lungs screaming in protest. "And I didn't kiss you to manipulate you, Nyx. *You know that.*" He stepped closer. "Look me in the eye, and tell me that my kiss felt different." I stayed quiet, arms shaking. "You *can't.*"

I moved towards the window. He observed my every movement, cautious as if he was dealing with a wounded animal. I detected the sound of a car and peered out the window, seeing Grayson and Sebastian pulling out of the driveway.

"You hate me," was my feeble reply.

He forced a laugh, breezing over my statement. "I hate what we've done, how we handled everything."

"Don't you understand how *stupid* this all looks?" I sought, not glancing at him. "I've never given you a reason to forgive me. Am I just supposed to *trust* that you genuinely wanna help? Well, excuse me if I'm finding that hard to believe."

He sighed, forcing out his next words. "I don't hate you." No, but whatever he felt came close. "I just wanna help."

My eyes stung and my voice was a whisper now. "I'd like to believe that, I really would." But, I couldn't. I'd heard those same words before, from Nate. And my life was ruined even more than it already was. Less money, more humiliation. I didn't want to go through that again. "I'm gonna save you the effort, Beck. You wanna know why I didn't want to label what we were?"

His dark brows came together into a profound furrow. "What are you talking about?"

Perhaps, if I gave him what he wanted, he'd end the rouse. I didn't care what he did with the information, I just wanted him gone. I couldn't have him up my ass with questions, professing to care and making me fall for him all over again—only to leave. I upped my gaze to his.

As strongly as I could, I spoke, "My dad beats me." His eyes shadowed further. "I'm a grown woman, and my dad beats me to a fucking pulp if I put a toe out of line. How can I fully trust a man when one beats me the moment I get home?" I paused, letting the words sink in. "Happy?"

The thread was being towed on again. Broken was the wrong word to use. My dad hadn't broken me. He'd torn me to fragments with each bellow, each blow, and each time I'd ventured to stitch myself back together again with this fragile piece of thread made from my will. I'd tied it into a knot, but when Melissa had slapped me that night, she'd unlaced it.

For the first time, I had let myself cry; in front of Beckham of all people. Prior to that, he'd had no interest in my life and me after my supposed betrayal. Men enjoyed fixing something they considered broken. I didn't want him to try and fix me. I wanted him to take the information he wanted and leave.

"I'm far from fucking happy, Nyx!" Beckham flared. "And it pisses me off that you think I'd take pleasure in your pain." He traversed the span of his room and my eyes pursued him. His body was quivering with subdued anger. "*Jesus.* Whatever happened between us would never be reason enough to want you constantly in pain."

I shrugged. "Could've fooled me." I'd always been reminded of how much Beckham hated me each time he looked at me. He never sought to disguise his resentment, up until recently. "After all, I nearly cost you your captaincy." He ceased pacing to glance at me. "Even though I knew how much that captaincy meant to you, I still threatened to ruin it. So why would you help me? Why would you care?"

Instantly, he shook his head. "*Don't* do that." I pursed my lips. "Don't try and turn this into an argument. I'm trying to *help*, for fuck's sake. And you're making it so damn difficult! I want to help you. Nobody deserves to be in your position. I don't care what you did in the fucking past and *nothing* you say is going to change anything."

I stared at him, his chest rising and falling rapidly. His face was pinched and his gaze was imploring. I hated that my dad made me feel like I didn't deserve help. Because this was the outcome; many, many, *many* frustration-filled disputes when somebody wanted to help me—which was rare. I'd had a similar conversation with Nailea once before.

I leaned back against the window ledge, not knowing how to react. My body was so tired of this shit. My mind was exhausted. I was spent. I recalled back to a few days ago; when nobody had been in my family's business, when it was just something Annie and I had to deal with. We were okay with it, it'd been that way for years. I had this facade that I put up at school and everyone thought I had my shit together. Nobody could see through it. But then I'd gone and made myself look vulnerable.

When I dragged myself back to reality, Beckham was right

in front of me, his palm cupping my cheek. "There's nothing you can do to help," I told him honestly, voice showcasing my fatigue. "If we get help," my eyes moistened, "we'll lose Indic and Poppy. And I *can't* let that happen." I shook my head, sniffling. "They're just babies. I don't wanna lose them."

"You won't lose them," Beckham said, but I knew he was lying to make me feel better.

I would lose my baby sisters. They'd be taken away and a good family would adopt them and they would hate me for not doing better to keep them close. After this morning, I knew we had to speed up our plan, take out a loan, *anything*. We needed to get away from our dad.

"Is our truce still in place?" he asked suddenly and I looked up at him.

My nose scrunched. No matter how stubborn I was, I had to admit that Beckham appeared genuine in wanting to help. I recalled Indigo's words about how I was always stony with Beckham because I was scared. All the possibilities of what he could mean to me scared me.

"For the time being," I whispered. Beckham shook my hand, a gentle look in his eyes. "I need to get home to them," I mumbled, clearing my throat. Beckham nodded, stepping back and gesticulating to the mugs. A small but grateful smile rose on my face and I gulped the hot chocolate. "Thank you, by the way," I spoke woodenly. "For earlier. With my dad."

I didn't even want to begin to imagine what would've happened if I'd gone home with him. His anger was intense, worse than ever before.

But Beckham had put him in his place. If I wasn't as hurt

as I was by my dad's actions; I would've taken pleasure in seeing him being the prey for once. It was weird to think of him like that because he'd always been this big guy in the house that used his strength to his advantage. But Beckham was bigger, stronger.

The threat he'd issued my dad had given me hope. My dad was scared of him, that much was clear to see. And fear restrained people I would know. The image of protection Beckham offered both called and intimidated me.

Beckham scowled. "I hate him."

A laugh bubbled in my throat. "Finally, something we have in common." He smiled, finishing his drink.

After we consumed the hot chocolate, Beckham directed me to his car and locked the house. When I inquired where his housemates were, he told me that they regularly went to get ice cream late at night. That was probably supposed to ease my nerves. The drive to my place was rigid and I attempted my best to calm myself down. The only person who ever drove me home was Nailea. The house was in a sketchy neighbourhood with even sketchier people.

Central City East; a neighbourhood in downtown Los Angeles. Most commonly known as Skid Row, the epicentre of LA's addiction crisis. Drug abuse was as normal as breathing here, probably why my mom had had such easy access. It was basically filth compared to Silver Lake, Beckham's neighbourhood. Instead of putting my address on his phone, I described the directions to him. It gave me something to do other than stress.

"Can I ask why you got arrested?" he urged as we paused

at a red light.

I shrugged. "Beat up my dad's new car." No further explanation. If I was going to explain this to anybody first, it needed to be Annie. I could feel Beckham's gaze on me, and then his hand on my thigh. He gave a sympathetic squeeze and left it there. "The light's green, idiot." He chuckled, proceeding to drive. His hand stayed where it was, providing me with some warmth.

Soon, we pulled up in front of the dismal house. He didn't say anything, thankfully. There were people roaming around outside, mostly groups of teens looking for somebody to mug. Beckham trailed me out of the car and, voice filled with humiliation, I advised him to make sure it was locked. We didn't need his vehicle getting hot-wired and stolen. He laughed, following me to the door. Annie's truck wasn't in the driveway because my dad had taken it as punishment.

Digging into my backpack, I unearthed my keys and unlocked the door. The aroma of brownies hit my nose and I smiled to myself. I ushered Beckham inside and shut the door. He peeped around, gazing at the pictures of my sisters and me.

"Nyxie!" A bullet of energy raced towards me and Indigo jumped. I caught her just in time, burrowing my face into her neck. She clung to me and I did the same to her. "Daddy said you weren't coming home tonight," she whispered against my neck and I stroked the fluffy material of her onesie.

"I can't stay away from my favourite girls for too long," I teased, moving back to stare into her pretty brown eyes. "Why's there chocolate all over your face?"

Indigo beamed bashfully. "Annie's making brownies." She

noticed Beckham. "Ew. What are *you* doing here?"

Beckham smiled, tipping forward to tousle her hair. "Nice to see you too."

His actions were slow and gentle, and I felt that tingling sensation in my chest. He didn't want to frighten Indigo. I carried her into the kitchen, finding Poppy on the counter, her face concealed in a huge plastic bowl.

Her onesie was the same as Indigo's. The latter plunged to the ground and seized the bowl from her sister. Poppy looked up, face camouflaged in chocolate. She noticed Beckham and grinned. "Hello, Mr Beckham."

"Miss Poppy," he nodded.

I motioned for him to take a seat at the table before asking, "Where's Annie?"

Just as the words left my lips, Annie tripped into the kitchen. If I'd thought the girls were dirty, Annie blew them out of the water. It looked like somebody dropped a bag of flour on her hair. Chocolate stuck to her face and apron.

Annie gasped when she saw Beckham. "I didn't know we were having visitors."

Indigo licked chocolate from her fingers. "There's no visitors." She pointed at Beckham. "Just that guy." I laughed softly as the two glared at each other. Annie was grinning at me and I felt my heart decline.

Slowly, my laughter died down and Annie noticed. She took in my bandaged hands, my swollen eyes, and suddenly overanalysed Beckham's presence. Just like that, she cleared her throat and walked to our room. I looked at Beckham and he shot me a thumbs up. I offered a smile before following

Annie. Once we were safely in our room, I shut the door.

"Dad called to say you had literature camp. I knew that was a lie. What happened?"

"I got arrested," I began mildly and her eyes filled with distress. "Because I beat up Dad's new car. I noticed it this morning when Nailea picked up breakfast on our way to class." Annie looked disoriented, probably because our dad always drove his rusty old car. "After practice, I had her drop me at the supermarket close to where I saw the car. It was still there and so was he."

She touched her lips, features clouding with uncertainty. "I don't understand."

My voice trembled with the gravity of what I was saying. Annie had always held out hope that our dad would change, that he'd be a proper dad again. She thought if we behaved how he wanted us to, he'd recognise we were perfect like he wanted. It was a silly dream of hers, one she wouldn't let go of.

And I was about to slaughter it.

"It was in a nice neighbourhood," I persevered, walking towards her and holding her hands in mine. "I know what he does with the money we give him." Money that we worked hard for to make him happy. A lump developed in my throat and each word was uncomfortable. "He," I choked on my words, "he has another family, Annie."

I watched the life leave her eyes. But she was still breathing, still standing. Her body was convulsing, she was crying, she was falling. My arms were encompassing her and we tumbled to the ground as she wailed into my chest. She clawed at the sweater I was wearing, pulling me, pushing me. It was the worst kind of cry, the soundless one. Her mouth was open in anguish, but I couldn't hear anything. My ears were ringing.

I couldn't find it in myself to tell her more. I couldn't tell her that he had a wife, and two perfect little girls around Indigo's age. Two girls that looked exactly like him. I couldn't tell her that that's probably where he went when he didn't come home. I couldn't tell her that he'd looked content with his family. They hadn't looked petrified of him. I couldn't tell her that I'd witnessed him taking his girls for a stroll, laughing, smiling as he directed them into the house.

I couldn't tell her that I'd sobbed as I reached for the spray paint I'd bought at the supermarket. I couldn't tell her that I'd decorated disgusting words on his car, that I'd struck the windows in with my fists, punctured his tires. I couldn't tell her that it had felt like my world was falling apart, like we were doing everything for nothing, seeking his approval for nothing.

He had his perfect daughters. He didn't want us, never wanted us.

Never had he looked at any of us the way he did those two girls. I couldn't tell her how I'd screeched at him when a neighbour had called the police, how I'd wailed like a baby when his new wife had questioned who I was. She didn't know about us, didn't know about the daughters he beat. I couldn't tell her how I'd willingly gotten into the police car because I couldn't stand to look at him. I just *couldn't.*

She didn't deserve that torture when she'd spent years trying to be a good daughter. Our dad had the fucking *audacity* to get pissed at her for seeking a father within Uncle Robbie as a young girl but then went and had a whole other fucking family. *Replacing* us.

He was a hypocrite of the worst kind.

I dragged Annie's practically debilitated body to the bed, feeling myself quivering. Annie was crying into her cushion as she told me to check on the girls, and reassure them everything was going to be okay. But how could I? Wiping my face, I shut the door on her excruciating cries and shuffled to the kitchen.

Indigo was in Beckham's arms, playing on his phone. Poppy was on the counter, slicing the fresh brownies and the smell intensified. It seemed like Indigo was taking pictures of the brownies, urging Beckham to help them start a business so they could help make money. He promised her he would. The two girls quickly fell into a discussion about their logo and customers.

Beckham saw me hiding in the hallway and put Indigo on the counter before walking to me. He didn't say anything, cupping the back of my head and dragging me to his chest. I'd once said that I only hated Beckham because he hated me, and that was what I always told myself. But, at that moment, I knew for sure that I didn't hate Beckham. I hated what he represented; somebody who cared about me. The men in my life—at least those that had claimed to love me—only ever treated that love like a transaction. I'd give and give and give to make them happy, just like how a business needed revenue to stay afloat. I'd give and receive nothing at all. Love shouldn't take from you. It should give.

And it terrified me that I felt all the strength Beckham was trying to give me through a singular embrace.

Chapter 18

Beckham

The auditorium was stuffed with people who came to see the fashion show, looking very energetic for a Monday evening. In just a week, Nyx had managed to plan the entire thing. The decorations were amazing and the food was ordered from a list of small businesses. Nyx's involvement in the entire community was going to stack up some serious points, but I knew it wasn't all about the points to her. She genuinely enjoyed hosting these events, organising it all, and then watching her artistry come to life.

I could hear the crowd applauding as another one of my team members took the stage. The designers really exceeded themselves and it was obvious that they'd have one hell of a career after school. Jai wandered past me, donning a brilliant white suit. Jasper's looked the same, except his was a dark blue colour.

Oliver paraded in a green suit and his second outfit was a tiny black dress that he *forced* his brawny body into. The crowd went ballistic with applause and Oliver lapped it all up, grinning. A few more guys showcased newly made jerseys that supporters of the Trojans could wear to games. There were plenty of those, enough for everyone to go around.

Girls from the volleyball team had volunteered to model as well. Even Nailea was here, wearing a bedazzling red dress that many people were already bidding for. It was a smart move on Nyx's behalf. She knew that if Nailea was seen wearing something, everybody would suddenly want it.

Jasper marched out with his second outfit of the night, an emerald evening gown draping from his lean body. It had a glittery trail that Oliver held up when they sauntered onto the stage. When Jasper and Oliver were together, they always gave me a headache. It was like the two were constantly high in each other's presence. Oliver tousled his red hair, striking a pose and winking. Jasper held his head high, hands on his hips and beaming at everyone.

Sebastian grimaced when it was his turn because he didn't want to model. He stood at the curtains, refusing to unveil himself to the audience. I didn't see his problem—he looked good in his suit. After many more arguments with the designers, Nailea rolled her eyes and curved her arm through his, hauling him out. He nearly slipped over Nailea's new silver dress before finding his footing. I chuckled as she accompanied him around the stage, waving at the audience. He didn't look happy but got his job done.

"Prince Charming!" Indigo bellowed from her seat in Beth's lap. Poppy sat next to them, filming everything. Annie was there too, holding a bag of popcorn.

Sebastian's lips quirked slightly at the sight of Indigo. He let go of Nailea and plodded down the steps, reaching a hand out for Indigo. Her chubby cheeks turned red and Sebastian shovelled her into his arms.

So much for hating kids.

Poppy, Beth and Annie clapped as he carried her away. When he hopped back onto the stage, Indigo was burying her face in his neck as the audience cheered along with her sisters. He whispered something to her and she gently lifted her face to stare at him. He muttered something again and she glanced at the audience.

And then she grinned, waving avidly.

Sebastian hooked his arm through Nailea's before they vanished behind the curtain with Indigo. The latter grinned when she spotted Benson at a desk, marking off the outfits that were modelled already. Recently, she'd taken to calling him Santa, much to his annoyance. She sprinted towards him and scrambled onto his lap so she could stare at the lists. Benson handed her a pen and showed her where to tick off.

Nailea and Sebastian disappeared to get their next outfits. Nyx then arrived backstage, being fussed over by some designers. My breath left my body when I took in her outfit. She wore a deep blue silk dress that was backless and plunged low in the front. A lace cardigan was over it, but I could see hints of her skin through it. Her hair was pulled into an elegant bun, allowing her features to be ogled at.

"I was wondering when you'd look at her like that again."

I tipped my head, locating Grayson next to me. He was donning a grey suit with a black shirt and matching shoes. Like me, he'd been hiding and wouldn't step foot onto the stage.

His words suddenly hit me and I scowled. "Fuck off."

Grayson chortled, laying a hand on my shoulder. "The last time you looked at her like that was before Nate." I shrugged his hand off, prompting him to smirk. "And she didn't even know."

He hummed to himself as if the world was a show he enjoyed watching. Grayson usually came in handy when he marked every little detail, like Sebastian, but it got vexatious quickly.

I hated thinking about Nate. People always said to move on, but I couldn't bring myself to, not when he was the reason for my team's pain. He may have been gone, but he'd still left his mark. I could see it when Jasper expected me to yell at him, or when Oliver and Jai involuntarily became too competitive with each other. It would take a while for things to go back to normal, and I was doing my best to help the team in every way that I could.

My attention stirred to Nyx as the designers quarrelled with her because she wouldn't take off the lace cardigan as it covered the style of the dress. There was a weird glint in her eyes as she stood steady, refusing to remove the cardigan.

"It looks fine like this," she contended, crossing her arms obstinately. Whenever she got like that, it was difficult to get through to her. She'd made up her mind and the designers were fighting a losing battle.

One designer huffed, parodying Nyx's stance. "No, it doesn't. It's *ruining* the look." Nyx grew antsy, begging them to let her keep the cardigan. Begging. Nyx didn't beg.

Indigo darted towards me and raised her hands so that

I could pick her up. I frowned because I'd thought the little demon despised me. And I was standing next to Grayson, somebody she obviously preferred over me.

When I elevated her, she whispered into my ear. "She's got a really ugly bruise on her back." I closed my eyes, sighing. Nyx hadn't mentioned what happened after her dad had finally returned home. I assumed it was too painful for her to talk about. Or she didn't want me to get involved again.

Handing Indigo to Grayson, I strolled towards Nyx and settled my hands on her shoulders, nodding my head at the designers. They'd been wary of me throughout the show because whenever one of them tried to get me to go onto the stage, I flipped them the bird. Nyx stiffened as I gently peeled the cardigan from her skin. I kept myself pressed close so that her back was only for my eyes.

Once the cardigan was off, I found the purple bruise on her lower back. Indigo was right when she'd said it was ugly. The edges were yellow and the closer it got to the centre; it deepened to several shades of blue and purple. I didn't want to envision what her dad had done to leave a brand like this. Twirling her around, I splayed a hand over the bruise, concealing it from everyone's view.

"C'mon," I hummed and directed her towards the wings. We stopped at the curtain, waiting for Jasper to finish his dramatic production. Although the skin beneath my hand was creamlike, I could still sense the distress it had gone through. "Does it hurt?" I urged, watching Jasper strut his stuff in a pair of wedges as the audience laughed, pretending to throw money at him.

Nyx shuddered, blinking hastily. "It always hurts," she responded without looking at me. "Even when the marks have long left my skin. I still sense his hands."

It was just us in the wings so she didn't bother to whisper. She dipped down and began pulling up her dress until it was bunched around her waist. I cleared my throat and looked away. Too much confidence was never a bad thing, but I always dreaded the day Nyx stripped naked in front of the entire school.

Her black thong was exposed and she took my free hand, leading it to her hip. Just beneath the waistband, I felt a smooth bump on her hipbone that I'd never noticed before. Or maybe I had, but chose to see it as a childhood scar. We all had one of those.

"What's that?"

She attempted a smile and I knew this was her way of letting me in. "My dad burned me with a cigarette when I was ten. I—"

I pressed my lips against hers and her dress fell back to her feet as her hands went to my hair. Mine slid to her ass, one covering the sordid bruise as if I had the mystic ability to make it vanish. She melted in my arms again, just like the first two times, and I tugged her closer, moving my lips against hers. Her mouth opened and I thrust my tongue inside. As I kissed her, I made a vow to myself to never pick up another cigarette, not when something as insignificant as that could cause a woman so much pain.

When I drew away, her eyes were still closed. I took a moment to gaze at her creamy skin, long lashes, button nose and plump lips. I'd despised this girl for so long because of what she'd done. But I was beginning to think there was more to the story than what she allowed me to read.

"Do you miss it?" I asked abruptly, frantic to know the answer. She blinked in bewilderment, tilting her head. I cleared my throat before muttering, "Us. Do you miss it?"

Nyx smiled, one filled with memories. "You sound a little desperate, Hunt," she taunted, looking reluctant to spill how she was truly feeling. I should've expected it. "Are you sure you wanna know the answer?" I nodded. She pursed her lips, eyes closing in deliberation. Or maybe she just didn't want to meet my gaze. "You were the first man I'd ever felt safe with," she expressed in a quavering tone, no matter how hard she tried to stabilise it. "So what do *you* think? Do I miss it?"

"I'm sorry." It seemed to be the only words I could form; like my body was making up for all the times I should've apologised to her but hadn't. "If I'd stayed, maybe things would've been different," I told her truthfully.

She would've trusted me enough to eventually know more about her family. Money wasn't an issue for me. I would've used all that I had to get the Taylor girls away from their abuser.

"*If*," she whispered, pithily glimpsing over to where more students took to the stage. "*If* my mom hadn't been a doormat, she would've taken us with her or gotten us out of that situation. *If* I hadn't met Nate and cared so much about him," I bristled, "I would've left his problems and focused on my own. *If* I wasn't so terrified of letting you in, maybe you could've helped. There's no end to the ifs, Beck." She closed her eyes again.

I spoke without thinking. "There didn't have to be an end

to us, though."

If we'd just handled things differently. *If* she'd told me why Nate was more important. *If* I'd allowed myself to stay instead of leaving, to listen.

"*Maybe*," she murmured, pulling me from my thoughts. Her eyes were open now, watching me in understanding. I bit back a curse because she knew what I was thinking about. She removed my hands from her and stepped back. "But I can't bring myself to say sorry." My jaw twitched as I stared at her. "As much as you want to lie to yourself, you know you still somewhat resent me for it."

I crossed my arms. "We're not the same people we were last year. Change is inevitable."

She shook her head, pursing her lips. "But, if given the opportunity to rewind time, I'd do it all again." Her words held an underlying meaning, one I couldn't figure out. "You got what you wanted, which was the captaincy. If even one variable was changed, the outcome could've been way different. Maybe Nate would still be here, maybe he would still even be captain."

Our truce had stated that she wouldn't bring up Nate to piss me off, but I could see this wasn't one of those times. I knew she mentioned him to keep me at bay, to switch from a regular conversation to an argument that would allow her an escape, and it always worked. But as I stared at her, I saw something my anger hadn't previously allowed me to see. My mom had said Nyx kept me at bay because she was scared of being hurt again, but there was something else. I could see it.

The answers I needed were *in* what happened with Nate. And because I despised him, Nyx knew I would never want to dive into my past with him.

It was a test.

She was checking to see if I'd repeat my past mistakes. My hatred for Nate had made me walk away from her before, all because I wouldn't ask questions. But not this time.

My mouth opened to say something, but I was interrupted by the appearance of Jasper as he motioned for us to take the stage. I settled my hand on her back, covering the bruise.

"One day, you're gonna tell me what actually happened with Nate."

She floundered, clearly not having expected that. "What are you—"

"Trust is a two-way street, I understand that." I glanced down at her with a smirk, noting her wide eyes framed by long mascara-coated lashes. "This is me saying I trust you."

And then I guided her onto the stage.

The rain was hammering on the roof of Daisy's Delicacies where I sat after practice. The boys had all headed to Jai's place for a movie night, since it was a Friday, a few days before our next match against UCLA. Although the fashion show was another smash, Benson was right when he'd said we couldn't rely on the points accumulated by Nyx's events. We couldn't risk slacking.

The next match was an away game and we were departing Sunday afternoon and staying at a hotel to be on time for the match in the morning. It was a mere seventeen-minute drive to UCLA, but the school didn't have their own ice rink. They trained and held games at The Cube Santa Clarita, a rink about a forty-five minute drive away. I was going to lose my mind in a bus with Benson.

My brain was hurting because of how long I'd been working on my essay. It was for my class in star and star formation. We had the decision to select a star to work on and I'd chosen the binary star because I'd felt like it related to me. If you could relate to something, it was easier to write about it. I typed a few more words onto the laptop, grabbing my pen and making some notes in my journal. Reaching for my coffee, I saw Annie over the screen of my laptop. She was taking the order of an elderly woman, but she kept peeping out the window, waiting for something.

She was friendlier than her sister, presumably because Nyx was always the one who shielded her sisters. When I'd arrived, Annie had grinned at me as if I was an old friend. She didn't seem to mind that I knew what I did, or that I'd heard her crying that night. She was also more trusting than her sister; I realised. I took another sip of my coffee.

"Slight warning," Annie said as she stopped next to my table. "Nyx is on her way and she's not too happy with you." I snorted. She wasn't ever happy with me. A cloth hit me in the face and I glared at Annie. "I'm serious."

It was weird seeing Annie return my glare. She had the face that just made you want to give her the world and the gaze of somebody seeking to give and receive affection.

"Don't tell me you girls swap secrets at night?" I teased, rolling my eyes. "What did she say about me?" Part of me was serious. I wanted to know what Nyx told her sisters about me.

Ever since I'd first met Indigo, I'd been intrigued. If she knew me based on what she'd overhead Nyx saying, I could only imagine what Annie knew. The latter examined her surroundings, probably in case Donovan caught her conversing with the customers. He was still a shit manager and I wouldn't be shocked if his business went bankrupt soon. People stopped coming because of his ludicrous prices and his treatment of everyone. His mother would be disappointed.

"Nothing," Annie revealed and I frowned. "*That's* the problem. Usually, she complains about you trying to force your way into her life." I said nothing, still firm in my decision to trust Nyx. "I'm guessing you stopped forcing."

Women were so fucking complicated. "Shouldn't that make her happy?"

The brunette gave me the stare of a discontented mom. "No, idiot." I threw my hands up in exasperation. "Men are so stupid." Saying nothing else, she left.

I scowled at the table, wondering why Nyx was so fucking difficult to figure out. For the next twenty minutes, I could get nothing done because whenever Annie passed me, she muttered *'idiot'* under her breath. It didn't help that Beth was working the cash register and she kept laughing at me.

After another few minutes, Annie's truck was stationed outside and Nyx jumped out, tugging her hood up to shield herself from the rain as she speed-walked towards the door. It'd been uncomfortable between us—on her end—since the fashion show, which had been four days ago. This was probably because she hadn't expected me to be a good dog and lay down. Instead of using Nate against her, I chose to trust her, something that my mom was hounding me on.

She'll tell you the truth once you stop treating her like a criminal that wronged you, dumbass.

I loved visiting my mom, nothing like a lecture from her to whip me back into shape. Once I'd taken her advice, Nyx began acting weird. I gave her space, only speaking to her if it was important and regarding the team. The bell above the door jingled upon her entrance and she shook the rain from her hair. She waved at her sister, but her destination was unmistakably me. I didn't look at her when she slid into the seat opposite me.

"You haven't been answering my emails," she commenced without greeting as she scoured through her backpack, pulling out her notebook. "So I assumed it would be better to deliver this in person." She pushed a page towards me. "This is a list of young boys from a struggling middle school. It's for my next event."

I continued typing. "The last one just ended."

The skin of my cheek burned where I could feel her glare. "Yes, but I'm trying to plan everything out. For the next event, it's just going to be you and your team teaching these boys how to play ice hockey." I saw her shrug from the corner of my eye. "We won't be making any money because the lesson will be free." She grinned suddenly. "Unless you count the brownies that Indigo and Poppy will be selling at their little stand."

I folded the page she delivered to me and tucked it into my journal. "Thanks." And then I concentrated on my essay again. Nyx didn't disappear, even after five minutes of me typing away. I paused. "Was that all?"

She glowered at me. "What's your problem?"

"I don't have one," I informed her, glancing at my notes for a second. She opened her mouth to say something, but I beat her to it. "I offered you help, and until you trust me enough to accept it, I'm showing that I trust *you*. That means no longer behaving like an asshole."

"I believe you when you say you wanna help." I still didn't look at her. "It's just difficult to accept it. Wanting you to hate me is a defence mechanism. It's easier that way."

"And how is me hating you easier?" I questioned rhetorically, gripping my pen to write something down. My mind felt paralysed from overthinking.

She shrugged, numerous emotions passing through her eyes. "Somebody has to hate me for what I did."

"And you don't hate yourself for what you did?"

Her gaze met mine, clashing. "I can't."

She'd asked me what I had to gain from helping her, and now I wondered the same; what did she have to gain by helping Nate? We all knew he paid her for the resources and everything, but that couldn't have been enough. Startlingly, she didn't seem to hold him in the highest regard anymore. If she hated him, she wouldn't have helped him. But maybe she *had* liked him. And then something had gone wrong.

It was silent between us again until she spoke. "What are you doing?" This was her way of changing the subject, whisking our current predicament under the carpet. She seized my journal and I grunted in annoyance, having thought she'd leave if I kept my mouth shut. Her eyes examined the pages before she looked at me with a bewildered pout. "What exactly is your major?"

She'd never asked me that before, and that should've been a hint for me that she wasn't planning on staying. She hadn't planned on making me a fixed person in her life.

"Astrophysics."

Her eyes widened and she stared at me in surprise. "I was *not* expecting that. Holy shit. You're a little nerd."

"And you're a little bitch," I grumbled, still typing.

Few people knew what I majored in. They all just assumed I was a thick-headed fool there to play ice hockey. But I enjoyed what I studied. It was interesting and kept me on my toes; like the minx in front of me.

Nyx crawled underneath the table and then darted back up on my side, scooting against me. "Binary stars?" she pondered out loud as she looked at my screen, trying to make sense of it all. Her eyes were filled with curiosity, as if she'd never given stars a second thought before.

Growing up, my mom would always take me to the beach at night or we'd even lie in the backyard, trying to spot and name stars. It was where my love for stars had originated. With a sharp clench in my chest, I understood Nyx wouldn't have had something like that.

"Two stars orbiting a common centre of mass," I informed her, feeling her lean closer to squint at my laptop. I scrolled through my assignment and halted at a picture of a binary star system. "See that? The brighter star is listed as the primary star and the darker one is the secondary star." She nodded and I overcame a smile. "Binary pairs are ranked according to their orbit. I'm concentrating on close binaries. Stars in this system can shift their mass to each other and sometimes exert a gravitational pull powerful enough to pull the smaller star in completely."

I didn't tell her I imagined her as the primary star, the brighter one, luring me in with each passing day. It was one reason why I was puzzled about whether I hated her or still desired her. You could never really tell with tension, and there was always tension within a binary star system.

Nyx pulled a face. "So do they just continue to orbit around each other forever?" To her, it may have sounded confusing, but I liked the thought of it.

"If one star in a close binary system collapses in a supernova, the other star can be destroyed." Her eyes held mine as I explained. I noticed her shudder and wondered if the same thoughts were tearing through her head. "However, it *can* survive and *will* proceed to orbit the newly formed body, perhaps even passing on more of its material; helping their partner to rebuild, even at the expense of itself."

She smiled. "So, a binary star system is just a euphemism for a toxic relationship?"

Not really. If anything, it was a good thing. The stars helped each other, keeping one another afloat. People could learn a few things from them, how to trust and how to stick by when things became difficult. It was a lesson I apparently needed.

I chuckled. "Well, according to Sir William Herschel, a binary star is the union of two stars that are formed together in one system by the law of attraction." Something flickered in her bright eyes at the mention of the law. The apples of her cheeks were red and she wouldn't meet my eyes. "Sound familiar?"

An amused smirk formed on her lips. "Law of attraction," she mused, sinking back into the seat. The term was clearly familiar to her. It'd been popping up everywhere when I'd searched for an essay topic. Maybe the world was trying to tell her something, too. Nyx climbed over my lap so that she could leave the booth. Suddenly, she gripped my hoodie and yanked me close, her nose against mine as she smiled. "Don't ignore me, asshole. I don't like it."

"Don't be a bitch," I shot back, lips brushing against hers. "I don't like it."

Nyx grinned, stepping back and grabbing her bag. "Law of attraction," she echoed, still grinning. "You know, I attended a philosophy class where they spoke about it."

I raised a brow. "Did you now?"

She nodded, driving a hand through her wet hair. "Yeah, what's meant for me will find me and all that shit." I smirked. She picked up my pen, twirling it between her fingers. I watched her in amusement. "Say, if I lost this pen, if it was truly meant for me it would find me again, right?"

A laugh left me at the ludicrous analogy and I was unable to stop it. Nyx wasn't even attempting to be subtle. Then again, she never was. "I guess, yeah. Why?" I asked with a tilt of my head. "You lose something recently?"

Her eyes twinkled with barely restrained laughter. She ran her tongue over her bottom lip before asking, "Did *you*?"

My lips quirked. "Maybe," I shrugged. "I'm an idiot," she hummed in agreement and I feigned a scowl, "I lose a lot of things. We'll just have to see if the law of attraction brings any of my shit back." I offered her a smile.

She snorted, swaying on her feet. "Tinkerbell finds lost things, you know?" she spoke, referencing the nickname I'd once given her. It was fitting. "I could help you find the shit you're looking for."

Without looking at her, I said, "Maybe this time Tinkerbell's a lost thing herself." She stayed silent and when I looked up at her, her cheeks were flushed. I wanted to reach out and pull her into my arms. I'd missed it, missed the way I could make her blush. Only *I* could do that, she gave everybody else the death stare.

After we'd parted ways, I'd thought I would never be able to pull a reaction like that from her again. Nyx was biting her lip now, trying not to smile. And then she turned on her heel.

"Law of attraction!" she yelled suddenly and I snorted, questioning her sanity. She'd do whatever it took to avoid talking about her feelings.

Donovan peeked his head out of the staff doors. "Stop disturbing my customers!"

She held up two middle fingers and Beth laughed. "Suck my fat cock, Donovan!"

Before he could say anything else, she left the cafe, trudging to the truck. Her hood was down, and the rain completely drenched her. As she hopped into the vehicle, she caught my eye and mouthed something. I didn't have to hear her to know what she said.

Law of attraction.

I turned back to my essay, laughing. Annie paused next to me again, waving as Nyx drove away. "You know, she's already had that happen to her, the whole exploding into a supernova thing. Last year, when everything fell apart," she mumbled and I apprehended she'd been eavesdropping. Her deep brown eyes landed on me and she squeezed my shoulder in comfort. "And you're proving to her you survived it."

Chapter 19

Nyx

Poppy and Indigo had been up late last night, having a Barbie marathon on my laptop, so it was no surprise that they were sleeping in. What was a surprise was the man sitting opposite me, peacefully eating breakfast. He had a plate of scrambled eggs and bacon with a cup of steaming coffee. I forked some bacon into my mouth, keeping a wary eye on him. He hadn't slept here last night. I would've heard him come in.

"This is amazing," he spoke around a mouthful of food, the bruise at his cheekbone dancing with each chew. "Compliments to the chef."

Annie was behind the kitchen counter and she looked at me with wide eyes, miming with her hands as if asking what the fuck our dad was doing home. Scrambled egg shot off from her fork with her wild movement and she bent to pick it up.

We hadn't seen our dad since the night he'd came home to deal with me after I'd destroyed his car. Perhaps it had been naïve of me to think that Beckham's threat had cautioned him.

I still couldn't touch the broom after he'd beaten me with it. Annie had kept the girls in our room and I'd tried my hardest to not make a sound. I never wanted them to have to hear my cries.

A bonus point was that it pissed good old Matty Taylor off I didn't make a sound of agony.

Picking up my fork, I chewed around some eggs. "Your wife doesn't cook for you?" I sought absentmindedly, reaching for my orange juice. Annie hopped to her feet, mouth open. She looked at our dad, anticipating him to lunge across the table.

He didn't. I thought he'd be unsettled about us knowing about his other family, yet he wasn't. If I wasn't so good at reading him, I wouldn't have picked up that he was gloating. He was proud of his other family, loved them more than us.

Inquiries were working through my mind about why his life hadn't worked out here. It felt like my family was nothing but a trial run for him, to see if that life befitted somebody like him. And then when he'd apprehended he *did* want a family, he preferred others.

Somebody needed to let him know that this wasn't *The Sims*. There were no swapping families after you got sick of them

A wicked smirk formed on his lips, made even more ghastly by the black eye he was sporting. "Not really," he answered, nibbling at his bacon and crunching in contentment. "If you hadn't noticed that day you kindly destroyed my new car," I smirked, "she lives in a pleasant neighbourhood so she's rather well off. Has her own cook."

It was supposed to anger us because he was living lavishly whilst we struggled. Regrettably for him, I didn't care and would've let the comment spiral down my back. But I marked Annie's crestfallen expression. She tried to hide it, preparing the lunchboxes for the girls for when Georgia took them to the park with Julie later today.

"If she's so rich, why do you still take money from us?" I demanded, keeping my gaze levelled with his. If I dropped my stare, he'd think he won. And I would never let him.

He placed his cup of coffee down, fists clenched. It delighted me when he got like this. He sought to give off the impression that he was in a jovial mood and refused to let me get to him. But I always did. I was like an annoying rash. In your asshole. He'd mistaken my heartbreak for fear that day he'd picked me up from the station.

But I wasn't scared of him.

"Are you trying to start a fight?" he asked.

A father trying to start a fight with his daughter. How cute. I shrugged. "If there's a worthy opponent, then sure." His eye twitched. "But, I don't see any. *Pity.*"

"You're testing me, Nyxie," he tutted, shaking his head whilst speaking in an admonishing tone. "I thought you learnt your lesson about disrespecting me."

"And I thought *you* learnt your lesson that I'm not a little girl anymore." I gesticulated to the split lip he was sporting. "Matches the one you gave me when I was eight." He clutched the end of the table, prompting my cup of orange juice and his coffee to flounder. "It's repugnant that you have to hit a woman to feel like a fucking man—"

My dad slammed his hand on the table. "You better wash that mouth of yours!"

Tilting my head, I blasted back, "It's gonna stay dirty whether or not I wash it because I suck my boyfriend's dick with it." Everything went still. Annie froze as she poured herself juice and my dad appeared to be containing an outraged bellow. "You remember Beckham, don't you?"

I didn't bother to conceal my smile. My dad knew better than to maintain this dispute when he knew I could easily involve Beckham's dad. I wouldn't, but he didn't know that.

"I don't approve of your boyfriend, Nyxie, treating me the way he did," he tutted, keeping his anger in check as he shifted tensely. The very mention of Beckham seemed to put him on edge, making me think that his threat hadn't gone unheard after all.

"Your opinion means squat to me," I easily replied before nodding towards his black eye and bruised cheekbone. "The fuck happened to your face? I gave you the split lip—you're welcome, by the way—but I think I would've remembered if I rammed your face into a pole."

My interrogation pissed him off. Did the man really think we wouldn't question his appearance? He looked as if he'd gotten hit by a truck and I didn't miss his wince each time he shifted in his seat.

Before he could say anything, Annie appeared with more bacon. She laid it on his plate, smiling. Peacekeeper, as always. Just like she'd hoped, he calmed down.

"You know, Annie," our dad began, picking up another piece of bacon, "speaking of *respectful* boyfriends; a colleague of mine has a son your age." When he wasn't looking, Annie pulled a face and I rolled my eyes. "I think you guys would make a perfect match."

Anybody who was friends with him was insane, so I sure as shit wouldn't let him set Annie up with anybody that he knew. Besides, she had Beth.

"You don't know her, so how would you know if they're a perfect match?" I questioned lightly.

My dad glared at me. "I know *my* daughter." His words were suddenly heated.

"Still jealous of a dead man I see," I hummed. Everything went hushed.

Annie's mouth was open in surprise at the fact that I'd dare mention the man he hated the most. He'd never gotten over how much we'd preferred Uncle Robbie over him. The latter had done duties that were supposed to belong to our dad. *Pathetic.* Our dad was pathetic and instead of appreciating that we'd had somebody when he'd gone rogue—he chose to be jealous.

I watched his eye twitch, his chest vibrating with restraint. I waited for him to start yelling. Weirdly enough, he didn't. But the smirk on his face made me wonder who truly had the upper hand. He continued speaking as if I didn't just provoke him.

"I know that Ted's son is a better person than the last asshole that broke her heart." Annie tensed as he pointed at me. "And if I remember correctly, *you* brought him into our lives." My frustration grew. He just *had* to bring that up.

Annie blanketed my mouth with her hand to prevent me from retaliating. "Dad, please," she begged the ruthless man that was glowering at me. "Let's not bring Nate into this. It's in the past and I'd like for it to stay that way."

I pushed to my feet and went straight for my room, shutting the door behind me. Why did it feel as if all my fucking problems began and ended with Nate? He was a major obstruction between me and Beckham.

I thought back to what he'd said about binary stars. Last night, I'd been on my phone; investigating as much as I could. The law of attraction meant that like attracted like. It was vexatious to think that Beckham and I were still attracted to each other. And I couldn't forget the effect of his kisses on me. I didn't enjoy having a weakness and I needed to figure out how to get rid of it.

Beckham could end up being my downfall—*again*.

The door to the room opened and Annie slipped inside. I abhorred hearing Nate's name on her lips. It was painful to hear the heartbreak in her voice, even after all this time. She opened her mouth but I articulated before she could. "Annie, *don't*."

She didn't listen. "I'm sorry."

"Try saying that without looking like you're a breath away from bawling your eyes out," I expressed, making sure that I had everything packed. "I've told you before, there's nothing to be sorry about." We'd had this conversation one too many times.

Annie groaned, tugging at her short hair. "There's a lot to be sorry about, Nyxie."

"Yeah," I nodded, "I'm sorry that I ruined your relationship with the one fucking man you were able to love and loved you in return," I fired at her, feeling my eyes sting. My dad knew it hurt both of us when he brought Nate up, and he still did it. When I heard a sniffle, I knew I had to leave. The guilt was suffocating.

Her hand was suddenly around my wrist. "Funny," she stated, but her tone conveyed that she didn't find it funny at all, "I was about to tell you the same thing." I froze, seeing my reflection in Annie's moist eyes. "Nate *chose* to leave me—"

"And Beckham *chose* to leave me," I finished, annoyed that we were still on this topic.

Yet, Annie wasn't done. "Beckham wouldn't have felt the need to leave if I didn't let you go along with that foolish plan to help Nate—"

"And Nate wouldn't have felt the need to leave you if I hadn't *formulated* that foolish plan in the first place," I cut her off, breathing heavily. We stared at each other, both of us practically overflowing with pent up emotion.

She spoke first. "But ask yourself which one of them is back." My lips parted, but no words came out. "Nate *knew* about our home life and he still left me because his pride was hurt. Beckham knew *nothing* about your family and he left because his pride was hurt. Now he knows and he's back. Are you really gonna let that go to waste?"

Childishly, I grimaced. "You know I wouldn't let myself be happy if you weren't." It was an immature response, but the truth, nonetheless. "My plan was supposed to benefit both sides, Annie," I sighed, "Beckham got what he wanted, but is that enough? Was the captaincy worth the expense of your relationship?" She opened her mouth but I spoke again. "I'll answer it—it's *not* worth it. But hey," I laughed sarcastically, "at least we're even."

Annie bristled, her nostrils flaring. "No, *don't* do that. Do not put us in the same boat, Nyx. Nate and Beckham are two different people. *We* are two different people. Just because my relationship didn't work out does not mean you should jeopardise your own," she scolded, stepping closer to me. "I don't want you risking your happiness for me because you already did that before. You have the chance to be happy again and I have Beth now—"

"It's selfish," I interrupted, shifting uneasily. How could I move forward knowing that I was the reason it all happened? "I know you have Beth and I'm glad you do. But your relationship wasn't the only thing that suffered at my hands. Our family did too. Remember when I got sued?" Annie flinched. "Yeah, I was the reason for it all. This is my punishment and I'm not going to be selfish again by wanting more than I deserve."

Something bizarre flickered behind her eyes but it was gone before I could identify the sentiment. "Sometimes, you have to be selfish, Nyxie. Sometimes you have to put yourself first, for once. People make mistakes, people hurt other people—it's the way of the world. But we move on, we learn and we grow. Don't punish yourself, it won't change the past." She squeezed my arm. "You've taken enough punishment. Maybe it's time for a reward."

And then she left, hearing our dad call for her.

Her words played in my head. Annie was my best friend, I knew her better than anyone else. And the words she'd just left me with, she'd uttered them with knowledge. But never once had Annie been selfish. It was unheard of in the Taylor household. Almost as if the universe was listening to me, Annie's phone flashed from its place on the dresser. I stared at the vibrating phone for a good few seconds. *No*, I had no right to snoop through her things. From where I was standing, I could see it wasn't a saved contact, just a phone number. I didn't make a move. Instead, I monitored the phone like it was a bomb that could go off at any second.

The vibrating stopped and I could hear our dad conversing with Annie, not a care in the world. When it was just the two of them, he seemed almost more content. None of us had that same feeling with him, not even Indigo who looked like him.

A message suddenly flickered onto the screen.

Anniecat, just a few more weeks. Georgia's got it all under control. I'm sorry I couldn't do more for you girls, I really am.

The screen went black, but I felt the vomit in my throat. Anniecat. Only our mom had called her that. Our mom. She was messaging Annie. Anger formed deep in my gut, anger at the woman who had birthed us. I wondered if she'd targeted Annie because she knew she'd get sympathy there. Me? I wouldn't pick up the fucking phone. Georgia moving to town suddenly no longer felt like a coincidence, her eagerness to help us.

The word *selfish* could only be associated with our mom. Did Annie sympathise with her for being selfish and leaving? It made sense but I didn't know how Georgia could be involved in it. My brain ached and I swore softly. Another time. Annie and I could talk when our piece of shit dad wasn't home. Mentioning our mom around him would only trigger the idiot.

And the things he could do whilst controlled by rage at my mom—it could be more damaging than ever.

I picked up my suitcase, furnished with necessities for the next day. We'd be leaving for the city of Santa Clarita later. I was *not* looking forward to spending almost an hour with those nincompoops in a small space. It was only the first and second teams, but that was still way too many men for me to deal with. I seized the handle of my suitcase and hauled it into the hallway. The girls were still asleep when I entered their room so I kissed their foreheads.

My dad stared at my suitcase when I hugged Annie goodbye, trying to ignore the heavy feeling in my chest. "And where are *you* going?" he asked.

"To do my job," I easily riposted as Annie handed me the truck keys. I'd drive it to the rink and then Nailea would take her to pick it up later. We'd had a spare key made the other day. My dad's anger built and I gave Annie a look, telling her she could explain my internship to him, but *not* to mention the money. "I love you," I told her and she kissed my cheek. Smiling at my dad, I stated, "See you when you need money again."

I shut the door on whatever he was saying, stored my suitcase in the passenger seat before hopping in. Turning the keys, I pulled out of the driveway and made my way onto the road. Hopefully, the drive would calm me down, stop me from overthinking. I reminded myself to text Nailea and thank her.

My phone rang and I dug into the pocket of my skirt, seeing the name 'Santa' flash on my screen. "Santa's come to the perfect hoe. What can I do for you?"

"You're insane," Benson retorted and I could hear skates on ice in the background. He was no doubt trying to get a last session of practice in. "Please tell me you're on your way."

I laughed. "*Yes.* I already told you I'm joining you on this trip." He sighed in relief and I laughed harder. His relationship with the boys may have been getting better, but I knew he wouldn't survive a bus ride with them all on his own. When I wouldn't stop laughing, Benson hung up.

We all favoured home games, not only because there wasn't a need for a long trip, but because all our supporters would be with us. Few would drive for an hour to watch a game. The thought of running into Nate also crossed my mind. I didn't know what I'd do if I saw him. Part of me would want to disregard his presence, but also attack him. Contrary to what many believed, Nate had the potential to be a good person.

He just chose not to.

A huge bus was stationed outside of the rink and I pulled up next to it. I delivered my suitcase to one guy that was helping to load everything. A spider-shiver wriggled down my spine when I stepped inside. The rink was always ice cold, opposing my sunny outfits. Despite it being winter, it was still fairly hot outside. The glacial atmosphere inside the rink howled at my pleated skirt and tank top. At least I wore a denim jacket over, but it was no help.

The second team was on the ice, Benson skating after them and barking orders. It had been my suggestion to work on them first this morning. The first team already got so much attention. Although the second team was just substitutes, it didn't mean that we could neglect them. It was *guaranteed* that they'd get ice-time, and they needed to be ready.

Jasper was the first to detect me and he grinned. I smiled in return. He was one of the first men that I hadn't despised immediately. The guy was hilarious as fuck and had the ridiculous ability to make me laugh every single time. He was sitting with Oliver, the two observing practice. Grayson was on the ice because he rarely ever got substituted and played every game. Sebastian was leaning on the bar, eyes narrowed in thought as he watched his substitute, Levi, skate. The latter hadn't given me lip again and I had a feeling that was due to Beckham.

The captain in question stood shirtless, wearing his signature grey sweatpants. He held a towel to his face, mopping sweat. Even though it was freezing, I could see how moist his skin was and the same could be said for Jai. They'd probably been in the rink gym. Jai looked on the verge of having a stroke and he thumped onto the bench, fanning himself. Beckham laughed at his teammate and the sound nearly caused my knees to buckle. I mentally criticised myself.

When Jai sat up to throw Beckham with his sweaty towel, he noticed me and winked, flirty as ever. Beckham turned around and his eyes met mine. So many unspoken things passed between us and when his eyes darkened; I knew he was thinking about the last time he'd kissed me. His eyes dropped down to my exposed legs and I crossed my arms.

Ever since he'd mentioned binary stars, I couldn't stop thinking about it. Or him. I felt that gravitational pull he was talking about—I'd *always* felt it.

Before I dissolved into a fucking puddle, I left and went

straight for Benson's office. I didn't enter, though, just stood there hyperventilating. Tired. I was tired, that was it. Blaming my not-so sudden attraction to Beckham on my exhaustion seemed like the best idea. I pitched against the wall and dozed off for what felt like a minute when the sound of footsteps reached my ears.

My eyes opened and I watched Beckham saunter around the corner. A block formed in my throat as I watched him fix the drawstring of his pants, his stance casual and tattoos dancing with the movement of his arms. He was yet to locate me and I suddenly wished I could walk through walls so that I could hide.

Since when did I fucking hide? I was heavily attracted to him. There was no hiding that. Imprudently, I thought it'd pass. Beckham was an attractive man. I'd seen other attractive men before. So what made Beckham so different? I knew the answer to that.

He was my first. The first guy I'd ever let close. His touch was the most gentle I'd ever experienced. The first man I'd felt safe with. There was history; that was more than enough.

Beckham ran a hand through his hair, glimpsing around—and then his eyes found mine. Instantly, I looked away, paying close attention to the wall opposite me. Beckham's chuckle carried across the space between us and I felt myself quiver.

"If I didn't know any better, I'd say you were hiding," he stated, shoving his hands into his pockets. The corner of his mouth tipped into his cheek, forming a smirk.

Clearing my throat, I responded, "I need something in Benson's office." Like an idiot, I gesticulated to the office door and he grinned. There was an awkward silence and I knew he was doing it on purpose, trying to make me uncomfortable. Well, it was working.

"You should get back to your team," I pronounced resolutely, eyeing the door and contemplating dashing through it. Benson wouldn't mind me hiding there, seeing as he was on the ice.

He narrowed his eyes, mouth set in a straight line. "Do you want me to go?"

"Yes." A low grunt left his mouth and I proceeded. "I'm sure practice sounds far more appealing than arguing with me."

And I *was* going to start an argument to get him away. He knew I started arguments because I didn't know what I'd do if I let him get too close again. Something stupid, most probably. Frustration coursed through my blood. There was no telling what I'd do.

Instead of snapping at me as I presumed, he laughed, a deep sound that made my chest ache. "And are you gonna start an argument—"

"You *know* I will," I cut him off.

Beckham eyed me for I moment and I felt exposed. "There's that defence mechanism again," he articulated over me when I attempted to argue. "I wonder what'll happen if I get past it." In three strides, he forced himself into my space, hands framing my hips. He pushed me against the wall, nose skimming the side of my jaw. I shuddered, hearing him chuckle to himself. "Wonder what'll happen if I don't let you bait me with an argument," he hummed, pressing kisses to my neck and I couldn't help but sigh.

"Beck—"

"You can't deny that you're attracted to me, Nyx. Instead of fighting it, let's see what happens," he grumbled, hands roaming my body. His thumb brushed my bottom lip. "Open up for me, sweetheart."

"*Beck*," I hissed when he bit the skin of my neck before running his tongue over it to ease the prickling. When it stopped, he bit into that same spot, no doubt leaving a clear mark. "We can't do this. This is a bad fucking idea—"

He stilled. "Nyx—"

I tried to move away but was confined between him and the wall. "Emphasis on *bad idea*."

"Can you stop thinking about what happened last year, for once," Beckham all but growled, grip tightening around me. "I'm not talking about the past. This is right now."

Sagging in his hold, I closed my eyes. I dropped my head against his chest, feeling my resolve disintegrate. "I fucking hate you," I mumbled, trying to mean every word.

Beckham pressed his body against mine and I felt the bulge straining against his pants. Another tremor. "Just this once." I shook my head in response, sighing when his fingers trailed up my leg.

He raised my leg, wrapping it around his waist and thrust, pressing his bulge against my warmth and I choked on a moan. I could no longer hold back, not when my body and my mind were on conflicting sides. I needed them to work in sync to focus. So I'd give in. "Just this once, *asshole*."

Beckham ground against me, making another feeble cry leave my mouth. I'd never wanted somebody so desperately before. "Just this once." His free hand collared my throat.

"Mouth, baby."

And then his tongue was inside my mouth, battling with mine. The kiss was exactly how I remembered it. He nipped at my lips, groaning when I tried to take control. I sucked on his tongue, moaning. If anyone turned the corner they'd see us. The risk of getting caught thrilled me. Picking up my other leg, he bucked furiously against me. His skin was warm underneath my touch, courtesy of his time in the gym with Jai.

We were dry humping like two teenagers who'd just discovered sex. "*Shit*, Beck," I hissed when his fingers clutched my ass tightly.

"I knew you'd melt again," he grumbled against my lips as I tugged on his hair. "Because you've been aching for this. You've always been mine." A humourless chuckle left his swollen lips. "Isn't that right, Nyx?" I nodded, too focused on rubbing myself against him like a cat. "Use your words, baby."

"*Yes*," I moaned when he palmed my breasts. I felt the familiar tingle in my spine, signifying that I was close. Beckham sensed it too, slipping a hand under my skirt and into my panties. "*Fuck*." He rubbed furiously at my clit and I nearly sobbed. "Beck, I'm gonna—"

"Yo, Beck!" Jasper hollered as he rounded the corner, eyes aimed at the paper in his hands and not yet spotting the predicament I was in. Beckham halted his actions and I dropped my head onto his shoulder, trembling because of my release being interrupted. "Benson's got a list of the team at UCLA. He wants you to look through it and see if you can remember any of their weaknesses on the ice—" He glanced up, mouth going slack at what he was witnessing.

Then an amused grin emerged on his lips.

Beckham withdrew his hand and I whined, making him chuckle. “I hate you.” I directed my words at both of them. “I really do.”

I also refused to lift my head because the cognisance of what I’d just done hit me hard. The shame was threatening to drown me. How desperate was I?

Answer: *very desperate.*

Ungracefully, I unwrapped my legs from Beckham, my body still quivering lightly. I felt drowsy, as if I was minutes away from passing out.

Jasper was beaming like an idiot. “I fucking knew you guys were back together.”

Irritated, I remarked, “We were never together in the first place.”

Beckham’s hand was suddenly in my hair, turning me to face him. His pulling at the strands was *not* helping my situation. “I’d like to hear you say that to my face.” My eyes narrowed and I could hear Jasper chuckling. “Jasper, you think of Nyx as your sister, right?” he asked without looking away from me.

“Is that a trick question?” Jasper questioned in confusion. Beckham tilted his head slightly to glare at him and Jasper laughed awkwardly, no doubt thinking of the time we’d made out at the club. “*Of course* she’s my sister, man. Like a totally hot stepsister.” He smirked at me. “I’m bisexual for a reason, darling.”

Finding my moment to shine, I looked at Jasper, a teasing smile on my face. “What are you doing, stepbro?”

Jasper looked ready to burst into laughter but his smile slipped when he caught Beckham's aggravated gaze. "*No*, not at all. Completely biological. Nyx is like my biological sister, no incest over here. No, sir—"

"Jasper?" Beckham called over my laughter.

He stopped his rambling. "Yes?"

"You might wanna fuck off," Beckham responded smoothly. "Unless you think it's normal to watch me finger your sister?" Jasper didn't need to be told twice, already scrambling away. I was about to follow, but Beckham dragged me back. "We're not finished here," he murmured, palming my nape.

"As if," I scoffed, still feeling on edge. Beckham burst into deep laughter, dabbing a light kiss on my lips. His free hand trailed down my stomach before returning beneath my skirt. I sucked in a breath when his fingers found my clit again. He found my opening and slipped one finger inside and I clutched his bare shoulders, not trusting my legs to keep me upright. "*Beck*."

He shushed me, lazily working his finger in and out before adding another. I clenched my teeth, feeling my release come alive again. "So tight, *fuck*. Almost forgot what you felt like." A loud moan left me and he consumed it by kissing me again. "That's it, baby." He moved his fingers faster and faster, pushing me to the edge. "Come all over my fingers. That's my girl." My release slammed into me and I cried out. He gripped my hair to keep my head up so he could watch my orgasm take me.

My skin was tingling as Beckham kept his hand in my panties, making me shiver with aftershocks. Trying to catch my breath, I leaned my head against his chest, panting. I couldn't lift my head to meet his gaze because I felt that familiar sensation inside of me. It was still there, even after all this time.

Intimacy was difficult for me. The only man in my life did whatever he could to hurt me. I wouldn't let boys in high school close enough to leave a peck on my cheek. Yet, I'd kiss Beckham with my dying breath. Being with him gave me hope, it was why I could be with others after we'd separated, why I could move on. But it just didn't feel the same; I had to admit it to myself. *I had to.* It was why that feeling was back, a *knowing*. This was what I'd been missing.

I slowly fixed my skirt and underwear as Beckham stepped back slightly. Still breathing awkwardly, I asked, "We still hate each other, right?" He grinned at my attempt at downplaying what happened. Feelings were a fucking nuisance. "Because I'll still fucking kick your ass."

"I'm counting on it, Tink," he answered with a huge grin and I scowled.

I shoved his chest and he chuckled. "This changes *nothing* between us," I affirmed steadily, but my professional tone only appeared to entertain him because he laughed harder. "I'm serious, asshole." I tugged at my skirt. "Let's head back separately. I'll go first. How do I look?"

He snorted. "Like you got fucked." I ventured to push him again, but he only pulled me to his chest. "I may or may not have left some marks." He ran a finger over my neck before fisting my hair after I'd just attempted to fix it. Before I could say anything, he leaned down and pressed his mouth to mine. "You know what I realised," he mumbled against my lips, "I've never seen you sporting anybody else's hickeys before."

Yanking his hair, I replied, "Don't flatter yourself."

"How can I not?" he asked with a smirk, pulling back slightly. It felt like he was able to read my mind. He was right though, as much as I hated to admit it. No other guy had ever left a hickey on me because I wouldn't let them.

It made me feel like they were trying to place a mark of ownership on me. So why wasn't I ever opposed to the idea of Beckham leaving one on me?

As he moved to brush the hair from my face, I noticed the split knuckles of his right hand. It was a coincidence. It had to be a coincidence. Still, I asked, "What happened to your hand?"

Beckham stilled, gazing down at me with an unreadable expression. "My answer depends on whether you're gonna get pissed or not."

"Why would I get pissed?"

He smirked. "Because you don't like being a damsel in distress." Flicking my nose, he added, "I promise I didn't do too much damage."

"Understatement of the century," I scoffed, recalling my dad's black eye. "Where'd you even find him and why—"

"Grocery store," he answered. "He and I had a little chat. The fucker seemed to think I was joking when I said he'd have hell to pay if he touched you again."

I bit my lip, feeling an unexplainable wave of gratitude wash over me. "You didn't have to do that, but thank you." He didn't say anything, his hand still holding my neck. "What *did* you do, by the way? He looked horrible."

Beckham laughed. "Hey, not all of it was me. He had that split lip before I fucking touched him." I crimsoned. He froze, lips parting in confusion before realisation dawned. He raised a singular brow in question and I nodded. "Good girl."

Wow.

I wiggled out of his hold and headed for the bathroom, knowing that he was following me, the idiot. My panties were ruined—even more so after his praise—and I needed to change into a fresh pair on the bus, like right now, whilst there was nobody there. Beckham watched me slip the soiled panties off from underneath my skirt and, just as I was about to fling them in the trash, he gripped my wrist.

Frowning at him, I watched as he took the flimsy black material before tucking it into his pocket, maintaining eye contact. Without another word, he spun on his heel.

"Where are you going?" I questioned.

He smirked, gesturing to his pants. "To take care of this." I gaped at him as he left. Once out of his presence, I took in a deep gulp of air. My feet led me to the benches where Jasper and Oliver sat.

"Hi," I croaked out, my voice suddenly disappearing. I swayed on my feet before sitting down between them. Jasper was giggling like a little girl, and for a second I thought he knew I was commando.

Oliver eyed me weirdly before laughing. "You look like you just got fucked." I blushed, recalling Beckham saying the same thing. "Nice." Jasper handed him some money and I frowned. "We had a bet going on," he revealed. "About how long it would take Beck to make his move to get you back."

I glared at them both. "I said around the time of our second match. Jasper over here said around our first match." He smirked at the scowling man on my other side. "And he lost fifty dollars because of it."

I punched Oliver's shoulder and he pouted. Taking the money from him, I handed it back to Jasper. "*Technically*, he made his move in that toilet two days after your first match. So you owe Jasper fifty dollars."

Jasper whooped, pulling me to his chest. "I knew you were my biological sister for a reason." I smiled as he kissed my head repetitively, Oliver frowning in bewilderment. My face was still red when I left them to go to the bus because I couldn't stop thinking about what had occurred between Beckham and me.

We'd said *just this once.*

But the pounding in my chest, the ache between my legs said otherwise.

Chapter 20
Beckham

There was one thing that always exasperated me about those coming-of-age books and movies; the friendship aspect of things. I'd always detested the way those stories played out. You'd be standing in line at a grocery store, wanting to buy a carton of milk or some shit, and then the cashier would say something about how that batch of milk was expired. And the only other person in the line who had expired milk was this dorky person who laughed at the misfortune you both walked into. The cashier would then take you to fetch new milk and you and your new friend realised this was the start of a glorious friendship.

That wasn't how it worked in the real world.

But if it had happened to you, congrats bro, you were one of the lucky ones. Many of us didn't have that privilege. The world wasn't the same as it had been during the time our parents were growing up. Kids had started gossiping and bullying as young as four years old. It was horrifying to sit through a class and constantly stress about whether anyone was talking about you behind your back. Making friends was tough. There wasn't a love-at-first-sight thing going on. I could honestly say none of my friends had trusted one another when we'd first met, or liked one another. It took time. Even if we'd had a meet-cute, we were still wary about the next person.

Grayson was the perfect example.

We hadn't started off great. I'd been a spoilt only child, I'd admit that, and he'd come from a struggling family. We'd met back in middle school and hadn't necessarily liked each other. Sometimes, you had to go through the worst to discover who you could truly rely on. That one day in middle school, when Grayson had appeared looking like the living dead, his friends hadn't bothered to question him. They hadn't questioned when he'd missed a few days or when he'd spent lunch sobbing in the toilet.

Nobody had said a damn thing.

But I'd heard my dad talking about the Carter family one night at dinner. I hadn't understood what he was going through, nobody had. All I'd known was that nobody deserved to suffer through something like that on their own. I was the worst at advice and I soon came to discover that was *his forte.*

I'd been by Grayson's side through the worst, watched him claw at his bedroom walls, and struggle with drugs and drinking through high school. I'd never told him what to do. It was an unspoken rule between us. There was a difference between telling someone what to do and letting them see things from your viewpoint. I hadn't told him to stop drinking and smoking, but I'd made it clear what would happen to him, and how his parents would feel. I'd followed the rules of our friendship.

If only the fucker would do the same now.

"Are you telling me to forgive Nate?" I sought, not attempting to conceal the outrage in my voice and character. My dad had suggested the same thing before.

We'd arrived at the hotel just over an hour ago. The drive was supposed to take about forty-five minutes but had taken over an hour because Benson had gotten lost. He didn't trust technology enough to use a GPS and then he'd taken a wrong turn.

It was dark outside and Benson had recommended we all get some rest. Grayson was rooming with me and he was currently sprawled across his bed, gazing at me with those *oh-so-perceptive* eyes of his. The moment Benson had declared that I'd be staying with Grayson, I knew I was going to get a speech. I'd been predicting it since the fashion show. He'd been giving me shrewd glances ever since, informing me that he was preparing a lecture.

"That's *not* what I'm saying."

"Then what?" I pressed, sagging back against the headboard.

I was already pestered because Nyx had snubbed me through the entire bus ride as she sat with Jasper and Oliver. She may have urged *just this once*, but I knew that was far from the truth. If the ongoing glimpses she'd sent me told me anything, it was that she wanted more. And it *terrified* her. So she'd elected to pretend that I didn't exist.

Grayson sat up. "Don't you think you deserve peace?" He tilted his head, looking genuinely concerned. As if I wasn't at peace with myself. "What will you benefit from hating him for the rest of your life?" I looked away. "You may try to hide it, but it's always on your mind. I see it when you're training, when you're talking to Nyx."

I scoffed. "Thanks for that life lesson, Mother Teresa."

"Look, all I'm saying is that you can't expect to move forward with Nyx when you're still thinking about the past," he vocalised, wiping non-existent dust from his bed. His words thumped something deep within me and my chest throbbed, like concrete drying inside me. Everything felt heavy.

Instantly, I sat straighter and scowled at him. "And who says I wanna move forward with Nyx?"

As far as anyone knew, we hated each other and we never gave the impression of otherwise. Well, except maybe Jasper. He'd had the absolute fortune of seeing me knuckle-deep inside her.

Grayson gave me a look, nose scrunching. "Do you think I'm stupid?" I said nothing because he was the furthest thing from stupid. "You don't hate her." He said the words with weight, daring me to contend. "You never really did."

Smoothing a hand over my face, I groaned. "I did. For a brief period."

And we both knew what brief period that was. It was just around the time she'd turned her back on me and went scrambling to help Nate. When that had happened, I'd taken what little admiration I had for her and buried it, buried it with my own hands and watered it with the hurt I'd felt. And from that, hatred had grown.

"If a stranger was to steal your laptop and phone," he started and I frowned, "you'd be upset but get over it. You'd say that life happens or maybe he needed money for his family." I was about to interrupt because I was confused as fuck but he continued speaking. "However, if somebody you *loved* hurt you, you'd automatically hate them."

I rolled my eyes, not startled at his cogitative standpoint. "So the lesson to be learnt is that I'm in love with Nate? *Nice.* Always thought he had a great ass."

"You hated Nyx because she hurt you," Grayson proceeded as if I didn't say anything. "She hurt all of us by choosing Nate. But, it's been months, Beck. People change—"

"If people change then why isn't she willing to move past Nate either?" I demanded gruffly, towing at my hair. It was the one thing that'd been pounding on my mind. That defence mechanism. I wanted to know why she needed me to hate her and I was beginning to think I'd never get through to her.

Grayson shrugged. "What happened between her and Nate has nothing to do with you." I chilled, looking at him in confusion. He was speaking as if he knew something I didn't. "She had a choice, she chose the one she thought would be the best for everyone. But everything she's done has led her here, back to us. Things worked out so let's just fucking move on." I pinched the bridge of my nose, feeling my head spin. "There's also this thing called fucking communication."

"I know what communication is, Gray," I riposted.

He raised his brows, fabricating shock and I wanted to punch him in the face. "Oh, you do? Well, that's a mighty fucking surprise considering you haven't done the one thing that could fix all of your problems. *Talk to her.*"

"How about *you* talk to *River*," I shot back and he gasped dramatically, turning crimson. "Yes, I went there." Grayson was glowering at me. The door opened and Sebastian strolled in, holding a cupcake. "Where the fuck did you get that?"

It was only then that I discerned he was wearing swim shorts. "Never mind that," Sebastian answered, motioning his head towards the door. "Benson just went to bed and some of the guys are gonna head to the hot tub."

The idea sounded great, but as the captain, I knew Benson was right when he'd said we needed the sleep. He and I may not have seen eye to eye all the time, but when it came to the well-being of the team; we could agree on many things.

"Guys, we have a match tomorrow," I told them, tilting back against my bed again.

Sebastian and Grayson shared a look before the former stated, "Nyx is there."

My body jerked but I didn't get up. Two minutes of tense silence must've passed before Grayson changed into swim shorts and followed Sebastian out, but not before the latter hurled his cupcake wrapper at me. I scowled, throwing it into the tiny metal bin.

I knew Grayson's advice was coming from a place of love and concern. He knew that all my problems with Nyx originated with Nate and if I didn't let go of that animosity, I couldn't move forward, as much as I wanted to. But even if I did trust Nyx, I feared that she'd keep that defence mechanism up—so what would be the point? I stood up and stepped to the balcony.

When I peeked down, I could see some of the guys in the boiling tub. But Nyx wasn't there. I could see Jasper and he plucked Oliver from the hot water before launching him into the probably freezing pool.

He hadn't mentioned what he saw, and I wondered if Nyx had told him not to. I didn't necessarily want the guys to know what went on between us because gossip like that would spread like wildfire. They'd no doubt assume she'd gotten her internship like that. I didn't want to be the reason for another rumour.

"I think Grayson and Annie are scheming," Nyx spoke as she entered my room, wearing a short satin robe. She looked freshly showered and ready for bed. Holding her phone up, she laughed. "I just got a call from Annie. Something about communication?"

I snorted, closing the balcony doors and wandering back inside. "I thought you were ignoring me."

She cast her phone onto Grayson's bed and sat down. "Would you have preferred I jumped you in front of everyone?" I quirked a brow, wondering what she was trying to achieve. Glimpsing at me, she grinned. "What? You expect me to sit in an enclosed space with you after you finger fucked me against a wall?"

No filter, whatsoever. Gesturing to the room, I responded, "This is an enclosed space." My words sounded rough even to my own ears. She had a plan, it was evident. No wonder she'd avoided me; she'd been plotting.

Nyx smirked. "But we're alone." She cleared her throat, going into her professional mode. I was surprised she didn't have a clipboard with notes. As she articulated, she gradually unknotted the string holding her robe together. "So, I was *thinking*," I swallowed, "since this attraction between us is making it difficult to ignore your existence."

Her robe fell to the ground, exposing her black lace underwear. Her bra had a tiny bow in the dip between the two cups and a matching one was at the front of her panties. My jeans grew tight as fuck as she sat down at the edge of my bed. She definitely had a plan. And part of it involved seducing me.

I tried to maintain eye contact and not have my gaze roaming. "Nyx, what the fuck are you doing?"

She frowned. "Oh, I thought this was what you wanted. I suppose I could always go find Jai. He seems like he knows how to have a fun time." The little minx knew exactly what she was doing. I stepped closer until she had to tilt her head to look up at me. "So, are we doing this or should I find somebody else?"

I knew her better than that by now. In the past, I'd have let her trick me without even knowing it. Like when she'd used me at the party, danced with me. But the thing about using the same trick all the time meant that I could now see it coming from a mile away. She thought she could control what happened between us.

Anyone who knew Nyx Taylor knew that she liked being in control. She was used to it. If something scared her, she'd try to tame it. She'd grown up being terrified of her father and now she made it her mission to succeed at everything she did, to not let men put her down. This attraction between us alarmed her, made her melt in my arms—and she didn't like that all too much. This was her attempt at taming it. But I wouldn't let her be in control, not at all. Because she had nothing to fear when she was with me.

And I intended to show her that.

"Nice try," I murmured, sketching featherlight touches on her lower back. Gently moving her, the back of her knees hit the bed and she had no choice but to sit down. "Whatever happens between us will be on *my* terms." She tensed, scowling up at me. "Because you always have an ulterior motive. Elbows. *Now*," I whispered, seeing her lean back and prop herself up on her elbows. Sliding my hands beneath her, I clutched her ass and dragged her to the edge of the bed.

Nyx shuddered. "I'm still in control here. This was *my* idea." She was grasping at air now, desperate for some form of power.

"This wasn't your idea. This was your *plan*," I emphasised, hooking my fingers through the thin straps of lace covering her and dragging it down, tossing it behind me. "A plan to try and dwindle this need you feel for me. You were certain that if you did things *your* way, your body would be content and want nothing more to do with me."

Her legs were dangling from the edge of the bed and I spread her thighs, seating myself between them. I'd started what happened between us in the hallway and she clearly believed that the only reason she wanted me again was that her pride was wounded. She'd *let* me touch her, *let* me take control, and now she wanted that control back.

"Since when did you become a professional at reading me?" she questioned, contempt in her voice. I could feel my jeans grow tight at the sight of her. If there was one way to die, this would be my pick. Raising a hand, I parted her folds, spotting the moisture accumulating there. "Are you gonna stare at me the entire time or actually do something?" Nyx queried, my eyes snapping to hers. She lifted an obstinate brow. Smirking, I gently nipped the inside of her thigh. "*God*, you're an asshole," she hissed.

"I've barely touched you and you're already so wet," I hummed, tilting forward to lick through her slit, feeling her quiver. "The things I could do to you." She bit her lip to contain a gasp and I smiled against her as I buried my face in her pussy.

Nyx was far from ashamed, finding no problem with voicing what she wanted. And I did exactly as she asked, groaning when she yanked harshly at my hair. She squirmed and curved her back, moaning uncontrollably as I ate her out. I lapped at her, sucking her clit into my mouth and revelling in the full moans that left her mouth.

"Shit," she cussed, throwing her head back. I shifted my tongue inside her and groaned deep in my throat. She was a whimpering mess, but I wasn't about to hold back. She thought she could brush this under the carpet. Well, she couldn't. "*Beck.*"

Her legs clamped around my head and I tapped her thigh. "Wider."

Nyx palmed the back of my head and spread her legs. I nearly laughed. Nyx Taylor spreading her legs for me. She let out a sound that nearly had me coming in my fucking pants like a young boy watching porn for the first time.

"Why did I hate you again?" she pondered out loud and I chuckled against her, savouring the way she trembled. I could spend hours between her legs, listening to her moan, watching her writhe.

There was something so stimulating about the sight of her

at the edge of the bed with her legs spread for me. My hands made their way underneath her bra until I was cupping her breasts, tweaking her nipples.

"Fuck," she whined. "I guess that mouth is good for things other than spewing absolute shit."

I suckled her clit. "Even seconds away from an orgasm, you're still a bitch." She grinned, pulling my hand so she could suck a finger into her mouth. I swore. "Fucking minx."

"You should consider a career in prostitution," she blasted back, wiggling when I pinched her ass. "You'd make some serious cash."

"Fuck off," I mumbled, biting her thigh.

"How about you *get* me off?" she suggested, her words fading into another moan.

I paid attention to what had her on the brink of screaming and repeated those actions. Pulling away slightly to gaze at her, I shoved a finger inside and curled it. Nyx's mouth dropped open and her eyes fell shut, her chest rising and falling rapidly with each pant.

"So pretty," I mused, adding another finger and plunging into her. It was mesmerizing, watching her tighten around the digits. "That's it, baby. Can you take another one?" She nodded, features twisting with pleasure. I added a third finger, crooking them slightly, and she moaned my name. I groaned as she tensed. "Good girl."

"I'm gonna—"

"*Come*," I grunted, doubling the pace of my fingers. Nyx pressed a hand to her mouth and I hissed. "Don't cover your mouth. I want to hear you." She practically collapsed into the bed as she convulsed with her orgasm. I watched her eyes glaze over. "That's my baby. Come all over my fingers." I scissored my fingers and she let out a strangulated sound.

Nyx gripped my hair. "Wait," she wheezed and I paused, moving back to look at her. "Come here." Nonchalantly, she dragged me towards her and then pushed me onto my back. I was smirking, not at all astonished that Nyx would have an idea of her own. "Stop looking so smug," she stammered. "Can't have this being an unfair exchange. That's not how this works."

She unzipped my jeans, freeing my dick and taking it into her hands. A throaty moan escaped me. "*Shit*, baby." All air left my lungs as she squeezed me, her tongue whispering over the head. "Suck." I nearly lost it when she finally sealed her lips over my dick, sucking me deep.

I hoisted her by the hips and had her pussy hovering over my face. There was no way I was done with her. Control needed to stay in my corner. Not wanting to be outmatched, I clamped my lips around her clit and felt her moan around me.

The vibration sent a shiver down my spine. I clutched her ass cheeks and spread her wide, breathing cold air onto her clit. I could scarcely concentrate with her sucking me off as if her life depended on it. Three fingers slipped inside her again and she whimpered, fisting my length in the creamlike skin of her hand. I watched my fingers sink inside her, feeling her clench around me.

"Fuck, you taste so good," I muttered, biting her ass cheek and hearing her moan. My release was near and I could tell she was fast approaching another orgasm. But I didn't want it to end. She bobbed her head; I felt myself hit the back of her throat. Fuck, she didn't even gag. And that's when my resolve broke. I groaned deeply and she sucked whatever I gave her into her mouth. Simultaneously, Nyx quivered as she orgasmed above me.

Nyx sat up and twisted around, straddling me. My eyes rolled to the back of my head as I felt her rub her warm and wet pussy over my dick. She moaned, placing her hands on my chest. "Beckham, please—"

I gripped her hips, stilling her. Neither of us were thinking straight, too high on each other. And that was bad. It was like all the tension between us fried our rational thoughts. "We can't—" My own hiss cut me off when she dragged the head of my dick through her slit.

What was I saying again?

I kissed her throat when I dragged her down, sucking at her skin. Finding her mouth, I plunged my tongue inside. I roughly ground against her and she squeaked, gripping my shoulders tighter.

Our kisses and touches were desperate, frantic. Nyx leaned down, placing her forehead against mine. There was a battle in her eyes, showcasing her internal conflict. Her body wanted me, but her mind was still hesitant.

"Please," she whispered, still grinding against me.

I shook my head. "I don't have a condom, baby."

It took way too much energy to deny her, but it needed to be done. She wasn't thinking clearly and I feared she'd come to regret the decision to have sex with me in the morning. Messing around was one thing, sex was an entirely different game. Her orgasm was fucking with her head.

Not liking the rejected expression that appeared on her face, I kissed her, showing her I felt the exact same way about her. But we didn't need to rush things. I kissed her exactly the way I would've fucked her for the first time in almost ten months. Slowly, lengthening each second. Nyx moaned.

"Easy, sweetheart," I murmured.

"Get inside me, dipshit," she grumbled against my lips, grinding against me again. I could hear how wet she was and it made my decision all the more harder.

And my dick.

I chuckled. "Nyx, calm down."

She groaned in exasperation and launched herself next to me, landing with a huff. After a few seconds, she turned to face me, not at all concerned about her half-naked state. Despite the circumstances, I'd missed that adorable look of pleading she used to give me.

It was back now, her eyelashes fluttering. "Don't look at me like that, you little minx."

"Just listen, I've got a hypothesis," she beseeched with dazed eyes.

Dipping my head, I glanced at her. Her face was still flushed and her eyes were glossy. There were marks covering her neck and I wasn't looking forward to her spotting them in the mirror. "You've got a hypothesis?"

Of course she had a fucking hypothesis.

Nyx nodded, brushing hair out of her face. "If this is supposedly the law of attraction at work," cue air quotes, "then shouldn't we just—boom!" I watched her slam her hands together and I blinked. She waited for my response, but I didn't know what was happening. "Me," she raised one hand, "and you," she raised the other. "Boom!" She slammed them together again.

"You want us to murder each other?" I asked. I knew what she was implying, but it was beyond comical watching her get frustrated with me. "High five?"

Her eyes narrowed like a snake. "You *know* what I mean, fuckwad."

I shook my head. "No, I don't—"

"Liar!" she exclaimed and I burst into laughter, pushing to my feet and buttoning my jeans again. "We should just fuck. Then maybe this feeling will go away." I wanted to tell her that she didn't sound like she wanted the feeling to go away, but she'd yell at me. "I'll come up with a better plan soon enough."

"You do that," I returned, grabbing a towel and strolling into the bathroom.

It was smaller than the one I had back home yet managed to look more luxurious. White tiles covered the walls and floor with gold ornaments. It was quiet in the room and I wondered if Nyx left. As much as she'd argue against it, seducing me wasn't the only reason she was there. She genuinely wanted me, it was clear by the way she'd yielded so easily. That was a conversation for another time.

Once the water was hot enough, I undressed and moved into the shower. I wet my hair and examined the shelf of products. Many of them looked like they smelled like fruit. I was proven correct when I opened a tube and got a whiff of strawberry. And then the shower door opened.

I turned as a fully naked Nyx stepped inside, shutting the

glass door behind her. She didn't say anything, she didn't need to. In the blink of an eye, her legs were around my waist as I pressed her against the wall, my mouth attached to hers. I kissed her thoroughly, running my hands all over her. If this feeling was going to go away the moment we had each other, I was going to enjoy it as much as I could.

It felt *right*, having her in my arms again.

My hands tightened in her wet hair as she suckled the skin of my neck, leaving marks of her own. I could barely even shower with her latching onto me, but I didn't care. Not in the slightest. Once I was done showering, I wrapped Nyx up in a fluffy towel, carrying her back to the bed. She used a spare one to dry her hair as I dried myself, slipping into a pair of sweatpants.

One of the things I'd noticed about Nyx was that when she was exhausted, it was more challenging to camouflage her emotions. So as I ruffled my damp hair, I could see the look of affliction on her features. She was back in her underwear, the satin robe loosely belted around her waist and giving me an eyeful of her tits.

"Why do you always have that look on your face after spending time with me?" I teased, disposing of our towels into the hamper.

Nyx looked up. My words only hit her a second later and a delicate laugh left her. "No, I, uh," she wavered, flushing slightly. It was difficult to imagine this was the same girl who'd initiated the sixty-nine with me. "I was thinking about what you said the other day, about me trusting you. Annie's been encouraging me to do so, but I feel like she's—"

"Hiding something?" I finished for her, taking a seat at the edge of the bed. Nyx nodded, looking ashamed of her thoughts. "Yeah, I kinda got the same from Grayson. Initially, I thought he was crushing on her." She frowned in inquiry. "But as much of a gentleman as he is, Grayson's not looking for a relationship, trust me. And he'd never disrespect Beth like that. Friends? He can never have enough of those."

The blonde pouted. "Annie doesn't have any friends besides Beth. Well, Beth's a little more than a friend now, I guess." She appeared to be thinking something through. "But why Grayson and not Nailea?" she asked rhetorically. "Nailea's been around her more than him."

"Grayson," I began with a sigh, "he's a peculiar one, to be honest. You know he's the most feeling out of all of us, the mom-friend if you will." Nyx nodded. "Let's just say he has this weird ability to sense when something's…" I trailed off, floundering to phrase my words without hurting Nyx.

She sat straighter, looking distressed. "When something's what?"

Her emotions were clear as day, something that I never even knew I'd missed. The very fact that she was talking about her feelings, about her problems with me gave me hope.

"When something's wrong," I concluded, pinching the bridge of my nose. "Or better yet, when somebody's hurting."

Grayson was like the fucking Dumbledore of the hockey team. Sometimes it felt like he could read everyone's minds. It was him who'd always encouraged me to speak to Nyx, to talk to Nate and settle things.

I saw the combination of emotions in Nyx's eyes. "If Annie's hurting, why wouldn't she tell me?" I didn't have the answer to that and neither did she. Nyx wanted the truth, but the truth seemed to excavate a ridge of insecurities. "Maybe I should ask Georgia. Something weird is going on there, no matter how hard I try to ignore it," she mumbled more to herself than me.

"Georgia?" I pulled a face.

Nyx was rambling now, anxiously tugging at her damp hair. "Georgia Lowe. She's a parent at Poppy's school, and helps out when we need it sometimes. I think Annie's been talking to her about our—"

She was going so fucking fast but all I needed to capture was the beginning. "Did you say Georgia Lowe?"

The name sounded familiar and I wracked my brain for it. My mom's friend? She could be part of her cooking club, or maybe something else. My mom was part of too many fucking clubs.

"Yes," Nyx responded, freezing at the expression I wore. "How do you know her?"

"*I* don't," I answered, eventually acknowledging where I knew her from. I'd seen her around the station before. "But my dad does. Georgia's a social worker."

Chapter 21

Nyx

It felt weird, thinking that you knew everything, only to find out you knew nothing. The moment the words had left Beckham's mouth, I'd been able to feel a string being tugged inside me, a string stitched into every encounter I'd had with Georgia. Our first meeting, her offering to help, offering to host sleepovers. It had never occurred to me I should piece it together. Why should I have to? Georgia was a friend.

But pulling it all together was inevitable and as I sat there, allowing myself to really *think* about Georgia Lowe, I could see the fissures in the portrait that I'd put together. Where had she come from? And why had she arrived at the perfect time? If she was a social worker, why weren't my baby sisters taken away yet? Why wasn't my dad arrested? Was she even helping us?

It was an hour later and I sat in my designated room, legs crossed and phone clenched in my hand. My thumb hovered over Annie's contact. She'd no doubt be awake, probably baking. Whilst I was overthinking everything, my finger slipped and I watched the phone ring. Immediately, I ended it after one ring, throwing the device a foot away from me.

A second later, my phone was ringing and I suppressed a groan. “Hey, Annie,” I greeted, putting the phone on speaker and letting it lay in front of me.

“Hi,” she returned with a yawn and I could hear her moving around the kitchen. “Everything okay? Or did you butt-dial me again?” I couldn’t find it in myself to laugh along with her, too many questions swirling around.

I forced a laugh. “Yeah, um, I just got into bed now. Figured I’d give you and the girls a call.”

She was silent for a moment. “Um, it’s just me tonight, actually.” I frowned, automatically assuming the worst. “The girls are at Georgia’s for the weekend. She picked them up earlier.”

Okay, that did *not* make me feel better, especially after discovering what Georgia was. There was no way Annie couldn’t have known. So the question was: why hadn’t she told me?

“Annie,” I murmured, feeling my eyes sting with unshed tears. She hummed. “We tell each other everything, right?”

Another tense beat. “Of course. Is everything okay?”

With no idea how to phrase my question, I just threw it out there. “Did you know that Georgia’s a social worker?”

The insecure part of me expected a tense silence, one that allowed my sister formulate a lie. But she didn’t miss a beat, her voice as gentle as ever.

“Not at first, no. But everything changed a few weeks ago, after that first call from Mom.”

The phone call that I’d begged her not to tell me about.

Young me had been upset over the fact that her mom had left and wanted nothing to do with her. “And I begged you to never mention anything regarding her around me.” I was beginning to regret that decision now.

Annie hummed. “She explained that Georgia was there to help us, seeing as she couldn’t be. I wanted to tell you, I really did—”

“But I wouldn’t listen,” I finished, feeling horrible. “I let you deal with all this crap on your own.” My eyes burned and I hugged a pillow to my chest.

“Nyxie,” Annie began, her easy tone making me want to bawl. “You were hurt. If you wanted nothing to do with Mom, I couldn’t fault you for that. What did I tell you the other day? I’ll tell you everything you want to know when you’re ready and not a moment before—”

I sniffled. “Annie—”

“I knew this day would come, knew you’d eventually overcome the hurt and want to know what happened,” she continued, leaving no room for me to be angry at myself. “I’m your big sister. I shoulder what you can’t until you have the strength. That’s how we work, remember?” I nodded, although she couldn’t see me. “I want you to know that you can always come to me. If you have questions, ask them.”

My throat ached as I thought of everything Annie had to shoulder on her own, all because I was a petty bitch. “For now, I just wanna know what Georgia’s purpose is.”

“To be honest, I don’t even fully understand. I recommend talking to Georgia, but what I do know is that Dad knows she’s a social worker.” My jaw slackened. “It’s why I didn’t suspect him of having another family," her voice broke at the reminder, "because he usually disappears to compulsory counselling that Georgia makes him go to. When he lashes out, the girls are technically in Georgia's care until his therapy sessions ends, but to not frighten them, she leaves them with us whilst Dad is gone and passes nights with her off as sleepovers. Ever since she's been in our lives, he's been making an effort to not hurt Poppy and Indigo. They're minors, you see, so he doesn't hurt them as much as he hurts..."

She didn't want to say it. So I did. "Me. As much as he hurts me."

"We willingly stay with him," she said, that sentence carrying so much weight. "Georgia's there to protect Poppy and Indigo. The counselling is compulsory, only when Dad refuses to attend and constantly or purposefully hurts the girls can Georgia take them away. But the thing is, the sessions have been working, and that scares me because—"

"Because you don't want them to stay in his care," I mumbled, feeling my head spin. "Annie, I can't believe you've been struggling with these worries all on your own."

She forced a laugh. "Somebody has to be the mom, huh?"

"Thank you for telling me," my words were soft.

There was rustling on her side before she said, "thank you for asking."

That one sentence made my chest ache. This was only some of the weight I was taking from her. I didn't want to imagine what else she had to do as the mother figure in our household.

"Annie?" I said suddenly and she hummed again. "I don't want you to feel like you can't tell me things." Or feel like she had to listen to my petty requests, especially if it meant suffering for her.

"I *know* I can tell you things, Nyxie," she responded, her voice dripping with sincerity. "Which is why I'm telling you that I'm thinking of asking Beth to be my girlfriend."

Now that took my breath away. "You're ready to make it official with *Macbeth?*"

And then the cackles came, Annie hastily speaking over me about how much of a great person she was and how she felt it was the right time with her going to an event that Beth's maternal family was hosting and all. But I was too far gone, too elated at the fact that Annie was finally taking what she wanted from life. Beth was good for her, that much I could gather.

She spent the next few minutes expressing her outrage for somebody named Vivian, Beth's mother. I listened to her speak, promising myself that I wanted her to always sound this happy. If that meant putting on my big girl panties when it came to my mom, then so be it.

It felt weird, thinking that you knew everything, only to find out you knew nothing. But perhaps not knowing everything was for the better. Important facts would reveal themselves when the time came, and because of my experience with the law of attraction, I believed the universe knew exactly what it was doing.

The match had been going on for almost two hours already.

I'd forgotten how invigorating it could be. I felt each scrape of skates against the ice in my teeth and I felt my heart soar each time somebody from our team scored. The guys were putting in their all. The Bruins clearly upped their game since the last time we'd gone against them, but so did our Trojans. I'd been so close to launching myself onto the ice whenever the other team scored. But I knew Benson had trained them to the best of his ability.

He may have arrived empty-handed, but he'd been willing to learn. I knew that the team had the best coach in him, although I would never admit that to him. He'd never let me hear the end of it.

Just five minutes ago, Sebastian had to be taken off the ice and replaced with Levi. From the moment we'd driven to the rink, I could tell there was something wrong with him. He wasn't normally chatty, but this time was weird. It looked like each time he'd opened his mouth; he'd turned an alarming shade of green. Like the dedicated player and alternative captain that he was; Sebastian had still played the game. But although people regularly called him an angel, the guy was still human and had nearly thrown up his guts on the ice when a Bruin had slammed into him.

After I'd gone with him to the toilet and he'd coughed up the rest of his breakfast, I'd found out that he'd eaten a cupcake with buttercream frosting last night. Since he wasn't lactose intolerant, the only plausible answer was food poisoning.

"Wasn't the cupcake sour?" I inquired as I sagged against the wall, watching Sebastian take huge gulps of his bottle of water.

He was still wearing his uniform, but the skates and helmet were removed. His face was pale and I could only imagine how his abdomen was hurting because of the heaving. But then again, he had abs of steel.

He gurgled the water, grimacing as he swallowed. "I thought it was supposed to taste like that."

Now I understood what Grayson meant when he said Sebastian ate everything. I'd seen it with my own eyes before. He would always have some form of food in his hands.

"Well, now you've probably got food poisoning," I appended, hearing the audience collapse into cheers. A poignant look passed over Sebastian's features. He wouldn't be able to get back onto the ice, not when he was sick. Well, that was a lesson learnt. "This is why you shouldn't eat everything you see."

His glass-like eyes snapped to me and the corner of his lips quirked. "Somebody should tell Beck that." I tensed. "Didn't he like eat you out last night?"

Oh. My. *God.* I knew people gossiped all the time, but I didn't think Beckham would tell his friends about what had happened between us.

"Do you not have anything better to do with your life?" I seethed through clenched teeth. My body felt feverish all over and not in a good way.

Sebastian must've seen the murderous look in my eyes because he raised both hands in surrender. "Chill, dude." I scowled at him. "He didn't tell us," he chuckled, "we kinda just *knew.*" That wasn't helping things. "Besides, we need you so it's not like I'll run to Benson with this information." I didn't respond. "As long as you don't backstab us again."

And that sparked a fire underneath my ass. I stood straighter, studying him before stopping at his eyes. "Was that your attempt at a threat?" Sebastian shrugged. "Listen to me, asshole, I don't take threats lightly. Try it again and I'll make your life hell."

I knew I had too much anger because of one diminutive threat, but it was so much more than that. All the team saw was me supposedly turning my back on them, but they had no idea what *I* had gone through because of it. They weren't the only ones that suffered.

And I was getting a little sick of the judgement.

"Beck might be bewitched by your pussy but I'm not as trusting as him," he informed me, looking all too presumptuous for somebody who'd had his head buried in a toilet a few minutes ago. There was a hint of teasing in his tone, veiled with annoyance. "He made the mistake of trusting you once before. I don't know what the fuck your plan is because you've been helping us so far—"

"Speak to her like that again and you'll leave this rink missing an appendage."

Both Sebastian and I turned to the end of the hallway. And there stood Nate Wyatt, ornamented in his new school gear. He looked exactly as I remembered, from the rumpled brown hair to the sparkling green eyes. Those same eyes had once been filled with love for my sister, even for me.

He wasn't looking at me, but rather at a scowling Sebastian. The latter's mouth dropped open, but no words left him. Even I was at a loss for words. I understood there was a possibility of running into Nate, but I didn't think it would actually happen. The blonde must've been thinking about many things. This was the captain that had put his team through hell. This was also the guy they supposedly believed I'd helped.

Sebastian glanced from me to Nate and I felt myself roll my eyes. "Oh, I see," the blonde grumbled, looking like he was about to barf again. He nodded to himself, glancing at me one last time before heading back to the match.

"That was a dumb move," I articulated without looking at Nate. Sebastian already thought I had ulterior motives, and Nate standing up for me only fanned the flames. It even disturbed me. We didn't part on the best terms. The last time I'd seen him was probably when I'd chewed his ass out for breaking my sister's heart. "If he wasn't sceptical before, he definitely is now."

Nate strolled past me with the confidence of a God. He was always like that. It was one of the many things we had in common. "Walk with me." I bristled at the command but followed him anyway. If there was a time to get things off my chest, tell him things I hadn't had a chance to, now was the time. He paused at the foyer doors and then whirled around, soundlessly examining me. "Are you okay?"

"Why'd you defend me?" I countered his inquiry with one of my own. He didn't react, but his eyes flared. So many unsaid things.

"Nyxie," he started in a tasteless tone and my shoulders tensed at the nickname. I'd once allowed him to use it because he was family. "You just never learn, do you? You'd let an arrogant bastard like Sebastian Hayes treat you like shit even after all—" A look of realisation surfaced on his features when I didn't oppose, and then he chuckled. "You didn't tell them."

I tugged at the Trojan jersey I was wearing. Looking at Nate was like looking my past in the eyes. "What I do is none of your business."

He nodded, pouting. "True. But what's a villain without a redemption arc?" There was a smile on his face now, one that made me see exactly why Annie had fallen for him. She'd first spotted him at the grocery store where she'd previously worked. Nate was always aware of his surroundings and he had easily put two and two together; Annie was my sister. His advances had never been bad.

Nate had loved her.

As much as I should've fought against it, we were both villains. It wasn't a nice thought, but it was the truth. We both had done bad things to help the people we loved. Nate's dad didn't reciprocate those feelings and never would. Beckham didn't even know the full story.

"That's funny," I grumbled, eyes narrowing. "I'm not the only one hiding my redemption arc, am I?" It was his turn to tense up. Because I'd grasped that he was a good person; he just buried it very well. "I'm surprised you haven't joined the hockey team."

It was my crack at hurting him, hurting him the way he'd hurt my sister. All I could see was the heartbreak in Annie's pretty brown eyes when he'd left her without a word. My baby sisters had loved him and he'd left as if he hadn't been there to begin with.

All because of a man who didn't deserve his respect, his

admiration.

Hockey had been his life and it was a surprise to many to see that he hadn't tried out for the UCLA team. Like Beckham, his dad had played hockey when he was younger. The difference between Nate and Beckham, however, was that Beckham's dad hadn't forced him to do anything he hadn't wanted to.

But he fired back with a low blow of his own, one that made me recoil. "I'm surprised you haven't told Hunt that everything you did was for him." I had to remind myself that it was illegal to murder somebody. The one person, other than Annie, who knew the truth. Loud cheers broke the stiff air and he quirked a brow. "Who do you think won?"

Without missing a second, I answered, "My boys."

Nate grinned, stepping closer. He placed his hands on my shoulders and leaned down to my height. "All of this hurt for a guy who told everyone I was paying you to sleep with me." I rolled my eyes. "You didn't know?"

"Are you saying Beckham started that rumour?"

I'd already surmised it was him so whatever Nate was seeking to accomplish with that information wouldn't work. I knew Beckham was an asshole so I automatically thought the worst of him. It helped in situations like this.

Now Nate couldn't take me by surprise.

He nodded. "Well, that's what I've heard—"

And because I knew him so well, I apprehended he was nervous when he began scratching the back of his neck. It was a habit Annie had found utterly enchanting. I thought it was stupid. It allowed people to have the upper hand on him.

"And what was your source, *www.trustmebro*?" I riposted,

feeling the opening of a headache developing. "And don't pretend you care, you little bitch. Not after what you did to us."

Nate gawked at me. "After what *I* did? Everything that happened to your family was *your* fault and you fucking know it. All you've been doing is trying to shift the blame to me, but it was *you* who nearly ruined your family's life for some asshole who walked away without a backward glance."

It was always the same story; us transferring the blame to each other like a game of catch. Annoyed, I responded with, "You could've said something. Went against your dad but you let him do what he did, let him ruin our lives. *Suing* me for defamation? Really Nate? Was our situation not bad enough and then you let your dad take more money from us?"

He shook his head. "You did that yourself. All of that effort and Hunt still doesn't trust you, right? So what was the point? You caused the rift between me and Annie—"

"That was all you, Nate," I cut him off. "If only you stood up against your fucking dad. My dad may beat me, but I *never* cower. If only I could say the same about you."

This was the Nate nobody knew, the one that was always stowed in the dark. This was the Nate who was exactly like me; an abused child, deep inside. I channelled my anger and hurt differently. I put it towards succeeding. Nate, on the other hand, still strived for favour from his dad. And as long as that proceeded, he'd have no real friends. I'd discerned right off the bat that his dad's mission was to isolate his son because my dad had tried that once, too. Only, I had siblings.

Nate was alone.

His eyes gravitated to his feet, his throat bobbing. "We're

not the same person."

Swallowing, I spoke, "I did you a favour because I loved you. Annie loved you and I'd do anything for her, even risk my own fucking happiness. Do you think she enjoyed watching your dad constantly criticise you? Force you to play a sport you hated? Fucking beat you each time you opened your mouth against him?"

Nate boosted his emerald gaze to mine. "I didn't deserve her, Nyxie. I didn't deserve any of you, to be honest."

"But Annie *loved* you," I flung back, watching his eyes moisten slightly as he looked away. "You know, Beck and I may not have worked out, but I thought for sure you and Annie would've. Then you left her—"

He groaned. "My dad—"

"Fuck your dad, Nate." I interposed. "I risked my own fucking relationship so that you and my sister could be happy and how do you repay me? You break her fucking heart." My heart was banging wildly against my ribcage. "You've always despised hockey and as long as you were around your dad, you'd never escape him. Now, you're out of his sight. Ask yourself who put that distance between you and your *abusive dad*," I finished, wiping at my burning eyes.

"My dad couldn't stand the embarrassment after I lost the captaincy," he stated in a coarse tone, shoving his hands into the pockets of his jeans. "The only option was to transfer. The UCLA coach also had a few words with Coach Ford." He shrugged. "I'm not allowed to join the team after how I treated the Trojans."

He didn't look too sad about not being able to play. Not

at all. I'd intended to get Nate away from his dad and hoped that he and Annie would try to maintain their relationship. It hadn't been in my plans to ruin their relationship. That had all been Nate's dad.

"All you had to do was let Annie love you, let her care for you," I said with a sardonic laugh, slowly shaking my head. "Nate, I know what it's like to feel like nothing, to be told you're nothing by the very person that had a hand in creating you. I knew that he was going to shit on you for losing the captaincy, but what're a few minutes of a drunken asshole berating you when you know that you'll never have to go through that again, that Annie, the girl you loved, was going to help soothe those final wounds?"

He stared at me, remorse evident in his leafy eyes. "I let him get to me."

When I'd thought about running into Nate, I wanted to hate him. I wanted to hurt him, yell at him. Even if I'd had a hand in what had happened with my family, so had he. He could've prevented it, served as a blockage because he'd had the power to do so. But all I saw was that frightened boy, again.

All I could see was me.

"Yeah, I figured."

He sighed. "I should've known it was a bad idea when I hired you to plan my events for the captaincy." A rough laugh escaped his lips. "I mean, you were always Hunt's girl, even if you didn't acknowledge it." He smiled slightly when I flushed. "Having you as his supposed enemy only fuelled his desire to win. Let's not add the fact that you—"

"Let's not revisit what I did exactly," I stated with an

embarrassed groan. When it came to people I cared about, I could be vicious. My situation with Nate was a prime example. "If it helps, part of me *does* feel bad about the position I put you in. But it all brought you here, with a few costs."

On both sides; because I had some costs too.

Nate nodded, his eyes becoming dazed. "Annie being one of the costs." I looked away at the pain in his voice. "Does she hate you for it?" Before I could respond, he chuckled. "That's absurd. Annie can't hate anyone, not even if she tried."

"She doesn't hate me," I confessed. "Because she knows that my goal wasn't to break you two up. But she's still upset that you left so easily after what your dad did. If you'd just sat down and spoken to her, she would've listened."

He cleared his throat. "Can I be honest?" I nodded. "I felt like a coward, running away from my dad. Annie deserves better than a pushover, one that couldn't even stop his dad from trying to ruin his girlfriend's life. It's one of my biggest regrets."

"Nate—"

"You sabotaged my chances of staying captain," he stated and I wrinkled my nose at the reminder. "But you did it for Hunt because he deserved that title. You did it for me because you wanted me away from my dad. And you did it for Annie so she could be with me without my dad breathing down our necks." I shifted uncomfortably with my past actions being revisited. "I was jealous of your strength, especially after discovering your true intentions. And I couldn't even stop my dad. My apology is worth dirt but I'd like to offer it to you anyway."

I didn't know how to respond. He moved closer, hand

reaching out to me. I stared at it for a while, stared at that soft look in his eyes. It was the same look you'd see on a toddler after they were yelled at for making a mess. It was a look of defeat. It was a look of utmost regret. So I let him pull me into his arms.

If not for me, then for him.

Because like I'd told Beckham before—Nate had nobody in his corner, nobody to help him out of the dark room he'd locked himself in.

It wasn't my place to forgive him for what he'd put the guys through. That was between them. But it was my place to try to forgive somebody who had once been my brother.

"I'm sorry," he whispered into my hair, squeezing me. I could hear the emotion wrapped around each word.

"I'm sorry too," I mumbled, burrowing my face into his chest. His arms were firm around me, keeping me in the familiar hold. "And I know you're only prolonging this hug because Beck's watching." Nate erupted into laughter, stepping back but keeping his arm around me. "I fucking *know you.*"

Nate shrugged, eyes crinkling at the sides. "What can I say? Old habits die hard," he said, referencing the times he had made Beckham jealous.

"Did you come to scold me?" I demanded without turning around, knowing that Beckham was lurking in the shadows. He wasn't as slick as he thought. The sound of his thick uniform was enough to alert me to his presence. "Come to question whether I'm working with Nate?"

Beckham stepped closer. His stormy eyes were trained on Nate, but there was no animosity. "Wyatt."

"Hunt," he replied with a nod before turning to face me. "Thanks for the talk. I'll see you when I see you, Nyxie." Before he could walk away, he stopped, glancing at me one last time. "I'm attending therapy, by the way."

The smile I sent him was genuine. Some words went unspoken. He didn't want to be like his dad. A small nod was sent in Beckham's direction. It wasn't an apology. In all honesty, I didn't think Nate was capable of apologising to the boys yet. That would be like apologising to somebody for stabbing them whilst still holding the knife. Nate needed to get rid of the knife, get rid of the negative thoughts and anger his dad had taught him was normal. The therapy was only the beginning, and it was conveyed in that nod he'd sent Beckham.

It was a promise that he would return to pay his debts. He didn't say anything else, just disappeared through the doorway and into the parking lot. There was a look of understanding as Beckham watched Nate drive away. He must've heard a good portion of the conversation for him to look at him with anything but contempt.

This was the same guy who had put his team under intense emotional strain. His arm coiled around my waist, pulling me against him. I could see the questions swirling around in his eyes, but he didn't know where to start.

"He's right," he declared. "Having you as my enemy made me want the captaincy even more."

I tried my best not to blush because if he'd heard that far into the conversation, he'd surely heard Nate refer to me as his girl. That I'd even sabotaged Nate.

"Good," I hummed, attempting a smile.

Beckham stared down at me and then he grinned. "We won." There was no doubt about it. I could still hear the cheers going.

"I know," I murmured. Placing my hands on his chest, I mumbled, "I know you won."

His voice was a low murmur as he said, "And I apparently have you to thank for that." Adoration filled his eyes and I smiled up at him, some tension leaving my body. "You really sabotaged him?"

I smirked. "Say it."

Suddenly my feet were off the ground, my legs wrapped around his waist as he cupped my nape, making sure that I maintained eye contact. "You little minx." What used to be an insult now held so much meaning. "You're not gonna explain further, are you?"

Laughing, I muttered, "I've got to hold something over your head, right?" The corner of his mouth lifted. "Baby steps, please." My eyes drifted back to where Nate once stood. "I've got a lot to think about."

Chapter 22

Beckham

Guilt; it had been my best friend for the past few days. I felt like I was trapped inside a complex maze, forced to accept the reality of the situation. There was no way to escape my guilt unless I confronted it. But I was terrified of what I'd find at the heart of that maze. It was why I'd been all over the place since our last game against the Bruins, although it was a win. My mind kept deviating back to that brief moment between Nate and Nyx.

When Sebastian had first told me that the two were together, a spark of rage had blazed inside me. The vulnerable side that I fought to hide had jumped into gear and I'd immediately thought of the worst likely scenario. I'd thought that although I was making progress with Nyx, Nate could easily take her away again. But then I'd apprehended the idea was preposterous. Nate's hands had been on her shoulders, but she hadn't been hostile. She'd looked hurt. Obviously, the green monster inside of me had strived to get to the surface, but I'd contained it.

My unnecessary anger would only cause problems when the obvious solution was to talk things through. *Communication*, Grayson always reminded me.

I hadn't been able to hear much of their conversation because I'd stood quite a distance away, and the audience had still been celebrating our win. At first, I hadn't moved closer because I'd apprehended it was a good thing. It was better to ask her about it than to eavesdrop. Countless movies proved that eavesdropping was bad because you'd end up getting the story completely wrong.

It was like picking up a new book and trying to figure out the entire plot merely by going off from what you read of the blurb. My plan had been fine until Nyx's expression had contorted into one of pain. That's when I'd stepped closer and grasped something monumental.

If only you stood up against your fucking dad. My dad may beat me, but I never cower. If only I could say the same about you.

After that, I hadn't known how to react. We all lived such privileged lives that we never cared to peek outside of our bubble, afraid that it would pop. Never would I have suspected that Nate Wyatt was a victim of abuse. His expression had said it all when Nyx had confronted him. I thought back to the past two years he and I were on the same campus.

There'd never been any bruises and he'd never reached out to anyone. But then again, neither had Nyx. I felt stupid for not discerning these things, too caught up in my own shit. Nate had still hurt my team, but a bully only became one because they were bullied themselves. It didn't justify his actions against us, although it made me question everything.

That's where the guilt came in.

The obvious answer was that Nyx had commiserated with Nate because they were comparable and had corrupt home lives. And I'd spent all my time hating the two of them. Well, I had a valid reason to despise Nate because of how he'd treated us like his puppets. But all this time, I'd believed Nyx had turned her back on me when she'd only been trying to help somebody who she'd seen herself in.

There were people outside of the bubble I lived in. Perhaps it had had nothing to do with me at all, just her wanting to help Nate by getting him away from his dad. So she'd sabotaged him.

That was something I still couldn't wrap my mind around.

"Why's your heart beating so fast?" a dozy voice piped up with a tap against my chest where her head was resting.

I peeped down at Indigo, who I held in my arms as I sat waiting in the food court. For a Friday afternoon, the mall was relatively peaceful. Back when I'd been in high school, the mall was always filled with teenagers, highlighting my argument that teenagers were fucking scary. Walking past a group of them was like hiking past a pack of wild animals.

"Aren't you supposed to be asleep?" I countered her inquiry with one of my own.

Nyx had left us just five minutes ago to get some groceries and Indigo had declared to be too exhausted to walk around the supermarket. So I'd stayed in the food court with her and she'd said she was going to take a nap because school was *so* tiring. When I'd asked her what she did at school that was so tiring, she'd told me that dealing with other human beings was what distressed her.

"How can I with your heart drumming in my ears?" she questioned whilst rolling her eyes and I smiled. Indigo really did have Nyx's personality. Poppy was more sweet and quiet, like Annie. Nyx and Indigo could never keep their mouths shut about what they were thinking. "Are you thinking about Nyxie?"

Grimacing, I watched her brush hair out of her face. That question came out of nowhere. "Why would you think that?"

Indigo shrugged, which I discovered was a habit she had when she thought you were being silly. "Your heart's beating fast. Annie says if you think about someone you love, your heart beats fast." I nearly stopped breathing. Were all Taylor girls this blunt? "Annie says you love Nyxie—"

"Okay," I cut her off and prayed to God my face wasn't as red as it felt. I needed to have a word with Annie. My face inflamed further when I wondered if Annie had told Nyx the same thing. "Enough of that."

She blinked up at me, seeming pestered. "Why else would you offer to take us to the mall? Shouldn't you be at a club or something?"

This was merely another step in righting my wrongs, making up for all the times I'd been an asshole to Nyx. Now, more than ever, I needed to make up for my blunders because there was an enormous chance all of my resentment and rage had been for nothing. Not even a chance, it was a reality. Despite Nyx not yet being ready to explain, it was obvious that I'd been wrong.

And I was going to grovel the fuck out of this situation.

"Can't I be a nice person?" I riposted, finding offence.

Indigo stayed silent for a minute, peering into my fucking soul as if she was searching for answers like some sort of therapist.

Once she nodded to herself, I found myself fearing what she was going to say. "I know what it is," she stated resolutely, and I waited patiently, wanting to hear what she had to say. "You want to mate with Nyx—"

I began convulsing violently, startling the girl in my arms as I choked on air. She hit my back when I tried to get air into my lungs. My throat felt raw as I coughed and people began to look over. Indigo beamed at them and showed them a thumbs up.

"I want to *what*?"

She shrugged again. "*Mate*," she echoed slowly. "You want to have babies with her. That's why you're helping her, because you need to impress her. It's like a mating dance."

My tongue felt numb and I didn't know what to say. Luckily, I didn't have to say anything because Nyx was walking towards us. Hopefully, Indigo would keep her mouth shut about our previous conversation.

I turned around when I saw Nyx getting closer, empty-handed. She constantly carried herself as if she had an audience. There were always a few eyes trailing her and I couldn't blame them.

She sighed, looking just as annoyed as Indigo. "Okay, a bad idea going for groceries first. The lines are so long." Checking her phone quickly, she tucked it back into her jeans.

Those jeans would honestly be the death of me. It had to be

a new pair because I'd never seen her in it before. It was a dark blue colour and practically painted onto her legs. Plus, it did wonders for her ass. My dick had nearly saluted her when I'd arrived at Daisy's Delicacies to pick her up. I'd had to remind myself that we were in the presence of Indigo.

"Now what?" Indigo urged her sister, tugging at my earlobe.

"Now, we get some other things," she said, gesturing for me to get up. "Poppy needs new kneepads for her next volleyball match and *you*, little miss," she kissed Indigo's head, "need a new leotard and tutu for your recital."

Nyx had mentioned Poppy was at volleyball practice this afternoon. It was why she didn't have the truck because Annie needed it to go to Poppy's practice after her shift. I stood up, hoisting Indigo in my arms as she clung to my neck. Nyx led us to a store with sparkles in the windows. The mannequins wore elaborate costumes and Indigo clapped at the sight of them. It looked like the store stocked all kinds of supplies for dancers because the space was humongous with different sections dedicated to different types of dance genres.

"When's the recital?" I questioned, following behind Nyx as she examined the racks. She held up a few and compared them to Indigo. The latter was small for her age and Nyx strolled towards the younger ages.

"Sunday," she returned, eying a sparkly purple leotard. "By the way, you boys have next week free. The fundraiser's only the following weekend and the next match is the next week." My relief must've been evident because she laughed. "Benson and I thought you all deserved it. I'll leave it to you to tell your team."

The past four weeks had definitely been rough on us with practice every day and attending fundraisers plus matches. I could just picture their excitement once I told them. Hockey wasn't everything for us. We had classes as well, and I knew quite a few of the guys were behind on assignments and lectures. An entire week off meant catching up on everything and unwinding.

Indigo saw something, squealed, and kicked her legs for me to put her down. I nearly toppled over when her foot hit my dick. She apologised softly but Nyx was howling with laughter. I'd been slammed into the plexiglass during matches, hit with a hockey stick against my jaw, and not even those hurt as much as getting kicked in the dick.

"Can I try this one?" Indigo urged, holding up a white leotard with little diamonds stitched all over. The sleeves were long and made of lace.

Nyx struggled to speak through her laughter as I cupped my crotch, so she nodded. When she followed her baby sister to the fitting rooms, I cursed under my breath because that kick had hurt like a bitch. Part of me wondered if she'd done it on purpose. I wouldn't put it past Indigo.

There was an elderly lady gawking at me as she picked out a pair of tap shoes, probably for her grandchild. She glanced down at my hands on my crotch, pulled a face and then scurried towards the other side of the store. I probably traumatised her. After taking a few deep breaths, I headed towards the fitting room.

"Are you sure you don't need any help?" Nyx asked through

the shut stall door. "I'm gonna look for a tutu that goes with your leotard. *Lock* the door and stay put until I return." Indigo yelled her agreement and Nyx backtracked, nearly crashing into me. "She's got a solo," she told me with a grin, whirling around and making her way towards the tutus. "So she gets to wear whatever she likes."

The pride was clear in her eyes and it brought a smile to my face. "Of course she's got a solo," I mused, blinking at the vivid colours of the surrounding tutus. Some were long, some short and flowy, whereas others were poofy like a ballgown. "Next you'll tell me that Poppy's the captain of her team." Nyx froze, smiling. "No fucking way."

She smirked, favouring back against the shelf. "What can I say? I'm not the only sibling that strives for success."

There was a faraway look in her eyes, one that always seemed to catch her when she was happy. Like everything else, there was a more profound meaning behind it, a deeper reason why the Taylor girls strived for the best.

The guilt came rushing back alongside regret. Each wave was colder than the last and I dreaded that by the time the full truth was unveiled, I'd be nothing but an icicle solidified in my own mistakes. Reaching out, I tugged her closer and she floundered into my chest. Nyx looked up at me, bewildered.

"I'm sorry, baby," I murmured and her brows furrowed. "It shouldn't have taken me this long to realise there was obviously more to the story—why are you smiling?"

"Because you're an idiot," she returned, still smiling. "You're a real fucking idiot. Since when do you care about what I think of you?" I shrugged, my action broadening her smile.

Startling me, she tugged me down to her height, pushing my lips against hers. "You've been less unlikeable recently," she mumbled, looking disturbed. "And I hate it."

I chuckled, sliding my hands down her back. "I'm sorry?" She pulled a face. "If it helps, you've been less unlikeable lately too."

She tutted in displeasure. "You know, this could easily be resolved if you considered my hypothesis." I rolled my eyes, and she jokingly punched my shoulder. "It makes sense. Think about it. After we have sex, we'll go back to being normal around each other—"

"This sounds like a bad movie plot," I proceeded, squeezing her ass. I'd been wanting to do that since I'd first seen her in those jeans. She pouted at my words.

I had to hear about her hypothesis each time we saw each other and I never gave in. It made little sense. I'd fucked Nyx Taylor before, and you didn't just move on with life after doing something like that. If anything, the attraction between us would intensify after we had sex again. This wasn't a movie where everything miraculously worked out after a badly thought-out plan. Then again, Nyx was desperate to go back to having no weaknesses. And attraction seemed to be a weakness for her.

Before she could quarrel, I kissed her again, relishing the way she melted in my arms. Her hands strayed to my hair where she tugged at the messy strands as I dragged her closer. If I was ever worried about Indigo's kick breaking my dick, I knew now that my concern was needless.

A throat cleared. "Shouldn't you be saving that for the

bedroom?" I detached my mouth from Nyx's and recognised the elderly lady.

Nyx spun around in my arms and demanded, "Shouldn't you be picking out your tombstone?" The elderly lady gasped in aversion and I was torn between apologising and laughing. With one last huff, the woman hiked her bag with her purchase further up her arm and then left the store. Nyx looked back at me. "What?"

I shook my head. "That was rude."

She rolled her eyes and shifted her attention back to the tutus, settling on a white one. We went back to the fitting rooms and Nyx knocked on Indigo's door, telling her to come out. The tiny girl stepped towards where we sat, her hair all over the place. She had a good eye because the leotard was really pretty.

"Come here," Nyx told her, gesturing for her to step closer. When she was close enough, Nyx held out the tutu and Indigo slipped her legs inside. "Well, *look* at you," she stated with a big smile, causing Indigo to flush. "I guess this is the one?"

Indigo nodded and I grinned at her. "Well, don't you look pretty?"

I poked her cheek and she scowled, despite the blush coating her cheeks. "I will literally eat your finger." Her stomach growled suddenly and she tapped it as if it was a monster. "Can we get something to eat that won't turn me into a cannonball?"

Neither of us corrected her because she already stomped back to the fitting room.

"I meant to get something *immediately*," Indigo complained from her seat in the shopping cart, "not *after* we get groceries." I poked her nose whilst shifting the cart through different aisles, attempting to find Nyx.

When I didn't spot her in the cereal aisle, I groaned. "Where'd she go?"

Indigo gave me a look. "You should try shopping with Annie. She walks like a *snail*."

"And this one's like a damn bullet," I appended and she snickered into her hands.

Nyx kept disappearing. Then she'd pop up with a few things, throw them in the cart and then vanish again. Considering that it was pointless walking around looking for her, I grabbed a few things of my own that I wanted to buy, throwing in some candy for Indigo, seeing as her sister had a limit on candy in the house.

Everything today felt a little too domestic for my taste; shopping with Nyx. Just a few minutes ago, a woman had stepped up to me and said that Indigo looked just like me. The little girl had glared at the woman until she walked away and we had both promised to never speak of that moment again.

"How about cookies?" Indigo proposed, shifting in her seat so she could browse everything on the shelves. "Chocolate chip." I pushed the cart, looking for the cookies. "There it is!" She pointed to the top shelf and I reached for it, tossing it into the cart.

"Beck?"

Both Indigo and I turned our heads, spotting the tall

woman with slightly greying brown hair. She was adorned in her usual long sundress and cardigan.

I blinked. "Mom?"

Of all places and times to run into her. Indigo pouted, her thin little brows furrowing as if she couldn't possibly believe that I had a mother. Knowing her, she probably believed me to have popped out from an alien egg.

"Mom?" But then she looked at me, repeating the word slowly. "*Mom.*" Her features conveyed that the words felt unnatural on her tongue, and I felt some part of my chest squeeze painfully.

My mom glimpsed from me to Indigo and then smiled that tender smile of hers, one that I'd seen many times as a young boy when I'd stupidly injured myself.

"Well, this is a lovely surprise. Never thought I'd see the day you shopped for your own groceries." She laughed, turning to Indigo. "Hello, sweetheart. Are you a friend of Beck's?"

I clenched my jaw as Indigo snorted before saying, "He *wishes* he was my friend." My mom laughed, showcasing that she always found delight in little kids. It was why she was a teacher. Just when I thought Indigo was becoming better at getting along with me, she articulated again. "But he's dating my sister." Heat flared in my cheeks, like a flame being lit there by Indigo herself.

"Beck!" My mom looked at me with wide hazel eyes. "You have a girlfriend and you didn't tell me?" I opened my mouth to say something, but she spoke again. "Is this why you haven't been home to visit in the past week?" And all of this was happening in the candy aisle.

Indigo grinned. "Her name's Nyxie. Just earlier, they were kissing in the store. His hands were on her butt and everything—"

Through my embarrassment, I glowered at her. "You *left* the fitting room after Nyx told you to stay put?"

She shrugged. "You guys were a few feet away. All I had to do was stick my head underneath the door. I was wondering why you were taking so long. Turns out, you just wanna make babies—" Not the *mating* thing again.

"I'm becoming a grandmother?" my mom asked with a provoking grin. She knew very well how disconcerted I was at that moment and she was savouring it.

Growing up, she'd purposely try to make me shy in front of my friends or tease me. Having her and Indigo gang up on me was my worst nightmare. I could only imagine what would happen if Nyx was added to the equation. Each of them had a knack for making me want to peel my skin from my body, purely for their amusement.

Cursing underneath my breath, I seized a lollipop from the shelf, unwrapped it, and put it in Indigo's mouth. "You," I told her, "shut up." Then I twisted to my mom who was laughing. "Nobody's pregnant." Indigo took the lollipop out of her mouth to say something. "*Shush.*" She put it back in, rolling her eyes. Clearing my throat, I stated, "It's nice to see you, Mom."

She stepped forward, opening her arms and I hugged her. In regular mom fashion, she pinched my cheeks. The scent of cinnamon embraced my nose and I fell deeper into the hug. My mom always smelt like cinnamon.

"It's nice to see you, too. Your dad gets more visits out of you because you visit the station but you're too damn *lazy* to drive and see me at the house unless you need a good lecture. How have you been doing since the last time we spoke?" There was a knowing look in her eyes, a subtle question asking if I'd sorted things out with Nyx.

"Great. Our last two matches were a win and I'm on a break for a while." Again, there was an underlying meaning to my words. I was making progress with my girl and wouldn't rest until she and her sisters were safe.

"Good. That means you can visit your poor old mother," she replied with a nod of her head. I knew she didn't *need* the visits because she was a busy bee, part of many clubs; including sports, books and cooking. But I was her only child and she enjoyed my company, probably because she found happiness in humiliating and lecturing me. "I've missed you, Hammy—"

"Hammy!" Indigo bellowed, nearly choking on her lollipop as she cackled. "This is *gold*."

I scowled at my mom as she laughed into her hand. "Nobody *ever* called me that."

It was a random name she'd loved to bring up whenever I'd had a girl over at the house, whether it was for a project or just to hang out. Suffice to say, they never returned after my mom had brought out that horrible weapon of hers; *Hammy*.

"Nice tits!" The disturbance came from further down the aisle and my mom gasped, tightening her cardigan even though the man wasn't speaking to her.

Completely forgetting that she was in the middle of digging my grave of mortification, she declared, "The *nerve* of some men to harass young women. I should kick him where the sun doesn't shine." Indigo stared at her in reverence and I sighed. New friends bonding over violence, how exciting. My mom frowned. "Well, she doesn't look happy."

I looked towards the commotion and groaned. "Oh, *fuck*."

Indigo poked my chest. "Bad word. You owe me a dollar, Hammy." Handing her a dollar, I pushed the cart closer and my mom frowned at my concern. She'd be finding out soon enough.

"Repeat what you just said," Nyx responded with narrowed eyes, standing taller despite her lack of height against her opponent. The man opposite her was dressed in a suit, similar to the ones the men at the bank wore. He wore a name tag, but I couldn't make out the name from where I stood.

He grinned placidly at her, looking nonchalant in his business suit and shopping in the candy aisle. "What?" he sought with a chuckle. "I just said you have some nice tits."

My hands clenched around the handle of the shopping cart and my mom's eyes zeroed in on the movement. Indigo bit into the lollipop, the crunch sound filling my ears as Nyx stared at the man. She had nice tits, but I doubted she wanted to hear that from a stranger. As much as the flimsy tank top she wore emphasised her assets, it didn't give strange men the right to objectify her.

"And do you think it's okay to tell a woman that she has nice tits?" Nyx was scowling at him now, gripping the carton of milk in her hands. "How would you feel if I walked past you and said I liked the fucking shape of your dick?"

I heard my mom snort at her inquiry and I glanced over at her. This was not how I was expecting her to meet Nyx.

"Just thank me for the compliment, fucking hell," the man shrugged, reaching for a bar of chocolate on the shelf.

Nyx glared. "*No.* I *won't* thank you." He glared back, becoming annoyed. "Because that's all this is for you, a *brief* moment for you to objectify a woman, make her feel uneasy. But are you the only man on this fucking planet?" He went to articulate, but she acknowledged her own inquiry. "No, you're *not.* And you're also not the first strange man to tell me I have nice tits. So thank you for making me feel even more uncomfortable than I was before!"

He stepped back, raising his hands in capitulation. The regret was visible in his eyes. He'd made a big mistake by provoking Nyx. "*Jesus*, I'm sorry. Can't you take a joke?"

Nyx laughed, disturbing the man. "Yes, because the '*f*' in sexual harassment stands for funny." Her eyes dropped to his name tag. "And I'm assuming the '*f*' in Frank stands for fucking asshole." I chuckled at the expression he wore. He probably wasn't expecting to be chewed out by somebody nearly half his size. She opened the carton of milk. "Here. Since you like tits so much. Have some milk."

Indigo cackled evilly as she watched her sister spray the man with milk. He barked obscenities and dropped his chocolate, hurrying away. At some point, he slipped and tumbled into a nearby shopping cart. Even my mom couldn't hide her laughter and neither could the other passing customers. Nyx placed the empty carton on a shelf and sauntered towards me. She looked exhausted, as if dealing with that man had taken all of her energy.

I opened my arms and she walked right in, falling against

my chest. Indigo was counting on her fingers. "You cussed five times," she told her older sister, "you owe me five dollars."

The blonde groaned, pulling away slightly before stating, "I hate men." I laughed, rubbing her back soothingly. That's when she noticed my mom; who was grinning at us like a creep. I prayed internally that she didn't say anything to humiliate me.

My mom pulled Nyx away from me and enveloped her in a hug, confusing me. "I knew I recognised you." The two stared at each other and I frowned in dismay. How the fuck did they know each other? "But I had no idea you were dating my son." My mom's smile grew, nearly splitting her face in half as Indigo smirked.

Nyx swallowed. "Dating. *Your son.*" She looked at me and I looked at Indigo. It was her mess.

Not noticing the awkward atmosphere, my mom clapped happily. "How does supper at my place sound? We'd love to hear all about the girl who stole Hammy's heart."

Fuck. My. Life.

Chapter 23

Nyx

If you'd told me a few weeks ago that one day I'd be on my way to have supper with Beckham Hunt's parents, I would've punched you in the throat. Then removed your windpipe, used it as a flute and played a tune as I tap-danced on your grave. Okay, that was a little dramatic, but I was *freaking out*. Never would I have thought that I'd *ever* meet Beckham's parents. The closest I'd gotten to it was that one time I daydreamed I'd murdered Beckham and they came to my execution as I paid for my crimes.

Of course, I hadn't known what they looked like, so my brain had filled in the blanks.

Not even when Beckham and I had been somewhat together had I ever imagined meeting his parents. That was a milestone of sorts I hadn't wanted to reach. It meant things were getting serious and that scared me. If I already hadn't wanted to *label* us, imagine how I would've felt about meeting his parents.

His mom had looked painstakingly familiar and I couldn't

place my finger on it. It was only when Beckham had driven me home that I realised she'd been one half of the couple that always had breakfast at the cafe. She was the same woman who'd questioned me about her son without even telling me she was his mother. I'd known there was something up with her.

She looked youthful, with creamlike skin and a great sense of style. I'd been so immersed in my stupor that I barely paid attention when she'd said she would meet us back at her home in a little while for supper. *Girlfriend.* She thought I was Beckham's *girlfriend.* Indigo had had a merry laugh about it on the way back home.

Beckham had waited in the kitchen as I went to my room to change. I'd made him promise that he'd clarify things with his parents at the supper. Having dinner with a friend was fine but I was in no way taking it further than that. Halfway through my panic attack on what to wear, Annie had arrived home with Poppy.

"Try the blue dress," Poppy pointed to the one I tossed onto the floor. Her skin was tinged red with her activities at practice, making it appear as if she had a disastrous sunburn. She was still wearing her uniform, too excited about my so-called date to go and change or even look at the new kneepads I'd bought her. "It matches your eyes."

Indigo sat at the edge of my bed, a bag of candy in her lap, provided for her by Beckham. "No, she should wear the silvery slip dress," she shook her head, bouncing with enthusiasm. Annie was going to have her hands full with her tonight. "It matches Hammy's eyes."

Poppy did a double-take, gawking at Indigo. "Hammy?"

I disregarded them as Indigo frantically told her sister all about her adventures at the mall. Although, her version of events was completely exaggerated compared to what had actually happened. The two consumed candy as I fretted about what to wear. Eventually, I settled on the blue dress, because it was informal, and paired it with sneakers and tights (seeing as it was kinda chilly). To make up for my lack of silver, Indigo planted a silver heart necklace around me to equal Beckham's eyes. I left the two sugar-high kids in my room and went to Annie, who was talking to Beckham.

"I'm done," I announced, reaching into the fridge to take a sip of a bottle of water. My throat felt drier than dirt. All the water succeeded in doing was turn my throat thick, like sand turning into mud. Silence was all that embraced me, and I halted midway through a sip and looked at Annie. She was smirking, holding a steaming mug of coffee to her chest. I glanced at the only other person in the kitchen.

Beckham was staring at me with a weird look in his eyes before he looked at Annie and then at his feet. My stomach did a ghastly flip and I shoved the bottle back into the fridge.

Annie snorted and then placed her mug down to squeeze me. "Have fun."

I yelled bye to my baby sisters and left the house, following Beckham to his car. He opened the passenger door and I stopped. "What's wrong with you?" I asked.

He finally met my gaze and squinted at me as he held the door open. "Opening the door for you?"

My lips tilted into a teasing smile. "Are you trying to

manipulate me—"

"Oh my fucking—just get in the car, Nyx," he spoke with a deep groan, tossing his head back in exasperation. I crossed my arms, wondering why he was being beyond charming. There was only so much *nice* Beckham I could manage. "Get in the fucking car before I strap you to the seat with rope."

I rolled my eyes. "Kinky." Sauntering past him, I climbed into the car and he shut the door, walking around before hopping inside. "This isn't a date," I felt the need to remind him.

He didn't reply, only scowled at me and started the car. I didn't speak on the way to his parent's house, my throat rammed with nerves until there was no space for words to shift through. It was a surprise I was breathing evenly.

"Who's Uncle Robbie?" Beckham asked after about five minutes of me panicking. I hid a smile at his question, knowing that Annie had probably told him one of her stories. Or a lot, considering how long it had taken me to get ready.

"He was my mom's best friend, passed away when I was younger," I answered, turning to look at him and forgetting about my previous apprehension. "Annie speak about him?"

He nodded, seemingly satisfied that he'd distracted me. "She mentioned that he would've enjoyed terrorising me before he let me take you out." I laughed quietly. "When I asked who he was, it seemed to open a flood of stories." That was said with a smirk and I laughed harder.

"She takes any opportunity to talk about him. Usually only with me because Poppy and Indigo weren't born yet when he died."

Beckham lowered the sound of the radio. "She says you don't remember him."

"I don't remember anything before the age of seven," I mumbled, realising that I'd never mentioned this to Beckham before. "Around the time of my seventh birthday, I was in a car wreck—"

"You were *what*?" Beckham asked, disbelief etched into his features and I smiled at his confused frown.

"I was in a car wreck. I'd gotten a concussion that left some effects, unfortunately."

He was still bewildered. "That's why you can't remember?"

I nodded. "Retrograde amnesia. I can't recall any of my memories that were formed before the accident. Annie still has hope, though."

Beckham blinked. "You were in a car wreck." He looked suddenly tense, his grip on the steering wheel tightened.

I couldn't help it, I laughed. "Beck, it's not like I remember the accident. You can calm down. I'm not about to freak out."

His body eased slightly. "A car wreck."

"I got off better than Uncle Robbie though," I attempted a dark joke, one that Beckham didn't appreciate. His eyes filled with understanding. Some part of me wanted to cry, but there was no reason to. I'd be crying for a man I didn't remember. Sensing my inner turmoil, Beckham placed a comforting hand on my thigh.

"I wish I remembered him," I admitted, more to myself than Beckham. "I never told Annie this because she wears that look of pity—which I *hate*. I pretend that it doesn't bother me, that the fact that I can't remember him doesn't unnerve me.

But he loved me enough, was with me enough times for me to begin calling him *Dad*. I wish I remembered him because he was more of a father to me than my own. He cared for me when my real dad was still debating whether we were worth it or not. And he doesn't exist anymore, not even in my memories." I rubbed my eyes in aggravation. "It's stupid."

Beckham changed gears before he squeezed my leg. "It's not stupid. In fact, I think it's amazing. You miss him although—"

"Although I don't remember him," I scoffed, comprehending that it sounded dumb. What was there to miss?

"No. Your brain might not remember him, but a heart never forgets," he said firmly before wincing almost dramatically. "*Fuck*. I didn't just say that. You didn't hear that shit." He looked pained. "Holy fuck. I did *not* just say that. What the actual fuck?"

I was smiling so hard, watching him fight the urge to shudder. "Thank you." He cringed, stepping on the gas and I leaned over to peck his cheek. "That quote of yours is going on a t-shirt."

He huffed. "Fuck you, Taylor."

Grinning, I settled my hand over his, turning to stare out the window. Beckham's face was so red and I decided to not tease him further. Unbeknownst to him, his supposedly *cringey* words had meant something to me. So he escaped my taunts; this time.

The drive was lengthy and I shook my head when he took a detour into the fancy neighbourhood of Glendale.

Everything looked straight out of a movie. Even in the light of the slowly setting sun, the street looked clean enough to eat from. The grass was such a vigorous shade of green that I had to blink a few times to make sure it was real. Trees created an archway of sorts along the street, giving everything a tranquil feeling.

Beckham pointed towards a house with a spacious garden. If I closed my eyes, I could imagine rich blossoms and swaying trees. But all that I saw was death, *literally*. The flowers were withering, the vines that coiled around the house looked more like maggots trying to plod through the fissures. The sight made me quiver.

After a rigid moment of censorship, Beckham hummed, "Grayson's house."

My mouth parted in surprise. It was eerie to think of vivacious Grayson Carter once living in a house as dismal looking as that. But then again, he was a third-year student and had moved away from his parents long ago.

I licked my lips, trying to articulate around the blockage in my throat. "The garden must've been really beautiful at some point."

Beckham passed me a look that I didn't understand and nodded. We drove a little further down the street. Everyone looked friendly. There were some people tending to their gardens, taking a stroll or even lounging on their lawn as they watched the sunset. We pulled into a long driveway of a three-storey house. The structure was old, yet it was evident the property was well cared for. I took in a deep breath and then climbed out of the car.

Beckham strolled around to my side, setting his hands on my shoulders when I took in a deep breath. "Hey, chill out."

"*Chill out*," I parodied in a high-pitched voice and he chuckled, leaning down to kiss me. I allowed him to, even dragged him closer until I realised where we were. Elbowing him away, I said, "Don't kiss me." His lips were swollen and he looked dazed. "Your parents are gonna think we're together, asshole."

Beckham rolled his eyes and I saw somebody sitting in a sun lounger at the house across the street. She was wearing a bikini, trying to get the last of the sun. The sight kinda threw me off because we were in the middle of winter. The girl's hair reminded me of the Weasley family from Harry Potter. It was a blinding shade of orange. She noticed me looking and so did Beckham.

"Hey, River!" he called, waving a hand and she grinned as she reciprocated the action. An unusual feeling slithered up my throat, the same way the vines were snaking up Grayson's house. Beckham discerned the look I was giving him and smirked. "Jealous, baby?"

I huffed. "Fuck off."

He tossed an arm around my shoulder, escorting me to the door. "Put away those claws. She's Sebastian's little sister." The feeling went away and Beckham grinned at my controlled appearance. He opened the door, allowing me to enter first. "My dad's car's not here yet but he's probably on his way." The house was even more pretty on the inside. Elegant. I was afraid to touch anything, afraid that I'd contaminate it somehow. "Mom!"

As Beckham called out for Helen, I gazed at the walls that we passed. Professionally taken family photographs ornamented the walls. There were plenty of Beckham; their golden child. Many incorporated Sebastian, Grayson and Beth, seeing as they'd grown up on the same street. His parents looked in love in every photo of them. He guided me into the living room where he motioned for me to sit down.

Helen tripped into the room, an apron bound around the same dress she'd worn earlier, only the cardigan was removed. Her hair was tied into a bun at her nape, and she beamed at the sight of me.

"There she is!" she exclaimed. "I'd hug you but I was busy with the steak and I wouldn't want to get sauce all over you."

I merely smiled, almost trembling with nerves. "You have a lovely home." Was that a dumb thing to say? I'd witnessed it in a movie before. I wasn't a girl that guys usually brought home to meet the parents so I had zero practice with what was happening.

Thankfully, Helen looked pleased with my admiration. She gave off the same energy as the sun. "That is the most delightful thing you could've told me. Thank you, sweetheart." With the enthusiasm of Indigo during a sugar rush, she beckoned me forward and ushered me into the kitchen. "I've heard *so* many great things about you."

Beckham groaned, following us. "Mom, *please*."

"Go away," she swished her hand as if she was sweeping off a gnat, and I couldn't help but smile. "It's the first time I'm properly meeting your girlfriend. It's been over a year since you first spoke about her? How are we only meeting her now?"

Over a year. There was a fluttering sensation in my stomach but I schooled my features, willing the feeling to go away.

"About that," he replied, scratching the back of his neck as he cleared his throat. Helen froze and so did I. "We're not dating." Helen looked between us repeatedly and I held my breath. He should've added something a little more because now it sounded like we were only fucking around.

"As you may recall, I'm helping the team during championship season," I appended with a grin, taking a seat on a barstool that Beckham held out for me. "Event planning."

Seeing my flushed face, she sighed in understanding. "Oh, so we're in *that* phase of the relationship." I frowned and Beckham looked at his mom with a dead stare. There was no relationship to begin with. "So, who's the one unwilling to admit they've got feelings for the other? My money's on my boy." She waved another hand, scorning Beckham's look of disbelief. "The entire world would be able to see that he's in love, yet he wouldn't say a damn—"

"Nobody's in love," Beckham interposed instantly and I felt my cheeks boiling again. "We're just friends." I cleared my throat awkwardly. Were we even friends? Eh. Helen's smile didn't leave her face and it made me apprehensive. She was nodding but didn't reveal her thoughts. "Understand, Mom?"

Shrugging, she answered, "I understand just fine. Now, go get the grill going before your dad arrives." Beckham glanced at me and I nodded, showing that I'd be fine. Once he was gone, Helen giggled. "Do you mind waiting until a little later for a tour? I'm starving and want to get the food done as soon as possible."

I shook my head. Helen spoke a mile a minute and it was an effort to keep up with her. Her hands moved with every word and there was always a smile on her face. She was a highly animated talker. Beckham had told me she was a teacher and it made so much sense. Her classes were probably so much fun. Indigo would have the time of her life if Helen was her teacher.

Not even five minutes later, the front door opened. Footfalls played through hallway, keys settled on a wooden surface, and then a tall man entered the kitchen, decked in a police uniform. He had the same dark hair and silvery eyes as Beckham. When his eyes descended on me, he looked far from startled and smiled. He strode over to Helen and planted a kiss on her lips.

"Anthony Hunt," he said in a rough voice, holding a hand out to me, which I shook gingerly. "You must be Beck's girl. Nyx, is it?" The man was intimidating as fuck and I couldn't find it in myself to correct him, terrified that he'd arrest me. It was clear where Beckham got everything from. His dad was a gigantic man, hinting back to his days as a hockey player. "It's good to finally meet you."

The way he phrased it made me shudder in trepidation. "Beck's outback with the grill," Helen stated, tapping her husband's arm. "You should help him."

"I'll get changed first," Anthony motioned to his uniform. With one last smile, he retreated upstairs. Helen watched him leave, eyes levelled on his backside and I coughed around a laugh.

"Married for 25 years and I'll never get sick of that ass. *Especially* in that uniform," she muttered and I couldn't hold back my laughter this time.

I wondered what it would be like to have what they had.

The two were clearly in love after all these years. And it would forever be immortalised in the photographs of them. I thanked her when she delivered me a glass of orange juice.

"25 years is a long time," I mused.

Marriage never appealed to me, probably because I'd had a poor example of it. In 25 years, I could be so much more instead of being tied down. Annie seemed more like the type to marry and have kids. My marriage would never work out because my husband could never restrain me. And I'd seen first-hand what happened to relationships like those. Perhaps the lonely life befitted me. My sisters would have kids and I'd have a big family, just not one of my own. The thought of having one disturbed me a little.

I was gonna be the cool aunt for sure.

Helen nodded with a faraway look in her eyes, presumably reliving her favourite moments. "It sure is. But I remember every second. How long have your parents been married?"

Her question was asked absentmindedly. My smile drained, but fortunately, Helen didn't notice. She was moving the steak to a clean tray and I was thankful for that. I didn't want her to see the moment of dread in my eyes.

"They got married when I was seven, but they aren't together anymore," I apprised her, having to scrape the words from my tongue. I hated talking about them. "My mom left five years ago."

Wiping her hands on a cloth, Helen frowned, seemingly doing the calculations in her head.

The sombre expression told me everything I needed to know. She apprehended that Indigo had just been a baby when my mom had left. But I didn't want pity. We were doing fine without her and I believed we'd soon be out of the clutches of my dad. The taste of freedom was mouth-watering, just out of my reach. For so long, it seemed like an unattainable goal and now we were so close. My dad could run off into the sunset with his new family. My mom could do what she wanted once she left rehab. I didn't care.

Annie still cared. It was obvious. But she'd soon see that hoping was futile. There was no hope for Matthew Taylor. Poppy had never liked him, not after he'd berated her solely because she looked like our mom. I could see the hope slowly leaving Indigo too. No matter her age, she was clever enough to understand a father wasn't supposed to act the way he did.

"Her loss," Helen responded with a disdainful look, displeasure glazing her words like a poisonous cake. "Indigo's got one hell of an attitude and Annie makes the best coffee I've ever tasted."

I grinned. "There's Poppy too. She's the shy one."

"A house full of girls," Helen was beaming again. "It must drive your dad nuts." I didn't reply, just nodded. "I'm satisfied with my two big boys. Do you mind taking this to Beck?" She held out a tray with the steak.

"What happened to Hammy?" I inquired, prompting Helen to laugh as I wandered away, following the directions she'd given me. I spotted measurements against the wall from when Beckham was a boy. The latest measurement was taken when he'd turned 21. I smiled.

The rest of the house was even more gorgeous and I had to clench my jaw to keep my mouth from dropping open when

I entered the backyard. I first noticed the hot tub, and then the large pool. There was a garden to the side with a dainty little fence and a sign that read: *Helen's Little Corner.* There were three sets of handprints on it, the third was a small pair. My eyes watered slightly as I took in everything before me. I wondered if this was where Beckham had laid stargazing with his parents and discovered his fondness for stars, where Helen had taken him to play when he was a toddler. Or where Anthony had taught him the basics of hockey.

This backyard was like Pandora's box, except it was stuffed with memories. And I'd just opened it. I could feel my throat locking with the inconsistencies between my childhood and Beckham's. He had parents who loved him. Sure, my mom would try to protect us from our dad, but she had still left. She'd given up.

A stubborn tear slipped out of my eye and traced down my cheek. The tray was abruptly taken away from me and settled on the picnic table. And then Beckham was in front of me.

"What's wrong?"

I despised that question because whenever someone asked me that—everything would leave me in a torrent of emotions. The dam would just burst. Usually, I was strong enough to stop it, but not now.

"Why couldn't I have had this?" I questioned in a tiny voice, feeling more tears escape. Beckham frowned as my voice cracked. "What did I do in my past life to have deserved what happened to me? What did we do?" I sniffled, pestered when my tears wouldn't stop. "There's no rage within these walls."

He wiped my tears. "What are you talking about?"

When he cupped my face in his hands, I laid mine over his. "There's no rage within these walls," I repeated, blinking to free myself from the useless tears. "When I walked into your house it was silent. When I walk into my house I can hear the remnants of the yells, the violence."

"Nyx—"

"The walls are like sponges. They've swallowed everything my dad ever said and each time I open those doors, I can hear it," I murmured, shuddering.

Beckham cursed and pulled me into his chest.

My voice was deadened against his sweater. "There're no holes in the walls here, holes that need to be fixed by hanging something over it. The kitchen feels warm like your mom is always baking something." I sniffled again. "I *never* had that. My dad scared my mom away. She was a coward and *ran* but not before pushing my grandma away. And my dad beat me because he hated the life he was living. He was always scolding the little ones. *Why*? I could never understand it. I could never *understand* why he'd do that—"

Beckham leaned down to stare into my eyes, his voice steady. "If you can't rationalise why your dad did all that he did to you, it's because you're *not* like him. You're *nothing* like him, baby. Understand that."

His words reverberated through my mind. I'd spent years trying to understand why my dad resented us. His betrayal hurt the worst, the moment he'd first raised his hands on me. It was like being propelled from a plane without a parachute before you were ready. When I'd first been pushed, I'd thrashed and yelled for help. My dad was on the plane, and he was the one that had pushed me. He'd watched me fall into a pit of despair. As I'd taken in my surroundings, I'd found Annie alongside me. As the years went on, Poppy had fallen too, and now Indigo.

I'd always been afraid of what would be at the bottom. I think I'd hit the ground first when I'd seen my dad with his new family. Every bone in my body had fragmented on collision, but I'd felt *nothing*. My body had already been comatose because I'd been anticipating the pain, the only sister not clinging to hope as if it would crystallise into a parachute and save me. Annie had fallen next, when I'd told her. Seeing Beckham's home made me apprehend what I wanted, what we deserved. Although I was crying, it furnished me with a new purpose. This was what we *deserved*, and if our dad wasn't going to give it to us, we'd provide it for ourselves. I was *going* to find a new house and we *would* leave our dad in the dust.

By the time Poppy and Indigo landed, Annie and I would be there to catch them.

"I loved him," I managed to get out after a few seconds of Beckham just swaying with me. It felt good to say the words out loud. I'd been stifling it for so long, disgusted with myself because how could I love my abuser? But he was my dad before he was my abuser. "I loved him *so much*."

My face scrunched in agony and I fought back heavy sobs. Beckham kissed the top of my head and I could've sworn his eyes were soaked with tears.

"I envy him because he had the absolute privilege of being loved by you." I held him tighter. "Because I've seen what you're willing to do for the people that you love. I've seen the pain you're willing to endure to help them." He swore softly. "Jesus, you risked everything when you decided to help Nate; because you loved him, because you loved your sister."

My eyes felt blinded by flashbacks from last year. I saw the team glowering at me whenever they saw me. They didn't know that I'd never chosen sides, not when I'd wanted to help both. I'd wanted to save the Trojan boys from their torment whilst saving Nate from his as well.

Sabotaging Nate had led to my family paying the price. Richard Wyatt had used his position as a lawyer to sue me for defamation after having found out I'd been ruining his son's reputation. So much money lost when we could've escaped our dad already.

But like I'd told Beckham, I couldn't hate myself for it. I couldn't hate myself when he'd gotten the captaincy and Nate was free. Now that Annie was dating Beth, I couldn't even hate myself for what had happened between her and Nate—she was happy now. Georgia was silently helping us, and the girls were happy.

I glanced up at Beckham as he wiped the remaining tears from my face. Maybe there was no longer a need for hatred, for animosity. Maybe there was no reason for guilt. And maybe this was the universe giving me a second chance, one that I could finally take without worrying about anybody else.

Maybe it was my turn to be selfish again; this time without ruining everything.

Chapter 24

Beckham

"Second-year sports management major," Nyx answered my mom after she gulped down the portion of food she was eating. There were twin stains of red on her cheeks, courtesy of the crying she'd done previously. My parents didn't question it and I had a nagging impression they thought she was red because we'd been doing something sexual. Not even close. As much as I was aching to have Nyx in any way, she was hurting and this wasn't the time.

My dad's brows nearly darted into his hairline at her rejoinder and he looked at me with deep eyes. The man looked like he stepped straight out of a caricature. All he was missing were the exaggerated lines and features. Desperate that Nyx didn't see his reaction, I instantly shook my head, and he glimpsed back at his food, disguising his laugh with a cough. He'd heard about her before, but that was back when I was completely obsessed with her. Then that had changed to hatred. All that I'd ever done was whine about her.

My mom had heard the same criticisms but apparently, a woman's mind worked differently so she had an entirely separate view of Nyx compared to what I did. My parents had heard everything there was to hear about Nyx Taylor.

My mom, seeing as she already knew who Nyx was, maintained the conversation. "You sound like you know what you want to do."

Nyx turned even redder. For somebody who enjoyed throwing her achievements around, she blushed a lot at the mention of it.

"I've known what I wanted to do for a long time. It wasn't possible to risk not knowing. I had a deadline for scholarships and college applications. If I picked wrong, it wasn't like I could redo the year. Hopefully, by the time I graduate, I can get into sports PR management—"

"You'll get in," I appended, reaching for my glass. The table went hushed and my dad was grinning. Nyx looked befuddled, and I cursed under my breath. "I mean, you've had a lot to do with the team in the past year or so. You've attended every game and you wrote those awesome articles on our matches in the school magazine—"

Her lips parted in astonishment. "You read those?" *Double fuck*. She turned to my mom who was grinning too. "I didn't think anybody read those. My articles were always too precise and detailed that they seemed a bore to read."

Yet, I'd read every single one.

"That's exactly the type of attitude you need in your career choice," my dad responded after clearing his throat. "There's no such thing as too detailed. If you always put your best foot forward, nobody can ever doubt you. Take Beck for example," he said with a smirk, flinging me a look. I tensed. "My boy wasn't even the captain, yet they were treating him like one—"

"Yes! You see because you showed you cared from the very beginning," my mom interjected excitedly. I sighed, sharing a look of apology with Nyx. I was their only child so they took any opportunity to gush over me. It happened all the time, specifically at my mom's club meetings. "I remember they threw you a party after that one match," she proceeded, tapping her chin in reflection.

Nyx's shoulders stiffened and I gaped at my mom, silently telling her to shut up. The party had happened the night of her birthday and I'd told her it was when I'd fucked Avery Malcolm. We didn't need to bring back those angry thoughts of hers. We'd come a long way since that day.

"That's so sweet of them," Nyx muttered after shifting in her seat. I knew I shouldn't have told my mom what I'd said in that closet with Nyx. She probably thought that I'd taken long enough to explain myself.

So she was taking the reins. And she sealed my fate when she spoke again. "It was, wasn't it? Too bad he didn't go."

I heard the tiny intake of breath. Nyx turned to me. "You didn't go?"

My mom was smiling but I glared at her. She stood up unexpectedly, inviting my dad to help her carry the dessert tray. The two of them vanished, leaving me with a frowning Nyx. Her eyes were beseeching, wanting me to verify what my mom had said. In the end, I nodded.

A glare appeared on her face. "You told me you fucked

Avery Malcolm that night at the party."

A shrug was what I gave her. "I say a lot of things." She pinched my arm and I yelped, stroking over the red spot. "What the fuck? I didn't go to the party, okay?"

"Why not?" she pressed. "It was a party thrown in *your honour.*"

I groaned. "Nyx, it was at a *club.* How the fuck was I going to call you with all the commotion happening?" Her lips parted in shock. "I stayed home so that I could call you the second after midnight. Can we not talk about this?" I asked, feeling my face heat up the longer she stared at me with that delicate look in her eyes; a look reserved for those she cared about.

I'd missed an eight-hour party so that I could talk to her for an hour on her birthday.

"What about Avery Malcolm?" she insisted, staring at the plate in front of her.

I didn't say anything, not wanting to confess that I'd lied because she had hurt my pride. I felt a soft hand and turned to feel her framing my jaw. In the blink of an eye, she was out of her seat and on my lap, her arms sheathing around my neck. And then she kissed me.

Her lips were silky against my own and I held the back of her head, keeping her close. The kiss was gentle and slow, something I wasn't used to with Nyx, not for a long time. When she pulled away, her forehead was against mine.

"What was that for?" I whispered, squeezing her hip.

"For not fucking Avery Malcolm on my birthday," she expressed with a faint laugh, her words carrying only a sliver of what she had tried to say through the kiss.

I grinned stupidly, helping her back into her seat when I heard footsteps approaching. My mom entered the room, carrying a peppermint tart, but the smile on her face told me everything I needed to know. Nyx's cheeks were red with mortification, probably sensing my mom curbing her cooing.

"I heard you're helping this Coach Benson with the matches?" my dad spoke as he sat down, placing a chocolate cake in the middle of the table.

Nyx laughed, the soothing sound gliding through the tense air. "I only gave him my notes, but I mainly plan the events. The first time I tried to train them, one of the guys hit on me instead of taking me seriously—"

"She broke Jai's fingers," I mused.

The memory brought a smile to my face. I'd never tell her that, but watching her put Jai in his place had been a major turn-on. In fact, everything she did was a turn on and many of the guys would agree. Other than the fact that they hadn't trusted her in the beginning, the guys also hadn't wanted her around because how was somebody supposed to concentrate with Nyx Taylor running around the rink?

"*Sprained*," Nyx supplemented with an abashed smile.

She didn't look too proud of her actions. The pleasure had only been in her eyes for that few minutes after she'd hurt Jai. But when I'd seen her tending to him, enveloping his hand, I'd known she had felt distressed. Thinking back now, after I knew what I did, she didn't want to be like her dad, to get her point across through brutality.

Melissa was a whole other story. That was revenge.

"And I helped him bandage it. He needed to be knocked

down a peg or two."

My mom was laughing now, nearly suffocating. "Am I correct in thinking that you've knocked quite a handful of guys down some pegs?" She had no idea.

I used to think it was a sport of Nyx's to embarrass the guys around campus when they tried to make a fool out of her. Even during the period when the team had been pissed at her, she gave just as good as she received. And those guys could be unmerciful, but Nyx had held her head high.

"Men," my mom resumed, ready to offer her story. "This one time back in high school this guy wanted to go down on me—"

"That's our cue to leave," I stated, scrunching my face as I stood up and carried some dishes into the kitchen. Trust my mom to speak about her sexual history. She was always too comfortable, but that wasn't something I wanted to hear anything about. Trying to quell the vomit clawing up my throat, I practically ran away.

A few seconds later, my dad followed me, his eyes wide. Woodenly, he placed his dishes on the counter, nearly dropping his glass, and I laughed. As a cop, he was always the most composed person in the room. But right now, he looked completely ruffled and I had a sense he'd heard something he wasn't supposed to.

"You okay there, Dad?" I questioned absentmindedly, filling the sink with hot water.

He was nodding and then shook his head swiftly. "What the fuck is a sixty-nine?"

"*Shit!*" I yelled when I stung my hand in the scorching

water, detecting laughter coming from the dining room. Quickly running it under cold water, I veered to the bewildered man. "Where did you hear that?"

Memories of a naked Nyx entered my mind and I nearly dropped the cloth that I reached for. This was the worst time to be reminded of what had happened between us.

"Your mother mentioned it just as I left. The way she said it made me think she wants to try it soon—"

"Dad, *please*," I pleaded, ready to throw up in the sink. He wandered to the fridge and then gulped down a bottle of water as I examined my hand. "I don't want to hear about that."

Being an only child wasn't the dream, as everyone thought. I was constantly caught in the middle since my parents didn't have other kids to gossip with. But I wanted to hear *nothing* about what went on in their bedroom.

My dad nodded to himself, looking a little traumatised. I took the bottle from him and drank some water to pacify the vomit that was screeching to be freed.

"So that's her?" I stopped my actions and could hear the grin in his voice. This man was up to something. He wasn't using his cop voice, but his character said enough. "I don't know what I was expecting, but it wasn't a pixie-like woman. With the way you spoke about her when you were competing against Nate, she sounded like the devil reincarnated."

I began scouring the glass cups. "She's hiding that side of her," I quipped, hearing Nyx giggle at something my mom said. A weird sensation bloomed in my chest, the same one I'd felt when she'd stepped out in that dress. More than anything, I'd wanted to kiss her, right then and there. But I'd been stopped by the knowledge of something always on my mind. "I hurt her."

He frowned. "Beck, I'm sure—"

"Dad," I cut him off, sending him a bitter smile. "Trust me. I hurt her, probably way more than how I was hurting. I walked away when she probably needed me the most, all because I was fucking jealous. She hated me because of it."

The shit I'd put her through, I didn't deserve forgiveness. She'd been going through one of the gravest times in her life and I'd made it infinitely worse by being an absolute dick for no reason. She was being abused and I'd added bullying into the mix.

"You know what I did. The rumour—"

"Wasn't your fault," he concluded my sentence, pitching against the counter. "Stop blaming yourself. You were the only member to speak to her other than Nate. And he was gone. So who was the next best source? People will only believe the rumour if it came from somebody trusted. That was you."

I'd heard that before when I had initially told him about the latest rumour suddenly circulating campus with my name fastened to it.

I groaned, feeling my throat close. "She didn't deserve any of that. Remember when I said she turned her back on us?" He nodded. My throat throbbed with the words I didn't want to speak, words that had been playing on my mind on a loop.

"Beck, what is it?" he inquired, voice communicating his concern.

"Dad, she didn't turn her back on us. In fact, she sabotaged Nate to boost my chances of getting the captaincy," I told him, leaving out the part where she'd needed to help Nate as well. "And I feel like shit because of it. I could've stopped the team from bullying her because I was the captain but I didn't." I planted my hands on the sink and took in a thick breath. "I don't even know why she's here. She could've said no. There's no reason for her to be nice to me after everything I put her through."

My dad was soundless for a minute. "I hate to be the one to tell you this but I told you so." I glowered at him because I didn't need a lecture. I'd gotten many from my mom already. "I told you not to do anything stupid and just focus on saving your team." I cursed quietly. "You won, you had the captaincy but you made things worse by practically bullying that girl inside and stressing over Nate. You won."

I shook my head before whispering, "I didn't." He crossed his arms, gesticulating for me to speak louder. My words came out more potent the next time, tired of being kept quiet for so long. "I didn't win."

His eyes hooded. "You had the captaincy—"

"But I thought he had her," I choked out, closing my eyes momentarily. There was a rigid silence, one that scraped its talons on every inch of my skin. "Shit," I spoke after I understood this was his plan all along; to admit what I couldn't last year when I'd first found out Nyx was helping Nate. "Did mom put you up to this?"

He shrugged, grinning, and I wanted to dig a hole and die in it. "I always knew there was something else to it. First, you were okay with me paying for the position and you didn't care about what people said, not at all." I bridled. "Then suddenly you're ready to compete for the position like a lion that hasn't been fed in years. Tell me why." I scowled. "It's because of her, isn't it?"

"Fuck off," I snarled, prompting him to chuckle heartily. "You *know* how I felt about her."

My dad nodded, a little smile on his face. "Yeah, I do. I also know that seeing your girl aiding your enemy is enough to light a fire under your ass. You fought so hard *because* she was on the opposing side." He gave me one last look. "It's obvious why she did that." I frowned, brows crimping. "She knew you'd fight for her."

And I had. I'd fought for her under the pretence that it was all for the captaincy. But my pride had been wounded and I'd walked away. Not this time though. This time, she was going to know deep in her bones that she was mine and only mine.

The ride back to her place was stiff, making me wonder what she and my mom had spoken about. Nyx had been fine, up until my mom had inquired if she could get a moment alone with her before we left. I knew I should've objected and insisted we get going. Because now Nyx was being awkward as fuck. That behaviour carried straight into Saturday.

It was currently just past midnight and all the Taylor girls were staying with us. We'd obtained tickets to Indigo's recital; we being me, Grayson and Sebastian. Later in the day, we'd leave straight from our place as it made things easier. Instead of meeting at the auditorium, we could all leave together. The plan was good, but the only one who had a problem with it was Nyx.

And I knew my mom had something to do with it. I just knew it.

Grayson and Sebastian were dispersed around the living room, attention on the horror film playing in front of them. Sebastian was sprawled out on the fluffy carpet, blonde hair slovenly from twisting around in his blankets. Grayson was in an armchair, hands resting behind his head and eyeing the movie in amusement. If you asked me what was happening in the movie, I wouldn't be able to tell you because I'd been lost in my thoughts the entire time. I kept thinking of my conversation with my dad and trying *not to* think of the fact that Nyx was upstairs in a spare bedroom.

I was so close to giving in to her fucking hypothesis because it had been hell trying to stifle what I was feeling. I could understand why she wanted it to go away because it was bothersome as fuck. Every single time she walked into a room, it was like my entire body wanted to surge for her.

"Nyx?" The voice belonged to Grayson. I snapped out of my daze and saw both Sebastian and Grayson looking at the blonde girl who materialised as if she knew I was thinking about her. "You okay? You look a little hot."

Pressing her hands to her face, she probably felt that the skin was on fire. Sebastian turned back to the movie when a woman's scream tore his attention from Nyx.

My gaze hauled across her body, taking in her boy shorts and tank top. She held her breath when my eyes stopped on her nipples. Then my lips tilted into a delighted smirk. I knew exactly what she was going through. Because I was going through the same thing. It was why I was attempting to watch a movie with the guys. Each time I closed my eyes, I saw her.

"I'm fine," she said after clearing her throat. She didn't even realise she was staring at me; intensely. Sebastian glanced between me and Nyx with a smirk before he turned back to the movie again. He was enjoying seeing Nyx ruffled because she was still giving him a hard time for being an asshole at the last match. Grayson was still worried, pushing to his feet and stepping towards her. My smirk dropped.

"I'm just thirsty, Grayson." Sebastian snorted at her words and so did I.

"Do you want me to get you a glass of water?" Grayson proposed, holding out his hand.

Okay, he was genuinely a friendly person. But his voice was higher than usual and when Sebastian laughed, I knew he was up to something.

I stood up, cracking my neck which was numb from sitting in one position for so long. "Sit your ass down, Gray," I told him as I walked towards Nyx. "She's *my* guest, so that means *I* have to take care of her." Sebastian choked at that and Nyx crimsoned.

Grayson stared at me, grinning. He sighed and was about to pull Nyx in for a hug but I scowled at him. There was a firm silence. And then Grayson chuckled before taking his original seat. Turning on her heel, Nyx entered the kitchen and I followed behind.

"I can get a glass of water myself," she muttered, probably not liking the fact that she was alone with me. Ever since

Friday evening, she'd been doing her best to dodge me. "You don't need to take care of me."

She sounded annoyed and restless. It looked like she was having some sort of withdrawal symptoms, but I knew she didn't do drugs. The answer was obvious. She was horny.

I apprehended then what Grayson had intended. He'd noticed she'd been avoiding me and the thing he constantly preached about was *communication*. He *knew* I wouldn't let him be alone with her when she was wearing that outfit. He *knew* I would stand up. The fucker gave me a chance to be alone with her.

Too bad talking wasn't in either of our plans.

I sagged against the opposite counter, watching as she opened the fridge and poured herself a glass. My mom must've told her something hair-raising if it caused her to disregard her need and try to elude me. I'd thought we were past the avoiding stage. But my mom had just taken us back a few steps.

Just as Nyx took a sip of her water, I said, "You're wet." It was a statement. One that made her choke on her water and begin coughing.

Water spilt onto her top and she glared at me, words dripping with frustration. "Well, now I am," she hissed, dabbing at the front of her top. "Thanks to you."

In a fluid movement, I was in front of her, backing her against the counter. The smell of strawberries hit me, her usual smell. The conversation with my dad had made me recognise that I wanted her even more than before. Because I always had. She'd just never been properly within my reach, something always keeping us apart. Whether it was Nate or her trust issues, I could never reach her.

And now I could.

"I'm talking about your pussy," I hummed, grazing my nose against the side of her jaw before nipping her ear. "Thanks to me?" She stayed quiet. "Answer me, Nyx."

"You're quite full of yourself, aren't you?" Her voice came out unstable because I began suckling at her throat, leaving marks. Marks that everyone would see.

More gunshots rang throughout the house, louder than before. I had a feeling the guys knew exactly what was going on in the kitchen and put the TV louder.

I mumbled against her skin, making her hiss. "Just say the words and you can be full of me too." Because I was ready to give in to that hypothesis. She let out an instinctive moan and quickly clamped a hand over her mouth. I chuckled, trailing kisses all the way from her neck to her mouth. "You said I don't need to take care of you. Is that true?" She nodded and I stared her dead in the eye. Unyielding Nyx was back. "So you don't want me to take care of you? Don't want me to relieve you of that ache?"

Nyx quaked when I cupped her over her shorts. She couldn't deny the magnetism between us, couldn't contain it as much as she wanted to. "There's no ache." Her tone was chiding. Abruptly, I slipped my hand into her pants, sliding my fingers through her folds. This time, her words came out as a moan and I smirked. "*Beck.*"

"I'm right here," I whispered, gently playing with her clit. "Your pussy's so soft and warm." I plunged a finger inside her, making her grip my shoulders with everything that she had.

"And *wet*." Another finger. "Who made you wet, Nyx? Tell me."

I scissored my fingers and her legs began quivering. I could hear the squelching sound my hand made, how wet she was. She must've had a wonderful dream.

"You," she managed to say through clenched teeth, shuddering when I began moving my hand faster. I wondered how much it took for her to say the words. "Always you."

That made the feeling inside my chest fracture. The desperation in her voice nearly made my knees buckle.

"Good girl," I murmured. And then I towed down her shorts and panties before placing her on the edge of the counter. Nyx barely had a chance to blink before I was down on my knees, face concealed between her legs. *Fuck*. She moaned and jerked at my hair as I ate her pussy. She pulled me closer, clamping her thighs around my head. "My baby tastes so good." My words were a growl, sending vibrations through her entire body. She was trying her best to not make any sounds, afraid that the guys would hear.

Her body began trembling, hinting that she was about to reach her climax. It was clear she was ready for it, aching for it. But then I pulled away.

"What the—" I shoved two fingers back inside her, moving in and out at a furious pace. "I want you to come all over my fingers." She moaned, biting into my shoulder to deaden the sound as she jerked.

"Shit, Beck," Nyx groaned as her back arched, pressing her face into my neck. She tugged at my hair, my fingers burying deeper inside of her. I used my thumb to flick her nub, hearing her whimper against me. "Oh, god, *yes*."

"Do you wanna come?" She nodded, tears pooling in her eyes. "Come for me, baby."

And she let go, crashing into her release. My hand never stopped moving, riding her through the wave. She sagged against me as my free hand rubbed her back. The other pulled out of her and she watched me lick my fingers clean.

"That's disgusting."

A loud laugh left my lips before I pressed my mouth to hers. "I was eating your pussy a few seconds ago and you think me licking your taste off my fingers is disgusting?" She shrugged, nuzzling her face into my neck. "You tired, baby?" She nodded. "Let's get you to bed."

I pulled her pants up and instead of carrying her back to the room she was staying in; I took her to mine. She didn't protest, just let me place her on the bed. Before I could move away, she tugged me to her. And then her mouth was on mine. She dipped her head, prompting our tongues to graze against each other. Her hands moved to take off my shirt, wandering the skin that she found. A deep noise left my throat and I dragged her against me. I cupped her breasts as she whined into my mouth.

"I need this to go away," she muttered against my lips, drawing me closer even though I was already pressed against her. "This constant feeling of wanting you. *I hate it.*" I knew exactly what she was talking about. "Maybe it's only here because we have a history? And if we just take care of it—"

"What if it doesn't go away?" I uttered the issue that had been troubling me and she froze, hands caught in my hair. The question had been hovering in the air for quite some time and both of us were too afraid to reach for it. “What if we have sex and this feeling doesn’t go away?”

Nyx beamed, nodding to herself and beginning to play with my hair again. She didn’t sound too terrified, not like I’d expected. In fact, she approached the question with familiarity. I needed to have a talk with my mom because, knowing her, she’d asked Nyx if we were sexually involved.

“It’s a hypothesis for a reason. There’s a chance that I could be wrong.”

She didn’t proceed, although it was apparent there was more to say. If her hypothesis was incorrect, then we were just two people who craved each other even after all this time. And Nyx didn’t know what to do with information like that. Because it scared her, just like it had the first time.

Tilting back, I stated, “After the recital.” She pulled a perplexed expression. “After the recital, you and I are having sex.” She wrinkled her nose, stunned that I was giving in.

“And if the feeling doesn’t go away?” she demanded after thinking it through.

I smirked, pulling her towards me again. “Then, you’re mine.”

Chapter 25

Nyx

"Okay, nobody's here right now," I muttered, shoving and twisting the key. The door wouldn't open and I was beginning to get annoyed. "Fuck this bitch ass door—"

Beckham took the key from me with a laugh, easily opening the door and I sighed in aggravation. "I guess I'm just experienced in inserting things."

I frowned at him, a little startled. "Refer to vaginas as keyholes again and I *will* murder you."

He laughed harder, following me inside. We had a limited amount of time together. After Indigo's recital, everyone had gone back to his place for dinner, dinner that Beckham and I were tasked with ordering and picking up. Surprisingly, the guys had had a great time at the recital and I wouldn't tell them, but I was glad they'd attended.

Indigo had needed everyone there. Everywhere she'd looked, she'd seen families clustering around her friends. She'd seen enthusiastic dads tossing their daughters into the air as they squealed. She'd seen emotional mothers crying and fawning over their daughters. I knew it would unnerve her. It always did. The same thoughts had ran through my head during high school, when my parents hadn't attended my debate competitions or when I'd given speeches. Surrounded by all those people, I'd never felt so alone before. And I didn't want Indigo to feel like that. She was too young, too pure.

I'd told myself I wouldn't cry. I'd *promised* myself I wouldn't cry. But the moment Indigo had stepped onto the stage looking like a baby swan, there was no holding back the tears. The fall had been gradual, slow streams running down my probably red cheeks, and every few seconds, I would reach up to wipe it away. I'd done better than Annie, who had tried her best to stop her ugly crying. Indigo was perfection and I wanted her to always know that. I'd cheered when she'd done five consecutive pirouettes after she'd been struggling with it for a few days.

"That's my sister!" Poppy had roared, nearly leaping out of her seat and Beckham had had to pull her back. Indigo had been laughing, skipping to the front before dropping into a middle split and then rolling into a backbend.

The tears had returned again when I'd seen her gigantic grin as she twirled and the audience applauded. Just earlier, in the dressing room, she'd gotten cold feet. And there she was, enjoying every second of her solo. When the final timbre of the piano had died down, we'd been up on our feet, screaming her name and Indigo had been crying, trying to laugh through her tears.

She'd had a family there to support her.

Even Georgia had been there with Julie. I'd done my best

not to behave awkwardly, trusting Annie when she'd said she had everything under control. Georgia had given me an understanding smile and an encouraging pat on the shoulder. I just needed to figure out when I could talk to her.

For now, sex.

"Did you order the food?" I demanded, placing the keys down on the table.

Beckham nodded, taking off his jacket. "Yep, we've got forty minutes." I checked each room, making sure that my dad wasn't home. We didn't need him walking in on me having sex with the son of a cop. "You know, I don't think normal people *plan* when to have sex."

"This was *your* idea," I riposted, starting to rethink the normalcy of this plan. "The hypothesis was mine." Beckham was sitting on the couch now, looking all too comfortable.

Why wasn't he nervous? Because I was nervous as *fuck*.

I'd always said I would never admit it, but Beckham was handsome. His hair was just the right length, always falling messily on his head. His eyes were the shade of a raging storm and fuck, I wouldn't even dare go down the path of the tattoos.

A throat cleared and I glanced at him. My cheeks flushed because I'd been fucking *gawking* at him like an idiot.

"You look a little tense." The teasing in his voice was unmistakable whereas the smirk looked permanently engraved into his stupid face.

I shrugged. "Tense? I'm not tense."

What the fuck was wrong with me? Okay, this was Beckham. Good old asshole of a man, Beckham. And as soon as this desire for him went away, we could coexist peacefully.

No more unnecessary hatred and no more unneeded attraction.

My chest constricted, making it feel as if I was about to have a stroke. Beckham stood up and walked towards me, making me back into the counter. I felt like prey. I was usually the fucking predator. He caged me against the counter and I held my breath.

"Breathe, baby." Slowly, I let out a breath, causing him to chuckle low at my apprehension. I took in another deep breath because this was just *Beckham*. There was no need to be nervous. We'd done this before. "There you go, deep breaths." My body felt lighter with each exhalation. "Good girl."

His lips grazed the shell of my ear as he spoke. I stopped breathing again. How did he expect me to inhale and exhale when he did shit like that? I quivered when his teeth skimmed my ear.

"You're an asshole," I whispered.

He moved lower, caressing my neck. "I think I should put that on my resume because you keep saying that." I clutched his shoulders when my body sagged as he nipped the skin of my neck before sucking it into his mouth. "One word," he murmured, kissing my jaw. "One word will determine how we spend the next forty minutes. Do you want this?"

"Just shut the fuck up and kiss me."

"That wasn't one word," he said with a taunting grin. "Yes or no?"

I glared at him. "Yes."

"Good girl." And then his lips met mine. His arms went around me, tugging me closer. I moaned against his mouth, pulling at his silky hair. He bit down on my lip and I moaned again. "I'm sick of you pretending that you don't want me."

He lifted me onto the counter and I smiled. "The same gocs for you." Pitching forward, he kissed me again, tongue traversing every inch of my mouth and I sighed, breathing heavily through my nose. Beckham moved back down to my neck where he'd left the original mark and began sucking again. "*Beck.*"

"I'm right here," he whispered as he bit me again. There was so much substance to the way he said it, that he was with me. "I don't think I'll be able to stop." His eyes were flaring and I could hear the need dripping from his voice. We were in the same boat.

So I said, "Then fucking don't."

He picked me up and then stepped over to the couch, sitting down. Our kiss was messy, a disorder of tongues and teeth but I didn't want it to stop. He kissed me like he was chasing after his last breath. I began rubbing against his thighs. All that separated me from him were my panties and his jeans. My skirt was bunched up around my waist.

"That's it, baby," he grumbled, squeezing my hips as he kissed my neck. "Get yourself nice and ready for me."

I seized his shoulders, moving against him and whining when he stroked his thumb over my nipples. His fingers then moved up my thighs, playing with the band of my underwear. I moaned, hearing him chuckle at my desperation. I could feel the wetness pooling between my legs and I was on the verge of begging.

"Please, Beck. I need you. *Now.*"

He merely moved my hips again, grinding me over the

bulge in his jeans. “Yeah?”

When I scowled, he chuckled again and stood up. I resorted to kissing his jaw as he carried me through the hallway to where he remembered my room was. He placed me down on one bed, having to unwrap my arms and legs from him because I wouldn’t let go.

When he stepped back to pull off his shirt, I found myself saying, “I never dated Nate.”

Although it went without saying, it felt right to state it.

Beckham froze, his shirt partially over his head. Slowly, he towed it over and then flung it to the floor, staring intensely at me. He gulped. “What?”

I attempted a smile, panting. “There was never anything between me and Nate. He was dating Annie.” He was still staring at me as if I suddenly transformed into an alien. “Based on what you know, it’s obvious there was only ever familial love between Nate and me, but I just wanted to clarify. I didn’t want that hanging over your head,” I confessed, a lump suddenly in my throat. “You always said you wouldn’t take Nate’s sloppy seconds—”

“I—”

“But he’s never had me,” I stated and saw his entire body tense. I had no idea what was going through his head but I needed to get this off my chest.

Just as I was about to get up and lock myself in the bathroom for being an absolute fucking idiot, he spoke. “I never fucked Melissa.” I blinked. “She came over with Sebastian, made a move on me and fell asleep in my bed. I slept on my couch.” He cleared his throat, looking slightly guilty. “And when I kissed her at the club, it was because I hoped that if she *thought* she had the upper hand on you, even just for a moment, she'd leave you the fuck alone. Not my best moment at all."

I couldn't hold it against him; that he'd kissed her. I'd basically eaten Jasper's face off that night.

I grinned. "This communication thing isn't too bad, I guess." And then I tugged off my panties and skirt, and kicked off my shoes before leaning back on my elbows. "Now let's do this—"

I slumped back against the bed as he hovered over me, lips pressed to my neck as his hand hunted down my leg. His nose skimmed my cheek and I shuddered. When his fingers found my clit, I moaned loudly.

"I need to be between your legs," he murmured, moving lower down my body until his face was between my thighs. I sat up slightly to remove my sweater and unclip my bra. Whatever he saw there made his eyes darken with lust, a groan of appreciation leaving him. His tongue slid through my folds and I sank back again, back arching. "So sweet," he grumbled against me.

A second later, he slipped two fingers inside me and began pumping. It felt like all the air left the room because I couldn't breathe. All the teasing caught up with me. The kissing, the grinding.

"*Shit*," I hissed.

"Come on, baby. Be a good girl and come for me."

My fingers found his hair and I gripped it harshly as my back arched again. "*Shit*, Beck. I'm gonna come—"

Pleasure slammed into me like a truck and it felt like I was fucking floating. My eyes shut when my vision became blurry. Beckham stood up and hovered over me again, kissing me.

I bit his lip and he grunted. "Fucking minx." I wrapped my arms around him, holding him close. My body was still reeling with the effects of my orgasm.

"Beckham," I whispered, nipping his lip again.

He smiled against my mouth, unbuttoning his jeans and kicking off his shoes. I made the task difficult with my grinding against him and he chuckled. I whined when he pushed away from me and dug into his wallet for a condom. It was finally happening. I watched him slide it over himself whilst holding eye contact with me.

This was fucking happening.

I leaned back as he walked towards me and breathed deeply. A second later, he was between my legs. "You ready?" he questioned softly, brushing my hair out of my face. I nodded. He gripped the base of his cock, dragging it through my wetness. "Fucking hell," he groaned, jerking slightly so he could press against me.

My nails burrowed into his shoulders as he gradually pushed into me. He paused when I hissed. The idiot was big. I mean, I knew that. I'd had his dick inside me before. But that felt like forever ago. He forced my lips apart, burrowing deeper until he bottomed out completely.

"Oh my *god*," I moaned, arching slightly. He held me in place, hands gripping my waist as he began thrusting. "Holy—"

"*Fuck*," he hissed, my body rocking against his as he swivelled his hips and a silent scream left me. The arch of my back left the bed completely when he hit a particularly good spot. Tears were pooling in my eyes and I whimpered, reaching for his shoulders. “That feel good, baby?” I nodded, unable to form any coherent words. He jolted his hips forward and my breath left me in a choked moan. “Easy, sweetheart, that’s it.”

My hands met the sheets, gripping them between my fingers. “Please, don’t stop.”

I was being stretched in the best way possible. He leaned down, lips meeting mine in a breathless kiss. I circled my hips against him, hearing him groan. The kiss was scorching hot and I felt him grinding against my clit. I wanted more because it felt like he was doing everything. And I wasn’t one to be outmatched. Tapping his shoulder, I forced him to turn over so I could straddle him.

Beckham smirked at me as he pushed back against the headboard. I sank lower, feeling the head of his dick slip inside me. The pain was short-lived, being supplanted by an extraordinary wave of pleasure. My knees buckled and I gasped, burying my face in the crook of his neck as I lowered myself completely. The stretch stung, making it feel as if I was about to be split in half.

An animalistic groan left Beckham and his hands were clutching the flesh of my ass. “Jesus, fuck,” he groaned, circling his hips, and I moaned. “You’re taking me so well.” He was so deep inside me that it felt impossible. The feeling was overwhelming; being filled to the brim. Bliss poured out of my moan as Beckham pushed me against him. I was frozen, trying to stabilise my mind. “Move, baby.”

His voice was muffled, pinched. Setting my arms on his shoulders, I raised myself slightly, eyes trained on his. But

Beckham wasn't looking at me. He was looking at where we were connected, his cock gradually sliding out of me. With another groan, he gripped my hips and slammed me back down on him.

I whimpered, eyes clenching shut. "Beck," I moaned, rolling my hips slightly before replicating the process. It was a continual sound of flesh against flesh. The slapping sound resonated through the small room, drowned out only by Beckham's rumbling grunts and my moans. "*Fuck*, that's so deep."

"Just like that, Nyx," he praised, prompting me to move faster. My legs felt paralysed by the pleasure rushing through my veins. "There you go—*fuck*," he cursed when I involuntarily tensed around him. My mouth was parted, moans emerging as Beckham and I moved in sync with one another.

My hands roamed up his broad shoulders, shifting to cup his face. His stubble was scratchy, providing a ticklish sensation against my skin. I placed my forehead against his, palpitating with the effort of riding him.

"*Shit*," I whined when he elevated his knees, hitting a deeper spot within me. Beckham was gazing at me, eyes cleared of its natural storm. All that greeted me now was pure silver. "That feels *so good*."

He slapped my ass, smirking when I squealed at the unexpected move. "Who would've thought Nyx Taylor could ride a man this good?" he inquired in a low tone, groaning when I clenched around him again.

I sighed, tossing my head back. My voice was breathless when I remarked, "I'm just full of surprises."

Beckham's thumb found my clit and I jolted. He stared at it as he stroked furiously. "You're full of something, alright." I didn't have the energy to call him out on the pride in his tone so I let it slide. I'd never felt so utterly intoxicated before. In one fluid move, Beckham flipped me over, placing himself between my legs.

His restraint snapped as he slammed into me at a merciless pace. My senses felt stripped from me. My ears were buzzing and I could barely see through the pleasure of it all. Beckham was pressed so tightly against me, I didn't know where I ended and he began. I locked my legs around his hips, pulling him closer even though there was no more space between us.

His abs stroked my stomach with each move and the hair on his chest tantalised my peaked nipples. I was past the point of pleasure now, plunging straight off the cliff of overstimulation. I was high on my own personal drug, a drug that'd I'd been abstaining from for so long.

Until now.

All that was leaving my mouth was his name, like a breathless chant. The words leapt from my lips, gliding through the tense air. There was a tightening sensation from deep within me and I willed it to go away. I didn't want this feeling to end, this feeling of fullness.

"Beckham." His name was the only thing I knew. It was just me and him, rutting like animals on my bed. His skin was moistened with sweat and so was mine. I yanked at his hair, pulling a deep growl from the back of his throat.

His hands slipped underneath me, cupping my ass and heaving me against him. I nearly passed out at the feeling.

“That’s it, baby. Move with me.” His voice was hoarse, like pure gravel. There would surely be bruises on my thighs because of the way he was gripping me. His palms suffocated my ass, gripping it as if it was his salvation. “*Nyx*,” he groaned into my neck and I bit my lip. “Are you gonna come for me?” I was so close to sobbing.

The sensation in my stomach unwound and I shook my head, not wanting it to end. “No, Beck”

He pulled back, gazing down at me with lust-filled eyes. His pace intensified and I cried out. “Come for me, Nyx.” I shook my head, making him growl. “*Do it*.” I gave in, moaning uncontrollably as I squirmed underneath him. My orgasm viciously crashed into me and I could barely hear the scream that left me. Pleasure wept from my every pore, every nerve. “That’s my girl.”

My eyes snapped to his, something building in my chest as my nails scraped down his back. It was a feeling I tried to suppress. “Who said I’m your girl?” I asked breathlessly, air returning to my lungs.

He flexed his hips, emphasising that he hadn’t orgasmed yet and was still filling me up. “Whose cock is inside you right now?”

I scoffed jokingly. “That question’s irrelevant. I could easily replace it with somebody else’s dick tomorrow.”

Beckham’s hand shot to my throat. I froze but the smirk was still etched into my mouth. His nostrils flared, sensing the amusement I was radiating. With his other hand, he pulled out of me, leaving me empty as he dragged the head across my overstimulated clit. I suppressed a whimper.

"Maybe I should just leave my mark," he whispered, kissing my jaw. "Brand you so that others know to stay the fuck away." He hissed as the head of his cock penetrated me again.

I seized the sheets in my hands as he pumped slowly. I couldn't even respond to his previous words as my eyes rolled to the back of my head, body arching to fit against his like two puzzle pieces. Beckham didn't hold back at all, relentlessly grinding against me. My limbs felt like jelly but I kept my ankles secured behind him, reluctant to let him go. His mouth found mine, tongue slipping inside and exploring to its heart's content.

The intimate feeling emerged inside me. I scratched his back, marking the skin with my nails, and he swore loudly, pulling my bottom lip between his teeth.

"You're gonna come again, Nyx," he grunted against my lips. Beckham ploughed into me at a pitiless pace, making me chase after another orgasm. "Again," he grunted. "Come for me." When my pleasure hit me, I fell into the void of flames, branding and consuming my body in sheer euphoria. Beckham's body tensed and then I felt his cock pulsate with his release. "Fuck, baby, that's it. Just like that." His deep moans filled the air and I nearly cried at the feeling hastening through me. "*Shit.*" He groaned against me, moaning with his release.

He collapsed on top of me, nearly cutting off my air supply. But I didn't mind, binding my arms around him and stroking his back as he panted heavily into my neck. I felt the indents of my nails and I smirked. He wasn't the only one who'd left marks. His teammates would surely question him in the locker room and I could just laugh at the thought of his response

"I can feel your satisfaction, you little minx," he grumbled, flexing his back muscles, and I snorted. "If anybody asks, I can just say that I had some fun with a puck bunny." My smile dropped and he raised his head, grinning tiredly at me. "Not so fun, is it?"

I scowled, shoving his shoulders and he chuckled. He pulled out of me as he rolled over, making me whine at the feeling of emptiness. He stood up to dispose of the condom and I watched his ass. The man was so fucking lean and every bit of him was sculpted to perfection. The tattoos on his arms danced with every movement and when he turned around, showcasing his magnificent length, I was suddenly ready to take him again.

The thought alarmed me. This was supposed to *eliminate* the tension between us, put a stop to it. But that feeling was still there, concealed deep inside me. I felt my heart rate spike, anxiety filling my lungs like water. If anything, that feeling amplified.

I wanted him more than before, I couldn't deny that. Selfish. I was willing to be selfish again and take something for myself now that there were no consequences. The fearful part of me, the girl scared of being hurt again had hidden behind my dumb hypothesis. If this feeling was to go away, it wasn't a good idea to go back to Beckham.

But this feeling was still very much present, the intensity of it suffocating me.

When I glanced up, Beckham was staring at me as he slipped on his boxers, understanding in his eyes. "Beck—"

"I'm gonna go pick up our food," he cut me off, pulling on his jeans next. I took in a deep breath, trying to calm down.

His phone began vibrating and I knew our order was ready. Once he pulled his shirt on, he stepped closer to the bed where I sat, still naked as the day I was born. "When I get back, we're gonna talk about it. Sebastian can fucking wait for his food."

Talk about it.

That terrified the shit out of me. There was nothing to talk about. Except, maybe the fact that I wanted to yank him by the shirt and smash my mouth to his. He must've read my mind because his hand slipped to my nape, albeit gently, and kissed me. I moaned, trying to pull him closer, but he stepped back, smiling. He looked as baffled as me, which helped nothing.

His leaving so soon after we'd just fucked probably looked bad. But I understood the message clearly. He was giving me space, time to come to terms with what I was feeling. I'd expected the annoyance to come back full force once the desire was out of the way. But the barrier between us was dwindling, hanging on by a thread.

And Beckham knew that. He laced his shoes, grabbing the car keys on his way out. When the front door shut, I let out a frustrated scream.

The point of sleeping with Beckham again was to relieve the ache, but now that fucking ache was the size of Mount Kilimanjaro and the only fucker who could climb it was that arrogant asshole. I'd been lying to myself all this time, fooled myself into thinking I didn't care about him, that I hated him. But one could easily mistake hatred for something else. A feeling could only intensify if it was already there.

I loved Beckham Hunt.

There was no way to pinpoint when it had happened, but

the fact stayed the same. This was bad. This was so fucking bad. Of course I loved him. It was the only plausible reason as to why he scared me so much. The knowledge was always there, buried deep inside and I'd been too much of a coward to acknowledge it. This was bad. There was nothing stopping me from being with him now, except maybe the toe-curling fear of him leaving again, of giving my absolute everything to somebody who wouldn't treasure it. Trauma was a bitch. Beckham could leave when it became too much. He could leave at the slightest misunderstanding. That would hurt less than him not returning my feelings.

Oh my God.

My face felt feverish and sweaty. I stood up, slipping into clean underwear and clothes again. I washed my face, but the redness stayed, the bruises on my neck stayed. Fuck. He wasn't exaggerating when he'd said he'd leave a mark. Five minutes later, my phone dinged. I had a message from Annie that said we should pick up an extra burger because Julie was staying with us. The second message came through from Beckham and my heart fluttered.

Just so we're clear, your hypothesis was bullshit. You're mine.

I shuddered, plopping onto the edge of my bed as I thought things through. He had the potential to break me and he didn't even know it. The thought terrified me. I must've sat there for about ten minutes when there was a hasty knock on the door. Frowning, I stood up and headed to the living room. We never received visitors and everybody we knew, knew that we were at Beckham's place.

My dad had probably forgotten his key, the dumbass. There

was a dull ache between my legs and I slanted against the wall as I opened the door. Georgia was on the other side.

"Nyx?" she greeted me in surprise and I frowned, wondering why she was at the house. She knew we were celebrating at the boys' place, she'd *dropped* Julie there.

Which meant she wasn't at the house to see any of us. "What are you doing here?" I questioned, eyes narrowing.

She glimpsed around uneasily, checking for intrusive neighbours. I heeded her gaze, knowing what this neighbourhood was like, primarily when it came to my family. Everybody wanted to know what happened in the Taylor household.

"Come inside," I advised, allowing her to slip past me.

Georgia scrunched her nose. "It smells like sex in here." I pursed my lips, but she'd already spotted my subtle limp. A loud cackle ricocheted through the air, courtesy of her. "Ah, I see. No wonder you're home."

I winced as I took a seat and ignored her smile. "Why are you here?"

"To see your dad," was her straightforward comeback and I scowled at the mention of him. "I'm gonna assume you know I'm a social worker," she broke the ice, taking a seat at the counter. "It's gotta be the reason you looked so peeved by me during the recital like I was suddenly an outsider. But I want you to know, Nyx, I'm always gonna be on your side."

My mouth was parched and the words felt rough. "Annie says my mom left you to help us. Is that true?" It was difficult to imagine my mom wanting to help when all I could remember was her leaving.

Judging by the way Georgia was staring at me, I could tell she was glad she ran into me. She nodded, giving me a commiserating smile. "Your mom and I go way back, fell out of touch after high school but reunited about two months ago." Her brown eyes clouded with memories and I found myself wanting to know everything about their relationship, everything about who my mom was before she became a shell of herself. "A group of friends and I opened a private practice, and a while back, I got a call from your mom. She told me she was in rehab and read about the opening of my practice in the newspaper. There was no beating around the bush, she asked me to visit her and when I arrived, I barely recognised her."

A scoff fled me as I remembered how my mom had looked the years preceding her disappearance. "I remember the drugs, it's one of the worst memories for me," I conceded. "Can't even pinpoint exactly when she started using. But the alcohol made it worse. She was always out of it and no help against my dad."

The older woman nodded in understanding. "I'm not going to lie to you and tell you she's a good mother, Nyxie. But she came to me, asked me to do whatever I could to protect you girls."

Irritation sparked inside me. "Why didn't she ever try to do anything?" After Indigo's birth, all I could remember was my mom being forced around by my dad all the time or snorting coke. "Why didn't she stand up to him? And why did it take her *five years* to do something? The longest program is ninety days, I checked when Annie first told me where she was. What was she doing for five years?"

An unnerving silence passed. "Relapsing." I swallowed

roughly. "She was relapsing, Nyx. It takes some people longer to heal." Georgia looked suddenly pained. "I came here to speak to your dad about the next step forward. Your mom, she was released about a week ago." My blood went cold.

I cleared my throat. "She's out?" Georgia nodded. If my mom was out then it meant she'd finally gotten her shit together. This must've been what Annie meant when she'd said we had to figure out where our mom fit into our plan of leaving. Because there was always a chance of her returning, no matter how much I refused to believe it. "Where's she now?"

Georgia took a moment to assemble her thoughts and I shifted uncomfortably. "I was hoping to speak to your dad first before you and Annie," she began and I looked away at the mention of him. "As you know, I'm evaluating him. The past two instances when he hurt Poppy and Indigo while I was on the case, he was forced to attend compulsory therapy. Those sessions were helping. However, I only recently discovered his other family. His wife has been made aware of the person that he is." *His wife.* "And of course, she's not exactly happy. As far as I know, she's filing for divorce."

"Lucky her," I muttered. At least she had the sense to leave him.

Georgia sighed. "Your dad is unstable right now." I snorted. "With his wife leaving him and the situation with your mom, I think it would be best if we remove Poppy and Indigo from his care permanently."

Her words were like a gunshot in a silent room. I was barely aware of my hand going to clutch the front of my shirt. This was what we'd been trying to prevent. We wanted to be free from my dad before anybody tried to take our sisters away, when Annie and I were certain we could provide for them and be their legal guardians.

"What?" My voice trembled.

"I've been biased this entire time," Georgia continued, placing a hand on my knee. "When your dad goes to therapy, the girls are temporarily out of his care and are *supposed* to stay with me. But I let them stay with you and Annie, popping in now and then to check up. But now that it's certain Matthew Taylor can no longer care for the girls, they have to be taken out of this house permanently."

I was shaking my head. "They're not going to my mom, right?"

She squeezed my leg. "They'll stay with me, sweetheart. At least, until a potential guardian can take them in—"

"And how long will that be for?" I urged swiftly, trying to figure out if I could ask Benson for my payments early. "Because I could try and secure an apartment—"

The older woman gently shushed me. "As long as it takes for you to get settled and out of your dad's reach." I nodded absentmindedly, relief washing over me. Georgia was doing us a huge favour by taking them in. She was doing this as a friend and not a social worker.

When Georgia shifted to get up, I found myself asking, "And what about our mom? Are you not gonna let her try to get her daughters back? Visits?"

That was if she *wanted* to be back in our lives. Her presence could prove to be a hindrance.

There was a moment where Georgia's lips parted but no

words came out. I waited until she had what she wanted to say. "As I said, your mom has been out for a week. She promised to keep me updated."

She didn't even need to continue. The moment she uttered the word *promised*, I knew my mom had bailed on her.

Unamused, I shook my head and muttered, "She ghosted you, didn't she?" I was already scoffing before she nodded. When Georgia continued to stare at me, I raised a brow. "What? It's not like it's a surprise."

"Nyx," she said my name firmly and I felt the hairs on my arms stand to attention. "I don't know how to tell you this—"

But she didn't have to. She didn't have to finish her sentence—because I could see it in her eyes, in her posture, hear it in her tone and feel it in her presence. I stood up, ignoring the dull ache between my legs, and began to pace. My hands were shaking, my eyes were burning, but I refused to let myself cry. Georgia merely watched me as I traversed the length of the living room, arms folded across my chest.

"It doesn't make a difference," I muttered eventually, making Georgia frown. "It's not like she was part of our lives anyway—"

"She was still your mother, Nyxie," she said in a soothing tone, one that grated at my anger.

I shook my head furiously. "No. No, she wasn't. Biologically, she was my mom, but she never deserved that title." There was a weird sensation in my chest, one that I couldn't name. I didn't care about her, I didn't care about Eliza Taylor. But something inside of me was aching. Something inside of me was hurting.

Georgia stood as well, looking like she wanted to pull me

into her arms. "Nyxie—"

"She didn't call you because she wanted to be better for us," I spoke over her, leaning against the wall. "She called you because she didn't care enough to *be* better for us. Nobody else. She had nobody else so she dumped us in your care because she didn't *plan* on coming back." My chest was burning. A dad who fucking hated us and a mom who couldn't give a shit. "*God*, her death was probably an accident. She probably thought she was finally free of us. She thought she'd done her part by contacting you. She thought the burden of her girls was gone. She thought—she was—she didn't want us. She—"

When I sank to the floor and wrapped my arms around my knees, the sobbing came. It came and it didn't end for a while. I cried for little Nyx who used to love the fact that she looked exactly like her mom. Words crawled up my throat, words I yearned to utter to a woman who no longer existed. I wanted to tell her that I hated her, hated what she'd become. I wanted to thank her for teaching me what not to be.

Desperately, I wracked the deepest parts of myself for good memories of her but I came up empty, gasping for breath. So I clung to the pain she'd left me with. Because that was all she'd ever given me. I only had pain to remember my mother by.

Georgia sank down next to me, pulling me into a bone-shattering hug as I sobbed into her peach-scented scarf. I cried for the juvenile part of me that had secretly held out hope her mom would return. I cried for Annie who obviously believed our mom could be better. I cried for Poppy, a girl who grew up hating both of her parents. I cried for Indigo.

In the silence that followed my weeping, I murmured, "She

never met her. She never had the chance to know her."

Georgie swallowed. "She didn't need to. Indigo has you and Annie. You're more than enough."

I sniffled, wiping at my swollen eyes. "I don't want to be there when you tell Annie."

Georgia only nodded, stroking my hair. Annie and I felt differently about our mom so our reactions would vary. I couldn't offer real comfort to my sister, not when I couldn't give a shit about our mom. More than anything, Annie deserved to put the thought of Eliza to rest with good memories, and Georgia could give her that. But not me. We sat like that for a long while, long enough for me to wonder what was taking Beckham so long.

Beckham.

The moment his name whispered through my mind, I realised exactly what sensation was happening in my chest. They said the person you loved most was your mother, a love so intense that it took up the most space in your heart, regardless of other people you cared for. But that space had been hollow for me, filled with a faux version of what I truly deserved. It felt like the ghost of my mom's whispered words of affection were fading now that she was gone, her manipulative love being forced out by something genuine.

Beckham was taking up that spot in my heart now that he had permission to. He wasn't replacing her, but rather filling the void that she'd left behind. The thought soothed me more than it scared me. So I clung to Georgia until I could find myself in the arms that truly gave me comfort.

Chapter 26

Beckham

I was so fucking in love with Nyx Taylor.

My dad knew, as dads always know, that I'd been in love with her since the very beginning. Even the other night, he'd emphasised it with my initial reaction to Nyx helping Nate. I'd been hurt, and thought that the girl I loved was nothing more than a figment of my imagination. But she was real. So very real and so very *not* my enemy. The realisation had hit me the second after I'd stood up from her bed. It didn't feel right. It didn't feel right leaving her. When I'd turned around, I'd seen the panic in my eyes reflected in hers. That moment, so insignificant yet simultaneously monumental. I could still see it.

Her face was red and sweaty, blonde hair in tangles because of how I'd gripped it. She was completely naked in the centre of ruffled sheets, her body and emotions completely bare to me as something passed between us—a whispered secret that only we would ever know.

A thousand memories of her raced through my mind, and

I fell in love with her all over again. Loving her was always the easy part, but admitting it to myself was an entirely different game. The majority of my frustration this past few months had come from my urge to subdue it. Even when it had seemed we were on opposite sides, I always found myself a little in love with her. The way she raised a brow when she couldn't believe I was being an idiot. That look in her eyes when she insulted me and she could *feel* me wanting to laugh.

Or that small smile she had whenever she won our battles of banter, as if her subconscious reminded her I wasn't angry, just in love with her.

I'd known that I loved her the second I saw her, ornamented in fluffy clothing at what was our first match of the school year. She'd looked like a literal marshmallow, hair tucked into her beanie, heavy clothes and cheeks red with the frigid air. When I'd first spotted her in the audience, I'd gotten thrown to the icy ground. I'd glanced up and caught her eye—she'd smirked before looking back at the notebook in her lap. Nate had admonished me at the end of the match, but at least I'd gotten her attention.

After that, I'd started noticing her everywhere. She'd been a freshman and I'd thought perhaps she would need guidance being shown around campus. It had soon become quite clear that she didn't need help from anyone. She'd made it obvious by chewing the head off every guy that hit on her. I'd kept my distance, observed from afar. And then I'd made my move, dedicating all of my free time to her.

Thinking back, I wish I'd labelled what we were, made her my girlfriend. I wondered if things would've been different if

I'd stayed, listened to her or helped her instead of leaving like a heartbroken coward. I scowled at the memory of my actions.

"I know that look," a soft voice spoke as I leaned against the wall, waiting for my order. I had to place an extra order for Julie, and the place was packed so now I had to wait a while. "You fucked up, didn't you?"

My brows furrowed and I glanced at the woman who stood next to me, dressed in a lengthy coat with a scarf bound around her neck. Leather boots were on her feet and she had a fashionable pair of sunglasses atop her silvery hair. She didn't look a day older than thirty, but her greying hair and maturing face said otherwise. This was a woman who moisturised as if her life depended on it because her skin was smooth. Benson could learn a thing or two from her, seeing as he was slowly turning into a sea serpent.

I'd noticed her earlier, walking in with a bright smile on her face although she'd nearly been bulldozed by the sheer amount of people. What I hadn't noticed, however, was when she'd made her way over to me. I must've been deep in my thoughts to miss her approach.

"Excuse me?" I urged blandly, not wanting to offend her.

People jostled past us, wanting to get in line for food. Project Burger. Annie had said this was Indigo's preferred place to eat at because they supposedly had the best burgers. I understood now why I had to place an order through the phone because this place was bursting at the walls with people.

"Ms Lewis," she introduced herself, although I didn't ask. Ignoring my look of confusion, she proceeded. "I was saying, I know that look. It means you fucked up." I stared at her, wondering how she got all that from a mere scowl. "You good?" She seemed slightly amused.

I stared at the tall woman with her long grey hair. Her features were tender, as if she was genuinely intrigued by what had me so disrupted.

"It's nothing," I returned, shaking my head.

Except it was everything. My mom had a right to be disappointed in me when it came to how I'd handled things with Nyx. When she'd supposedly helped Nate, I'd tried to stifle what I felt for her and converted it into contempt. But that unneeded anger was leaving my body, breath by breath.

"Doesn't seem like nothing," Ms Lewis mumbled with an entertained smirk. She flapped a hand, chuckling. "Take my advice, son. Apologise. Even if you don't know what you did. It's the easiest route." If I squinted, Ms Lewis reminded me of my mom. She had the habit of engaging in intricate conversations with literal strangers. "My husband never apologised after he stuck his dick in another woman. Joke's on him because not even five months later, I stuck him six feet under the ground."

My lips pursed, eyes glazing over with horror. "You *murdered* him?"

Ms Lewis chuckled again and shrugged. "Didn't need to. Cancer did it for me. Runs in the family, I guess." I stayed silent, allowing her words to bob in the space between us. "Enough about me. We've got at least another few minutes before our food's ready. Wanna tell me what's up with you?"

After she revealed that little fact about her husband, my body eased slightly, which was ironic considering that she purposefully implied that she murdered him. A joke, perhaps.

She'd offered a piece of information and was asking for some in return.

Was I really about to talk to a literal stranger?

Well, Grayson was unavailable. So yes. I always scolded my best friend for being too philosophical, but life was biting me in the ass and I was in desperate need of advice.

"It's not that easy." How did I apologise for all the hurt I'd put her through? She'd let me tyrannise her about being with Nate when she'd known the truth. "A sorry isn't enough." I would know, I've been apologising so fucking much but it didn't ease my regret.

"You'd be surprised," the older woman reflected, tucking her glasses into her little handbag. "A sorry means *everything* if you're willing to put pride aside." Her brown eyes examined me and then she hummed. "My husband never saw the wrong in what he did. Have you admitted to yourself that you were wrong?" I nodded, remembering all the nights I'd spent beating myself up for how I'd treated the girl I loved. Her next question took me off guard. "Are you ready for anybody else to know?"

I froze.

And she grinned.

For as long as I could remember, I prided myself on doing the right thing. My mom always quipped that it was because my dad was such a moral man, always followed the rules, became a cop. I didn't fret about the whispers when people had found out that my captaincy was *almost* bought. Because I knew it was the right thing to do to get rid of Nate. But now, it meant that I'd hated Nyx for nothing, my team had hated her for nothing, we'd put her through hell for *nothing*. They always followed the lead of their captain.

I was their captain. And I'd hated Nyx.

Yes, I'd thought she'd turned her back on my team who meant the world to me, but most importantly, I'd thought she'd also turned her back on me. And that hurt more than anything else. I'd been jealous. It was time to admit it. I'd been *jealous.* And I'd let that impede everything.

Beckham Hunt had been reduced to a mindless fool by envy.

Was my judgement even dependable? How could it be dependable if I let emotions get in the way? The question jabbing holes in my chest was whether my team would trust me to make healthy decisions from this point forward.

"Exactly," Ms Lewis articulated again after I was hushed for a while, obviously thinking things through. "Your apology won't mean anything if you're not truly sorry and ready to face the consequences. I hate bringing him up because he was a fucking asshole, but, once again, my husband didn't see the wrong in what he did but even if he had—he never would've let anyone else know he'd made a mistake." She scoffed. "An honourable man, supposedly. Honourable my ass."

I weighed her words. "If he was truly sorry. *Truly.* Would you have forgiven him for his mistake?"

Her lips quirked. "It's only a mistake if you don't learn from it." I glanced away, chest feeling heavy. "He used to wear that same look around the house, the little scowl you're wearing. It's why I approached you." I was about to interpose and argue that, unlike her husband, I was sorry, but she recommenced speaking. "He may not have thought much of me, but he wore that guilty look for our daughters. Can you imagine their little hearts being broken by their dad before a lover?"

An image of Nyx and her sisters infiltrated my mind. I saw Nyx and Annie crying at the sight of Indigo twirling on stage. I saw Poppy screaming her head off as she cheered for her baby sister.

And then I nodded. "Yes. I can."

Ms Lewis had a faraway look in her eyes. "Although he felt guilty, he couldn't admit to everyone that he was wrong. He took that guilt to the grave, never apologised. I pray that it's eating at his decaying body." Her lower lip shivered and she appeared to want to say more, but stopped herself short, settling for something else. "Men like that give women representations of everything a relationship shouldn't be. But it gets normalised, makes them feel as if they should feel worthless and be in constant pain."

I thought of Nyx again. I'd already proven what a heartless asshole I could be. If I could take everything back, I would. She hadn't deserved to be treated the way she'd been, as if she wasn't worth staying. Her dad had already done enough damage. I didn't need to add more scars to her collection.

"She means a lot to me. My girl, that is."

"Then fix it," she acknowledged with a compassionate smile. "How long have you been together?"

My face went pinched at the inquiry and Ms Lewis gave me a sideways glance. "We're not exactly together," I cut myself off, shaking my head, "well, we're together *now*."

If she'd have me.

"Does this lover of yours have a name?" Ms Lewis

demanded, checking the time on her wristwatch.

I couldn't stop my smile. "Nyx. Her name's Nyx." Even saying her name brought on a surge of delight that I'd been denying myself for so long.

She nodded, grinning. "Make things right. And Project Burger is the perfect starting point. Their burgers are magic." I squeezed her hand. "And thanks for the talk. I needed it just as much as you did." A worker called out an order number and Ms Lewis stood straighter. "That's me." She pet my arm. "Good luck."

Before she could step away, I held out a hand. "Beckham Hunt." She gripped my hand and shook it as she smiled. "Thank you."

She laughed again. "My pleasure, son." She whirled on her heel, but paused. Then she smiled and nodded. "Annabelle Lewis."

I watched her saunter towards the counter for her meal. And then she was gone. It was only ten minutes later that my order was finished. Once I had my order, I made my way back to Nyx's place, Ms Lewis' words still working through my mind. I wondered if she was a guardian angel or something because she'd said exactly what I needed to hear when Grayson wasn't there.

When I parked outside of Nyx's place, she came scampering out of the house, her bag clutched in her hands. She darted towards the car like a bullet, hopping in before I could even turn it off. I frowned as she shut the door, clumsily climbing over the console to settle in my lap. Then her face was buried in my neck, her body sagging against me.

I'd been gone for only an hour. Confused, I wrapped my arms around her. "You okay?"

She shook her head. "My mom overdosed on cocaine last week. They only just found her body." She said it so casually that I was about to ask if she was joking.

She stayed silent for almost ten minutes before she explained her conversation with Georgia. But no matter how much she tried to drive the point home that she wasn't hurt, I knew she was. There was no sadness at the revelation of her mom's death, only hurt at the fact that she hadn't tried. She elaborated on the role Georgia played and what she understood now.

"She never cared enough to stay," Nyx muttered, playing with the lobe of my ear; a habit that I'd noticed Indigo had too. I glanced down at her, at the small frown on her lips. Another wordless conversation passed between us, and then Nyx was saying, "She never cared enough to come back." *But you did.* She didn't continue, yet the ghost of the words she wanted to utter was there.

"Do you and Annie need a place to stay?" I asked, realising now that Georgia was taking the girls, the eldest sisters had no reason to stay with their abusive dad anymore. That filled me with relief. Although I'd promised Nyx that I wouldn't involve my dad in her business until she was ready, it still scared me that her dad could hurt her whenever he felt like he could. My constant threats would only keep him at bay for so long.

She shrugged. "Probably. Georgia still has to tell Annie, though, and I have no idea how we're gonna tell Poppy and Indigo."

Almost hesitantly, I pressed a kiss to her head. My nerves made it feel as if every affectionate action would expose the fact that I loved her. "You can stay with us." In fact, having her close would make me feel a whole lot better.

Her eyes lifted, the blue standing out against the redness from crying. "Thank you." It was one sentence, but I could feel everything else she was trying to say.

I leaned down, my lips briefly brushing hers and she smiled. And that's how we stayed for the next few minutes, completely silent yet souls breathless after running a marathon we couldn't complete last year. Hurdles that we hadn't expected had popped up, hindering us from completing the race. But now we did. We crossed the finish line we were too scared to. It was an unvoiced achievement between us, communicated by a gentle kiss.

Her hand in mine was my medal, showcasing that it all had been worth it. My hand on her jaw was a promise. She was mine as much as I was hers.

"I can confidently state that Indigo is the most talented Taylor sister," Oliver proclaimed, sauce dribbling from his mouth like blood. He was lounging on the carpet, a plate with his burger and fries atop his crossed legs. Unannounced, he and Jasper had arrived at my house a few minutes ago, claiming to have been passing by. I knew that was bullshit.

They wanted food.

Grayson was willing to share his meal with him whereas

Jasper shared with Nyx. Nailea arrived shortly after with pizza and plopped herself on the carpet by Oliver. Jai had a date, and I was sure he'd tell us all about it in the morning. He did, nevertheless, leave a dollhouse for Indigo to congratulate her on her solo.

Indigo giggled, dipping her fry into ketchup as everyone agreed with Oliver, including her sisters. Poppy was next to her with Julie on her other side. The three girls had a couch all to themselves with a big, fluffy blanket. Grayson and Sebastian were squashed on a couch with Jasper, Annie and Beth at their feet, the latter having shown up after her shift.

Jasper gulped down a bite of his burger. "Nyx sent me a video of your performance and all I could think about is *why* you aren't a professional ballerina yet." He was speaking directly to Indigo, who blushed profusely at the compliments she was getting.

"My thoughts exactly," Grayson added, winking at Indigo.

"You did great," Beth said after taking a sip from the milkshake she shared with Annie.

Indigo gave an adorable grin, watching how comfortably Annie sat in her arms. "Thanks, Macbeth."

I felt Nyx quiver against me, highlighting that she thought along the same lines as me. Indigo was thanking Beth for more than the compliment. She was thanking her for putting that smile back on Annie's face.

The rest of the meal was eaten alongside loud laughs and pathetic jokes made by Jasper. Nyx was laughing at everything, a carefree smile on her face despite the looming arrival of Georgia to speak to Annie. For this one night, Nyx told me that she would keep a secret from her older sister because she didn't want to ruin what was a joyous occasion.

Once we were done, Sebastian set up the TV as we all watched in expectation. Nailea aggravated him by calling him an idiot when he couldn't switch the tv on. It took Nyx threatening to throw them both out to get them to shut up. Nailea muttered a curse in Spanish that had Sebastian's eyes bulging.

Annie stood up and walked towards the TV. Her brown eyes found Indigo's, matching. She clasped her hands together when they began shaking. "As you all know, this is a big occasion. It was Indigo's *first solo.*"

"The first of many!" Oliver cheered and Sebastian whistled, suddenly no longer angry. The latter had come a long way for somebody who'd claimed to despise kids. He seemed to cherish Indigo and got along well with her.

I knew, however, that it was still tense between him and a certain blonde minx. For his sake, I hoped he apologised soon. I didn't like the idea of one of my best friends and my girlfriend being at each other's throats.

Because I was going to make Nyx my girlfriend this time around.

"And Nyx and I decided we'd finally answer a question she'd been dying to know the answer to," Annie continued, a timid smile on her face. The guys shared bewildered looks.

Indigo, on the other hand, was far from disconcerted. She nearly fell from the couch with enthusiasm and shrieked. "Finally! It's only been *two years* since I first asked you!"

I turned to Nyx, whose head rested on my shoulder, and

quirked a brow. "She wants to know why she's named Indigo."

When Annie summoned her forward, Nyx dug into her bag and passed her a little hard drive. Grayson rammed it into the TV and passed the remote to Nyx. The anticipation grew, and even *I* was apprehensive about what was going to happen.

"This video was taken on the day you were born," Annie said, making her way back to Beth. Indigo's grin grew at the new information, obviously excited. Nyx clicked a few buttons. The screen went black. And then we were gazing at a blank wall.

"*The day has finally arrived*," an unknown voice expressed, one that had us all going silent. *"Eliza's vagina finally decided to spit out the last of the Taylor girls."* Nyx snorted loudly at that and Annie blushed, glancing at the three young girls but they were more focused on the screen. *"First up, we have our favourite Anna Banana who's becoming a big sister for the third time. Tell us how you're feeling, Annaconda."*

Everyone, besides Nyx and Annie, let out sounds of surprise as the camera stirred to meet a very youthful Annie, around the age of eighteen. Her brown hair was even shorter and her eyes weren't as dim as they were now. She was leaping with nerves, face red and eyes wide.

"I'm nervous. Mom's been in there for quite some time," she countered in a tremulous voice, but she was beaming. *"I'm hoping this one looks like me. Too many blondies in the house."*

"I have a feeling you'll get your wish, Anna Montana," the woman replied. The screen blurred for a second before switching on again. *"It's four hours later and Eliza is pushing harder than that time I was constipated."* I snickered at that and Nyx grinned.

"I now call to the stand Nic Nac the Tic Tac."

Nailea practically screamed when a tiny Nyx arrived on the screen, long blonde hair and bright blue eyes. If you didn't look close enough, you'd think you were staring at Poppy.

"It stinks here," tiny Nyx spoke to the camera, looking like she was in the mood to cause havoc. *"And I saw a doctor pull a nurse into the closet. The doctor was wearing a ring,"* she drifted closer to the camera, eyes wide, *"but the nurse wasn't—"*

"Enough of that, Nicky Mouse," the camerawoman cut her off, sounding frightened. *"Let's go check on your mom."*

"Who's the camerawoman?" Jasper asked the question we were all thinking, throwing an arm around Nailea who snuggled into his hold. Sebastian glared at them both and I held back a smirk.

Annie grinned. "Our aunt. She studied film, and because of that, was always taping everything. We were the main actors in every one of her homemade movies."

I could tell everyone had more questions, like why there was no mention of their dad yet. Grayson knew snippets, probably having heard from Annie, and Nailea knew more than she let on. The frown on Beth's face told me that Annie had already told her everything.

The screen went black again. When it turned back on, we were looking at Nyx, who kept a six-year-old Poppy on her lap. Julie squealed at the sight of her best friend and Poppy laughed, poking the dark-skinned girl in the arm before grinning.

"Here we have our Popstar, the main Popsicle, the one and only Pop-tart. She's minutes away from becoming a big sister. She—" There was a piercing scream and then the screen went black

once more.

This time, when the image cleared, we were gazing at a blonde woman in a hospital bed. Doctors moved around her but she was smiling through the pain. Her face was crimsoned and moistened with perspiration, perks of going into labour. In her arms, she held a tiny bundle in a pink blanket. The woman was sobbing, but that wasn't what I was focused on.

Indigo stole the words right out of my mouth when she pointed at Nyx, although her eyes were trained on the screen. "She looks just like you." Nyx's smile dropped when Indigo's eyes watered. Her next question had my heart stuttering. "Is that mommy?"

The room was even more soundless than before. It felt like nobody was breathing. Indigo couldn't even remember what her mom looked like because she'd been abandoned before she could even grasp a proper memory. At nearly six years old, she was essentially seeing her mom for the first time. There were no pictures of Eliza around their home, I'd checked. I didn't know whether that was a mutual decision the adults had made or if it had something to do with their dad.

Annie swallowed roughly before saying. "Yeah." She cleared her throat, gazing at her mom. "Beautiful, isn't she?"

Indigo nodded, finally ripping her eyes away from the screen to stare at Nyx. "She looks just like you." Her words were a murmur, dripping with reverence.

It was as if she couldn't believe her eyes, couldn't believe that she'd spent so long trying to picture her mom when she had the real thing in front of her. Despite the constant teasing arguments and faux rivalry with the youngest Taylor, I wanted to squeeze her against me. She would never know her mother.

"I know, sweetheart," Nyx said with a petite smile. "Trust me, I *know*." Indigo wiped away tears. "But look, it's *you*." She pointed at the screaming bundle of pink. "You nearly turned us all deaf." Annie laughed, agreeing. Little Poppy was the first to climb onto the bed to see her new baby sister. Annie sat at the foot of the bed and Nyx huddled into her mom's side. The Taylor girls, all in one picture.

"Wait!" the camerawoman bellowed, being hushed by Eliza. *"I need to be in this too."*

"Let me," a familiar voice spoke up and I frowned, unable to place where I knew it from. The camera was then transferred, and soon, the original camerawoman was entering the frame. She wore a bright red tracksuit and a patterned scarf around her neck. Her head was bare of any hair, but she had on a cute headband with a big red bow.

"Scoot over, LolliPop. Make space for your favourite aunt," she stated, binding her arms around the small blonde.

Little Nyx snorted. *"You're our only aunt."*

Indigo tipped her head in bewilderment, glimpsing at her sisters as the film played on. "I don't remember her." If she didn't remember her own mom, it wasn't a surprise she couldn't remember her aunt.

Nyx was smiling, but her eyes were rimmed with tears. "That's mom's younger sister. She had cancer. Died the day after you were born." A loud laugh got our attention and we watched the hairless woman coo at the new baby. "Her name was Indigo."

Tears were streaming down Annie's face as she watched

the bright woman laugh in wonder at the infant, and I knew Nyx was stifling it. Even Poppy looked on the brink of sobbing. Because they were old enough to remember her.

The first Indigo.

I wanted to comfort Nyx, but the older Indigo implored, *"COME on momma bear. Don't be such a bore. You never wanna be in my films."* There was some muffled arguing. And then the camera was being laid on a table. *"Yes!"* Some doctors laughed as they scampered around the room, but I was frozen, watching as Ms Lewis made her way to Eliza's side.

"Who's that?" Indigo urged, pouting at the unfamiliar woman.

Poppy was the one who spoke up, but I already knew the answer. "Grandma."

Chapter 27

Nyx

"Fucking *ow*," I buzzed when my elbow banged into the tinted window and my frown intensified when Beckham laughed. "You asshole."

Just as I went to protest again, his mouth capped mine as he dragged me closer. I slanted into his embrace, coiling my arms around his neck, making sure to not thump my elbow into the window again. It ached like a bitch and I didn't want to go through it again.

Beckham groaned, hands clutching my hips and moving me against him. I dragged myself over his lap, revelling in the loud moan that left his lips. Kissing was always satisfying for me. I'd kissed many people in the past.

But kissing Beckham was completely different, solely because of the way his kisses made me feel.

Detaching his mouth from mine, he moved his lips down my neck and I tilted back as he suckled on the exposed skin above my bra. And then my back knocked into the car horn.

The ear-splitting honk carried through the campus parking lot, causing me to shriek in surprise. Beckham was laughing again.

Cussing him out, I fixed my sweater and opened the door, nearly falling off his lap. I snubbed him as I climbed out of the car, staggering on my feet and trying to steady myself. Beckham had a way of making me woozy.

"Where are you going?" he urged, still laughing and shutting the door behind him, locking the car.

When he'd texted to meet at his car during lunch, I'd gotten excited because I had some tension I desperately needed to release. However, that was far from Beckham's mind. He wanted to talk about how I was doing since finding out about my mom's death.

The truth was, I wasn't doing too great. Annie had taken our mom's passing better than I expected and I had a feeling it was because she had somebody to ground her, keep her afloat—somebody that wasn't related to her. It was the same way I felt about Beckham.

Poppy and Indigo were freshly placed in Georgia's care, something that excited them because it was like a long sleepover. They understood it was for their benefit and adapted quicker than what was normal. I assumed it was because they hated our dad and we promised to visit them every day. They also didn't seem to care that their mom was dead, something I couldn't fault them for. Georgia said she'd let us know about the funeral.

Annie and I still hadn't moved out yet, in the process of boxing our belongings because everyone had been busy lately. Luckily, my dad hadn't come home whilst we got our shit sorted. But then he had arrived last night. I didn't want to talk about it and Beckham knew that which was why he'd let me climb into his lap so we could make out. It irked me that he was so fucking understanding. As much as I was annoyed, I needed his comfort, the sanctuary that he provided.

My dad had arrived, freshly divorced and widowed by two different women. And then his two daughters were missing as well. I'd forgotten what he looked like when he got that mad. It was like being in the presence of a demon, sucking all life from the room. His words had been pure malignity and his fingers coated with destruction as he lunged for me, yanking my hair and flinging me into the wall.

Whore, he'd called me. The same word had been uttered repeatedly as Annie tried to calm him down. *Just like your whore of a mother.* He rarely discussed her so him talking about her had taken me by shock. I couldn't even explain how much he despised my mom. It surprised me that he wasn't revelling in her death, considering how much he hated her—but it only fuelled his anger. Now that she was gone, he had the next best thing to hate. I would never escape that hatred, regardless of putting my dad in my past the moment Annie and I left.

"I need a moment," I responded to Beckham, choosing to take a stroll around the football field because the memory of last night shrouded itself around my lungs and now I couldn't breathe. Beckham wasn't stupid. He knew something was up, knew it from the moment I'd placed my lips against his instead of talking. "You can head back to class."

He accompanied me, tucking his keys into the pocket of his jacket. "Nyx, what's wrong?" He sounded concerned, *surpassing* concerned.

I continued walking, feeling that froth of anxiety swelling inside my chest. It was a frequent feeling, one I'd dealt with for many years of my life. I stopped at the furthest edge of the field, the most faraway point from the main building. All this open space enabled me to breathe. I was away from all the people, giving me the range to reflect, to make sense of my fucked up life. Beckham still stood idling expectantly and I shifted to face him.

"He mentioned you."

Beckham's eyes narrowed. "Who?"

I stifled a shudder. "My dad."

I watched Beckham's eyes shadow with confusion, the same look that I'd been donning since last night. Running a hand through my hair, I sighed. The *entire* argument had been about Beckham, but not in the way that I foresaw. I'd anticipated him to call me out for being with the son of a cop, or maybe even to bitch about Beckham threatening him.. Yet, it wasn't Beckham that was his problem.

It was *me.*

I'd be damned if I let you ruin that man the way your mom did me, he'd seethed at me, slobber covering my face.

You're already damned, had been my rejoinder, one that had him clasping my hair tighter to the point where it felt like my scalp was about to split. Like a professor giving a lecture, he'd spent so long driving home his point; that he wouldn't let me wreck Beckham. The insane motherfucker I called a dad was certain he saw himself in Beckham, was certain we'd end up exactly as they did. The only comparison was that they were both an only child.

But it *stopped* there.

My dad had revealed that I was doing exactly what my mom had done to him, enticing and *corrupting*. He'd maintained it was why he resented her; because she ruined his life, and left him with unruly kids. He'd only married her because she'd been desperate for her kids to have their father. He'd thought the kids would make her less clingy in their marriage than what she'd been when they were younger. But his hatred for her had still outweighed his duty as a father.

Whore, he'd repeated over and over again. Even when he tried to move on, the memory of my whore of a mom plagued him and ruined his marriage. He blamed her for everything. Even in death, she tormented him. When I relayed this story to Beckham, his body tensed in rage.

"Bullshit," he snapped, stepping closer to me with an aggravated expression. "Absolute *bullshit*."

I nodded. "I know, I mean, I definitely believe nothing he said about the two of you. It was just very random."

It alarmed me because I questioned if my dad was right about the part where I was like my mother. We were comparable in looks, and from what I remembered, personality as well. Before my dad had broken her completely, she'd stood up for us and taken the beatings so we wouldn't. She'd shielded us and enraged him so that he would forget he was angry at *us*. She'd been doing what I'd done for the past few years, putting the girls first.

And then she'd left.

Annie and I would come up with scenarios like pirates

abducted her and she was spending every second battling her way back to us. At least, that was what we'd come up with when we were around Poppy.

When it was just me, I questioned if she'd found a man better than my dad, one that wouldn't harm her, assured protection. I wept because if that was the truth, that man meant more to her than her daughters. She was willing to leave us with a monster so she could run off. She'd left us under the rouse to get better, but what if she actually just wanted to get away? What if she had somebody else waiting for her? Somebody that was more important than her kids?

Her decision was selfish, and I knew selfish all too well.

That was the part that alarmed me. Because I'd already chosen Beckham once before. And my sisters had suffered.

"You say you don't believe him," Beckham hummed, "but your face says otherwise." When I looked up, his eyes were glazed with confusion and hurt. "Do you think I'm going to hurt you?"

My eyes widened and I quickly shook my head, apprehending how it looked. "No, Beck. *No*, I don't think that." Seeing that he was still unsettled, I took his hand in mine. It was rough and warm and so much larger than mine. I laced my fingers through his. My heart was beating so fast because I knew what was looming. The talk. To explain to him why I thought I was like my mom, he needed to know what happened fully. "I think he's right about one thing, that I'm like my mom. *Selfish*."

I remembered nights spent huddled in the bathroom, Poppy in my lap and Annie's arms encompassing me as we heard glass being flung around, heard yelling. My mom had fought back and Annie and I wished that she'd leave him. We couldn't wait for the day she gathered our bags and left our dad in the dust. But then she'd left. Without us. And we'd stayed clutching each other in the bathroom, only Poppy had been in Annie's arms and I'd held a baby.

He scoffed, looking pestered through his furrowed brows and pursed lips. "That's the most *absurd* thing I've ever heard. Anyone with eyes can see how much you love your sisters, what you're willing to do for them—"

"You know that I sabotaged Nate," I cut him off, words trembling and shoulders tensing. "I sabotaged every event I threw for him, from stale food blamed on greedy vendors to upset kids of rich parents. I even altered the reports that he sent to Coach Ford."

The grass beneath my feet felt too soft, the air felt too intense, and the sky too polished. Everything was too much, yet too little at the same time. I stepped back, reaching for a leaf on the tree I was standing in front of, enabling Beckham to process the words I just released like a pack of famished wolves I'd kept locked up for almost a year.

The wolves were after one thing, the stupid misunderstanding between us. My words wanted to gorge it. All this time, I'd had the capability to sever the supposed rivalry between us.

Beckham shook his head. "I knew that already—"

I shredded the leaf into tiny little pieces, watching each tear. "Nate was dating Annie and they were head-over-heels in love with each other. I intended to *help* him, not help him win." I swallowed harshly when Beckham stayed soundless. I ripped another leaf. "His dad's a pompous man. If Nate lost the captaincy, he wouldn't allow his son to roam the hallways of the place he lost at. His dad was so disappointed that he no longer wanted anything to do with him—which meant Nate could live without his dad trying to control him."

Beckham was visibly shaking with everything he was feeling. He knew that I'd sabotaged Nate, just not the weight of everything that had happened.

"Nyx, that doesn't make you a bad person. It makes you a good person, actually, wanting to help him when he had nobody else—even at the expense of yourself. What I don't understand is why you never sought to explain—"

"Because I was scared!" I yelled back, voice quivering.

His expression turned into one of anguish. "*Why* would you ever have to be scared of me—"

I shoved his chest, although he didn't even stumble. The remnants of the leaf slipped from my hands. "Because love is fucking terrifying!" I exclaimed, making him freeze. "People write all those pretty poems but seem to conveniently leave out the fact that love is absolutely gut-wrenching. I'm *afraid* of what I'd do for you, Beckham," I said, breathing heavily.

His eyes were so soft that I wanted to cry. "Nyx," he muttered my name, not finding the words. So I continued speaking.

"I was selfish. Helping Nate only became part of my plan *weeks* later when I felt like a guilty bitch for sabotaging him even though I *knew* he loved Annie," I explained, nearly choking on my words as I recalled the heartbreak etched into every inch of Annie as Nate left her, left behind what they'd had. "Helping him get away from his dad wasn't the reason I *started* sabotaging him, Beck."

His turbulent eyes halted on me and I could see the contradictory emotions battling for dominance. His throat bobbed when he swallowed restlessly and I zoned in on the action because I wasn't tough enough to hold his gaze for that long, not when his emotions were so stripped.

In a second, his hands were cupping my face. His features were hopeful, yet terrified. "I just want you to know that as you speak right now, you hold my heart in your hands, Nyx. Before you even continue, I want you to know that."

I planted my hands over his, breathing slowly. "There were only three men I ever cared about. I can't remember *anything* about Uncle Robbie but I know he loved me. Then there was my dad. He looked at me as if I was nothing." I forced a laugh. "And then there was you." He closed his eyes, leaning down to lay his forehead against mine. My name left his lips in a guttural tone. "I guess I was just desperate for you to look at me as if I was something—"

"You are something," he vocalised, eyes still shut. "You've *always* been something to me, baby." I trembled, letting my eyes fall shut as well. "My desire for you knows no end. I was desperate to talk to you, be around you. I was desperate to make you mine before anybody else realised that beneath that hard exterior, beneath the bitchy comments and *kill-all-men* attitude, beneath the scowls—there was *you*, bare of any armour."

Tears were dripping from my closed eyes, falling into his

hands. I felt more than saw his eyes open. His words penetrated my skin, allowing the negativity from my dad to flow out. His words embedded deep into my soul, substituting everything my dad used to torture me, to make me feel insignificant.

"I wanted you," I confessed quietly. "I wanted everything that you represented. Being with you gave me a sense of peace like no other. I had *nothing* to offer you in return, I didn't even know if I could love somebody other than my family, not after what I'd been through." He tried to intervene but I had more to say. "Still, I wanted to give you something. I agreed to help Nate after I overheard some of the older hockey players talking. Although you all were desperate, they wouldn't respect you as a captain if your dad bought the captaincy because you didn't fight to get them out of Nate's clutches."

I remembered my rage after I'd caught their conference. Although they were older, they weren't the ones who had worked their asses off to figure out a plan. It was the younger ones; Beckham, Sebastian and Grayson. The payment had been their last resort.

Beckham's grip around me tightened like he was waiting for me to evaporate and for him to discover that he'd been standing alone all this time. "So you had me believe you turned your back on me." I nodded, matching his gaze. "And I fought—"

"For the captaincy—"

"For *you*," he ended his sentence as he brushed away the last of my tears. "I was jealous of Nate because I thought he had *you*. We were never official and it just seemed so easy for him to take you from me. Why didn't you come clean afterwards?

Why'd you let me hate you?"

And here came the part that I loathed, the thoughts that kept me up at night. "I didn't deserve you, not when I ruined Annie's relationship. Annie knew what I was doing for you and she didn't try to stop me. Nate never liked hockey, so in her eyes, I truly was helping him. But when he lost, his dad moulded all of his anger into something else. And he broke Annie's heart, believed his dad when he said Annie was only with him for money." It was as if the words were scratching my throat because they felt biting. "His dad's a lawyer and I ended up getting sued for defamation."

"Asshole," Beckham grunted, arms going around me and drawing my body against his chest.

I sniffled. "We were already struggling, Beck. And I made things worse. The next few months were the *worst*. Indigo was frail from lack of food, even got sick." Beckham was practically reeling with outrage. I looked him in the eye. "But I couldn't regret what I'd done. Because you had the captaincy, your team respected you—"

"And you needed me to hate you," he echoed the words I'd once told him at the cafe. "Because you couldn't."

I shook my head, shaking. "I was *selfish*. My dad's right, I'm just like her." The resemblance was fucking uncanny. "I didn't know how greedy my heart was until I placed you above everything else." And I'd carried that, using it as a reason to keep him at bay.

Beckham's voice was rough when he spoke again. "I'm not worth all of that pain, baby. And I proved it to you this past year." His broken voice conveyed how truly repentant he was. "But you didn't intend to hurt your family. You intended to help two assholes who didn't deserve an inch of your love. You can't spend the rest of your life atoning for sins you didn't commit, Nyx, can't punish yourself." I buried my face into his jacket, trying not to sob. "The fault lay at the feet of Nate's dad. The beatings you suffered through bore the mark of your dad's hands." I heard what he didn't want to say out loud. *It wasn't Nate's fault either.* "You're nothing like your mom because she *left* you girls. You stayed." He gulped. "And you turned me into an enemy to put your sisters' happiness above your own."

I glanced up at him, eyes meeting his. There were so many things I could've said, things that I've only ever read or watched movies about. In the end, it came out as a simple sentence.

"I love you."

Beckham smiled. "I've always loved you, Nyx. I spent my time alternating between hating the fact that I loved you or loving how much I loved you."

My cheeks warmed. "That's a lot of love."

"Yet infinitely less than what you deserve," he continued, brushing hair from my face. "And I'll spend the rest of my life filling in gaps that weren't meant to be there in the first place."

The material of his jacket bunched in my hold, letting his words soak in. Beckham wasn't Matthew Taylor, and I wasn't Eliza Taylor. We were the furthest thing from them.

"Am I foolish for still wanting what my parents never had?"

I felt him shrug. "Am I foolish for hoping the girl I put through hell will still have me?" He pressed a kiss to the top of my head as I shook my head. His hatred had been a punishment I'd thought I deserved after what I'd let happen to my family.

But that family was happy now, on their way to healing.

"You've always been a fool, anyway," I mumbled into his chest. "I'm sorry that I kept trying to put distance between us recently, made light of what we felt. It wasn't fair on your behalf, making it seem like there was only a need for sex with us. I know now that it was because I was scared," I admitted.

"Nyx," he started, swaying slightly with me in his arms. "I'm telling you beforehand, I'm never going to leave. I don't care how long it takes but I'll earn your forgiveness bit by fucking bit." I suppressed a smile at his promise. "Now that I understand that you pull away because you're scared, I'm going to do whatever it takes to snuff that fear. There'll never be a decision between *me* or *your sisters*, their happiness or *yours*. It's one and the same." And the fucker just put into words that deep fear of mine. "I'll keep them happy to keep you happy, and vice versa. And I don't care how many reasons you throw at me to leave, I only need *one* fucking reason to stay." He placed a finger under my chin and tipped my head back.

"Sex?" I attempted a joke.

He grinned that boyish grin he kept reserved for his teammates. "Sure. If you replace the *S* and *E* with an *N* and *Y*." I tried so hard to keep my smile from appearing. It persisted, securing its grip around the edges of my mouth and towing upwards. Soon, with aching cheeks, I was smiling. "There's my girl."

And then he leaned down, pressing his mouth to mine. I sighed, reaching to tangle my fingers in his messy hair as his hands went to the back of my thighs to hoist me up. My legs swathed around him and he shoved me back against the tree, tongue slipping into my mouth. For the first time in forever, I allowed myself to kiss Beckham with no apprehension. In two minutes, he asphyxiated my deepest fear, *that I'd have to choose.*

There was no need to choose when Beckham was permanent.

"Can't believe you thought you lost," I mused as his lips met my cheek.

He pulled away, his gaze soft. No words passed between us for a few seconds. "I'm winning now." Before I could pull his lips back to me, a splatter landed just a few spaces away from where I was clutching his hair. "Did a bird just shit on my head?" I burst into laughter because there was no denying what just happened. A delicate dropping of white and green was splat in the middle of his head, soaking into his hair. "Just fucking great."

"*Hey*," I smacked his shoulder. "Bird poop is a good omen." He rolled his eyes, pestered that there was another being's shit on his head. When he tried to put me down, I bandaged my legs tighter around him, clinging to him like a koala.

"You're only saying that because you're not the one with shit on your head," he groaned, though he smiled when I scoffed. He tried to shake his head, but the poop was already drying. I snorted at his futile attempt to get rid of it.

"Symbolically, it's believed that when a bird shits on you, it means you have to pause and reflect," I told him, beaming at his exasperation. "You have to be honest with yourself and an important part of this is the cleaning stage—"

It was his turn to scoff. "When I have to clean the shit from my head—"

"When you're cleansing yourself and your soul," I finished, smirking triumphantly when he shut up. "But good luck will only come your way if you're open to receiving the greatness that the universe has to offer," I repeated the words that I memorised from the time I'd joined the philosophy students' meeting. As much as people liked to tyrannise them for being so philosophical, they made sense. And maybe, just maybe, I'd start regularly attending their meetings. "If you believe that good fortune is coming your way, it will. Your thoughts attract similar thoughts," I paused, blushing, "and people tend to attract people who are similar to them."

Beckham, despite having shit on his head, smiled. "I'm familiar with the law of attraction, baby." He kissed me again. "I'm very familiar with it."

Chapter 28

Beckham

Kids. *Everywhere.* Some were having their lunch break and gawked at me as I passed through the hallways, paper gripped in my hand with the number of the class that I was searching for. The school had potential. It was in a pretty area but the buildings looked aged as if they weren't taken care of. I'd been here before to coach some young boys alongside some of my teammates. Just last weekend, we concluded our third fundraiser, the coaching session. No money had been raised, but we figured that those kids deserved a chance at a sport they loved. Their school didn't offer hockey, so we volunteered to coach them.

As I turned another corner, I saw a giant banner with my team on it. I was in the middle, helmet in hand. On either side of me were Sebastian and Grayson, followed by Oliver, Jasper and Jai. Underneath it was; *support our boys in the fight for the Crosstown Cup!*

I grinned at the sight of it. When I got to the classroom I was looking for, I found it empty with a sign that said the kids were on a lunch break. Confused, I tried to make my way to the cafeteria, recognising the layout of the building. After five minutes of wandering around like an idiot, I found the big blue doors that spanned into the cafeteria. More kids were gawking at me now, probably recognising me from the banner. I found Poppy sitting in one corner, her right foot propped up on a chair, and Julie sitting next to her. The cafeteria went hushed as I entered but my focus was on Poppy.

She looked up when she saw me, beaming. "They sent *you*? I thought your match was taking place."

Julie waved at me and I flicked her head affectionately before responding to Poppy, "Ended an hour ago. Annie's got a shift, Nyx has class and Georgia's at work. So, here I am. Disappointed?" Poppy giggled, shaking her head. I glanced at her bandaged foot. "So what exactly happened?"

"She tripped when we were lining up for class," Julie informed me, her words a murmur as she gesticulated for me to drift closer. "Or better yet, *someone* tripped her."

Poppy gasped at her best friend's words, looking apprehensive and peeping around at the attention we were receiving.

One glower from me had everyone minding their own business, and I scowled when demanding, "Who?" The two girls stayed soundless and I turned to the blonde. "*Who* tripped you, Poppy?"

I'd already heard from both her and her sisters that she'd once had physiotherapy for a sprained right foot, and currently, that same foot was swathed. When Nyx had gotten the call from the principal to pick her sister up, he'd apprised her that

Poppy had tripped, and looking at the blonde now, she didn't tell the principal what actually happened.

Poppy pouted, melancholy eyes glistening. "If I tell you, you're gonna cause a scene, Beck."

I was damn right going to cause a fucking scene. She'd just finished physiotherapy and some *intellectual* decided to fucking trip her. Poppy's injuries could've been much more critical this time around.

I crossed my arms. "You decide. You can tell me who did it or I can tell Nyx that somebody tripped you." Her mouth dropped open at my threat, spluttering. "Three seconds. *Choose*." She glanced at Julie, who nodded rapidly, muttering to her that I was the better choice between me and Nyx, along with the allusion to a prior situation with somebody named Marcus. "One—"

"Poppy Watson," she whined to me, checking if anyone overheard her.

"There's another Poppy?" I sought.

Julie nodded, seeing as her friend was currently frantically examining the cafeteria. "Poppy Watson thinks she's the better Poppy." I rolled my eyes because middle school drama was weird as shit. "She isn't because she's the one who's vice-captain and *our Poppy's captain*—"

"She's on the team?" I interrupted, and they both nodded. *Fuck*. The little bitch must've had the motive to injure Poppy. "Do you by any chance have a match coming up?"

Poppy frowned, looking down at her lap. "Yes. And lots of high school coaches are going to be there. I was hoping I'd be one of their picks for a scholarship." Her voice broke. She didn't utter the rest of her thoughts, but I knew what she meant. The scholarship would've made things easier for her sisters.

And this other Poppy would be the centre of attention at the match, having to stand in for her absent captain. Kids could be fucking brutal.

After a few seconds of rigid silence, I spoke, "I'll discuss things with your sisters and Georgia." Poppy shook her head. "Because Poppy Watson won't get away with this. She *hurt* you."

She shrugged. "It's just a small sprain."

Her indifference scratched against my chest. The look Julie gave me flagged that this was a regular occurrence; Poppy backing down. I knew she was the bashful sister, the quiet one, but this was something else. This was years of conditioning by her dad. Swallowing the bullet of obscenities launching up my throat, I sank to my knees, planting my hands on Poppy's shoulders.

"Listen to me," I started gently, wanting her to take in every word. "*Nobody* has the right to hurt you. Do you understand me?" She wouldn't meet my gaze and I groaned, drawing her to my chest. Her arms stretched around my neck, and I stood up, bringing her with me.

Poppy adhered to me, her face in the collar of my jacket. I picked up her bag, hooking it over my shoulder. It was only then that I noticed their table was empty.

"Where's your lunch?" I urged, seeing everyone else eating.

Julie smiled tensely. "Poppy Watson threw it in the trash."

My rage mounted and Poppy stayed still. I muttered *bitch* underneath my breath and Julie let out a heartfelt laugh as she fist-bumped me. I fled the cafeteria, feeling everyone's stare. Travelling back to the main office, I found Poppy's teacher; Ms Hentley. I signed the forms needed to take Poppy.

Before I left, I stated, "In around ten minutes, there'll be a delivery for Julie Lowe from McDonald's. Make sure she gets it." Ms Hentley nodded. And then I left, locating my car in the parking lot.

When I put Poppy in the backseat, she strapped her seatbelt as I hopped in, starting the car. Frantic to change the topic, she queried, "How was the match?"

Meeting her stare in the rear view mirror, I smirked. "We won."

It was a close call between us and the Bruins, and Benson had practically been quaking with trepidation. Their team had gotten better in the past two weeks. I could tell Benson was regretting giving us a week off, because UCLA had unquestionably stayed training. But he also knew how important it was for us to rest, to take a step back.

We'd been one point ahead of the Bruins in the last few minutes. If it hadn't been for Grayson suspending their last shot, it would've been a draw.

Poppy scoffed. "Of course you won."

I grinned. "What's that supposed to mean?" She pulled a face and I chuckled. "Julie mentioned a Marcus. Wanna tell me what happened there?"

She crimsoned, concealing her face with her hands. "I hate confrontation." I'd noticed. "I think two months ago, this guy Marcus said Julie was really pretty. She was the new girl and I guess he liked her." She shrugged. "He said he'd consider hanging out with her if she dropped me because apparently, I'm ugly." I wanted to say something, but Poppy didn't stop talking. "Which is natural coming from somebody as good-looking as him, and I *knew* Julie thought he was cute. I didn't want her to choose—"

This girl was like her sister in more ways than just looks. She would've let her best friend leave her in the dust if it meant she was more content. Yes, they were still kids and crushes at this age didn't really mean anything, but it was a significant glimpse into the sacrifices Poppy would make when she was older.

"And how does Nyx fit into all of this?" I inquired, remembering Julie mentioning her.

"Julie told her," she grumbled and I laughed. Their friendship would last for ages if they kept putting each other first like that. "Annie's usually the one who picks me up and all the guys were crushing on her," she paused, rolling her eyes, "then they saw *Nyxie*."

I smirked. "Understandable."

"Marcus forgot all about Julie and decided that fantasising about my sister was better than actually hanging out with my best friend, somebody he had a chance with," Poppy revealed. A swift gleam of amusement arose on her features. "Nyxie confronted him in front of all of his friends about calling me ugly." Sounded like her. "She said, and I quote; Poppy has always looked exactly like me. Keep that in mind."

Deep chuckles left me as Poppy reddened again. "From what I've seen, your mom's genes are super strong," I told her, weighing how much Nyx looked like their mom. The latter had only looked older, more mature. But her features had showcased that she'd once looked exactly like Nyx. "And I've seen what Nyx looked like when she was your age," I appended.

"Like me," Poppy mused. There was no way she was ugly, the furthest thing from it. Her features at that moment were only a mere hint to what she'd grow into in the future.

I nodded. "Exactly. And I'm sure your mom looked the same at that age. So, basically—"

"I'm gonna look like Nyxie at that age," she concluded, appearing disturbed by the knowledge. If Poppy didn't like attention *now*, she was going to have to get used to it. Nyx garnered attention wherever she went, whether it was because of her words or her looks, it didn't matter.

Smiling to myself, I proceeded to drive as Poppy panicked morosely about the fate of her looks. Despite the stress of the day, she didn't look too unhappy. Nyx may have taken the news of their mom's death the best, but Poppy was a close second. Indigo didn't really care, too attached to her sisters and Georgia.

When I stopped at a red light, I promptly ordered Julie's food online. "You hungry?" I questioned Poppy.

But she wasn't listening to me. "Maybe I should dye my hair. Nyxie dyed her hair blue when she was my age."

"She what?" I urged through a laugh. Because *of course* she'd dyed her hair blue. I ordered another huge meal to be delivered to my place.

"My," she cleared her throat, "*parents* were so upset. But it turns out it was my grandma who bought the dye for her." Poppy shook her head with a smile. "At least, that's what Annie told me. I was only around five."

I nearly swerved us right off the road. Ever since meeting Ms Lewis at Project Burger, I hadn't known how to bring her up with Nyx. She'd never mentioned her before and I was doubtful of whether there was bad blood or not.

"Your grandma?" I pressed, wheeling another corner. "The one from the video the other night?"

"She was the best," Poppy beamed, "from what I remember. But I think she's dead now."

I tensed, because Annabelle Lewis was the furthest thing from dead. It appeared I was correct in thinking that she was estranged from her granddaughters. I didn't want to pry, but perhaps telling Nyx that I ran into her grandma was the best idea.

"I bet you miss her," I added, nodding my head as Nailea passed me in her own car, sending me an excited wave and I grinned.

Poppy was busy blowing kisses as Nailea disappeared before she turned back to my question. "A lot. Grandma would bring presents whenever my mom and dad were fighting. Sometimes she tried to help but my mom would yell at her."

Hearing Poppy speak about her parents felt weird. She was a child but had still lived through the same experiences as her sisters. It always seemed like their parents were a problem Annie and Nyx had to deal with, making them sometimes forget that Poppy was old enough to understand what went on.

"Your mom yelled when she tried to help?" I asked, suppressing a curse when we got caught in traffic.

She met my gaze in the mirror. "My mom did drugs,

Beck. If anyone tried to take it away from her, she lost it." Her lips tilted into a grimace as she paged through memories. "Grandma tried to take it away. If given the choice, I would've chosen Grandma over my mom."

Seeing that traffic wasn't moving at all, I turned slightly so that I could look at her. The girl's expression was a mixture of emotions. "I'm sorry for asking," I muttered, sensing that the topic unnerved her.

But then her frown deepened, eyes looking confused. "I should thank you for asking. Nyxie and Annie don't really talk about them to us. I know they're trying to protect us, but sometimes I have things to say, you know?"

The traffic began easing. "Things like what?" I offered her the chance she so clearly wanted; if her gaze was anything to go by.

"Like the fact that I'm glad my mom is dead, that we're away from my dad," she said without taking a second to ponder my question. "She was a bad person but she's gone now. But my dad's still here and we're still his kids."

Hearing the trembling in her voice, I said, "You're never going to go back to him." She gave me an appreciative smile, leaning to look out the window. "And I'm sure your sisters would love to hear your thoughts on what you think, trust me." She stayed smiling, muttering that she promised to speak to them.

We drove for another five minutes before I pulled up at my house. Poppy hopped onto my back so that I could carry her inside. She laughed when I pretended to flatten her on the couch. I was afraid the topic of her parents would upset her but she seemed almost lighter after expressing some of what she felt. I switched on the TV so she could be entertained whilst we waited for our food. Once it arrived, we didn't wait another second to dig in.

"I *love* their fries," Poppy told me, ramming her face full of it. "If I could eat one thing for the rest of my life, it would be fries. How about you?"

I nearly suffocated on my burger because the first thing that popped into my head was Nyx. And I nearly said it out loud. Clearing my throat to get rid of the lodged food, I answered, "Burgers."

Poppy nodded. "Good choice."

My face was definitely red and I swallowed some soda to calm down. The girl next to me didn't pick up on my flustered state, thankfully. She did, however, pick up on the designs on my right arm after I took off my jacket. I knew she'd noticed it before, but she never questioned it.

"Do any of your tattoos have meanings?"

If I had a dollar for every time a girl asked me that, I'd be dripping in wealth. The tattoos on my arm consisted of numerous drawings, some dates of special days. The drawings weren't anything personal, just things I found cool. When I told Poppy this, she sighed in displeasure. It was the general reaction I got when I revealed my tattoos held no significance.

"I love the crescent moon," she said absentmindedly, pointing to the little drawing on my right wrist. "When did you get it?"

"Last year, I think."

She pushed more fries into her mouth. "Did you know that

the crescent moon is the symbol of the primordial goddess of the night? Nyx was her name."

I turned my attention to the TV and responded, "No, I didn't know that." But judging by the smirk Poppy wore, she knew I was lying.

Tossing another fry into her mouth, she asked, "Do you love Nyxie?"

Unlike before when Indigo had brought up the topic of love, it didn't take me by surprise this time. In fact, it was like part of me was eagerly waiting for others to know.

My words left me smoothly. "With all that I am."

She glimpsed at me, nose crinkling as she phrased her next words. "Does that mean you love us by extension?"

The sound of the TV faded into background noise when I noticed how seriously she took her own inquiry. I thought of how to phrase my answer.

"Not by extension," I corrected, watching her pale brows furrow in confusion. "Individually."

The grin that she sent me was absolutely angelic. I felt blessed to be on the receiving end of a genuine smile from Poppy Taylor. Their dad didn't deserve something this beautiful, a love this pure.

Gently moving her leftovers to the coffee table, she launched herself into my hold, face finding the collar of my shirt as I wrapped my arms around her. Her eyes were closed, smile still on her lips. When tears began leaking from her eyes, she buried her face in my shirt to hide her emotions, and I took that as my cue to not question her. She stayed like that until she fell asleep, the day's activities finally catching up to her. In fear of waking her, I stayed like that for the next two hours, watching whatever was on the TV.

When Annie came home, Indigo was at her side, excited to be spending the rest of the day with her older sister before they returned to Georgia's place. The youngest Taylor dashed to the room Annie was staying in, ignoring my presence completely. Annie, on the other hand, stopped at the sight of the sleeping girl in my arms.

She sent me the same grin that her blonde baby sister had. At my confused look, she murmured, "Matthew Taylor doesn't give hugs."

Then she followed Indigo. It was a simple statement but it struck me deep. I glanced down at a softly snoring Poppy, comprehending that she'd never been hugged by a man that cared for her before. At the painful realisation, I pressed a kiss to her forehead.

I didn't love them by extension, that was the truth.

Each Taylor girl was unique in their own way, different personalities and quirks that pulled you in. They didn't deserve to be grouped together when it came to love. Their lack of it was enough of a reason to emphasise how much they deserved it individually.

And later, when a tired Indigo forced herself to my side, I held her in the same way my dad had held me when he put me to sleep as a child. The smile on her face as she fell asleep was a reward all on its own. If a smile from a Taylor girl could evoke such happiness within somebody—their love was a gift that few deserved.

Matthew and Eliza Taylor were idiots that didn't know

what treasures they had. They'd sought to bury them. Then along came an asshole with love he confused for hatred and a shovel in the form of persistence. He'd dug and dug, striving to find the blonde treasure he desired. He'd unearthed more than he anticipated, bringing treasures to light that could be cherished by him, his friends and family.

I'd never been more relieved to be that persistent asshole.

"A themed costume party?" Jai echoed, browsing through the page Nyx just delivered him. The entire first team was seated around our regular table at the cafeteria, being assembled by Nyx to discuss a few things. Four days after our match on Monday and everyone was still high on the win.

Oliver seized the paper, eyes skimming its content. "Sounds fun."

Jai glared at him, because before Nyx arrived, Oliver had agreed with his plan. To beg for a different fundraiser. "What happened to our plan?" he urged the redhead who passed the paper to Grayson.

"This sounds better," Oliver countered.

"I was thinking more of a car wash," Jai maintained, snubbing his teammate. Jasper snorted at his insistence, and Sebastian nodded along. Grayson, however, was the only one reading the paper properly, examining it even.

Nyx stopped her stroll around the table, her dress whisking against the very top of her thighs. It was a risky dress, a deep green that made her look like Tinkerbell. The little bun on her head added to the appearance. As it neared the end of winter, it was absolutely boiling outside. If I could crawl out of my skin, I would.

As promised to Poppy, I made sure that Nyx wouldn't go and confront Poppy Watson. Instead, the volleyball coach, class teacher and principal would handle the situation. She hadn't been a happy bunny when finding out somebody had hurt her sister. Though, I was happy to help her get rid of her stress.

"Why?" Nyx probed, levelling Jai with that icy gaze of hers. "If you want to see me all wet, just ask."

I scowled, but Jai reacted instantly. "Your pussy's overrated."

Just as fast she stated, "You're only saying that because you can't have it." Then, as if completely brushing off his existence, she proceeded with her meeting. "Tickets will go on sale tomorrow and the actual event will be held next week Friday, five days before your next match."

Grayson looked up from the paper. "It's Annie's birthday."

Nyx nodded, grinning as she stopped next to him. "So you're trying to kill two birds with one stone? A fundraiser and birthday party for Annie in one."

"The fundraiser is the perfect way to keep it a surprise. She can't know that this is anything other than a *fundraiser*," Nyx glared at all of us, daring us to tell Annie of her plans. "The money made from the tickets is going to the Angelica neighbourhood which, for those of you who don't know, suffered a major fire last week. Many families are left with close to nothing and whatever we make will help them try to get back into the swing of things. How does that sound?" Everyone nodded. "Good, we—"

She was stopped by the approach of Professor Coleman, who taught French, if I remembered correctly. He was a small and round man with a balding head, always dressed in glossy shoes and pressed suits.

His throat being cleared dragged our attention. "Good afternoon, boys," he acknowledged the team before laying his dull eyes on Nyx. "Miss Taylor."

I watched them eye each other and I groaned, already predicting an argument. The older man had a habit of pissing off the girls at our school.

"Professor Coleman," she granted him an obviously fraudulent smile. "If you don't mind, we're kinda in the middle of something. A meeting, actually."

Professor Coleman grinned just as plastically. "So I'm an *interruption*, how ironic. The reason I'm interrupting, Ms Taylor, is that I've received some grievances about your choice of outfit today."

Oliver passed Jasper some money and I scoffed at the thought of them betting on Nyx getting in trouble for her outfit. There was no dress code, not at fucking college. But Professor Coleman had been trying, for the past year, to implement one.

Nyx raised a brow. "And who exactly complained?" She didn't get a response. "Or is that just a euphemism for you can't keep it in your pants around a woman more than half your age?" She glimpsed down at her dress. "I'm nineteen years old, Professor. I find it highly inappropriate for you to be ogling me—"

"That's enough, Miss Taylor," he yelped, bridling at the attention being turned to him. "What I'm doing is my *job.*

The rule I'm trying to implement is for the benefit of our students. The amount of skin you're showing has proven to be a distraction to many of your fellow male students—"

I tipped my head, glowering at the man. "So, you're telling me that her clothes determine whether we get any learning done?" He returned my glare for interceding. "So I'm more entitled to education than her? Is that what you're implying, Professor?" Sebastian was smirking at the man's red face.

Grayson raised a hand, mocking the man's title as a professor. "And also, if you haven't noticed, it's scorching outside. Did you expect her to wear a tracksuit? If her dress makes you uncomfortable," Grayson chuckled, "with all due respect, Professor, I'm pretty sure you're the problem."

Nyx grinned before looking at a stuttering Professor Coleman. I didn't feel bad for him. He'd been a problem for some time now and many faculty members were hoping that his dress code idea would vanish over time.

Clearly not.

"I'm doing my *job*," he maintained, "either you follow the rules or leave."

Nyx crossed her arms obstinately. Jasper feigned a gasp. "Holy shit. She's got *skin*, can you believe it? It's too much for me." He fanned his face and Oliver snickered. "Nyx, I'm ready to leave my boyfriend because you, darling, have got skin capable of making a gay man straight."

I smirked, running a hand over my stubble. I'd give it three more minutes before Coleman was running away with his tail tucked between his legs. A regular occurrence when he tried telling the women of USC what to wear.

"Disrespecting a professor," Coleman mused. "Any more of this and you'll all be banned from the next few games." Jai nearly leapt out of his seat. "Miss Taylor," he ventured again, exasperated, but Nyx wasn't backing down. "I'm sure many of these people, myself included, could do without having to see the flesh of your ass each time you bend over—"

In a flash, I was out of my seat, seizing Coleman by the front of his preciously steamed shirt. I shoved him back, towering over him and stifling the urge to crush his face against the table. "And why exactly are you talking about my girlfriend's *ass*, Professor?"

"Beck," Nyx whispered in concern, placing a hand on my back. Even the guys were staring at me in dread. Taunting a professor was one thing, but physically threatening one could lead to expulsion. And for me, it could mean the stripping of my title as the captain of the hockey team. But Coleman was essentially harassing Nyx, a habit that he maintained under the guise that he was disciplining.

Coleman was nearly foaming at the mouth. "Get your hands *off* me, Mr Hunt." My hands had a mind of their own, contracting around him and hauling him closer.

"Not only are you blaming her for the perception of the surrounding students, but this *immortalises* rape culture," I groused, tugging at his azure tie. "And you know what I find fucking weird? No other professor has approached her about her outfit. You're not the only one here. If students had a problem, there's more than one professor to go to. The fact that *you* are here reprimanding her means that *you* are the one staring at her ass, *you* are the one who can't concentrate because you're too busy sexualising the body of a student who came dressed appropriately to the weather. She didn't put that dress on this morning with the intention of making *you* come in your fucking pants, Professor. She wore it because it's warm outside."

"Mr Hunt—" Releasing him, I stepped back, swearing when I realised many students were filming the entire ordeal. My team looked anxious, but I couldn't care, not when Coleman was still in one piece. "Your actions are going to have major consequences." He glanced at Sebastian. "I suggest you learn to be in charge for the next few weeks, Mr Hayes, because your captain is going to be unavailable. Twenty days, to be exact." I didn't react, but Nyx seemed to be struggling to decide whether she wanted to kiss me or kick me in the nuts. "Miss Taylor, you are to go to Dean Waverly's office for failing to agree to change your inappropriate outfit."

I wanted to strike his teeth out but Grayson pulled me back. Because I'd already worsened things for our team. Dean Waverly wouldn't even do anything. She'd merely apologise for the inconvenience. I hoped that they'd fire Coleman at this point, that this was the final straw.

Nyx scowled at the man. "So, my dress is the problem, then?"

Coleman clapped condescendingly. "I see you've got a brain after all—" He stopped speaking, probably stopped breathing. And I'm pretty sure we all did. Nyx clutched the hem of her dress and yanked it over her head, flinging it at the older man's chest. She stood in her sneakers and black panties with a matching strapless bra.

"You want my underwear too?" she provoked. There were hickeys on the swells of her breasts and lower stomach, remnants of our time in the storage closet earlier. When he didn't speak, she turned around, offering a generous view of her ass that sported hickeys as well. The guys whistled, tossing me amused glances. Before she left, she glimpsed at me. "You called me your girlfriend. Is that your way of asking?" She was smirking.

I shrugged. "What better way of saying I want to date you than by tossing around the professor that's leering at you?" I told her with a grin, overlooking the fact that Benson was going to be beyond fucking pissed.

"How romantic," she nodded to herself and then left, eyes on her until her presence was no longer in the cafeteria. Just as she passed through the doors, she raised her middle fingers at Coleman.

The older man tensed when he apprehended people were still filming. He threw the dress at me. "Make sure she puts that back on."

"I'm suspended," I reminded him. "You have no authority over me so I don't have to do anything you fucking say." With a twitching eye, he left through a different door, steam practically coming out of his ears, nose and ass. When he left, I faced Sebastian's gaze. I saw uncertainty. Until we sorted this situation, I was no longer part of the team. "Time to pull up your socks, *Captain.*"

Without saying anything else, I bunched Nyx's dress in my hands and followed the path to Dean Waverly's office. The area was barren, the receptionist behind her desk. I ignored her and peeked into the office. Only Nyx was there, seated with her arms crossed and an enraged pout on her face.

"Where's Waverly?" I asked, shutting the door behind me.

Her eyes shot to mine. "You're at peak dumbass. Benson's gonna be so pissed at you."

"In a choice of who I'd want pissed at me between you and Benson, I'd pick Benson any day," I responded, taking a walk around the office. "Where's Waverly?" I reiterated my question.

Nyx shrugged. "She just went into a meeting and I have to wait until she's finished." She spotted the dress in my hands and rolled her eyes. "He's so unnecessary. What even was the point?" When she stood up, I tilted back against the desk, watching her approach me. "You racked up some serious points with me, by the way. All of the boys did."

There was a proud look in her eyes. Those guys had come a long way, going from taunting her to standing up for her at the first sign of a threat.

I placed my hands on her hips, pulling her closer as I muttered, "As long as they don't get to redeem their points in the same way I do." She laughed, arms going around my neck. Slowly, my hands slid down, towing at her underwear. Her dress was on the desk next to me. "Maybe you should put some clothes on," I advised, wondering what the dean would think if she saw her sitting in her office wearing only underwear.

She tilted her head, fingers encountering the button of my jeans. "Or you could lose some of yours?" Her lips were suddenly against the skin of my neck and my grip on her tightened. "Waverly's gonna be away for a while and," she murmured, nibbling my skin, "I'm in the mood to fuck my boyfriend."

And there went my restraint.

After so long of not being able to have Nyx Taylor fully, she was mine. My dad would be disappointed in me, honestly. I had zero self-discipline when it came to Nyx, none whatsoever. With a teasing smirk, she unzipped my pants as I pressed my lips to hers in a bruising kiss. She moaned into my mouth when I eased my hands underneath her bra, tweaking the flesh in my hand. I felt her fingers teasing the skin above my waistband.

"If we get caught, I'm blaming you," I mumbled against her lips. She let out a faint, moaning gasp when my tongue intertwined with hers. We parted for a few seconds so I could tug my t-shirt off.

"If we get caught, we're probably gonna get arrested by your dad," she quipped and I pinched her ass in retaliation, not wanting to think about my dad when I was about to fuck her. She was grinding against me, eagerly pressing herself close whilst I dug into my back pocket, my hand trembling as I pulled out my wallet. "*Beck*," she complained in annoyance at me taking too long.

I chuckled, pulling a condom from the wallet. "What? Scared we're gonna get caught?"

Her eyes were defiant, seizing the condom from me and ripping it open. I picked her up, placing her on the desk and she lowered her panties. She watched me with dazed eyes as I dropped my jeans and boxers, sliding on the condom.

My hands smoothed up her silky thighs and she moaned, tossing her head back. Swiftly, I pushed forward, feeling her warmth swallow me and I groaned. If we got caught, there was no way I'd even be able to stop. My senses were overwhelmed by all things Nyx. I couldn't see outside of what was happening between us, couldn't hear more than her precious moans, couldn't see more than the look of pure need in her eyes.

A stuttered breath left her and she gripped my shoulders, nails digging into the skin there. She mewled and I moved deeper until I bottomed out. My stomach was clenched and I kissed her again, allowing her to adjust to my size. When I began rocking my hips, she moaned and I buried my face in her neck, gradually finding my rhythm.

"*Shit*, right there," she murmured, clenching around me. "Oh God, please don't stop."

She slid further on the desk, papers flying to the ground as I fucked her. Her legs curved around me, shaking when I found the perfect angle.

"Fuck, baby," I hissed, rubbing her clit with my thumb and she trembled.

There was rustling outside and we froze. Nyx spoke first. "Speed this up, bro."

"My dick is literally inside you and you're calling me *bro*?" I questioned.

"I'm gonna be calling you my ex if you don't get me off right now." Her words sounded like a threat but she was grinning. I pulled out of her and in one move, I spun her around, pressing her ass against me. "Okay, *wow*." Her surprise was evident when I pushed her flat against the table, my hand pressed between her shoulder blades.

She wriggled at my teasing touches, knowing that I was doing it on purpose. I angled myself at her entrance, hands grasping her hips. On the first thrust, I forced myself as deep as I could, quelling a loud groan. Unable to help myself, I leaned over, biting the skin of her shoulders to leave my mark. Her dress was backless, and I was filled with a sense of satisfaction at the thought of everyone seeing what I'd done to her.

Nyx was biting her hand, whimpering at the intrusion. Swallowing roughly, I questioned, "You okay there, bro?"

"*Asshole*," she swore, but her words came out as a whine when I moved again, fucking her harder.

I spread her cheeks, watching myself disappear inside of her. "I see your asshole. Want me to stuff that too?" She didn't get to respond because I grasped her hair, gripping the strands as I pounded my hips against hers. "Fuck yourself on me, Nyx," I grumbled, tugging her up so that her back was pressed against my chest. I kept a hand over her mouth as she slammed herself back on me, her head falling back in ecstasy. "*Jesus.* So fucking tight."

Feeling her tense around me, I knew she was close, knew she was experiencing that tightening sensation deep in her stomach. "*Oh my God*, Beck, I'm gonna—"

"All over my cock, baby," I groaned. "Do it." Her name was a guttural sound tumbling from my mouth as I ploughed myself deeper, spilling inside the condom whilst Nyx spasmed around me. "*Fuck.*" I pulled out, spinning her around so that I could kiss her. Our mouths were sloppy against each other. "Can't believe you made me fuck you in the dean's office," I murmured, making her smile. "Guess I'm not a moral citizen anymore."

She was dazed again, barely able to stand on her own and I

wanted to laugh. A few moments of silence passed, filled with us trying to catch our breath.

"Do you think it feels like this for me because you're my first?" Her question made my heart stop. "I mean, there's been others after you but nothing felt like *this*. How it feels with you."

I couldn't even be jealous, knowing that the others didn't even come close to me. There was more rustling outside and I could hear the receptionist trying to keep somebody at bay. Nyx gasped, shoving me away and I quickly pulled up my pants, hastily pulling my shirt over my head. Nyx slipped into her dress as I knotted the condom, keeping it out of view.

The receptionist was arguing with someone and I turned to Nyx. "I think it's just us," I responded to her previous question and she squinted in confusion. "I mean, you weren't my first, but everything I feel when I'm with you," I kissed her pout, "makes me *certain* you're gonna be my last. I love you."

She smiled. "I love you too, asshole."

The door opened and Coleman walked in, wrinkling his nose. He eyed our dishevelled appearances and scowled. I stepped away from Nyx, walking past him.

"If you were ever worried about her seeking male validation by wearing her outfits," I held up her panties, "now you know she doesn't need it." Nyx gasped in the background and Coleman turned red. I smirked, looking at Nyx who was trying to tug down the hem of her dress, realising she hadn't put her panties back on. "See you later, baby."

Chapter 29

Nyx

The light was just beginning to seep through the curtains, casting a golden glow right onto my face. The room back at my dad's place had always been dark, the window at an awkward angle that didn't allow any sunshine to peek through. *My dad's place*. It felt good, no longer having to refer to that hellhole as my home. This was a new book, let alone a new chapter of my life, and my dad was no longer a character that existed in this story.

I hummed sleepily, feeling a heavy arm wrapped around my waist and keeping me pressed against a firm chest. Warmth, I felt it all around me. And I loved it. Beckham was still asleep behind me, and I took a moment to bask in the heat that he radiated. Waking up like this, it was something that I had to get used to. I wasn't complaining at all, though. The only complaint I had was Sebastian sometimes bringing girls over and then fucking them at odd hours, his headboard banging against the wall.

Then again, he had to deal with me and Beckham. Poor

Grayson. And poor Annie too, although she spent most of her nights at Beth's new apartment.

Trying, and failing, to dispel my sleep, I wiggled slightly to get some life into my limbs. A deep groan rumbled from behind me.

I snorted, a laugh getting stuck in my throat as I felt something digging into my ass. That was enough to wake me up, having the same effect as three cups of coffee and a dip into an ice-cold pool. Testing the waters, I moved again. The groan was slightly louder, and Beckham moved closer, pressing his pelvis into me. This time, it was my own groan I had to curb. The arm that was at my waist moved higher, a hand suddenly gripping my braless breast. He squeezed, hips simultaneously jutting forward, and I bit my lip.

Well, somebody was having a very good dream.

His hips moved again, and I whimpered, wondering whether I should wake him or not. Before I could say anything, his lips were at my ear. "Morning, baby."

I could hear the smile in his rough voice, and it triggered my own. "Do you always wake up with a raging boner or am I being treated extra special?"

He squeezed my breast again, finger running lightly across my nipple. "This raging boner is your fault." I smothered a laugh, the sound turning into a breathy moan when he pressed his hips against me again. "Now are you gonna be a good girl and take care of the problem you caused?"

With my shirt bunched at my waist, his hand was suddenly in my panties, fingers making quick work of my already throbbing clit. "Beck," I mumbled his name, throwing my head back and feeling his lips meet my neck. "Shit."

When a singular finger probed my entrance, Beckham chuckled, his voice still gravelly with sleep. "Do you always wake up this wet or am I being treated extra special?"

"Asshole," I hissed, clenching my legs when he added another finger.

Beckham hummed. "Maybe. But the difference between you and me is that I fully intend to take care of this problem." He pressed a gentle kiss to my jaw. "And I'm going to enjoy it." He slipped his boxers down, grinding his bare cock against my ass as he fingered me faster. "God, you have no fucking idea what you do to me."

I tossed an arm back to grasp his head, keeping his face buried in my neck as I worked my ass against him. "*Oh.*" A complaint formed in my throat when he moved away to reach for a condom. The minute it was on him, I tried to straddle him, but he tutted. "*Beck*," I moaned.

He laughed against my jaw, slowly rolling us over so that he was between my legs. Not a word left his mouth as he pushed my shirt up further, quickly running his tongue over a peaked nipple. I squirmed underneath him as I framed his hips with my legs

"You're so fucking perfect," he muttered, leaving a hickey on the breast he was currently fondling. That pulled another moan from me, only widening his arrogant smile. He leaned back slightly before dropping a kiss to my lips. "I'm so in love with you."

The fluttering sensation rose in my chest, and I held him tighter, fingers playing with the hair at his nape. "Fucking whipped," I teased. "You're lucky I love you too."

Those were the last coherent words I could get out before he slowly entered me, gently rocking his hips. Then I was breathless, clinging to him with everything that I had as he maintained that slow pace.

"Shit," he swore, breathing deeply when I clenched around him. One of his hands slid underneath me, taking a handful of my ass to press me closer to him. The new angle allowed his thrusts to hit a deeper part of me, one that had me clawing at his back. I loved the feeling of him inside me, on top of me, against me.

I loved him so much.

With my legs around him as he murmured his love for me in my ear, I knew this was what all those poets wrote about. This feeling. Whatever Beckham made me feel was something people spent years searching for, something poets agonised over, trying to find the right words to describe. As beautiful as those poems could be, they didn't hold a candle to the actual feeling. Nothing ever would.

It was unparalleled.

My eyes rolled to the back of my head when he buried himself as deep as he could go. We could've stayed like that for hours. Time felt non-existent. My body jerked with every push of his hips. I was close, could feel it. And I could feel he was close too. My back arched as I practically sobbed his name when my release eventually hit me. His mouth deadened the scream that wanted to escape, and I felt him shudder atop me as he came. We stayed like that, both too dazed to move.

I stroked his hair, feeling his stubble tickle my neck. "I love you," he said, sounding sleepy again and I wanted to laugh.

"I love you too," I muttered, my smile nearly taking over my entire face. After a few minutes, Beckham pulled out of me and moved to get rid of the condom. Sleep called us both soon after and we welcomed it.

The sun was a little more aggressive when I awoke later, and I rolled out of bed whilst trying my best to not wake Beckham. Locking myself in the bathroom, I quickly freshened up and got dressed. The smell of scrambled egg was wafting through the house, and I was desperate to get to whoever was in the kitchen.

Once I was done, I made my way downstairs; still somewhat amazed at how easily I'd adapted to this house and mornings with Beckham. Annie's birthday and the fundraiser had passed by in the blink of an eye. It felt like time was moving faster now that we were no longer in my dad's presence. Living with the boys was better than I expected.

Annie and, surprisingly, Sebastian would take turns cooking dinner. The latter was the son of a well-known chef, a piece of information nobody had deemed important enough to tell me.

The truth was in his meals though.

Beth would join us most nights, and I found myself drawn to her bubbly personality. I could see why Annie liked her so much. She was a literal breath of fresh air, and it was beyond entertaining to watch Sebastian get irritated by her constant smile. Even now, the blonde angel was glaring at me as I sipped at my water—and I was enjoying it.

"The fuck are you smiling for?" he asked, moving around

me to get a tin of soda from the fridge.

"Sebastian, don't be rude," Annie scolded, distributing the scrambled egg into different plates. She'd taken on the role of mother hen, to nobody's surprise. I snorted at the disappointed stare she gave him, to which he responded with a huff. Being older than all the boys by three years, she had the motherly authority they couldn't oppose.

I smirked. "Yeah, Sebastian. Don't be rude."

Annie's glare turned to me. "*Nyx*," she uttered disapprovingly, causing Sebastian to snort. I grimaced, leaning back against the counter. "Stop provoking him."

It was Sebastian's turn to smirk. He flicked my head as he left the kitchen and I suppressed the urge to throw him with a plate.

Once he was gone, I looked at my sister. "Aren't you supposed to be on my side?"

She laughed, turning back to preparing breakfast. "I'm on nobody's side. And you really need to stop pestering him. Gosh, you're like Indie when she went through that phase of yanking Poppy's hair."

The memory brought a smile to my face. "We're having them this weekend, right?" I asked, trying to figure out if I had my dates correct.

Although they were staying with Georgia, the girls, including Julie, would spend some days with us. I for sure thought the boys would be annoyed with so many girls in the house, but it didn't faze them at all. In fact, it had been Grayson's idea so that we could spend more time with them.

Annie nodded, sparing me a quick glance. "We've got

Mom's funeral this weekend too."

My smile dropped. "We're going to that?" Immediately, I winced at how heartless my words sounded. But it was too late, Annie's frown was in place. "I didn't mean it like that. It's just, I don't exactly want to go, Annie."

Her gaze was understanding. "You don't have to. But I also don't want it to seem like Indie and Poppy shouldn't go because *we* don't want to—"

"You know Poppy doesn't want to," I interjected, reminding her of the conversation we'd had with her. We'd been so focused on protecting the girls that we'd forgotten Poppy had her own thoughts about our situation, thoughts she'd recently made very clear. "And Indie doesn't even know her," I added.

Annie placed the pan in the sink before she looked at me. "Then who's going to be there?"

The question made my muscles tense. My mom had nobody. She was cut off from our grandma, had no friends and her daughters didn't want to attend. I waited for the sympathy to hit me, but it never did.

"I'm not going," I informed her, my decision final. She nodded, not looking upset at all. "She wasn't a mother to us. If she had been, I would've attended."

"I know," Annie murmured. "I'm not attending because I'm her daughter. I'm attending because if I don't, there'll be nobody else there." Her smile was slightly teasing. "I'm taking one for the team because I know neither of us wants that on our conscience, that our mom's funeral was attended by nobody."

She didn't say anything else, beginning to place bread in the toaster. I pushed off the counter, eyeing her for a second.

"Mom never deserved you." I watched her tense, but by the time she turned around, I was already leaving the kitchen.

My feet led me to Beckham's room, the space we were currently sharing. I wasn't surprised by what I saw. His bed was made already because Beckham Hunt was a fucking neat freak. Everything he did was so precise, even when it came to cleaning his room. Each object had a place where it stood and if it wasn't there, Beckham would flip.

He was standing at the window when I entered, just ending a call. Because he was only wearing sweatpants, I could see the marks I'd left on his back earlier this morning, and I grinned.

When he spotted me, he grimaced. "That was Rick," he said, referencing the owner of Project Burger. "Still no sign of an Annabelle Lewis."

I pulled a face, plopping on the edge of the bed and ignoring the slight ache between my legs. When Beckham had first told me that he'd ran into my grandma, I hadn't believed him. We hadn't heard from the woman in five years and her running into *my boyfriend* of all people? It didn't seem believable. My doubts only became heightened after what he just said.

"You sure it was her?" I asked probably for the hundredth time since he'd first told me.

He rolled his eyes and I tossed a pillow at his face. "*Yes*, I'm sure. It was the exact woman from the video you played. Rick promised that he'd keep an eye out for her."

"Did she know who you were?" I questioned, trying to figure out why the fuck my grandma had been talking to him. He shrugged, mentioning that he'd told her my name. "It's not a very common name," I offered hopelessly. "She *had* to know who you were. And it can't be a coincidence that she's back after her daughter fucking overdosed. It's almost like she expected it."

Beckham neatly placed his pillow back and I hid the urge to laugh. And the urge to mess up the pillows again, just to piss him off. "You think she's going to the funeral? Maybe you can speak to her there."

I shook my head. "After my aunt's passing, my mom went downhill and my grandma wasn't willing to be dragged along. She'd lost both daughters a long time ago, there's no need for her to attend this funeral." The same expression of defeat that I wore appeared on Beckham's face. I poked his cheek. "Don't stress about it. She'll pop up eventually."

He pulled me into his arms suddenly, looking determined. "From what Poppy's told me, she's always been good to you girls. Your Uncle Robbie might be gone, but your grandma's still here. More than anything, you need somebody like her in your life."

I leaned into him, inhaling the fresh scent that he carried and realising that in the ten minutes I'd been downstairs, he'd already taken a fucking shower. The man was a morning person like no other, getting shit done the moment his eyes opened. I didn't know whether to hate it or love it.

I brushed my nose gently against his. "It's not a need," I told him, running my fingers through his damp hair. "Not when we've already got you and the boys. And Nailea. And Georgia." His lips barely touched mine. "And Beth," I added, making him laugh. "What?"

"You fucking hated Beth at some point," he said, pinching

my leg and I smacked his shoulder.

"No, I didn't—"

"You did."

"No, I didn't—"

He scoffed, looking offended that I would even argue. "You were jealous, baby. Admit it."

My lips pursed. "Jealous? As if." The asshole was fucking smiling. I tried to get out of his arms, but he only held me tighter. "Let go of me, loser."

Beckham nipped the skin at my jaw. "Not until you admit you were jealous."

"I was *not* jealous," I grumbled, quickly trying to think of something. "I was angry because you were annoying and Beth just happened to be standing in the shooting range."

He raised a brow. "Nice excuse."

"Fuck you," I laughed, managing to fall out of his hold. He didn't let me get far though, immediately enveloping his arms around my waist and pulling me back to his chest. "*Beckham*."

"When did you realise?" he whispered, spinning me around so I could look up at him.

I gripped his biceps, trying to hide my smile. "I had my suspicions after our first meeting. There was more sexual tension between me and her during that one argument than you and her probably during your entire friendship."

He stole a quick kiss from me. "I don't know how I never noticed it. Even my mom knew."

Sensing the subtle shame he carried at not knowing or noticing more about his friend, I said, "I don't think Beth knew fully either."

Annie had told me what her mom was like, a despicable woman who sought to control her daughter's sexuality. It had made her question what she felt, compared it to what her mom told her she was supposed to feel. That only led to a lot of confusion, confusion that Annie had helped her to unravel.

"I'm glad she's happy," he continued. "That they both are." He kissed me again. "And you. And your sisters. You all deserve it." Another kiss.

I rolled my eyes at his dorky smile, but it only mirrored my own. Because I could feel his own happiness, and knowing that it was fuelled by mine—yeah, there was definitely a poem somewhere out there about this feeling.

Chapter 30

Beckham

I was a demanding man and it had gotten me into many rough tangles before. Even my dad had told me to try and extinguish the monster. I tried to, and I succeeded. At least, that was what I thought. As a captain, I was used to getting my way. And it was never personal demands. I only wanted the best for my team.

Naturally, I felt the same way about Nyx. I wanted her to speak to me instead of bottling all of her emotions. With her dad still on the run, she was completely out of it. There was so much fear surrounding her; fear for what Matthew Taylor would do while in hiding. He could pounce on them when they least expected it. My dad and his team had said they had it under control and I believed them. But I could see Nyx felt guilty about making her problem everyone else's. The thought alone was stupid and I didn't know how to make her see that she deserved to be helped. Not only was she and her sisters important to us, but it was the right thing to do.

The rink was empty, although it would only be another

three hours before our fourth match against the Bruins would commence. Sebastian was all too keen to relinquish the title of the captain back to me. For an egotistical guy, he really had zero confidence in himself when it came to captaining. He was great at it, but he was wasting too much time in my shadow. He wanted to be there, veiling his talents. Something needed to be done about that.

Jasper strolled past me, holding a bottle of water in his hands. "What's up with Nyx?" he asked underneath his breath.

And that was what had been tormenting me for the past few days. I'd applaud her because she was striving to give everyone the impression that nothing was wrong.

I shrugged. "No idea."

He stared at me for a moment, but then made his way over to Oliver. I kept my eyes on him before turning away, swearing quietly.

"Beck," Grayson called my name, stopping next to me. "Benson wants to run through one last exercise with me. Do you mind picking Annie and Beth up?" My eyes caught Nyx, snuggled up to Jasper's side. "They've got a shift right now but they should be done in about twenty minutes. Beck?"

"Yeah, I'll go get them—"

"But they still have another twenty minutes on their shift—"

"I'll wait," I cut him off, marching to the locker room to get my car keys.

The noise in the rink was beginning to give me a headache and I just wanted to leave. Add the fact that I felt like the worst boyfriend ever. Once outside, I hopped into my car and made my way to Daisy's Delicacies. I hoped the drive would ease my nerves.

It didn't.

With an exasperated groan, I parked the car and jumped out, feeling like my body was on fire. But then I stopped, breath seizing in my throat. Because there, to the side of the building, was Annie caught in a heated discussion with Annabelle Lewis.

It was Ms Lewis that noticed me first. "Beckham Hunt," she stated in an amused tone. "I hear you've been looking for me."

When Annie located me, her eyes widened to threefold their size and for a second, it looked like she was about to start hyperventilating.

"How the hell did you find her?" I questioned Annie, ignoring the smile Ms Lewis was wearing.

"She literally just showed up a few minutes ago," was her rejoinder. It seemed like she was still trying to come to terms that I hadn't imagined meeting their grandma and was, in fact, telling the truth.

I turned back to the older woman, seeing her casually leaning against the wall. "Did you know who I was?"

She smirked. "Of course I did."

"And you knew I was looking for you?" I threw in another question.

This time, she shook her head. "No, actually. I always planned to come and speak to my granddaughters. You were a variable I didn't account for. In fact, *I'm* perfectly on time." Not once did she lose her smile.

Annie grimaced at her grandma's words. "You consider five

years later on time?"

It took everything in me not to laugh. She may have been the nicest of her siblings, but they'd been fucked over one too many times, had hope for people who didn't deserve it. Eliza Taylor seemed to have been Annie's last straw.

"Annie, there's much we have to discuss," Ms Lewis spoke, giving Annie's shoulder a sympathetic squeeze. It was like she understood exactly what she was thinking. "And I assure you that there's a *very* reasonable explanation behind my lack of presence in your lives."

The brunette next to me still didn't lose her snark, although she probably knew her annoyance was unnecessary. "Like what?"

Ms Lewis was quick to respond. "You *know* what, Annie. A restraining order." My arm around Annie's shoulders tensed and I felt her stiffen. "My daughter didn't exactly like me, and when I sought to take my grandkids away from her—"

"She lost it," I murmured, repeating the words Poppy had told me.

Ms Lewis nodded. "Her death allows me back into your lives. In fact, I've been here a few weeks before her death since restraining orders only last—"

"Three to five years," I finished again, seeing some parts of her story stitch together.

She grinned. "Smart man. I was just telling Annie what I was doing back in the city when you interrupted us." The girl in question paled. "It was the whole reason why I took the risk of coming back into your lives earlier than what was allowed."

Ms Lewis gave Annie a photograph. I peeped over Annie's

shoulder and she allowed me to look, passing it to me. "They look like Indie," she stated incredulously.

And they did. In my hands, I held a photograph of two girls who looked remarkably like Indigo Taylor.

"Those are your half-sisters," Ms Lewis explained. "When I recently found out Matthew had another family, I knew I had to watch from afar. He doesn't exactly have the best track record with daughters," she gave a half-hearted smile. "You girls had Georgia watching over you. They had no one."

Me, on the other hand, I was floundering at the new information. *Another family?* That fucker had another family when he couldn't even care for the one he already had? Nyx's comment about her dad having two surprises running around made more sense now. She'd seen him with his family and she'd freaked out. I returned the photograph to Annie and she took it with tremulous hands.

She stared at the innocent little faces, so much like Indigo. "What are their names?"

Ms Lewis pointed to the taller one. "That's Jade and that one's Rue. Lovely girls. Your dad plays pretend to the public like he always has, but he beat his wife. I fear that if they stayed in his clutches any longer, he would've taken to beating them too, his anger at the news of you girls leaving him getting the best of him."

Sympathy seeped into Annie's features. Their freedom could've meant the suffering of Jade and Rue. All because Matthew was a heartless asshole. I hoped that he was caught soon and placed in a cell where he fucking belonged.

"How do you know all this?" I asked her, articulating

because Annie looked like she was about to malfunction.

"I befriended their mom. She had no idea who I really was, though." Annie frowned at her answer. "I was the one who encouraged her to talk to Georgia. She needed to get herself and her girls out of that situation. I'd failed Eliza already, I couldn't fail her too."

Annie was trembling again. She was still clutching the photo of her half-sisters. "Why didn't he hit them?"

"Because they're not Eliza's daughters," was her easy response, one that made sense almost as much as it didn't. "Annie, I'm sure you've noticed that sometimes your dad will try to be better. But he always hated Nyx, and now Poppy too. All because they looked like your mom, something they can't control." She cleared her throat. "And I know you remember those times when Nyx had to stay with me after the wedding because your dad was so unstable, angry about her very existence."

It was the way she said it; with a deeper understanding.

Then abruptly, she remembered I was still standing there. Her eyes widened, but I had her. She didn't need to say anything else, at least not for me. I glanced at the photograph again, at Annie. My chest felt tight, my ribs threatening to ram through my skin. It was right there. It was always *right there*. Granted, I hadn't known that Matthew had other kids, but it made so much more sense now.

I cleared my throat. "Could you drop her and Beth at the rink once you're done talking?" I asked Ms Lewis.

My voice was unsteady and she picked up on it. By the rueful smile she gave me, she knew I'd figured it out. She nodded. I stared at Annie's terrified expression for a moment and kissed her head before bustling back to my car. The drive felt like years, probably because my brain was completely jumbled.

Nyx. My poor girl. She'd been through so much already and life just wouldn't stop shitting on her. This was going to break her.

And like most strong women, she'd feel the need to suffer through it all on her own, she'd push me away. But I wouldn't let her. I wouldn't let her isolate herself, take it all on her own. I couldn't let that happen. Regardless of having me, Nailea and the boys, people who loved her—she'd try to distance herself to save us from being pulled into her problems. There was no way I was letting her do that, and I needed to make that clearer than it already was.

Far from any possible wandering eyes, I parked the car. Taking out my phone, I sent a quick text to Nyx, hands quivering with the knowledge I'd uncovered. It took her five minutes to find me after she read my text. The passenger door opened and she hopped in, shutting it behind her.

"The match starts soon," she reminded me, confusion evident in her eyes. When I still didn't say anything, the sides of her lips tilted downwards. "You alright?"

"Remember when I first took you to my parents' place? When we first had dinner there?" I blurted, weaving together my words. Still slightly confused, she nodded. "I knew my mom spoke to you that night because you avoided me after that. There was the option of questioning her, but I figured you'd tell me eventually. Part of me already knows, but I'm going to ask you what she spoke to you about."

Her cheeks took on a red shade and she leaned back in her seat, fidgeting with her top. "She said you always had the best intentions and I had to remember that." I watched her swallow nervously. "I think it was the way she said it that freaked me out. Maybe she was trying to tell me that you loved me without *actually* telling me," she said with a laugh and I groaned at how intrusive my mom was.

"Her heart was in the right place," I attempted to ease her nerves. "I don't know how she does it, but she always knows things, without having to ask."

Nyx smiled. "I figured that out the second I complimented her house." She bit her lip. "There was this *knowing* in her eyes and she didn't want to frighten me. Before we left that night, she told me she'd overheard me crying, told me that if I ever needed anything I was welcomed there anytime. It scared me."

"You're afraid of people leaving you," I murmured and she nodded. "So you don't give them permanent places in your life. It was why we never dated."

She looked down at her lap. "I hate giving people ammo to hurt me. People I've trusted have held that gun before. And it hurts every single time. My mom, my dad. I can't imagine going through that again."

"Not everybody is gonna leave, Nyx," I spoke in the most gentle tone I could muster. Feelings weren't my forte either, but I was trying. For her. "Not everybody's gonna turn into a scar. You know that I love you. You know that the people around you love you and your sisters. You're always going to have us."

"But what if I don't?" Her words were accompanied by

teary eyes and she cursed softly. "I love you all, I really do. But there always has to be caution. Forever with somebody isn't guaranteed."

I placed a hand on her bare thigh, uncovered by her skirt. "And why would it not be guaranteed in this situation?"

"I've spent my whole life trying to prove that my sisters and I deserve love, deserve to be treated with care but nobody ever listened." She sighed. "For so long, it's just been us. And now there's everybody." *Overwhelmed.* She was overwhelmed. "My life is one big mess," she mumbled, throwing her hands up in exasperation. "And yours *isn't.* No matter how hard I try to push the thought away, it feels like all I'll ever be to you is a massive burden."

And there it was. Nyx had people who loved her. Me, my family, Nailea, Beth and the boys. Even Georgia. That was a lot of people to somebody who'd once had nobody. I was hoping the pessimistic thoughts wouldn't creep up on her, but it was expected. A burden. She and her sisters could never be burdens.

They were blessings.

"I wish there was a way for you to look into my mind," I cleared my throat, "to see how much I love you. You could never be a burden to me, Nyx. You never were. I tried to cover it up with anger because I was so fucking in love with you and everything you stood for." I forced a laugh, feeling embarrassed. "It still doesn't feel real, *this*," I squeezed her leg.

Her eyes watered and I counted the seconds it took for her to speak again. "I tried to rationalise why I'd risk everything to help you. But there was never an answer. No matter how hard

I tried, I could never get a fixed answer. Help Nate, help the team, help you. The answer was constantly evolving. I don't think I'll ever find out why." She squeezed my hand. "But you can never rationalise the things you do out of love. My mom took beatings for us because she supposedly loved us, then she left. My dad claimed to love us, but he beat us. What if love *isn't* enough to keep people?"

I leaned forward, cupping her face in my palms. "I love you. We all do," I whispered, watching her eyes shut, her lashes flitting against the top of her cheeks. "I don't just want this facade you put out there, strong, independent and no need for help. Whether you can do it alone or not, you don't *need* to anymore. I want the parts that you hide. I've looked at you with so many different emotions over the past year, resentment, admiration, dread—but never in the absence of love. You're a bitch, not gonna lie," she snorted, "but for valid reasons. And I want to know those reasons. But most importantly, I want to love you in a way that you deserve to be loved."

There was a long beat of silence as she allowed my words to caress her. Slowly, her eyes opened, a vivid blue meeting my gaze. "What belongs to me will find me," she uttered, a petite smile gracing her lips.

I grinned. "Simple law of attraction, baby. You're mine, I'm not leaving you. If you believe in anything, believe in that."

With that, I pulled her in for a much-needed kiss. I would never tire of kissing Nyx. For such an electrifying woman, her kisses were affectionate, passionate, tender. It was a preface to everything she burrowed inside, everything I wanted to know. Feelings weren't her area of expertise, but her kisses told me everything I needed to know, that she loved me.

Her arms went around my neck, clinging to me as if her life depended on it. My lips found her tender spot, just underneath her ear and she moaned when I nipped at it. Impatiently, I pulled her over the console until she was straddling me, her back against the steering wheel in a position we knew all too well.

As our lips met again, I slid my hands up the smooth skin of her thighs, feeling her shudder at my touch. Gripping her ass in my hands, I tugged her closer. Thank fuck my windows were tinted. She dropped her head onto my shoulder when I moved her panties aside, sliding a finger inside of her.

"Fuck," I muttered when she clenched around it. Slowly, I added another finger and she whined. "Easy, baby," I whispered, pulling her face to mine for another kiss.

Her hips bucked against me as my fingers moved faster, fucking her at a furious pace. It didn't take long for her to come all over my hand and I smirked. My fingers never ceased their movements, pushing her over the edge. Even when she finished trembling in my hold, coming down from her high, I continued to thrust them into her until she was a whimpering mess.

"Beck," she moaned as I crooked my fingers. "*Please*."

Her back curved, mouth parted in pleasure. Her eyes met mine, the blue colour tinged with a darker shade. That look she gave me was my undoing, filled with so much trust, so much love. Impatiently, I worked my cock out of my pants, looking for my wallet. Without needing to be told, Nyx raised the condom, just as feverish. I groaned when she slowly slid it over me, her hands smooth and warm.

I took off her camisole before cupping her breasts in my hands. My mouth clamped over a nipple, sucking and she arched into me. I pinched the neglected nipple and alternated between the two.

All while I was enjoying myself, Nyx ground harder against me. "My baby's impatient."

"*Beckham*," she complained. With a loud pop, I let go of her nipple and pushed her panties to the side again. I fisted my cock, lining it up with her entrance. Slowly, she sank down onto me.

"Fuck," I hissed. I gripped her hips, before slamming in. "Jesus, *fuck*," I groaned as Nyx cried out, clutching my shoulders for assistance. She was beyond wet, enabling me to slide in smoothly. I waited for a few seconds, allowing her to adjust to the intrusion. Her walls were clamping around me and I moaned. "So fucking tight. Fucking killing me."

When I gently pulled out and then pushed back in, her moans turned louder. I replicated the motions, slamming into her over and over again. She countered my actions, riding me. Heaven, absolute heaven. I wouldn't have a problem with dying like this.

I slapped her ass, prompting her to go faster. "Shit. Your pussy's so fucking tight." She braced her hands on my shoulder. "Ride my cock, baby."

Nyx threw her head back and raised herself slightly before pushing back down. I cursed and she stifled a scream. Up and down. She repeated it, improving her pace when it got more and more pleasant.

"*Beck*. You feel so good," she moaned, sinking down to kiss me. I cupped her ass and helped her slam down onto me. "*Yes.*"

"Fuck, yes," I growled through clenched teeth. "That's it. Squeeze my cock. Just like that—*Fuck!*" She tensed around me and I grunted into her neck, slamming into her. Her back curved and I took a nipple into my mouth again.

"I'm so close," she moaned and I quickened my pace, hands pinning her wrists behind her back.

My eyes were trained on her breasts as they swayed with the movement. She whimpered, sensing her climax slithering upon her. "You close, baby? You wanna come all over my cock?" She nodded, eyes watering due to her impending release. "Give it to me, Nyx."

I tipped over and my pelvis rubbed her clit with every thrust. It was the final straw. Nyx came with a scream, shuddering atop me as I proceeded to work in and out of her.

"Oh, God. Beck!" The sound of my name on her lips sent me over the edge. My vision went blurry, eyes rolling to the back of my head.

"Fuck!" I felt the rush of my come shoot inside the condom before I relaxed, sagging against the seat. The tinted windows were murky with our breaths and perspiration flowed down my back. I raised my head so that I could kiss her, slow and sweet. "I love you."

Her eyes were dazed and she was thoroughly fucked. Nyx looked at me, smiling. She needed to know all that she meant to me because her world was about to be tilted from its axis. She needed to know that she could count on me, that I would shoulder her problems so she wouldn't have to carry it on her own. She needed to know that she had people she could rely on because this was going to absolutely break her.

Matthew Taylor's genes were strong as fuck, each of his daughters the spitting image of him.

Except for Nyx and Poppy.

Because they weren't his daughters.

Chapter 31

Nyx

They weren't supposed to lose. That wasn't part of the plan. But as I watched UCLA score one last goal before the timer went off, I knew it was over. *One* point ahead. One damned point. It didn't help that everybody seemed to be caught in their own world. Perhaps the long break had been too much. Sebastian and Jai weren't able to gel well this match, almost as if they could sense their captain's unease. Their footwork was sloppy and they missed a few passes.

Jasper had been worried about me for a while now, I knew that. I wasn't behaving normally, too stressed about my dad being on the run. One thing I had to get used to was that I had more people who cared about me now. So when I began acting off, Jasper had picked up on it, and it showed during his performance tonight. His distraction was what caused his partner, Oliver, to get slammed into the plexiglass.

Of all people, I expected Grayson to remain the most focused, but even he was out of it. Throughout the game, he kept tossing concerned glances at Annie, who sat in the front row next to me.

Her features were contorted in dismay from the moment she'd stepped foot into the rink. Even though I was still high on Beckham's touch, her expression was like a cold bucket of water being poured over me. At first, I'd wondered if it had something to do with the girls, but she assured me they were safe with Georgia. Everybody seemed to be out of sorts.

I was snapped out of my daze by Sebastian slamming his locker shut. Two hours after the match had ended and the boys were still mad. I didn't know what to say to them. It was clear they were taking this loss super hard. The look in their eyes was the same as when they'd lost numerous matches last year, back when Nate was their captain.

The blonde angel sighed, running a hand over his sweaty face. Grayson sent him a look that said he felt the same way. Oliver was on the bench, frowning as Jasper shrugged his backpack on. Jai was silent, unlike himself. But it was Beckham that held my attention. He didn't look too irked about their loss.

Instead, he was concerned about me.

"Losses happen," Oliver muttered, standing up and grabbing his bag. "It was one loss. We have a lot more chances to make up for it," he then glanced at me, "plus, we have the points from our fundraisers."

Sebastian nodded, listening to his teammate. "But we have to ask ourselves why we lost. Why, after so many wins, do we suddenly lose? What are we suddenly doing wrong?"

"Nothing," Beckham added, his voice guttural. "I don't want *anybody* blaming themselves for this," he said, making eye contact with each member of his team. It was just them in the locker room, the other teams having left long ago after a few words from Benson. "We lost. We'll just try harder next time."

They stayed silent, contemplating his words. They were all still cooling down after a good lecture from Benson and I knew they didn't need another. What they needed right now was support. As the coach, it was Benson's job to reprimand them. But Beckham was more than a captain; he was a friend.

"Let's go. Movie at our place."

The guys shuffled out, making sure they had their bags. The rink was empty, tired employees left to pick up what the audience had left behind. Benson stayed in his office, no doubt going through my notes, trying to do better.

"Can you drop Annie and me back at our old place?" I asked Beckham, catching up with him, and he glanced back at me, features going tense. "We have to pack up my mom's things so we can sell the house."

It was something I wasn't looking forward to, especially with the knowledge that she was no longer with us. We had to throw out our dad's shit too.

"Twenty minutes," he said, peeking over his shoulder quickly. "I'm taking Beth home to her mom to pick up the last of her clothes, and then I'm coming straight back to you, okay?"

Knowing that his parents lived in Glendale, the same neighbourhood where Beth stayed, I sighed. "Beck, there's no need to rush. You can pop in to check in on your parents if you want. We'll be fine—"

"Twenty minutes," he said, voice firm as he gripped my

hips. "Understand?" I nodded in surrender because there was no way to sway him once he had his mind set on something. "Good girl."

Beckham threw an arm over my shoulders and headed for the exit. Annie followed closely, eyes darting around nervously as Beth spoke quietly to her. The parking lot was vacant too, filled with four cars. One was Benson's, the jeep belonged to Beckham, and the other two belonged to Sebastian and Jai. Jasper and Oliver hopped into Jai's car and Grayson into Sebastian's as Beckham informed them that we'd be late. The ride was silent, Beth trying her best to get through to my sister, but to no avail. I offered the girl a smile, silently promising to figure out what was going on with her.

Beckham dropped us outside, his face a mixture of emotions, emotions that he was begging me to understand as if it was a secret message. I couldn't figure out what it all meant, struggling to even figure out what *I* was feeling. The entire night was tense, feeling like a bomb ready to go off at any second. Beth pressed a gentle kiss to Annie's lips, the latter finally cracking a smile as her girlfriend whispered something to her.

After an astoundingly long embrace from my boyfriend, Beckham drove off and I shut the door behind me, eyes taking in the place I'd once called home. Annie headed straight for our parents' room but ceased in her tracks. I followed behind her, my breath hitching.

"What?" I questioned her, glimpsing around her shoulder to stare at what had pulled such a reaction from her.

And there he was: Matthew Taylor, lounging on the couch

with a half-empty beer bottle clutched between his oil-stained fingers. There was no car in the driveway, giving us no warning of his presence. His eyes were bloodshot and slightly swollen. Younger Nyx would've questioned if he was okay, if he was hurting. But older Nyx knew that he was a manipulative bastard.

He always did that, shed a tear or two to forcefully pull empathy from his daughters. We were supposed to believe he was in despair. He was a single father with four daughters, his wife was a drug addict who'd left him. It was excuse after excuse. And back then, I pitied him. But not anymore.

I felt my back pocket for my phone, ready to call Beckham's dad to tell him Matthew had finally appeared. Slowly, he elevated his red gaze. I expected him to start screaming, even hurl the bottle at me. It was usually during one of his intoxicated stupors that he heavily mistook me for my mom. But he didn't do anything, his eyes drifting to my practically petrified older sister. As if I was watching a tennis match, I looked between the two, wondering why their stare was so intense. An entire nonverbal conversation seemed to pass.

"I thought you were on my side, Annie," he expressed after an eternity, his voice seeming to break with each syllable that fell from his parched throat. A disgusting cough followed. "You were *supposed* to be on my side, Annie." This time, his words were more firm, and if he had more strength, he probably would've yelled. My stomach felt hollow at the tension that was in the house. "But you chose her," he spat in absolute revulsion.

I took a step back, dragging Annie with me as I questioned her, "What the fuck is going on?" She appeared shellshocked, unable to let a word slip past her lips. "Annie?" I reiterated, beginning to get fearful with her silence. "Call the cops," I whispered when I heard the sloshing of beer.

My dad stood up, teetering on his legs before righting himself. He raised a quivering finger towards Annie. "*Mine*," he accentuated drunkenly. "*My* fucking daughter and you betray me?" His eyes crossed until he was goggling at my sister again, a gruff laugh leaving him in a wheeze. "You choose them?" he wailed, waving a shaking arm in my direction as tears leaked from his eyes.

But I was no longer listening. Instead, I pivoted to Annie. She was already looking at me, apology in her bottomless brown eyes. I was muddled, my world was staggering, yet I understood nothing. I didn't understand my dad's words, I never understood him when he was drunk. But there was a pang inside of my chest, one that worsened with each breath. It was like my body knew something was wrong, acting like armour before any pain could reach the beating organ in my chest.

My body was telling me to *leave*.

Pathetically, I said my sister's name again. "Annie?" She'd always been my equilibrium, kept me afloat during the storm that was our lives. However, as we gazed at one another, it felt like I was being cut loose. And there I was, drowning all over again.

A loud *thunk* reached my ears and I shifted to see my dad, sprawled out on the floor. *Unconscious*. The bottle rolled away from him, leaving a stain on the carpet that I'd seemed to spend my entire childhood scrubbing. Annie reached for me but I stepped back, shaking my head. Everything was hurting and a hug from her would shatter me. I'd cry and I didn't need tears. I needed answers.

"Nyx," she murmured, but I held my ground.

The more I thought about my dad's words, the more it seemed to make sense. And I hated it. It was wrong of me to compare abuse, but Annie had it the easiest. I always thought it was because she didn't look like our mom, but he seemed to hold her higher than any of us, Indigo falling into second place.

The words felt foreign in my mouth. "Why's he saying that you're *his* daughter?" My breathing was rackety, each breath a near pant. A choked sound left me.

She mewled in despair. "Nyxie, I swear to you I didn't know." With each step she took towards me, I backtracked. "I didn't expect to see Grandma today but she was there and she—" she inhaled shakily. Tears were streaming down her face and I curbed myself from going to wipe them away. "Grandma told me what Mom had been keeping from us." Her next words were barely audible through her tears. "I would give *anything* to not be his daughter, to not be related to a monster like him. I hate that he loves me so much. I hate that he thinks he owns me." She shook her head. "I don't want to be his."

It all flashed by my eyes in a second, every time Annie stood back, when she went to our dad instead of mom. I'd thought it was because she preferred him, held out hope that he would change. But it was his way of staking his claim, trying to isolate her from me.

"Annie," I said in a distressed tone. "Annie, you're not his. You decided that the second you stood up for me the first time."

She was in my arms a second later, weeping against my chest as I held her the same way she'd held me all these years.

"I'm sorry," she cried. "I'm sorry for all the hurt you've had to suffer at his hands," she continued, words dripping with guilt. "Grandma planned to meet me here to tell you but I didn't expect him to be here. This was supposed to go better than this and I'm so sorry."

We must've stayed in that embrace for fifteen minutes, the silence filled with my dad's intemperate snoring. My older sister pulled away, looking suddenly anxious. Her jaw clenched and unclenched continuously. I could see her teeth grinding against each other.

There were tears in her puffy eyes. "Dad's always hated you and Poppy." I let out a humourless laugh. It didn't take a genius to figure that out. "It's," she sniffled, "I don't want to hurt you any more than you have been, Nyxie. But I want you to hear the truth from me, somebody who loves you instead of *him*," she pointed at our dad, "somebody who'll only use this information to hurt you."

More. There was more to the story that I hadn't captured yet. The sympathy in Annie's gaze told me that it was going to hurt. Childishly, I wanted to tell her to keep it to herself. If it meant sparing myself the pain, I didn't want to know.

Coward. For this *one* moment, I was okay with being a coward.

Then I thought of Beckham. I thought of the future I wanted with him. *Everything*. I wanted everything with him. Being with Beckham gave me a safe space, somewhere we could construct our future. The foundation was sturdy on his part. But I couldn't put my all in, not when I was still being held back by the unanswered questions in my past.

So maybe I needed to hurt. Maybe I needed to break. Maybe I needed to have everything I assembled on the ground my dad gave me to be destroyed. I used all of my devotion, my resources to construct a future where we were enough for Matthew Taylor. But it was never enough.

Demolition was the only way. I wanted all those resources back, all that love that I gave a man who never really cared. I would use it to build a better place, a future for any kids I might one day have.

But most importantly, for *me*. Wherever the future took me and Beckham, I'd want to look back and see that I put in *everything that I had, not what I had left*. So yes, maybe I needed to break before I could build.

"Tell me," I said to Annie in the strongest voice I could muster.

She must've seen the determination in my appearance because she offered me an encouraging smile. "Indigo and I," she commenced and I frowned, "are the only children Matthew and Eliza share."

I couldn't contain the bewildered expression I sent her. "Wait, what?"

Annie took my hand in hers. "Grandma told us the truth when she said Dad knocked Mom up in their senior year," she elucidated, squeezing my hand. "But she left out the fact that they'd separated *before* I was born. Mom moved in with Grandma so she could help raise me. It was during that time when Mom was with your dad; Uncle Robbie."

My world stopped. Uncle Robbie. My dad. I thought of the stories Annie always told me. I used to call him my dad. Annie had also mentioned thinking our mom and Uncle Robbie had once been together. But she'd passed that off as childish assumptions.

"What?" I questioned dumbly, not expecting an answer.

"When we were younger," Annie continued, "I thought you called him your dad because you were so little and I took to doing the same, but Dad only ever got angry at *me* because I was old enough to know better. I thought it must've been confusing for you, being with Uncle Robbie all the time when our real dad would appear once every few months. I thought it was clear you'd gotten attached to him and Dad hadn't been upset because you were so young. I just didn't know Uncle Robbie was actually your dad, Nyxie."

There was a ringing sensation in my ears. My eyes were murky and the floor was swimming underneath me. There was nothing to hold on to. There was nothing stable to hold on to. Nothing in my life was ever stable. I couldn't hold on to anything. Annie stepped towards me, but I lurched away, muttering to myself.

It had to be a lie.

It had to be a lie. But it was all right there, plain as day to see. But we never looked too closely. We looked nothing like him, not like Annie and Indigo. Even his daughters from his second marriage looked exactly like him.

Uncle Robbie. *God.* He'd died before he'd had the chance to meet Poppy.

"I'm sorry," Annie expressed with teary eyes, thinking that

I was trying to get away from her, that I was furious with her. The misery was unmistakable in her features and she looked on the brink of breaking down. "Now that you know nothing ties you to Matthew," she said in a tremulous voice, "I only hope you won't be too angry and want to distance yourself—"

"*No*," I cut her off, shaking my head as I leaned against the wall for support. "You are my sister, whether we share a dad or not," I declared, trying to sound as firm as I could. "He," I pointed a shaking finger at the unconscious man, "is nothing to me."

I thought back to the whips, his words of absolute loathing as he slapped me around. As he shoved me into the wall. As he attempted to drown me. And then I saw my baby sister, my little Poppy, bleeding through the same thing. I watched him cut all her hair off when she broke a plate by accident. I could see myself banging on the trunk of the car where he locked her for a full night after she'd forgotten to clean her room.

And then I cried, sinking to my knees. Annie shuffled towards me, but I nudged her away. I was still wailing, my throat raw. I clambered around on the ground, seeking to find the wall so I could stand back up. But I was drifting around aimlessly. I glared at the room we were in. I took in the furniture. This was always *his* house. And the moment my mom had left, Poppy and I never belonged. He'd always made it clear, but we never picked up on it. *Ruination*. He'd said we ruined everything. We ruined his perfect family.

Something inside of me cracked. And then I was running to the kitchen. I tugged open every cupboard. I tossed every single plate against the wall. Annie was shrieking, yelling at me to stop. I exhausted every drawer, hurling the contents around. On unsteady feet, I stumbled into the bathroom and dragged out the hammer that was under the sink. And then I was blasting the metal into the walls. I delivered blow after blow, simulating his hands as he struck me.

"Nyx!" Annie wailed, weeping.

But I wasn't listening. I *couldn't.* After battering the hammer through the walls, I crammed my hand through, trying to split it apart. My hands were rattling, my face wet with tears. I smashed it through the windows, rejoicing in the melody of the fracturing. I didn't feel the cuts on my hands. I didn't feel the blood dripping down them.

For a few minutes, Annie disappeared. And I was glad. I didn't want anyone to witness my breakdown. I threw Matthew's clothes all over his room. I grabbed a scissor, hacked them apart, stitch by stitch, the way he'd done me. I stumbled towards Matthew Taylor. He was on his back, completely knocked out because of how much he'd drank.

I was quivering as I descended to my knees, throwing a leg over his body. I could feel the rise and fall of his chest beneath me. My hand went to his throat. And then I was squeezing. His breathing became laboured until he could no longer inhale. And then his eyes shot open in trepidation.

"Nyxie," he choked out, hand raising to slacken my grip. But he was powerless. His body was feeble with the booze rushing through him. My grip tautened as I watched his eyes bug out of their sockets with the scarcity of oxygen. "*Please.*"

"You're a sorry excuse for a man," I muttered. He shook his head, slobber dribbling from his mouth. His body stilled when my grip tightened.

"You won't hurt me," he conveyed through coughs. "You can't hurt me because you know I had to do what I did." I raised a brow, wondering how he could even begin to defend his abuse. "Look how you turned out. You're so strong. And it's because of me—*Fuck*!"

My fist landed on his nose with a nauseating crunch. Matthew was writhing in pain. "*Oops*," I muttered, "hand slipped, Matty." He was wailing, tears trickling from his eyes.

"Nyxie, *please*," he beseeched, choking on his vomit. I tipped his head, permitting him to cough up the alcohol he'd been living on for the past few days. He was begging me, begging, in the same way, I had when I was a little girl. I stood up, heading to the kitchen to get a glass of water to toss at his face. When I returned to the living room, Annie was standing there with wide eyes, gaping at her crying dad. Beckham was next to her, his face blank.

"You're a piece of shit, Nyxie," Matthew cried pathetically, pushing to his feet. "After *everything* I did for you and your mom. She was a bitch that ran off with Annie! Came crawling back to me years later after your dumbass dad got himself killed. I took you little blonde beasts in when you had nobody! *Nobody* wanted you!"

"No dad has a right to hurt his daughter. But I wasn't even your daughter!" I yelled over him, releasing the glass of water and it narrowly missed my foot. "I wasn't yours to break, to beat, to completely fucking *ruin!*" My words were rusted, I was shouting, sobbing. A complete fucking mess. "Do you know how fucking long it took for me to let a man touch me?!" I hollered, shoving past Beckham to get to the crying man. "You fucking broke me to the point where I could never imagine myself in a fucking relationship. For so long, I'd been *terrified* of men."

"Nyx, please," Beckham sought, but I didn't listen. He pulled me into his arms and I trembled, screams crawling up my raw throat. "I'm so sorry," he whispered, kissing my head. I turned to see Matthew trying to stabilise himself. My outrage returned, anger for all the misery he'd brought into our lives.

I pushed away from Beckham and he called my name but I wasn't listening. My body was on fire, my organs were on fire.

Matthew was glancing around, still crying. I stepped closer to him and he froze, uneasy. "You broke me," I told him. "You made me feel worthless, like I didn't deserve anything!"

"Nyxie," he wailed, switching from anger to trying and appealing to pity. "Please, your dad wouldn't have done this." I blundered at his words. "Robbie wouldn't have—"

"Don't you dare say his name!" Annie hollered, her knees staggering as she pointed an accusing finger at her dad. "You have no right to mention him." *Robbie*. The name ricocheted around in my head. *My dad*. A dad I had no memory of.

Matthew fell back down again. "He wouldn't have done this," he sobbed pathetically. "Please. Nyxie, I know you're merciful—"

"Which one am I?" I questioned, stepping closer and sinking next to him. "Merciful or ruination?" The inquiry left me in a hollow voice and he jerked. "According to you, I believe it's the latter. I *cried*, wanting you to *love* me. I wanted to know why you *hated* me, and how I could be the perfect daughter. But *you* are the problem. You've *always* been the problem. So here, look what you've done. I'm a mess. Is that what you wanted? Are you happy?"

He gulped. "Nyx, we can talk this through—"

I laughed. Loudly. "Fuck you! *Fuck you* for all that you've done. The only good thing you've ever given me was Annie and Indigo. Everything else was just misery. Did you enjoy watching me cry, huh? Did you enjoy watching Poppy cry? Did you enjoy *breaking* us?" He didn't say anything. I looked him dead in the eye. "One day, I'm going to have a house. I'm going to have kids. And I'm going to *love* them," my voice throbbed. "My kitchen will smell like cookies. The walls will be full of pictures, the fridge filled with drawings. The house will be warm, everything this place *never* was." I spared Beckham a glance. "I will have an amazing man by my side. And he'll be the father you *wish* you could be."

The tears were still falling from his face as he listened to me, having his actions hurled back at him. "Are you going to kill me, Nyxie?" he asked, whining with the discomfort in his stomach.

My throat bobbed. "No. I'll let you think about your actions, Matty. Because they all have consequences." I pushed to my feet, glancing at Beckham. "Call your dad. I assume there's a prison cell with this bastard's name on it." My hands were shaking.

Beckham ambled into my room to make the call and I held out a bloody hand to Annie. The front door opened and my grandma slipped through it, her entire appearance a mess. My chest ached at the sight of the woman that had once cared for us.

"I came as soon as I could," she told Annie. "What—" Her gaze landed on a crying Matthew Taylor. His head lolled to the side. The fucker was unconscious again. Her blue eyes filled with tears. I could see it happen, see her relive the memories. Matthew had stolen her daughter from her, stolen her grandkids and left her with nothing.

And then she lunged for him

I tackled her to the ground and she thrashed in my hold. "Grandma, stop!" I screamed, but she still resisted. She managed to escape, crawling over to Matthew with tears in her eyes. I watched her hands wrap around his throat when I dived for her again. I kept her between my legs, gripping her arms and murmuring in her ears, "Breathe. Just breathe."

She was crying, the sound growing louder when Annie sat in front of us, trying to wrap her arms around us both. Beckham emerged, sending me a subtle nod to say his dad was on his way. My grandma stayed crying, calling out for a daughter she wished she could help.

I didn't know how much time passed. My ass was numb from sitting on the floor, my grandma in my arms and Annie's arms around me. Anthony Hunt soon arrived, taking in the scene with perplexed eyes. He shared a few words with his son and I caught 'statement' amongst them. Anthony heaved Matthew over his shoulder and hauled him to his car. Slowly moving my grandma into Annie's hold, I stood up, following Beckham outside and watching his dad place Matthew in the back.

What I didn't expect, was for Anthony to pull me into

an embrace. "You'll be okay," he whispered, sharing a glance with Beckham. "When you're ready, I need to ask you a few questions, okay?" I nodded against his chest. After a soft kiss to the top of my head, he let me step back into Beckham's arms. We watched him drive off, the silence killing me.

Beckham had witnessed me at my absolute worst. I didn't know what to say. Thankfully, I didn't need to. He spun me around so I could face him, wiping my tears. Three words. He said three words. And yet it managed to set me completely at ease.

"I love you."

When we walked back inside, my grandma was on the couch, staring into space and Annie was making tea. This house held bad memories and I could see it in my grandma's features. It was prominent in her posture, the way she glanced around as if she was in a foreign land.

"I don't know what came over me," she muttered after a few seconds, looking mortified as she ran a hand over her tear-stained face. "I just saw him, after five years, and I remembered all that he did and I just—I wanted to kill him—I can't—I just—"

"I know," I concluded, feeling Beckham's grip clench around my waist. She didn't have to explain. I knew exactly what had gone through her head.

Beckham leaned down to mutter, "We have to get this blood off you." I'd forgotten what had happened when I'd gone around smashing things. I glanced at the dried blood on my hands and allowed him to lead me to the bathroom where I'd made a mess earlier. I smiled sheepishly as he grabbed a cloth and wet it.

"I'm sorry that you had to see that," I voiced, watching him cleanse my hands. He halted, gaze meeting mine. It looked like he was about to repeat what he'd been telling me for the past few days, but I spoke again. "I'm not sorry that you're here though."

He smirked, going back to his job. "Good. I'm always gonna be here, baby. No matter what. I love you."

I smiled, feeling my cheeks flush. "I love you."

A kiss was placed on my lips before he cleaned my hands in silence, using a clean cloth to then wipe my face. My heart had calmed down, my nerves no longer feeling on edge. It was weird. After all that happened, I felt a little at peace.

It was probably because I knew the devil was out of our lives now.

The sound of the front door opening again made me frown. My first thought was that my grandma was leaving. Our relationship was splintered, but I wanted to try at least. Five years was a long time. It didn't need to be extended any further. Beckham trailed me as I peeked my head into the living room just in time to see Georgia enter with Julie and my baby sisters. My grandma gasped, placing her tea aside.

Georgia stepped closer, Indigo in her arms. The little girl was watching the blonde woman with wide, confused eyes. Poppy peeked out from around Georgia, holding Julie's hand. Her blue eyes landed on the figure.

Her yell was deafening. "Grandma!" Poppy was scurrying. "Grandma! Oh my God, Grandma!"

My grandma nearly collapsed. "Poppy!" I watched my sister

surge into the woman's arms, crying and shaking. She kissed her head, squeezing her. "My little Poppy-Flower. You're so *big*. When did you get so *big*?"

Beckham rubbed my back, pulling me close against his chest. I fell into his embrace, clutching him as if he was my lifeline. Indigo asked to be let down from Georgia, and then she was walking towards us. When my grandma saw her, her knees buckled.

"Grandma?" Another word barely passed her lips before she was in the blonde woman's arms. She was crying, seeing her granddaughter for the first time after five whole years. "My name's Indigo," she stuttered nervously. "I, um, I've always wanted to meet you."

"I would know you by your scent alone," she murmured, kissing her head. "There's no need for introductions." She caught my eye over their heads. So many unsaid things passed between us. Eventually, she settled on, "My *strong* girl."

When I pulled away from Beckham, my grandma was holding Annie. They made the perfect picture, together after so long. I didn't move towards them, but I could feel Beckham's arm around my waist, keeping me steady. Annie met my gaze, uncertain compared to my optimism.

"We'll be okay," I mouthed to her. "I promise."

Chapter 32
Beckham

It had been over a week since Nyx's world had came toppling down on her, since her grandma had plunged back into her life, since Matthew had been arrested. And most importantly, over a week since she'd last seen her sisters. I knew it was picking at her, not having been isolated from them for so long before. But I also knew she needed space. It was a privilege she'd never really had. It was always problem after problem and not for one second did she think to stop and take a breather. So when she'd asked for space, I promised that I'd do my absolute best to make sure she had it. It was the least I could do after everything she'd been through.

With permission from Nyx, Benson had been acquainted with the entire situation. The two hadn't gotten along in the beginning, but when I communicated the news, it looked like he was ready to go to battle on her behalf. But Nyx didn't want a fuss. She wanted peace and quiet. So Benson took up her spot as an event planner, managing to balance it with his position as the coach. Another match down plus one fundraiser. The match had been another loss, unfortunately.

The fundraiser lacked enthusiasm, although it was a success. And many people showed up too, having heard snippets of gossip about Nyx and they wanted to see how she was doing. As if I'd let them treat my girlfriend like a new artefact in a museum.

"Where is she?"

I peeped over my shoulder at Annie as she followed me into the rink parking lot. It was the same routine every day, one I wondered if she'd ever get tired of. Personally, it was becoming vexatious, her chasing me down. And she wasn't subtle about it either. She'd yell my name until I paid attention.

"Beckham!" Annie hollered, tracing my footsteps. I disregarded her, unlocking my car. "Beckham, please!" Her voice was beseeching, and when I peered at her, I noticed tears in her brown eyes. But it wasn't going to work on me. She'd tried that days ago already and her attempt was futile. "Where is she?"

"I already explained this to you, Annie," I countered, opening the back door and flinging my bag there. After the first few days, I thought she'd have given up. I'd forgotten how stubborn Nyx and her sisters could be. "This is getting old and you know it. So stop asking me—"

"Where is my sister?" she reemphasised, looking like a madwoman. It was her signature look as of late. "It's been a week, Beck, and I haven't seen her." Her voice was staggering and so was her body. The skin underneath her eyes was a dull shade of purple whereas the rest of her face was ashen. "I'm worried."

Sighing, I pitched against the car, staring at her. "And what makes you think I know where she is?" Annie blinked owlishly at me, not having been prepared for that question. It was the first time I actually engaged in a conversation with her instead of just driving off. "Did it ever occur to you that she left because she needed space? Give her time, Annie. Her whole life was turned upside down—"

"I don't want her to go through it alone," she cut me off, becoming agitated. Her voice went a few tones higher and her pale face turned a roseate shade. Angry. She was most definitely angry. "I'm so scared it's all become too much for her. Poppy and Indie miss her. And you won't *fucking* tell me—"

"Shut up," I said placidly, and she gaped like a fish, blinking again. Her using the girls to guilt trip me was a low blow. "Just *shut up*, Annie. You're giving me a headache." I opened the driver's side of the car and she watched me jump in. "She needs time. If you haven't noticed, she just found out most of her life was a lie. Did you honestly expect her to take it well?" Her censorship said enough and I chuckled darkly. "I know she's strong, Annie, but nobody's *that* strong."

"I'm just worried," she whispered.

"I know," I nodded. "Believe me when I say she loves you all. But she needs a little more time to sort out what she's feeling. Her questions need to be answered before she can move forward."

Annie stared at me, trying to make sense of what I was saying. I could understand that she was delighted to have her grandma back, truly, but Nyx and Annie were two different people. They didn't see it the same way. And I'd rather die than let Nyx's opinion be swayed by her sister. Because I knew that would happen. Nyx would do anything to make her sisters happy, even accept her grandma back without complaint if it would satisfy them. But she wasn't ready for that. Even a blind person could see it. Maybe it would've been a different story a few weeks ago, when she'd been excited about the prospect of her grandma returning.

But not now, not after what she'd just found out.

There was too much heartbreak, too many unspoken feelings and unaddressed issues. Until Nyx could disentangle everything she was feeling inside, she'd just have to stay away. One little tug in the wrong direction could compress the cluster to the point where she'd never untangle it. She needed time to sort through it, pick on each little knot with careful precision. Only she knew how to get herself out of that mess.

Submissively, Annie moved out of the way, enabling me to shut the door. I didn't feel guilty, not when I knew Nyx spent every night screaming into her pillow. She grieved for a dad she couldn't remember, and a dad who beat her.

Their house was sold, their things long moved out. The girls were still with Georgia and Ms Lewis was trying to adopt them. Annie hadn't been staying with us, finding her sister's absence too much, so she'd been staying full-time with Beth at her new place for the time being.

Nyx would only pop into campus to write her exams, seeing as we'd been in the final stretch of the winter quarter. Exams had given us something else to think about. Even the boys were relieved to be studying instead of practising. The quarter had ended a day ago and the brief break from everything was something we all needed. I chose to ignore the fact that the next quarter started next week.

I turned up the radio and rolled down the windows, needing to calm myself down after my daily discussion with Annie. When I stopped at a red light, I sent Grayson a quick text to let him know I wouldn't be home this weekend, instead, going to visit my parents.

Seeing all that Nyx went through made me more appreciative of what I had. I had a mom who loved to annoy the fuck out of me and a dad who was always ready with a good lecture if I behaved like an asshole. After a pleasant drive, I parked in front of the house and hopped out of my car, moving to get the bags that I'd packed last night. Without knocking, I entered the house, immediately getting a whiff of muffins. My mom was always fucking baking.

"Hammy!" she exclaimed upon noticing me and I rolled my eyes although there was a grin on my lips. Dressed in a picturesque apron and covered in flour, she looked a mess. "How nice of you to stop by."

Enclosing an arm around her, I pressed a kiss to her head and wiped away some chocolate that was stuck to the side of her face. "Hey, Mom. How was your day?"

My mom frowned at me, crossing her arms. I winked and she shook her head with a smile. "Don't pretend you're here to see me. She's in the living room." With an appreciative nod, I heeded her directions and went to the living room. The curtains were drawn and the TV was playing something although it was mute.

On the couch sat Nyx, a fleecy blanket enveloped around

her and her hair in a messy knot atop her head. She was staring off into space, her face red and eyes puffy. My heart clenched.

"There's my baby," I hummed in a soothing tone and she looked up. The smile she gave me was breath-taking. I thudded down next to her, and without a word, she crawled into my lap. Bandaging my arms around her, I inhaled her familiar strawberry scent. "How are you?"

Nestling into my hold, she responded, "I was just about to ask you that. How's the boys?" The guilt was apparent in her expression. Every day she would tell me that she'd hated leaving Benson on his own like that, no matter how much I assured her that he hadn't minded. "I miss them."

If only she knew how silent it'd been without her. We'd gotten used to her yelling insults when we made dumb mistakes. Benson's professional remarks never really helped. It was Nyx's taunts that really did the trick, and Benson just didn't have it.

"They miss you too," I told her, kissing her head. "Even Sebastian."

Without Nyx, it was like something was missing. She'd become part of the team, one of our own. Everyone could feel her absence. Even the guests at the fundraiser had noticed her disappearance. Her phone suddenly lit up from its place on the coffee table. The screen showcased a funny picture of Annie, and I felt Nyx stiffen in my hold.

"You don't need to answer that, baby."

She sighed. "I *miss them.*"

Her words were a little whisper. She didn't need to tell me that she missed her sisters. It was evident to everyone. Nyx had been staying with my parents for the past week, after my dad commanded that she come to them if she needed anything. My mom told me that Nyx would cry herself to sleep or call out to one of her sisters. It had taken a while for her to get used to being in a room alone, having shared one with Annie for years and then rooming with me at my place. When my dad worked the night shift, my mom would sleep in the guest room where Nyx was.

"I know you do," I answered, spreading a calming hand over her back. "But I don't want you deciding things based on what everybody else wants. You've been doing that for too long. Just this once, what do *you want?*"

Nyx went silent for a moment, pondering my words. "At first, I wanted my original plan back," she familiarised me, squirming with my sweater. "I wanted to buy an apartment and live there with my sisters, give them the life they've always wanted. But now my grandma," her voice broke, "my grandma is back. And that changes everything." She took in a deep breath. "Don't get me wrong, I love that she's back. I missed her so much, but with her back, I feel useless. My sisters turned to me in their time of need, always. Now they don't have to," she snorted, "I'm selfish, I know."

When her phone buzzed again, I stretched over and flipped it around. Five missed calls from Annie. "You're not selfish."

Nyx was the furthest thing from selfish. Everything she did was for her sisters. I was afraid to ask when she last did something for herself. The answer would most definitely upset me.

She gulped audibly, staring at the phone. "All these years, I did my best to protect my sisters, to love them when my mom couldn't, when my grandma wasn't there. Now she's back and it just feels like I did everything for *nothing*. Who needs Nyx when Grandma is back, huh?" Her head shook. "It's silly—"

"Your feelings aren't silly," I stated in a steady tone, seeing my mom enter the room with muffins. With a tender smile, she deposited it on the table and then walked away, pledging to bring back some hot chocolate. "Everyone's depended on you for so long. Of course it's gonna feel weird without that weight. I'm sure you had to get used to being in charge when your mom left. You made mistakes, learned to care for your sisters and be the adult until it became a second nature to you. The same applies here, you have to get used to Ms Lewis being back, giving her duties back to her, learning to be just Nyx. You've been a mother and a big sister, now you have to remember to be a daughter again. It's gonna take time, baby."

Nyx reached for a muffin, sniffing it before taking a nibble as she nodded to my previous words. "I'm glad she's back because now Pops and Indie have somebody else who loves them unconditionally. But with her comes answers I'm afraid of. All this time, I thought Matthew was my dad. I don't even remember my actual dad," she sniffled again, "I have so many questions, Beck." She took another bite, licking her lips. "I'm not ready for more answers. I'm just not."

I kissed the side of her head. "And that's okay."

"I'm gonna try," she announced, picking up a second muffin. "I'm gonna try, for my sisters. I have my own questions that I need to ask. Just, *not now.*"

After a few minutes, my mom stumbled back into the room, looking sheepish. "Do you mind moving this upstairs? I forgot I have a book club meeting in five."

I groaned. "*Mom.*"

Whenever she hosted the meeting, she made me stand in front of her friends so they could gush over me and how much I'd grown. I abhorred it. Some even still pinched my cheeks until they were red and gave me candy.

Nyx stood up, ignoring me as I reached out for her. "Don't be a baby, *Hammy*," she taunted, striding around the table with some muffins in her arms. I watched her leave, frowning, and my mom cackled, shoving two flasks of hot chocolate into my arms. With another groan, I followed Nyx to my room, seeing her staring out of the window, the muffins stacked on my desk. I placed the flasks next to it.

"What are you staring at?" I questioned, moving behind her and pulling her back against my chest. Following her gaze, I saw River seated on the lawn, soaking up the rays of the sun. That was known as her spot, the place she went to in order to get out of the house. "Have you spoken to here yet?" Nyx and River had opposing personalities, but hey, opposites attract.

She shook her head. "When she sees me taking out the trash, she turns this weird shade of red and runs away." That sounded like River.

I snorted. "That's because she knows who you are."

"Your girlfriend?" Nyx pondered out loud, turning around to face me. The smirk was inevitable, always appearing when she referred to herself as my girlfriend.

"Annie's sister," I corrected. The puzzlement on her face was amusing. "Back when we all thought something was going on between Annie and Grayson, Sebastian and I were talking to my mom about it. River overheard the conversation." I watched Nyx's jaw drop, realisation dawning on her as she pivoted to gaze out the window again. "From what my mom's told me, I'm pretty sure River's been in love with Gray since she was five."

Nyx cooed and I snorted again. "That's fucking *adorable.* Why aren't they together?"

My smile dropped slightly as I thought of my best friend. Nyx wrinkled her nose when she noticed my expression. "Sebastian might be called an angel because of his looks, but everything about River is angelic," I paused, wondering how to phrase my words, "Gray, he'd never go for somebody angelic, probably because he's the furthest from it."

"Oh please," Nyx scoffed, seeming to find my excuse preposterous. "Grayson's the sweetest out of all three of you." I gave her a look. "I'm serious, bro. I hated him the least because he's always been the nicest to me."

Rolling my eyes, I voiced, "Well, *bro.* He's *my* best friend, moved to the neighbourhood around when we were in middle school. I'm pretty sure I can tell what's a facade and what's not." She was quiet, trying to find the deeper meaning behind my words. "River's too good for him, and before you chew me out, that's his words, not mine."

Nyx stared at me intensely. "Gray *knows* River's in love with him?"

I shook my head. "I don't think he sees her as anything more than a sister. He probably thinks it's familial love."

She winced, glancing one last time at River. "That's tough."

Gripping her waist, I spun her to face me again. "Enough about River. I'm still stuck on the fact that you think Gray's sweeter than me—"

"That's so one minute ago, bro," she expressed, walking away from me and I smiled, watching her devour another muffin.

The moon gazed down at me as I slumped back onto my towel, arms curled behind my head. A chilly breeze wafted through the backyard, providing me with some relaxation. I could hear splashes coming from the pool, a melodic sound that'd been playing for the past ten minutes. My shorts clung to my body, the material becoming frozen the longer I lay in the icy breeze. But I didn't mind.

Other than the moon, the backyard was lit up by strings upon strings of fairy lights, set up by my mom. She'd insisted she had them laying around, but I knew it was a lie. My mom was never a great liar. A table stood to one side, embellished with different snacks and drinks. Again, my mom had claimed she had it laying around, but I'd seen the grocery bags in the trash earlier.

I gazed up at the stars, trying to spot some constellations. It was always a pretty sight, like sparkles scattered across a dusky fabric. I turned my head slightly to look at the clock against the door. Just a few more minutes before it was midnight. My attention was clutched by the silence. Sitting up, I glanced towards the pool, where Nyx was. I didn't see her.

Panicking, I stood up and walked to the edge, peering in. But I still couldn't see her. Just as I was about to call out her name, a hand coiled around my ankle. I bounced nearly a foot in the air and was met by boisterous laughter. Nyx was shifting wet hair from her face, beaming up at me.

"You bitch," I chuckled, splattering her with water as she paddled away. "You fucking scared me."

"That was kinda the point, bro," she shrugged, drifting on her back. "Get in here."

I shook my head at her, still grinning. I'd gotten so used to the perpetual frown, that it was weird seeing her smile. The week away from everyone was doing her good. Her sisters had their grandma and she could finally focus on herself, and heal on her own without having to take everybody else into consideration.

Sitting down at the edge of the pool, I placed my feet in the water. Nyx swam towards me, settling her arms on my knees. I swept the wet hair from her face. "Have you decided when you're coming back?" I urged, towing a strand and watching her wince.

She shrugged. "I was thinking next week, maybe?" Her voice held a veiled inquiry and I groaned.

"Nyx, I'm not gonna tell you when you should come back. That's an answer you need to figure out on your own."

"Fine, then next week," she declared doggedly, trying to look as confident in her answer as possible. "I miss the boys, I miss my sisters and I miss *school*. I never thought I'd be saying that, but I miss catching on shit in class with Nai." Her eyes went hazy. "Fuck, Nai. I miss her so much."

I gradually eased into the pool, sighing at the feel of the chilled water. "She misses you too. I'm sure she'll be happy to see you back, taunting people again. I miss that you."

"I do too," she said with a rueful smile. "I'm gonna get her back. I'm gonna get my life back on track and do what's best for me." She'd had another few hours to herself earlier to contemplate things and I was curious to hear the conclusion she came to.

Pushing away from the wall, I paddled to the other end of the pool and she followed. "Good for you, baby. You know you'll always have a place here, right?"

She snorted. "I know. But I feel too much like a third wheel. Did you know your parents have a date night every few days? It's adorable." I nodded because the two were still in love after all these years. "But I was thinking about getting my own place. It's high time I stand on my own two feet. I mean, instead of thinking of my grandma back as an intrusion, maybe it's a good thing?" I quirked a brow, wading through the water. "Because Indigo and Poppy have her now—"

"And now you can do what you want," I finished and she grimaced.

"Why the fuck does everything I say sound selfish?" Nyx exclaimed in an annoyed voice. "First I wanted everybody to depend on me and not my grandma. Now, it's like I want them to depend on her so I can be free. Fuck," she buzzed, leaning against the side of the pool to catch her breath. "I just can't make up my mind."

I swam closer, enveloping my arms around her waist. "You're torn between freedom, something you've never had, and wanting to be there for your sisters. It's gonna take a while to get used to the fact that they no longer only have you—"

"Yeah, I know. It's just a difficult concept, sorry if I sound repetitive." I pressed a kiss to her lips and she beamed. "I dunno, I guess I shouldn't try to plan everything out. Maybe I should just let things play out. What's meant to find me will find me, right?"

I kissed her again, tugging at the string of her bikini. "Exactly."

She screeched when a deafening alarm went off, followed by hysterical screaming. The backdoor shot open and my mom ran out, launching confetti everywhere. My dad followed closely behind, carrying a huge cake with candles. Nyx watched with tears in her eyes. She turned to look at me, lips parted in astonishment.

"Happy birthday, baby."

"I—you planned this?" she stammered, watching them set the cake on the table. My dad disappeared for a few seconds, carrying gifts that were dropped by the team over the past few days. One by one, they'd sneakily delivered it. We all knew she wouldn't be back by the time her birthday approached, but we still wanted her to enjoy her day, to know that she had all of us to come back to.

"The 27th of March is just as special to me as it is to you," I whispered, kissing her cheek. "Race you to the cake." I didn't give her a chance, already swimming to the other end of the pool. But when I got there, Nyx was already at the table, having climbed out to run. I laughed at her move and she grinned foolishly. My mom planted a party hat on her head, followed by a birthday sash. I climbed out, sauntering to the table where the cake was.

"You gonna make a wish?"

She glanced at all of us. And then shook her head. She blew out the candles, then shrieked when my mom thumped her face into the cake. "Happy birthday, sweetheart," my mom spoke with a roar, rubbing the icing all over her face. "The big twenty. How do you feel?"

"When you were twenty, we were already trying for Hammy, weren't we?' My dad tantalised, tossing an arm around my mom. Nyx's eyes widened and she blushed. I picked up the rest of the cake and smashed it into my dad's face. He pitched back before plunging into the pool. Nyx slapped a hand over her mouth to stop the laughs from escaping. "Asshole of a son! Helen, come help me." When my mom reached out a hand, he yanked her into the pool.

"Saw that coming from a mile away," I told Nyx, watching my mom try and swim away from my dad. "She falls for it every fucking time." But Nyx was no longer watching them. She was gazing up at me, tears in her blue eyes. Happy tears, of course. She'd done enough deplorable sobbing to last her a lifetime. "I know it's not the best birthday because your sisters aren't here but—"

Her arms went around my neck and I chuckled at the icing that was still all over her face. In the background, I could hear my mom cussing out my dad.

"I love you." That shut me up. She smiled at my quietness. "And I'm so damn thankful for you and all that you represent. I've got a long way of healing to go from here, but it makes it all the more easier to know that I have you by my side. I *love you.*"

I bent down, pulling her up so she could bind her legs

around my waist. Clearing some icing from her face, I muttered, "I love you too."

She tilted her head, lips settling on mine and I held her tighter. I disregarded my mom's wolf-whistle, grinning into the kiss. I overlooked my dad as he questioned my mom if she wanted to recreate what Nyx and I were doing. I could feel Nyx convulsing with laughter before collapsing into a fit of giggles when my dad said we wanted to get started on making Hammy Junior, or better yet, Pork Chop.

"Remember when you said that a star in a binary system could explode into a supernova?' Nyx inquired suddenly and I nodded. "I thought it's happened to me before. But I think this was it. I called it toxic when you said the other star gives off some of its mass to help the fallen star rebuild. It's not toxic, though, is it?"

Shaking my head, I stated, "It's not. It's something entirely different."

She nodded. "Law of attraction or love?"

I grinned. "Who cares? Either way, I'm winning."

Chapter 33

Nyx

I'd spent years imagining the moment I'd see my mom again. It was something I looked forward to; an end goal. I'd envision what I'd say to her, to torment her the way she had hurt us when she'd left. I could remember Poppy's screams. Sometimes I still heard it in my nightmares. I had it all planned out, truly. How could I not? When she'd first left, there was so much sorrow inside of me that it constantly felt as if I was suffocating. The first part of my plan involved questions, so *many* questions. Why did you leave us? Were we not enough? Did you not love us? Why would you leave us with him?

It was the inquiries of a girl who experienced so many controversial things and all she wanted were answers; answers that she never got. I became tired of seeking those answers and decided to make my own.

But as time went on, as I saw Matthew take his hatred out on Poppy and me, as I watched Indigo grow up without a mother, the sadness dissipated. A surge of bitter anger supplanted it, not even a blazing one. *Ice cold.* Fire meant emotion, passion. And I felt *nothing* for her. All of my emotions were solidified into little shards that I wanted to impale her with, emotionally, of course.

I'd planned to tell her about the girls she had left behind. I'd wanted her to know that Annie was a brilliant cook and could very well open her own restaurant one day. I'd wanted our mom to know that Poppy was fucking amazing at volleyball and that Indigo had a personality that could rival all the entertainers in the world. And me, I'd wanted her to know that I was tough, that I could rise to the occasion and protect my sisters like I always wanted to. I wasn't frail, wasn't the porcelain doll Matthew had made me out to be, a doll he'd smashed and glued together to his heart's content.

But then she'd gone and died.

What I had now was a grandma who'd been taken from us. My tongue felt too heavy for my mouth. It was difficult to hold onto my anger when it seemed like the universe was paying me back for the anguish I'd been through. There was just confusion now. Because I knew nothing about my life and who I was. The air in the place felt too muggy and my feet felt pulverised in my boots. I was all too aware of how wet my mouth was, of the blood rushing to my head and the sound of the clock on the wall. Each tick sounded through the tense air like a bomb. Yet, neither of us said anything.

The apartment was larger than I expected and situated in a bustling part of the city. It was a different kind of noise compared to a neighbourhood, and I could just picture Indigo waking up early, rushing to the window to watch people go about their morning once my grandma adopted them. My heart clenched at the thought of her. I pushed aside the guilt, telling myself that space was what I needed. It had been my mantra for the past week.

I need space.

I'd always made decisions based on what was best for everybody else. And I *couldn't* do that this time. Just this *once*, I needed to think about what I *needed*. And the answer was space. So I trampled that guilt, buried it and forced myself to not look back. Yes, I missed my sisters, but I also missed myself. I missed the sarcastic Nyx who taunted people. If Matthew couldn't dim my light over the years, I couldn't let a small situation like getting answers throw me off. I couldn't allow it.

My grandma sat on a pretty brown loveseat, her hands placed gently on her knee and head tilted as she gazed at me. She'd left an awkward teen behind and was now looking at a woman. Her blue gaze was piercing, and I turned away, staring at the numerous pictures of my sisters and me that bordered the walls.

I frowned. Many of them were old pictures of us, but some were recent. There was a picture from Indigo's recital and one from Poppy's last volleyball match. I swallowed roughly when I saw one that Annie had taken of me on my first day at USC. Annie and I were smiling like idiots at the camera.

Afraid that I'd lose my nerve, I said, "Tell me about my dad."

My grandma stopped, a fracture appearing in the peaceful facade she put out. Even I was stunned at how loudly I'd spoken. I might as well have just screamed. Slowly, she stood up and travelled towards a bookshelf. I watched as she kneeled, ransacking through a little box.

When she returned, she held out a tiny photo of a man with ginger hair and soothing green eyes. It triggered nothing. "Robert Aster." Her voice quivered again.

With trembling hands, I took the picture from her. My head was whirling. I felt like I was on a boat, crossing wild waves. My throat clogged and I could feel every hair on my arms rise. I looked at the picture as if it was a piece of gold that I'd just dug up.

My dad.

He was beaming at the camera, his eyes creasing at the sides in the same way that Poppy's did. I sniffled, repeating his name before I realised something. "Aster is Greek for—"

"For star," my grandma concluded with a watery laugh, dabbing underneath her eyes. "Nyx Aster. His little night star, he called you." The discomfort in my chest grew tremendously and I worried that I was about to go into cardiac arrest. "I always thought of him as a son. He was like a breath of fresh air after dealing with Matthew and Eliza," she proceeded, returning to her seat and allowing me to keep the picture.

Like me, she tried to feign indifference. "Is this the part where Matthew knocks my mom up?" I urged, running a thumb over my dad's smile as I remembered what Annie had told me.

She nodded, looking down at her lap and fidgeting with her fingers. "There's more to it than that, Nyx." Her shoulders were stiff with strain. "Eliza has always been obsessed with

Matthew, claimed to be in love with him. For what reason? I have no idea. She spoke about him all the time, throughout high school." Her eyes met mine. "But I was soothed by the knowledge that Matthew didn't return her feelings." Her voice broke. "I didn't know how obsessed my daughter was until it was too late. Scraps, she'd take *scraps* from Matthew as long as he gave her attention. She let him treat her like a dog, only ever calling her when he needed his bed warmed. As her mother, I was horrified."

"I'm assuming Annie was the outcome of these nights."

She nodded, looking slightly ashamed. "Matthew claimed Eliza swore she was on birth control but she lied—"

"*Shit*," I mumbled to myself. I didn't want to sympathise with Matthew, didn't want to understand him. Because no reason was ever good enough for abuse. But his anger towards my mom and his belief that she'd ruined his life—it was all beginning to add up.

Her lips quirked slightly at my muttered curse. "His parents disowned him because they didn't want anything to do with him and his supposed bastard. Your mom ruined his life by forcing her dreams of being with him. He didn't care for Eliza nor the baby, a fact that greatly upset her."

"And of course she didn't give up," I mumbled, frowning. If only she'd been that persistent when we needed her to get us out of Matthew's clutches.

"She did, actually," my grandma muttered. "She cut herself off from Matthew and dedicated her time to Annie and finding a job. Robbie was the son of a friend of mine and had been part of our lives since the day he was born." My breath hitched.

"He was ten times the man Mathew is. Without even blinking, he would babysit Annie whilst your mom went job searching. He'd drive me around town when I needed to get out of the house. He'd even take Indigo to school—" Her eyes teared up at the mention of her youngest daughter, the first to leave her. "Like I said, Robbie was a breath of fresh air. It wasn't a wonder your mom fell in love with him or that they ended up together."

I glimpsed back at the picture I held as my grandma sent me a soft smile. "Why does it sound like you're saying that with guilt?"

"Because I think your mom loved what Robbie represented; a good man. It gave her hope that Matthew would pull up his socks and upgrade from monthly visits to proposing marriage."

My heart gave a weird squeeze. "Did Robbie love her?"

My grandma shrugged. "He loved everybody, whether they deserved it or not. He had no regard for Matthew though. I had to make sure they never ran into each other during one of Matthew's visits."

"I'm finding it hard to believe that my mom didn't care about Matthew," I added suspiciously. For my mom to have gone back to an abusive asshole, she had to have been obsessed. What my grandma was saying, it didn't sound like the woman I'd known.

"Maybe she did, maybe she didn't. But I tried to limit the contact between them. I didn't want Eliza to be pulled back to him. And Matthew didn't really care either, so that helped. He only visited out of duty to Annie."

Frowning, I mumbled, "Poor Annie."

My grandma shook her head with a smile filled with

memories. "I didn't pity her. Robbie loved her more than Matthew ever could. He was a father before he even realised it, before you even came along. But boy, when you did," she grinned, "I'd never seen him that happy."

My mouth felt dry. "Annie's always reminding me about how much he loved me."

"He did. He loved you *so* much, Nyxie. I remember he took you everywhere with him. Your birth healed wounds he didn't even know he had—wounds inflicted by your mom." My jaw slackened in shock. "She asked him to not kiss or hold her in front of Annie in fear of confusing the poor girl. That should've been my first hint Eliza still cared what Matthew thought. He'd question Annie during visits, and he didn't want her to confuse Robbie for him; her dad. Eliza complied. Robbie didn't think much of it because he may have been Uncle Robbie to Annie, but he was still your dad."

"So my mom didn't want to give Annie the impression that her and Robbie were together?" I asked slowly, realising that she'd had that impression regardless.

She nodded. "Annie was still young, didn't understand romantic notions nor give much thought to it so the excuse was pathetic. Robbie knew that, which was probably why it hurt. As the years went on, I saw my little girl returning, Eliza was happier and Matthew's visits were becoming less frequent."

I changed my position on the couch, feeling my ass go comatose. "Then what happened?"

I watched her blink away tears. "Life was going well. Then Indigo got cancer." She stared at me for a long moment and then swallowed. "Your mom was never the same after Indigo got sick and it affected all of her relationships. Matthew took that as an opportunity to dig his claws into her."

Glancing at the photo, with a shaky voice, I asked, "And him?"

The silence was excruciating as I waited for an answer. Then she articulated. "Just after your seventh birthday, he'd taken you to the park. I remember you being sad because your parents were fighting. Robbie was worried about Eliza and the baby she carried but all she cared about was the fact that Matthew was lonely, that he had nobody and that they should help him. Eliza took Annie to visit Matthew. So your dad took you out for the day, even bought some clothes for your new sibling." My breathing slowed down. "A truck collided with his car," she paused, holding my gaze.

My breath left me in one whoosh. Although I knew what happened, it struck me all the same. Maybe it was because this time, it meant much more. This wasn't just Uncle Robbie. This was my dad. I couldn't breathe. Not at all. My eyes prickled and I blinked rapidly, not wanting to cry in front of her. I'd done enough crying over the past few weeks.

Whilst I tried to gather my thoughts, my grandma went back over to the box by the bookshelf. I disregarded her, feeling the lump push its way up my throat, triggering more tears. My dad wasn't even dead for long before my mom had gone back to Matthew.

Before she'd fucking *married* him.

"And she just went back to Matthew?" I asked, my disgust obvious.

She seemed slightly ashamed. "I hated her for it. But she

wouldn't listen, claimed you girls needed a father more than ever. I pitied both you and Poppy because you wouldn't know your dad." Her next words made bile crawl up my throat. "I know the amnesia made things worse for you because you couldn't remember the man your mom was trying to replace. One of the first symptoms we detected was that you couldn't remember what occurred *before* the accident. And you had great difficulty accessing older memories. They said it'd get better as time went on, but living with Matthew didn't really help."

"Get better?' I questioned.

She nodded. "We'd have to keep bringing up some things in your past as you grew older and I tried my best while I was still part of your life. But Matthew forbid it." Her gaze was remorseful. "Although, it's never too late to try."

A hand was in front of me. She was holding out another picture. Breathing laboriously, I took it from her and flipped it around. Staring back at me were two faces, mine and my dad's. I looked no older than five, donning a black dress with little stars on it. My dad had me in his arms, pointing at the camera and grinning. He was no doubt telling me to smile before the picture was taken. His green eyes rivalled my blue ones in brightness, like the sun gleaming directly onto a fresh leaf.

As if the picture triggered something within me, I could retrieve the moment of the picture almost perfectly. I could hear him. I could *hear* his voice, light and filled with love.

Smile for the camera, pretty girl.

And then I smiled, my mom capturing the moment in a timeless picture. I remembered it perfectly. And I was sure there were millions of memories with him I was suppressing because of trauma.

My grandma must've seen the recognition in my eyes because she responded, "I have an entire box of pictures of the two of you." I raised my head, feeling tears streaming down my cheeks. "Maybe it'll jog your memory? Annie was his daughter in every way but blood. But you, *you* were completely his. He was obsessed with you, could never put you down long enough for me to change your diaper."

She handed me another picture. In this one, I appeared at least two years old. I was asleep on my dad's chest, and he was knocked out too. Drool was trickling from my mouth and onto his bare chest. I looked closely, and on the left side of his chest, right where his heart was, were dark words tattooed into the skin. *Nyx Aster*, followed by my birthday. Daddy's girl. I was a daddy's girl.

"Thank you," I spoke after a while, clearing my tears. "For giving me clarity." She nodded, muttering that I could keep the photos of my dad. "Why'd you stay away?" Besides the restraining order, I wanted to add.

"I didn't want to," she responded smoothly, honestly. "I only wanted what was best for you girls and that best was *not* with Matt and Eliza. When I tried to do something, my own *daughter* took out a restraining order against me. Our justice system is pathetic and ends up hurting some people more than helping them." She raised a hand to dab at her eyes. "Regardless, the journey was dreadful, tumultuous for *all* involved. I just hope we can get better now, to heal. That's all I want."

Her words struck something deep within me because it was what I wanted too. "Time," I hummed, catching her attention.

"I'm gonna need time before everything will be okay."

Teary eyes followed her smile. "Time. I can give you time." We stared at one another for a moment. Understanding passed between us.

The doorbell rang suddenly and my nerves spiked, not anticipating her to have had visitors. She hopped to her feet and hastened to the door. When it opened, I watched her greet whoever was on the other side with enthusiasm, pushing all grief from her expression.

My heart plummeted as I saw her lead Matthew's other wife into the living room, accompanied by the two little girls that looked like Indigo. I picked up my bag and ducked out of the room, hiding behind my bag and swerving around them to move to the door. It was rude of me to not greet, but I was in too much shock. My grandma excused herself and followed me into the hallway.

"What the hell?" I hissed, hoping the woman didn't recognise me from that time I'd beaten up Matthew's car. That would make things a little too awkward.

I slipped the photos into my bag as my grandma gently shut the door behind her so they couldn't hear our conversation. She admonished my language and I rolled my eyes. Somebody needed to remind her that I was a grown woman.

"Fiona is her name," she said gently. "I'm helping her get through this. Matthew left her with next to nothing, having gambled a lot of her money whilst he was in hiding. She needs as much support as she can get. I won't let her do it on her own."

I nodded again, like an idiot. "That's good."

She smiled and I was about to awkwardly walk away when she stopped me. I raised a brow and she cleared her throat.

"I just wanted to wish you a happy belated birthday." I stilled. "It's been twenty years since you blessed our lives. Your dad would be proud of the woman you've become."

I didn't say it, but that was the best birthday present she could've given me. I'd spent years trying to be the ideal daughter to a man who didn't deserve it. He'd made me believe there was something wrong with me. But I had a dad. I had a dad, and he had loved me with everything that he was. I didn't get the chance to properly know him. Poppy didn't even get the chance to meet him. But he loved us, and that was a balm for all the scars Matthew had left us with.

"You wanna say a few words?" Annie asked, standing beside the little pile of dirt that topped off where our mom was buried. Her tombstone wasn't ready yet. All that was there was a little board with her information on it.

It was sad, I had to admit.

Beckham stood to the side, arms wrapped around a sombre Julie. Georgia was with them and so was our grandma. There were some benches that were occupied by Nailea, Beth and Grayson. Sebastian chose to stand, leaning uncomfortably against a tree. Although my mom's funeral had already passed, Georgia suggested that it would be a good idea if we all went to make peace with her—so we could move on.

Poppy was the first to step forward after Annie's inquiry,

all cosy in her thick jacket to combat the cold weather. I'd had a long talk with her the other night. She was old enough to understand what was happening, and I didn't want to keep her in the dark. She'd cried, as I'd expected, but along with that tears came relief.

"I'm sorry that we weren't enough," my blonde sister began, her hand clutched in mine. Immediately, I saw Georgia and my grandma wince. "I'm more sorry that you didn't get to see what happened to us. When you left, I was seven years old." Her lower lip quivered and I heard her sniffle. "I don't really remember you and I've stopped forcing myself to. I'm turning thirteen soon," her voice cracked. "I'm sorry you can't see me now. But I just want you to know that I no longer flinch when a door slams," she uttered proudly. "I'm not scared anymore. And I think that's something to be proud of. I think I'm probably the angriest—"

"Poppy," I intervened when I felt her begin to shake with rage, but my grandma stopped me.

She gave me an encouraging smile. "Let her bury it. It's time."

Poppy looked up at me. The two of us had been through the most with Matthew because of our mom. I couldn't imagine her carrying that much hatred for the rest of her life. So I nodded. She took in a deep breath.

"I have a lot of anger inside me. Grandma says it's because I was abandoned. But I don't think I was. I think I was freed from you. I only wish you could've had the same freedom from whatever tormented you." She stepped forward, crouching down to place a stuffed bunny on the dirt. "You gave this to me to protect me from the dark. It's time to give it back because I know it's dark where you are right now."

She didn't say anything else, moving over to stand by Julie. Her shoulders were shaking and she wouldn't meet anyone's gaze. Annie seemed to be composing herself.

"Indie," she looked down at the girl. "Would you like to go next?"

She shrugged. "How do I say bye to someone I didn't know?"

A loud crack of thunder filled the silence. I closed my eyes, feeling my stomach clench. Annie looked like she was fighting to find the right words. Neither Georgia nor my grandma looked willing to open their mouths, heartbreak keeping their words back. I glanced around, spotting Beckham consoling Poppy, the latter holding him as if she would sink to the ground if he let go. Julie was rubbing her back.

Grayson tipped his head, motioning for Beth to move forward. With a sigh, the tall woman stood up from her seat next to Nailea and moved over to my youngest sister.

"I don't think I knew my mom either and she didn't know me. At least, she refused to know me." She spared Annie a meaningful glance. "I've been putting this off because I didn't want to accept it, but I guess it's time to say goodbye to my mom too."

Indigo pouted in concern. "Is she dead?"

Beth smiled sadly. "To me. Like your mom, she didn't take the time to know her daughter. Which is a pity because we're both awesome." Indigo giggled. "So let's say goodbye together."

"You go first."

"Okay," Beth said. Instead of staring at the pile of dirt, she closed her eyes. "I'm sorry that our definitions of love aren't the same. Your love seeks to restrain. I know now what love is supposed to be. And I'm sorry you couldn't know it with me." She opened her eyes, a singular tear slipping down her cheek.

It was Indigo that wiped it away. She looked at where my mom's tombstone would soon be. "I'm awesome and I'm sorry you couldn't know me." That pulled some laughter from our group and Beth grinned, standing up with Indigo in her hold.

Annie slipped her hand into Beth's before saying, "I've already made my peace at the funeral." Her gaze landed on me, everyone seemingly holding their breath. "You ready?"

I licked my suddenly dry lips, stepping forward slightly. My heart thrummed restlessly, urging me to do something. I stared down at where the hole in the ground once was. My mom was buried there. Arms that I would once burrow into were now six feet under the ground. And I wasn't sad. I couldn't summon that pain at the death of my mom.

"When Georgia first told me you were dead, I wasn't sad," I said, staring down at my feet. "The guilt came next. I felt guilty because you're my mom and I'm supposed to mourn you. But it's not me that should feel guilty." I looked at the board with her name. "It's you. You should feel guilty because you have a daughter that doesn't care for you. Ask yourself why." Thunder crackled above us again, telling me to speed things up before it started pouring. Annie settled a hand on my back. "The sadness that I feel right now, it's not mine. I think it's yours."

The first drop of rain hit. "I think it's because you understand that most of my scars fade with you not being here. And that's alright. That's okay." Thunder crackled again. "I hope you're at peace. Because I am. We all are."

I didn't know how long I stood there, the rain beating down onto the earth. Georgia led my grandma and younger sisters to her car, mentioning something about dinner at her place. Poppy wouldn't let go of Beckham so he was forced to ride with them. He sent me a look and I nodded, a small smile on his face. Pride filled my chest as he picked Poppy up, carrying her to Georgia's minivan.

My mom had brought a man into our lives, and he'd hurt us in a way that I'd never forget. I'd brought a man into my sisters' lives, but he loved them. He loved them almost as much as he loved me. The vast difference between me and her made me want to scream in relief. The first step to her downfall was choosing Matthew. Being constantly told that I was exactly like her by Matthew, I think I'd proved him wrong by choosing somebody like Beckham.

The rain drenched me completely and I watched Sebastian hop into Beckham's car, having to drive it because the owner couldn't. Grayson followed him, beckoning for Beth and Annie to follow. My sister squeezed my shoulder.

"You coming?"

I shook my head. "I need a moment."

Nailea walked towards me, her curls plastered against her face. "I'll drive her."

Annie nodded in thanks before dragging Beth away, the two practically sprinting to the car to get out of the rain as they laughed. Another smile pulled at my lips. Annie deserved that.

I wrapped my arms around myself, seeing lightning strike between dark clouds. "You're amazing," Nailea said quietly, hooking her arm through mine. "I hope you know that." I rested my head on hers, seeing as she was too short for me to reach her shoulder. "I also hope you know that Beck wasn't lying when he said you don't have to do it all on your own. I'm here, Nyx."

"I know you are," I murmured over the sound of the rain. "And I love you for always going the extra mile. I love you for never asking questions but still helping. I love you for taking a chance on me. I love you for being my best friend."

Her grip on me tightened, followed by her teasing voice. "So we're using that term now? Am I allowed to call you my best friend? You think I deserve that privilege?"

Turning to look at her, I smiled. "You earned that privilege the second you decided to drive to Skid Row to get me and another thirty minutes through traffic back to school."

Her eyes watered. "I can't tell if I'm crying or if a really heavy raindrop just hit my eyeball." I laughed as her left eye turned red. She smiled through the pain. "I love you."

Having the admission said in front of my mom's grave held a deeper meaning. Somehow, I felt my mom's sadness increase. Because I was finally receiving the love I'd been deprived of.

And she was witnessing it, wherever she was now.

Chapter 34

Beckham

I stared long and carefully at all of the men packed into my living room. There were a lot of them, nineteen, to be exact. Settled comfortably on the couches were Grayson, Jasper, Jai, Sebastian and Oliver. In front of them, on the floor around the coffee table was; Elijah, Levi, Maddox, Aiden, Danny and Jonas—the full second team. I glimpsed at the others that were pitching against the wall. It'd been a while since all of us were in the same space since the rest were away for most of the time, playing community matches. But that didn't mean that I knew them any less than the two teams that I always played with. I was still their captain, and we all were affected by our recent losses against UCLA. It put them off which affected their matches against other schools.

"It's been a rough couple of weeks," I started, taking a second to run my eyes across all of their faces. Most of them looked defeated. "And I'm talking about more than just the losses." At those words, I peered at my first team and they stared back tiredly.

"Contrary, to what everybody else thinks, our lives most definitely do *not* revolve around hockey. We don't live and breathe on the ice." There were murmurs of assent. "We have lives outside of it, lives that are sometimes overlooked because of our dedication to the sport. And I don't think that's healthy."

Jasper beamed. "Preach, sister."

I disregarded him but couldn't stop the tiny twist of my lips. "Before I was captain," I didn't say Nate's name, not wanting to perturb anyone, "there was no such thing as breaks. We worked our asses off and received nothing in return, not even acknowledgement. The praises were taken by our previous captain." Some of them stilled. "But a captain is only as good as his team. And right now, we all aren't doing well. I want us to be able to say we're *okay* before we step foot onto the ice."

Jai leaned forward, elbows on his knees. "UCLA won't know what hit them after we come back." I nodded, savouring the fact that enthusiasm was being passed around the room. Some guys added in their own little thoughts and I watched, nodding.

"Once we're all back in shape," Aiden appended, "I bet there won't be any losses—"

"Don't jinx it!" At least fifteen of them barked at him and he raised his hands in capitulation, chuckling lowly to himself at the reception he was able to pull. I shook my head at him, smirking in amusement.

Probably struggling to figure out how to phrase his question, Jai peeped at me. "So, when can we expect the return of our captain's girl?"

"The captain's girl has a fucking name, Jairaj," Nyx

answered as she shifted through the front door, files clasped to her chest. Her tone was dripping in joviality which was why Jai didn't look abashed but rather sent her the biggest fucking smile that I'd ever seen on his face. "Her name's Froufrou," she renewed, taking a few steps into the living room before glimpsing at the rest of the guys and stirring the files to one arm. "For those of y'all that are confused, that's his butt plug he hides in his sock drawer—"

"You fucking liar," I cut her off, about to move towards her when Jasper abruptly bulldozed her.

The files plummeted to the ground and she was in his arms, elevated high in the air and being spun. Understandable, they hadn't seen her in a while. Her face was crushed into the side of his neck and he cupped the back of her head, kissing her hairline repeatedly.

"*God*, don't ever leave me again," Jasper told her, still kissing her head so his words came out warped. "I'm getting us friendship bracelets soon, how does handcuffs sound? That way, you can't leave me."

Nyx snorted, tossing her head back when Jasper shook her as if he couldn't believe she was in front of him. "Sorry, Jas. Only Beck gets to handcuff me." I chuckled when she winked at me.

The next to stand up was Oliver and he did the same, picking her up in his arms and dishevelling her hair. He grumbled something about missing the only other pretty person. Grayson soon followed, dropping a loud kiss on her cheek and hugging her tightly, although he'd seen her last week.

Jai then swaggered towards her and held out a hand. "Who would've thought I'd end up missing you?" But he embraced her anyway, wrapping his arms around her waist and lifting her, squeezing, and then dropping her. "You're an absolute pain in my ass."

Nyx shifted to me, face red from being suffocated by her boys. "I thought guys loved pains in their asses. Isn't that why you have Froufrou—"

"Shut up," I hummed, walking around Jai to drag her into my arms. She slumped into my embrace, giggling the entire time and I dropped my forehead to hers. "I hate you."

She stepped back, softly patting my stubbled jaw. "Cute."

When she whirled around, Sebastian was standing there.

"Good to have you back," he said stiffly. Rolling her eyes, she pulled him into a hug, one that he returned wholeheartedly.

After that, Nyx was welcomed back by each member of the team and she questioned everyone about what she'd missed. They filled her in on every single detail of their lives, loving that she was giving them her full attention. She was back, the vigorous Nyx, the funny Nyx. She was finally back.

And this time, there was nothing holding her back. No abusive dad, no missing mom, no heavy responsibilities to provide for her sisters. She finally had the chance to be a carefree twenty-year-old.

The development was only obvious to those who really knew her. Jasper was beaming from afar the entire time, seeing her joke around with the team. He caught my eye and tipped his head and I did the same. Whilst Nyx was enjoying herself, I picked up the files she abandoned and brought them to our room, piling them on my desk. As I passed the window, amongst the cars belonging to my teammates, I saw Nailea's car. I opened the window, ready to call out to her, but stopped.

Nailea looked like she was hyperventilating. She climbed out of her car, took two steps towards my house and then turned around. This process carried on for about five minutes. She placed a hand over her mouth and let out a repressed scream, stomping her foot. And then the tears came, pouring down her face as she furiously rubbed at them. But nothing she did would stop it. It was weird watching that because she was Nailea. There was never anything but a smile on her face.

Laughter came from downstairs before I heard a loud splash. They were moving to the pool. My mind was spinning, trying to figure out if I should talk to Nailea or not. The front door opened suddenly. Nailea was too busy berating herself and wiping her tears to know that Sebastian was marching onto the lawn to get something from his car. He halted when he saw her, but there was zero emotion on his face.

She hadn't spotted him yet, still crying. When she did, she looked mortified, cleaning her face. Sebastian didn't say anything, just observed her. Almost stumblingly, Nailea hopped back into her car, nearly tripping over her feet. With one last look at Sebastian, she reversed and raced down the street. He watched the fading car for a second before looking back at me. He knew I was watching.

Somehow, he *always* knew when somebody was watching him.

I shut the curtain, turning in time to see Nyx enter the room, her clothes and hair dripping wet. "Jasper tossed me into the fucking pool." I snorted, watching her strip out of the jeans and sweater before trudging to my drawer and snatching a t-shirt. I couldn't even find it in myself to ogle her, too busy thinking about what just happened. It reminded me of what had happened last year.

"Do you remember that rumour that spread about you?"

I didn't need to specify which one. Nyx slid the t-shirt over her head before shedding her panties and bra so they could dry. She raised a brow at the mention of the rumour as she reached for a clean set of underwear and put it on.

"You mean the one you supposedly started?" she quipped, grinning at me as she tied her hair up into a tight bun.

I nodded, still pondering. "I saw you crying." Nyx frowned. "That day in the empty classroom." She was gawking at me now, scepticism in her eyes. "I saw you crying and I've never felt guilt like that before. I felt worse because the rumour was pinned on me and in a way, it was my fault. So I put an end to the rumour."

Nyx took a step closer to me, nearly gliding in the puddle that she'd built with her wet clothes. "You *stopped* the rumour?" I nodded, barely able to say anything before she was in my arms, hers swathed around my neck and her legs around my waist. "*Jesus*, did you ever even hate me?" She was laughing.

I shrugged, pressing a kiss to her lips. "That's one of the world's mysteries, baby." I brought her over to the bed before sitting down. "How's Annie doing?" I urged.

She ran her fingers through my hair and I overcame a shudder. "She's good. Beth wants her to move in, and I can tell Annie's scared to leave us behind. Leave me behind specifically."

I nodded. "Yeah, I've noticed some of her stuff slowly being moved from the house. But she hasn't openly said she was leaving."

"She's scared to," Nyx said. "But I told her it's no problem. She deserves her happily ever after."

"And your grandma?"

"It looks like she's going to get custody of the girls. Poppy and Indie are ecstatic," she responded, glancing to the window. "I can't wait to go back to classes. Normalcy, I need normalcy now. And I called in, they're changing my name on the register to Nyx Aster."

I grinned, kissing her again. "At that club that we went to, your ID said Kennedy Taylor." It was something that'd been playing on my mind for a while. To me, she was always Nyx. There was no way she seemed like a Kennedy.

She rolled her eyes and I snorted. "Matthew had my birth certificate changed. The story I was told was that he didn't think Nyx was a suitable first name. But recently, my grandma said he wanted no reminders of my birth dad, even my name because he named me. And," she paused, "*speaking of Matthew.*"

Her features were pinched. "What?"

"Fiona, who's his other wife," I nodded, "she got a call from the prison he's being held at. There's supposed to be a court hearing in two months and she was worried they'd cancelled it or planned to release him or something." She was trembling and I could hear the anxiety in her voice. I ran a hand down her back, trying to calm her down. "But it was something else entirely." Another pause, one that had me worried. "He," she lamented, "he was brutally murdered when all of the inmates were being led back to their cells after lunch."

Absolute shock. Frost worked down my spine as I gazed into Nyx's eyes, at the muddle of emotions that I discovered there. "Brutally, you said?"

Brutal could mean something disturbing to us outside of prison, but to inmates, it was just a pinch.

She nodded. "I don't know the full story, but a group had been finding a way to smother utensils from the kitchen for about two weeks. *Knives*," she stressed. "Police are saying it was an inside job, someone on the kitchen staff had to be working with them. Whilst they were lining up they just," she shrugged, "*attacked*, I guess. Each member had a knife and they went for it. 178 stab wounds all over his body, his throat sliced and guts pulled out. A knife to each eye. They sliced his ears off as well as his dick—"

"Okay, fuck," I stopped her, quaking at the image of my dick being cut off. "I believe you now when you say brutal. And the police just stood aside?"

"I think you underestimate how many were part of this plan. The police reacted immediately but there were too many men to get around. The men that *weren't* part of the plan held the police back to prevent them from using their weapons when they realised that something big was happening. It was impossible to stop them." Her eyes found mine. "The moment they were satisfied with his mutilated body, the prisoners just dropped their knives and got back into line. The police were astounded that they didn't try to attack them. They just wanted Matthew. Word got around what he got arrested for, I guess. A lot of those men that went for him were fathers who had gone to extremes to protect their families."

And Matthew was a man who had abused his family. He was a disgrace of a man and the inmates thought a lifetime in prison wasn't enough for him. They were the judges and the jury that chose his fate. I thought about it for a second, still astounded by what she just said. *Murdered.*

Brutally murdered when he hadn't even expected it. I couldn't feel sorry, I couldn't. He deserved it for what he'd put the Taylor girls through. *Aster*, I corrected myself. All of them, even Annie and Indigo, were Aster girls.

"There's honour amongst criminals." She nodded with a small smile. "And how do you feel?"

It didn't take long for her to think about her answer. In fact, she answered speedily. "Grandma and Fiona won't let us see the pictures. Matthew suffered, *without a doubt*. They left his throat and eyes for last so he was suffering through most of the wounds." Her lips quirked. "I feel great."

Smirking, I stated, "Sociopath."

Her smile dropped and her features turned obstinate. "Just because I enjoy—"

"Watching vile men suffer, doesn't mean you're a sociopath," I concluded, delighted to see her laughing to the point where she nearly toppled off my lap. "Yes, I know, baby." She giggled into my neck when I pulled her closer and I grinned. She was most definitely back. "Do the little ones know?"

I felt her shake her head, getting a puff of chlorine from her hair. "Indie, Jade and Rue don't know. They think he's in prison. Grandma says she doesn't want to traumatise them.

And Poppy was eavesdropping." She pulled back so she could look me in the eye. Her features distorted into one of concern. "She was *ecstatic*."

Unable to help myself, I chuckled. "Definitely your fucking sister."

Nyx rolled her eyes, although she was smiling again. "Georgia says she went to bed without turning on her nightlight. That's never happened before because she'd been terrified of the dark for the longest time. When I saw her the next day and asked why she's no longer using her nightlight, you know what she told me?" I gestured for her to continue. "She told me she has no reason to be afraid because there's no monster in the dark anymore." Her eyes closed. "I don't know how I never pieced it together. The first time Matthew hit Poppy, it was the night our power went out. There were no candles because Poppy cut them all a while back to make snow for her dolls. Matthew was pissed and beat her. And she couldn't close her eyes in the dark again."

The only reason I wasn't pissed as hell was because I knew the fucker was already dead. And he'd *suffered*. "He deserved the death he got."

"He did. He most definitely did." She sighed, cupping my face. "Thank you for sticking around and helping me through my worst, even when I was an absolute bitch to you. Thank you for helping my family although you had no reason to, although I did what I did last year. My standards were so fucking low because of the image Matthew painted of men. The bar was so low that you could step over it. But *you*, Beckham Hunt, found a fucking plane and flew over that bar even though you didn't need to. You went above and beyond for me and I will never stop loving you because of it."

Her eyes were damp and I knew it was because she loathed talking about feelings. So I rubbed away the one tear that succeeded to escape and replied, "I will do anything for you. *Anything.*" I kissed beneath both eyes and she closed them, leaning into my touch. "I love you." I pushed to my feet and she squealed, holding me tighter. "Let's go check on our kids."

"Oh so you understood what I meant when I said Benson wasn't the papa," she taunted, trying to tickle me but stopped when I humorously threatened to fling her down the stairs like a beach ball.

When we stepped into the backyard, we found 18 idiots splattering in the pool in their underwear. Sebastian was probably in his room after what he'd witnessed with Nailea.

"They *are* our kids, aren't they?" Nyx mused. "I love them."

I dropped her to her feet, making sure my shirt covered what it needed to. "I love them too, but don't tell them that."

She grinned at me, turning to gaze at them. They looked felicitous, no longer under strain because of the matches. Hopefully, we'd be back on the ice in no time and better than ever. We still had many months left to win the Crosstown Cup, and we needed the break.

The first twelve weeks had already passed by in a blur. So much had happened in that time span, I'd overcame the obstacle impeding me from being with Nyx. And she'd managed to get out of that godawful position she was ensnared in.

A few months ago, it all seemed impossible. Yet, here we were, I thought as I gaped at her, watching her grin at the sight of my teammates. *Her teammates.* Because she was part of the team, there was no doubt about it. She would always be one of us and have a place among us.

Jasper was bouncing along the edges of the pool, shaking his ass. Nyx twitched beside me and I fought a smile. I knew exactly what she was thinking.

"Revenge, baby," I murmured.

With a loud laugh, she dashed forward and shoved Jasper with a mighty push. He screeched, flying back and splashing into the water. Before Nyx could let out a jubilant laugh, I was behind her and pushed. She landed in the water, breaking the surface to give me a mocking look of betrayal.

But she was stopped from scolding me when Jasper tackled her and the two proceeded to try and drown each other. I watched with a broad smile, feeling happier than I'd ever been before. As I stepped back to remove my shirt so I could swim alongside my pissed off girlfriend, I thought back to after I'd first met Nyx, that fateful November of her freshman year.

I'd gone home and I remembered telling Grayson that one day, Nyx would be my girlfriend. He'd nodded, believing me. It had taken a lot of tribulations to get where we were, a lot of obstructions. But we'd overcame them all and she was finally mine. I loved her with everything I was and she loved me in return. A simple affirmation was like an electromagnet. Like I'd told Nyx, what belonged to you would find you. And we'd found each other, eventually.

Simple Law of Attraction.

Epilogue

Nyx

SEVEN YEARS LATER:

I was going to be so fucking late. For the past week, they'd been hounding me; *be there at one, Nyxie.* It played in my head like a mantra, and I thought for sure I'd be on time. But it was past twelve and I was only rolling over in bed now, a cheerio stuck to my fucking forehead. With a disgruntled groan, I slipped out of bed and wiped the cereal from my head. Through dazed eyes, I glimpsed around the room, trying to figure out what the fuck was going on. My eyes crash-landed on the clock and I freaked.

"Holy shit!" I launched to my feet, stubbing my big toe against the edge of the bed. "Are you fucking kidding me?" I bellowed, venturing to lift my foot to scrutinise the damage but, incidentally, forgetting that my stomach was the size of a fucking beach ball. I stifled the urge to sob, moving to my closet to get an outfit. There was no time to waste. Passing the mirror, I stared at myself.

My hair was long and tangled after coming out of the bun I'd placed it in last night. There was chocolate on my face, I didn't know why. The strap of my bra was drooping off my shoulder, the material straining to support my milk-filled breasts. And the waistband of my shorts was rolled up just below where my stomach swelled forward. The skin was tight and smooth. I ran a hand over the humongous bump and found another cheerio stuck there. I popped it into my mouth before saying, "Twenty-seven never looked this good."

In record time, I cleansed my face and changed into a flowy sundress because pants annoyed the fuck out of me with this bump the size of Jupiter. I slipped my feet into flats and grabbed my phone, dialling the familiar number. When he answered, he was already chuckling.

I overcame the urge to scream when he said, "I'm assuming you only woke up now."

"Beck, you absolute asshole. I hate you so fucking much, you two-faced piece of shit," I spluttered, studying the room for my bag. I needed to leave right now because I was not in the mood to be teased for being late.

He snorted, and I could hear the sound of cars in the backdrop. "I love you too, baby."

I screeched into my hand and he laughed, enjoying my frustration all too much. "Shut up. Where are you?" Grabbing a brush, I put Beckham on speaker and quickly tamed my hair. "I was relying on *you* to wake me up."

He discoursed as I quickly made up the bed, disposing of the stray cereal into the bin. "I told you I had to drop my paperwork at the lab first thing in the morning."

He didn't take offence at me not remembering. He knew all too well what pregnancy did to my brain. The other day I'd been sobbing because I couldn't find my shoes only for him to point out that I was already wearing them.

"And I decided to save your grandma the effort, so I headed into town to pick up the cake. I'm on my way to her place right now. Think you can make it there in under five hours?"

I shook my head, snatching my bag and leaving the room. "I hate you so much."

Surprising almost everyone, Beckham hadn't wanted to get drafted into the NHL. During his fourth year of college and my third, he'd discovered that he enjoyed astrophysics and wanted to do it as more than just a hobby, he wanted more than that. He'd done his masters in astrophysics the following year whilst I'd obtained my bachelor's in sports management. It had taken him one year to complete his master's because he'd graduated with honours like the asshole he was.

The idiot was currently in his second to last year of studying to get his PhD. A lot of it revolved around him working as a research assistant at a private lab. The little nerd that he was. It hadn't taken me long to get picked up and I could boastfully say that I was the PR manager of the Westport Warriors, a local team that had *finally gotten drafted this year after years of hard work. Too bad my assistant had to fill in for me now that I was nearing the end of my pregnancy.*

"Your grandma just texted," Beckham announced as I wobbled down the stairs and climbed over the toddler gates installed there. "I've gotta make a quick stop to pick up the balloons. I bet you I'll still reach the house before you," he snickered.

I scowled, leaving the house and locking the door. "Jokes on you, asshole, I'm already on my way to the car." He was silent as I hopped into the driver's seat.

"Nyx," he began in a slow tone, and I frowned, clipping in my seatbelt. "You know I love you, flaws and all. We both know that pregnancy does things to you," like make me extra horny or scream at the mirror at two in the morning, "so I don't want you to feel guilty, okay?" It sounded like he was trying not to laugh, and I scowled. When he articulated again, my heart nearly fell out of my ass. "Baby," he chuckled, "we have a child."

"Oh my God!" I screamed, hanging up on Beckham's laughter and unclipping my seatbelt. I nearly fell out of my car in a hurry and dashed to the front door, unlocking it.

Heart in my throat, I climbed the stairs, manoeuvring through the hallways before halting in front of a white door. Shifting through, I scanned the area before my eyes settled on a white crib. Inside sat a toddler, no older than three, staring at me.

"Jesus, how could Mommy forget you, Percy?"

He raised his arms. "Silly mommy."

I nodded, picking him up. "Silly mommy, indeed." I pressed kisses to his dark hair, unable to believe that I'd nearly forgotten my fucking son. Beckham wouldn't let me live this down, he *wouldn't*. I'd be hearing about this for years to come. Shaking, I quickly dressed him as he asked me random questions. His favourite recently was to point at objects and ask what it was, followed by *why*.

Picking up his bag with extra clothes, I left the house,

Percy clinging to me and kissing my cheek. I'd been twenty-four when I'd had him, two years after I'd graduated. We'd gotten a good lecture about having a baby out of wedlock from my grandma, but Helen had just been ecstatic to have a grandbaby.

Soon after Percy's birth, Beckham and I got hitched in Vegas. We would be hearing about that today too, how everyone was robbed of a big wedding. But we could still have a proper ceremony, preferably after I popped out my beach ball daughter and Beckham graduated.

Percy asked if he could click in the strap of his car seat and I let him, kissing his head before I climbed into the car. Almost paranoid, I peeped into the rear-view mirror to make sure Percy was sitting there.

With a sigh, I started the car and drove to my grandma's house, barely a fifteen-minute drive. The entire way, Percy sang a song from an infomercial. It was a thing of his. Beckham knew I hated the annoying infomercial songs, so whenever Percy was fussy, he placed him by the TV and played fucking infomercials.

I parked the car and then hopped out, moving to fetch Percy. "What's that?" he pointed at the sky.

"Daddy's girlfriend," I countered, seating him on my bump so I could grab both our bags. It was a joke between us because Beckham spent a lot of his time staring at the sky through a telescope that the entire family had taken to saying he'd become one with it.

Percy coiled his arms around my neck, blue eyes gazing up. "Her name's Sky, right?" I loved that baby voice of his and hearing how well he was learning to talk. It made me want to squeeze his little face. "Why does daddy only think she's pretty when it's dark outside?"

"Because otherwise, he can't see the stars, munchkin." Without knocking, I opened the door and was met with a lot of balloons. It made me wonder why Beckham had to pick up even more. I dropped my bags on the counter and then shuffled through to the kitchen, spotting a short figure trying to lick the frosting from a cupcake. "Are you supposed to be doing that?"

Indigo spun around in all her *teenage glory.* The second she'd hit thirteen, we all had to respect her decisions and accept her as a grown woman; so she'd said. Her brown eyes flared with annoyance.

"I just want a cupcake."

"What's that?" Percy asked, pointing at his little aunt.

"A brat," I responded with a smile, and Indigo couldn't help but laugh, forgetting her previous annoyance. "Where's Rue and Jade?" I urged, referring to her and Annie's half-sisters. Each year that passed, their resemblance astounded me. Rue was Indigo's age, whereas Jade was a year younger.

She stepped closer and held out her arms for Percy, who beamed, practically vaulting into her arms. "They're coming over later."

Without another word, she tottered into the living room, where she had a stack of toys for Percy. I let her go, nervous to tell her I'd discovered yesterday that Percy was entering a throwing phase. It wouldn't be long till Indigo got a plastic truck to the eye.

I spotted a note on the fridge, one written by my grandma.

It said she was going to pick up Fiona, but she'd be back soon. And then out of nowhere, I had to pee. This fucking pregnancy bladder, I swear. Cursing underneath my breath, I wobbled to the guest bathroom and then wished I'd knocked. Squatting by the shower and inserting a tampon was Poppy. For somebody that hated tampons, she always used them.

"Oh *Jesus*, I didn't need to see that," I protested, moving around her to sit down on the toilet.

"Do you mind?" Poppy questioned as she stood, slowly tugging up her underwear.

"I just watched a tampon disappear inside you. I'm sure you can handle seeing my vagina," I returned, finished peeing and cleaning up. "Happy birthday, you bitch. How does it feel to be twenty-one?"

"Like my sister's boobs are currently leaking," Poppy shot back with a laugh as she washed her hands and I looked down to see two identical wet spots on my boobs. "Glad to see you made it on time."

"Shut up," I grumbled, washing my hands and leaving the toilet. I rounded the corner just in time to see Beckham place a cake on the table. He saw me and my lower lip trembled. "My boobs are leaking again," I whined.

He quite obviously contained a laugh and pulled me into his arms. "Oh no, my poor baby."

"My boobs hurt, I pee out of nowhere and I can't see my feet," I persevered, pressing my face into his chest. "You did this to me, you asshole." Probably deciding it was best not to tease me further, he led me to the living room where I could rest.

Percy looked up and pointed at his dad, more specifically the nametag around his neck. "What's that?"

Indigo answered, "An idiot."

Beckham glowered at her but she tossed him an innocent smile. Seven years and the two were still at each other's throats whilst simultaneously being best friends. I felt emotional all of a sudden because seven years had passed. I blamed it on the pregnancy hormones.

Poppy just turned twenty-one, and I thought back to that little girl that had followed me around and slept with a nightlight. She'd evolved so much in the past few years whilst simultaneously staying the same. Her eyes never lost their brightness, thankfully.

Indigo was literally the same, still a little bitch, and I loved her. My grandma had been getting some complaints about her at school because she was always starting arguments. But I knew it was just because she enjoyed arguing. I reminded myself to tell my grandma to sign her up for debate. Oh, who was I kidding? I was going to forget that reminder in the next five seconds.

Annie was living her best life and currently with Beth—her wife—trekking through some jungle with zero fucking cell service. I missed them so much, but they'd promised to be back soon so they could meet the new baby.

I was looking forward to having this baby, not only because I'd get to meet our kid, but it was an occasion that would bring *everyone* together. I'd get to see my busy boys again. Sebastian and Grayson were a constant in my life, and everyone usually hung out on the weekends. They'd meet up to play hockey, just like old times.

And I was pretty sure something was going on between Benson and my grandma, but I didn't want to think of it for fear of throwing up a lung.

The day passed in a blur. Georgia had shown up alongside Julie and the girl's boyfriend; Marcus. The latter had gotten over when I'd first met him, back when they'd been in middle school. Poor guy had been so scared of me for the longest time. Julie found it hilarious.

Poppy nearly died when she saw the Mercedes we'd all pooled in to get her. So much gratitude. The tears spilt down her face and I knew what she was thinking, because it constantly ran through my own mind.

Was this really my life? Did I really make it this far? It was difficult to believe that we'd managed to crawl out of that dark hole we'd been trapped in.

Once the sky dimmed, my grandma led everyone into the backyard for some hot chocolate. Fiona, Rue and Jade were there too. Beckham laid out a blanket for me where I could recline and he sat down with Percy between his legs.

The tiny boy pointed up at the dark sky. "Look, Daddy's girlfriend is back—"

"Daddy's wife," Beckham corrected with a snort. "And what's her name?"

Percy thought for a moment before he answered, "Nyx. Her name's Nyx." His eyes studied the vast space in reverence. "And what's that?"

Beckham grinned, running a hand over his son's fluffy hair. "Those are stars, buddy. Nyx protects and loves all of them,. Daddy's one of the stars because she loves him."

I rolled my eyes and he leaned over to kiss my cheek. Years later and I still couldn't believe his middle name was Rigel; named after one of the brightest stars in the sky.

The law of attraction really hadn't come to play with us.

Indigo pushed to her feet, pointing at the sky. "What's happening?"

Beckham had been telling everyone for months that something marvellous would be happening on Poppy's birthday, just when the sky would begin to darken. Suddenly, everything lit up. I watched as hundreds of falling stars shot across the shadowy space. They burned brilliantly and I could feel everyone's wonder. The stars passed through with a tail like the stroke of an artist's brush.

It was an astonishing performance as they whirled across the night sky. I turned my head slightly to see Marcus place a kiss on Julie's lips, the light of the stars gleaming onto them.

"Explain, Mr Scientist," Indigo said, poking Beckham's arms before sitting down next to him.

Beckham smirked. "It's the Perseid meteor shower, happens annually. We see the Perseids each year when Earth crosses their orbit."

Fiona nodded with a look of curiosity. Everyone turned to gawk at the shower, looking like it would never end. After a while, my grandma, Fiona and Georgia disappeared into the kitchen for some cake. Poppy decided to take Julie, Marcus and the girls for a late-night drive, leaving just my little family in the backyard.

"Daddy, what's that?" Percy inquired, looking at the

shooting stars.

I smiled, poking Percy's cheeks as Beckham went to answer. "That's the Perseid meteor shower," he explained, and the young boy definitely didn't understand what a meteor shower was. "It's called the Perseids because they hail from a constellation, which is one of Nyx's babies."

Percy frowned. "A constipation? What's his name?"

Already knowing this story, I spoke, "Perseus. The *constellation's* name is Perseus."

He clapped. "That's me." I nodded, kissing his chubby cheeks. "I'm a constipation!" he yelled, making me coo. "If Daddy's star and Mommy's night, what's sister be?" he asked, his words a slight disorder.

Beckham looked over at me and raised a brow. "Probably also a *constellation*."

Percy pushed his hair out of his eyes. "Can I pick?" We nodded and he pointed to the sky again. "Daddy, which constipation is that?"

It didn't take long for the answer to come together. He gave me that boyish smile that I'd fallen in love with so many years ago, his grey eyes twinkling like the very stars above.

"That's Cassiopeia."

I let out a gasp when Percy threw himself onto my lap, short arms trying to wrap around my stomach. He kissed the bump. "We're gonna be the best constipations, Cassie."

My eyes watered and I swore softly, hating that my emotions were all over the place. Percy continued speaking to his sister, pointing at different spots in the sky to explain constipations.

Beckham glanced over at me and winked. "I love you, Tink."

"I love you," I murmured in return, trying not to cry. That was futile because him calling me Tinkerbell reminded me of the first time I'd explained to him why I'd nicknamed him Annika. He'd insisted that we watched *Barbie and the Magic of Pegasus*. That led to weekly Barbie movie nights with my sisters.

Percy gasped, pulling me from my memories. "Ew, Mommy. Are you peeing again?"

My brows furrowed in annoyance at my bladder and I raised the skirt of my dress.

But it wasn't pee.

I looked at Beckham and he stared at me in amazement. He kissed Percy's head. "Well, buddy, looks like we're meeting Cassie soon."

Author's Note

Thank you so much for reading this story. Nyx and Beckham—*sigh*—they hold such a special place in my heart. I can't even begin to explain how much I love them, and I hope you do too. I was eighteen when I first penned their characters and now that I'm about to turn twenty, I can't help but look back and marvel at how much my characters have grown—not only my characters but my writing as well.

As always, there remains tons of space for improvement and I'm beyond excited to grow even more as a writer. And as far as debut novels go, I'm proud of this little baby. It may not be everybody's cup of tea—hell, sometimes my self-conscious ass even *hates* my own writing—but I'm proud, nonetheless. I'll remain proud, no matter where my writing journey takes me.

This isn't the last you'll be seeing of Nyx and Beckham as *Law of Attraction* is merely the first book in a series of standalones. My next book revolves around our favourite blonde angel and the gorgeous little troublemaker that never fails to exasperate him. Stay tuned for Nailea and Sebastian's *grumpy x sunshine* story: *Law of Polarity.*

If you loved this book, please consider leaving a review! If you want to talk to me or merely stay updated, then follow me on my Instagram: raeesahauthor

ACKNOWLEDGMENTS

I never would've thought this day would come; me being an actual published author. I started writing at the age of eight, although my work mainly consisted of cringey poems back then. This journey wasn't one taken alone, and I'm so grateful for those that have stuck by my side and encouraged me to follow my dreams.

Firstly, a huge thanks must go to my readers. I started out with nothing on Wattpad and as the years went on, my readership grew. If it weren't for my supporting readers, I never would've taken the leap and published. Knowing that they wanted my book is what pushed me. If you've read my book, I'm forever grateful. I love you guys.

To my parents. Thank you for always believing in me and my dreams. Thank you to my dad for remaining an unwavering system of support, no matter what. Anything I needed, you were there, ready to put everything on hold to help me. Thank you to my mommy for laying down the sturdy foundation for my dreams. Every whisper of strength and motivation allowed me to reach places you never had the opportunity to. I love you both—even though you always get annoyed with me because I talk too much.

To Raaiqah, my favourite (and only) sister. Thank you for not murdering me in my sleep after I spend hours telling you about a new idea. You're the funniest person I know and my number one fan. By the way, thank you for putting together the best playlist for this book. If anybody knows Nyx and Beckham as well as I do; it's you. I love you (without spaces in between).

To Diya. Words cannot express my love and appreciation for you. You've been a reader since the very beginning and since then, you've become a friend. I hope to have you by my side the rest of this journey.

And finally, to Ammaarah Adams. My best friend. Thank you for everything. Thank you for hyping me up all the time, for giving me confidence. I believe the universe gave me you after comprehending that I needed a friend equally as annoying as me. Years ago, when I was fourteen and your old ass was fifteen, I remember telling you that the jersey you were wearing was ugly. That must've been the first words I'd ever spoken to you, and right there, the law of attraction began working its magic.

ABOUT THE AUTHOR

Raeesah, more commonly known as Rae—as lovingly referred to by her readers—is a young author who always dreamed of one day becoming published. Her favourite genres are romance and fantasy. She hopes to finally pen the fantasy book she's been brainstorming for years. For now, she has romance ideas galore. When she isn't writing, she's reading one of the many books on her tbr.

Printed in Great Britain
by Amazon

14811115R00358